FAYE SNOWDEN

A KILLING FIRE

This is a **FLAME TREE PRESS** book

Text copyright © 2019 Faye Snowden

FLAME TREE PRESS
6 Melbray Mews, London, SW6 3NS, UK
flametreepress.com

Distribution and warehouse:
Baker & Taylor Publisher Services (BTPS)
30 Amberwood Parkway, Ashland, OH 44805
btpubservices.com

Publisher's Note: This is a work of fiction. Names, characters, places, and incidents are a product of the author's imagination. Locales and public names are sometimes used for atmospheric purposes. Any resemblance to actual people, living or dead, or to businesses, companies, events, institutions, or locales is completely coincidental.

Thanks to the Flame Tree Press team, including:
Taylor Bentley, Frances Bodiam, Federica Ciaravella, Don D'Auria,
Chris Herbert, Matteo Middlemiss, Josie Mitchell, Mike Spender,
Cat Taylor, Maria Tissot, Nick Wells, Gillian Whitaker.

The cover is created by Flame Tree Studio with
thanks to Nik Keevil and Shutterstock.com.
The font families used are Avenir and Bembo.

Flame Tree Press is an imprint of Flame Tree Publishing Ltd
flametreepublishing.com

A copy of the CIP data for this book is available from the British Library
and the Library of Congress.

HB ISBN: 978-1-78758-306-1
PB ISBN: 978-1-78758-304-7
ebook ISBN: 978-1-78758-307-8
Also available in FLAME TREE AUDIO

Printed in the US at Bookmasters, Ashland, Ohio

FAYE SNOWDEN

A KILLING FIRE

FLAME TREE PRESS
London & New York

To all of the fierce women I have known, including: Michelle, Viv, Lupe, Amy, Peggy, Sally, Carla, Donna, Renee, Rose, Julie and every single one of my Jessicas.

Keep kicking ass.

PROLOGUE

Floyd Burns' father was a black boxer who tried on his own name just like his son did. He called himself Lightning Burns because of what he thought of as the speed of his flying fists.

But he wasn't quick.

Lightning – his real name was Hamlet – was slow. But once he caught up to the poor soul unlucky enough to be in the ring with him, he'd pound and pound on 'em just like he was a human spike driver fastening a railroad tie. Everybody called him Hammer because of it. Nobody called him Lightning.

Not even his wife.

He didn't do much professionally, made a little money on the amateur circuit before settling down with his wife, Sarah, on a small farm where they grew corn and kept a few cows and pigs. Sarah came from one of them Okie families. Her people fled to California when the Oklahoma skies turned black and the soil became sawdust. She was as sweet and strong as a stereotype with narrow blue eyes that saw a lot but kept much of it to herself.

Floyd worried Sarah from the minute he was born. He slipped so easily from the womb that later on she would question if there was even one pang when he came into this world. His face was flat with calm as the midwife laid him on her belly. There was no lusty cry as there would be from her other children. He just lay there for a minute or two breathing softly with his eyes closed as if he was thinking on some extremely serious matter. When he finally opened his eyes, Sarah did see that one was darker than the other, but it wouldn't be until later that she fully understood that one eyeball would be a shimmering green and the other a blazing blue.

There would be the kids that were too scared to play with Floyd, not because of his eyes so much as for the way he was. How he would just sit back and watch things and not say a word for hours on end with them weird light-colored eyes. And as for the kids that weren't scared of him, Floyd found there would be a lot of pushing and shoving and a hard row to hoe.

But from Floyd there would be no tears, only that peculiar thinking look as if he hadn't quite made up his mind about the kind of world he had entered into or just how he would behave in it.

One day when he was sixteen, he didn't show up for dinner. Sarah had set his place at the table as usual on the first night he didn't show and then just as quietly picked the dishes up one by one when he didn't come in later. She washed and dried them as if he had eaten from them and put the plates back in the cupboard. She did this the second night too. She set Hammer's place, her own, the twins' places, and Floyd's. The dishes were laid out for the final time on that third night and when he didn't come home, Sarah once again washed the plate, the spoon, and the fork as if he had used them.

After she had finished the dishes she stood for some time in the open door looking out over the cornfield. A breeze rustled the tips of the stalks making the silk spark gold in the quilted darkness. The roof of the open country was so full of black that it made her feel as if she were in some movie theater or some giant tent with tiny silver dots painted on the ceiling to look like stars. She stood there for a long time watching the wind playing in the corn.

Then for an instant she let herself breathe a tiny sigh of relief at the thought of never seeing Floyd again. Hammer came and stood by her side, wondering why he couldn't muster up enough worry to go out and search for Floyd. He gave himself the excuse that it was from taking too many hits to the head. He wasn't in his right mind or strong enough to go and search for that boy. Besides, he couldn't leave Sarah alone with the twins. That just wouldn't be right. He put his hand on her shoulder, thinking that they had both just missed something terrible. But if anybody had come out and asked him what that was, he wouldn't have quite been able to put it into words.

CHAPTER ONE

Detective Raven Burns didn't know if she was asleep or awake. All she knew was that she was lying on her back with the music of Louisiana Zydeco playing loud in her ear. Eyes open, she watched the notes from the accordion swirl in neon red and green on the ceiling of her apartment in Byrd's Landing, Louisiana.

The nightmare was still with her, but fading. She had been dreaming about the time she had the chance to stop a serial killer but didn't take it. How her life and the lives of everyone whose path her father crossed would've been different if she had. But she wasn't brave enough.

Never mind that she was just a kid back then. Children could be brave. She knew who and what he was even at that young age, and yet she had allowed him to go on. Worse, she had even loved him as a father while he did so.

The Android on her nightstand played on with its Zydeco ringtone. Smooth vocals joined the accordion and before long she was wide awake. She picked the phone up and glanced at the time before pressing the answer button. The morning was barely an hour old.

"Wake up, sleepyhead," a voice said in her ear. "We caught one."

It was homicide detective Billy Ray Chastain, her Zydeco-loving partner who had been assigned the 'Walking to New Orleans' ringtone. She let her head fall back on the pillow and breathed heavily for a few seconds.

Murders came to Byrd's Landing one right after another. No sooner had she put one perp away than another one would pop up. It was like she'd been playing a macabre game of whack-a-mole ever since the Byrd's Landing chief of police lured her away from the New Orleans Police Department several years ago. The city had just ended the police services contract with the sheriff's department, and the chief, appointed as interim by the mayor, was trying to build the

Byrd's Landing Police Department almost from scratch. He wanted her. And she found herself back in Byrd's Landing battling memories of both her father and depraved killers.

During lulls when nothing much happened except for a bar fight or a domestic dispute, Raven knew that murderers like her father were still out there. She could feel them waiting. It's what had drawn her father to this Louisiana town. Anchored by a lake, bracketed by swamps and cut in half by the lazy, serpentine expanse of the Red River, it was an island unto itself. The town appeared to breathe in the darkness he so loved, find nourishment in the evil Raven had spent the better part of her life trying to defeat. If she was to ever get her father out of her system, it would be in Byrd's Landing.

"Where?" she said into the phone.

Billy Ray told her and she ended the call. She swung her legs over the bed and sat up. Sweating, dry-mouthed, she stayed that way for a full two minutes. She waited until the dream slid just beneath her subconscious, out of the way so she could get on with whatever business this warm July morning was about to bring her.

When she thought she had it together she took a five-minute shower so hot that her skin stung as if it had been punished. She noticed steam covering the bathroom mirror as she stepped onto the bath rug. She wiped the mist away with the side of her fist and studied herself in the low light. Two bulbs had burned out about a month ago but she hadn't bothered to replace them.

That wasn't like her.

The place was meticulously clean: the carpets vacuumed, floors swept, every surface wiped on a regular basis. That was one thing she got from her father, a habit she couldn't shake. Her desk at the station was the same. When her partner, Billy Ray, saw her efforts to keep the place sparkling, he'd accused her of acting as if she were cleaning up after a crime scene.

But she had a hard time replacing the lights in the bathroom. After all, that's where the mirror was. She stared into the one green eye and one blue eye peering back at her. The dream, never far away, resurfaced.

Fragments of images played slideshow fashion in her head – fire slithering along the grass, the white moon straining to send its weak light through a rare summer fog. And back inside the house, blood on the white stove, blood on the floor, and blood on the walls. That was the way she remembered the dreams, in fragments, like the letters her father used to send her from prison.

They were never complete letters, just juvenile scrawls on slips of paper with very few words. The notes came infrequently at first, but then a couple of weeks before he was executed, they came in a flood. There were times when she received two in one day. She remembered one particular scrap that arrived in an official-looking yellow envelope while she was still at the police academy. One of her instructors brought it to her in the cafeteria. Raven shouldn't have opened it right then but she did. She couldn't help it.

On a slip of paper no bigger than a Post-it note, her father had written a few sentences in cursive so small she could barely read it. Every word was spelled correctly except the word *killing*. He spelled that with just one *L*.

I never thought of kiling you, Birdy Girl. No matter what they said or what you thought, I never thought of kiling you, not once. Kiling you would be like looking in the mirror and slicing my own throat.

She threw all the notes away but that didn't matter. That last note especially had been with her ever since she read it, just behind her eyes whenever she shut them.

She gazed at her image in the mirror more intently. Her eyes didn't mean that she was like her father. They were probably just a trait from her paternal white grandmother, just like Raven's spirals of reddish blond hair and the gold undertones of her light brown skin. She told the face the same thing she told it every morning in case it got any ideas about who was in charge.

She said, "There are two 'L's in *killing*, asshole. Learn to spell. There isn't anything of you in me." She switched out what little light there was and padded naked to her bedroom.

She pulled on a pair of tight-fitting jeans and topped them off with a white T-shirt, smoothing it over her flat belly. She clipped her badge to her belt and stuffed her service revolver in the holster at the small of her back. Her personal weapon, a Glock 19, went into her shoulder holster. She thought about the Beretta 92FS she used to carry. It was now locked safely away in her desk drawer at work. She was glad that she replaced it with the Glock 19. Too many bad memories with that weapon, but she still didn't have the strength to get rid of it. Maybe someday, she thought, as she lifted a pant leg and strapped on a six-inch hunting knife.

As she shrugged into her jacket, she thought about how hard she had worked to leave behind the patrol officer's uniform. She had given herself four years in New Orleans to advance to the level of homicide detective. It had taken her two. And she congratulated herself on how far she had distanced herself from her father even though she was now back home in Byrd's Landing, Louisiana.

All the while she whistled 'The Battle Hymn of the Republic' until Floyd Burns – she would never call him *Fire* the way all the others did – pixelated into dust in her head.

She left her apartment and walked out into the brand new morning, the buzzing from the cicadas almost as loud as Buckwheat Zydeco's accordion. It didn't occur to her that the hymn she had been whistling to banish Floyd from her mind was one that he had always favored.

CHAPTER TWO

Raven pulled her red Mustang up to the iron gate leading to the Big Bayou Lake estate address Billy Ray had given her. The uniformed officer guarding the gate knew her, but he still checked her ID and logged her in before waving her through.

She followed the driveway for more than a half a mile with nothing but her headlights to guide her. The way was paved, but winding, and for a brief second Raven imagined herself lost in the pressing darkness of a predawn morning. She focused on what she knew about this part of town. She had been in the neighborhood before but never to this address. If she had her bearings straight, the lake would be visible from the back of the house at the end of the driveway. She had spent many childhood days on the shores of Big Bayou, and remembered the strands of Spanish moss trailing from cypress trees rising out of the flat water.

As she rounded the next bend, light coming from a massive brick house spread over her. Every window blazed with light. Someone, most likely the responding officer, had staked police tape all around the immense front lawn to delineate the crime scene. A double row of orange cones led to the back gate. The coroner's blue van was in the circular driveway, both back doors opened wide. A thin woman in work boots and a windbreaker peered inside. The only other vehicle was the department's lone, antiquated CSI van. Vehicles from the Byrd's Landing PD were parallel parked across the street from the residence. Raven slid the Mustang behind her partner Billy Ray's '67 Buick Skylark.

As she stepped from the car, her head filled with the constant hum she always experienced when entering a fresh crime scene. Her senses were on fire, ablaze with the yellow light coming from the house. The brackish smell wafting from the lake and the heat of the July morning darkness caressing her face made her feel as if she were all nerve endings. All cop now, nothing about the scene escaped her. She considered the cones leading to the back gate, and surmised that the primary scene with the body was on the other side of the redwood fence. She noted the boundaries of the crime scene – at least in the front yard – and didn't think that she would have expanded it any wider. The people on scene were all from the department. No civilians – not unusual for this time so early in the morning. She looked to the right and left of the house. Even the closest neighbor would not have been close enough to witness the murder.

"I'm guessing the chief isn't here?" Raven asked Billy Ray, who was walking across the paved road toward her with long, purposeful strides.

"No," Billy Ray answered. "It's just you and me, baby. I was the highest ranking on scene until you decided to grace us with your presence."

She looked at him then. Billy Ray was a tall man, about six four with rich, dark brown skin and features that were model-perfect. At first glance, he looked as wholesome as homemade ice cream, but he had searing brown eyes that could cleave a person in two. His intense gaze gave him a dangerous air. Raven often wondered if his fondness for bowling shirts and expensive pork pie hats, the one he had on now pushed back on his head, were Billy Ray's attempts to appear less edgy.

He had been her partner in New Orleans before she answered the chief's call to come back home to Byrd's Landing. But the town was more than she could handle alone. With one phone call from her, Billy Ray was by her side once again.

"You ready for the walk-through?" she asked.

"As ready as I'll ever be," he answered.

She cocked her head toward him as he began. "The sister found the body, female, around midnight and alerted the father. He goes out and checks before calling 911. Officers Hardy and Vernell responded." He waved his hand toward the back gate, where a lone officer guarded the entrance.

"Where's Officer Vernell?" she asked.

"Got her sitting with the family, making sure they don't talk to each other before we can get their statements. Not enough uniforms on scene to guard each one of them in a separate location. Didn't have the heart to put them in separate squad cars."

"Sister and father touch anything?" she asked.

"Said they didn't," Billy Ray answered. "Said they knew she was dead by the way she was lying there. I think they were too scared to touch her."

"Why?" she asked.

"Wait till you see," was all he said.

"Witnesses aside from the father and sister?" she asked.

"Maybe about three dozen or so but clueless as hell and they ain't here," he said. "They were having a Fourth of July barbecue, fireworks, lots of booze, the whole nine yards. By the time the sister found the body, everybody had jetted."

"What was the sister doing out at midnight?" Raven asked.

"Said she couldn't sleep. My guess is she was smoking something. Girl seems high as hell."

Raven nodded as Billy Ray went on. As she listened to his voice, which was both rhythmic and deep, she remembered when they became partners back in New Orleans. During their first week together, she had taken Billy Ray to dinner at the creole restaurant Dooky Chase. She winced at the impact to her cop's salary, but thought it was worth it to take him some place where they were unlikely to run into other cops. Besides, she had heard through the grapevine that Billy Ray liked to cook, and she was looking to score some brownie points. Dooky Chase was so famous for its food that it was once frequented by lions of the Civil Rights Movement. Everyone from Thurgood Marshall to Martin Luther King had been there. Even Barack Obama had sat at one of the tables with a bowl of gumbo in front of him. She thought herself lucky as hell to even get a reservation.

Over her double cut pork chops, and Billy Ray's redfish and eggplant, she said, "My father was the serial killer Floyd Burns, but you probably already know that. I watched him kill my mother. I was only five, don't remember much. And if it wasn't for the police reports that I've looked at since, sometimes I'd even question if it were real."

She watched him. He brought the rim of his beer glass to his lips, opened his mouth and emptied most of the contents down his throat. Raven went on. "I'm telling you this because there has to be an understanding between you and me. My other partner was so scared of me I couldn't walk in the room without him jumping out of his skin. It was annoying as hell. I need to know if you are going to be that way, because if you are, you probably want to ask the chief to hook you up with somebody else."

His intense brown eyes appeared to glow even in the brightness of the restaurant. He lowered the glass back down to the table a little too hard. It made a soft thump on the tablecloth. He looked at her, not quite drunk but getting there. Raven waited a moment. Then he said, "What's up with your eyes?"

She didn't say anything for a second or two. She wasn't sure that she heard him right.

"What do you mean what's up with my eyes? They're my eyes. Why are you even asking me about that?"

"Haven't you ever wondered?"

"Wondered what?"

"Why they are different colors and shit?"

"No, why would I?" Raven demanded sharply, because she knew it was a lie. She had always wondered, but not for the reasons he had probably thought.

"Ain't you ever looked it up on the internet?"

"No. Why would I look it up? My eyes are my eyes. You ever look up your eyes?"

Billy Ray shrugged. "No. But my eyes aren't different colors."

Raven shook her head. "Never crossed my mind to research my eyes."

"Well, I looked it up. It's called heterochromia. Two completely different-colored eyes. Very fucking rare. And rarer for it not to skip generations. Your daddy had it, didn't he? And you have it. You don't think that's strange?"

"I don't want to talk about this."

"Why? I thought we were sharing? I can't ask questions?"

"Not about stuff I can't help, and stuff that doesn't matter."

"And you could help your father?"

She said nothing. She waited for him to get to the point.

"It doesn't mean anything, your eyes. Medically, I mean. It could, though. But I don't think so in your case. Look how many miles you run every day. And you in good shape."

He leaned away from the table to get a better look at her lower half. "Real good shape," he continued. "But some people, Indians – not Indians from India but American Indians – they call them ghost eyes. Of course, you could be a witch too."

"I'm not a witch, Chastain. Not the last time I checked anyway."

"No? Ghost eyes, then," he said. "They say you can see into heaven and earth, good and evil at the same time by looking in the two separate places from each one of those eyes. You can see it all. Must be some kind of rush."

She leaned toward him. "Do you know what I see now, Chastain?" she asked.

"What?"

"My partner being an asshole."

After that encounter at Dooky Chase, they never had a serious discussion about her eyes or her father again. She was simply glad that Billy Ray wasn't afraid of her or, like some partners might, hadn't taken to calling her 'ghost eyes' as a joke.

★   ★   ★

She left the memory of New Orleans and Dooky Chase behind as the cadence of Billy Ray's sure voice brought her back to the Big Bayou estate and the murder scene. She stopped short of the entrance to the backyard and faced him. "Who's the victim?"

He returned her gaze with a steady one of his own before answering. "Hazel Westcott," he said.

Raven felt as if she had been punched in the gut. A trickle of fear light as a spider's leg crawled in her throat. She swallowed. Hazel Westcott had been dogging Raven in the year before Billy Ray came to Byrd's Landing, accusing Raven of things so horrible she couldn't even bear to tell him.

"Raven," he said, his voice grave. "You knew her, didn't you?"

She sighed, ran her hand through her spiraling hair. For a second or two, she thought about turning around and getting the chief on the phone, but the thought dissipated almost before it was fully formed. She was a good cop. She would do her job. But still. She sighed and said, "Did you notify the chief yet?"

"Yeah," he said. "Right after I called you."

"And he knew I was coming on scene?"

"Who else would he think would be coming, Raven?" he asked.

"Did he say he was coming down?" she asked. "The chief?"

He shook his head. "He said that he'd stay in town and manage things with the mayor there. Didn't want the mayor and the other hotshots getting in our way."

Raven nodded. There was her answer. If the chief thought there would be a problem, or he thought she would be anything less than objective, he would be on his way down. The chief's absence meant that he trusted her to do her job no matter who the victim was.

"He say anything else?" she asked.

"No," Billy Ray responded. "Said he was going to give Oral Justice a call, something about the community was going to be all over this."

Raven nodded. The chief was talking about Percival Oral Justice, a community leader who worked with the poor, especially troubled teens. Oral Justice was the unofficial liaison between the police and the community.

"You knew her," Billy Ray repeated, dragging her back to the question at hand.

She looked at him, still not wanting to tell him. Raven and Billy Ray had been in New Orleans together during the worst moment in the city's history. Katrina. They didn't know each other then, though they were both rookie patrol officers. He told her after they were homicide partners that he remembered seeing her after the levees had broken. She was leading a canoe in all her gear with muck up to her waist. An old woman with long gray braids sat in the canoe, her gnarled hands in a death grip on both sides of the boat. Raven believed that Billy Ray had seen her as a hero from the first moment he laid eyes on her. Even when she told him about Floyd, his initial view of her didn't change. After all, Floyd wasn't her fault. But Hazel Westcott was uncharted waters. She was unsure how Billy Ray would react.

.He waited. She put her hands on her hips and stuck a toe in the water. She said, "We had a run-in about a year ago, before you came up here to help me."

"That it? A run-in?"

Raven shook her head. "Okay, it was a bit more than that. She hated my guts, and I wasn't too fond of her either," she said. "And mostly everybody knows her father. Big shot in this town. Very wealthy. He owns Fast Money. Westcott is very well connected through his business and his charities. Man gives away so much money that they call him Big Daddy."

Billy Ray let out a cynical laugh. "You mean he owns those payday money loan stores and check-cashing places in the Bottoms? Son of a bitch would have to give to charity doing something like that. That's legalized loan sharking."

"Whatever it is, it's also political. He knows the mayor and the chief."

Billy Ray nodded "I figured the chief had some connection to the Westcotts when I talked to him earlier," he said. "How does he know Daddy Warbucks?"

"Not only the chief, but the mayor," Raven clarified. "Went to college with the mayor, I believe. He and the chief go some years back but I'm not sure from what."

"And your run-in with Hazel Westcott?" Billy Ray pressed.

She looked at him before quickly turning away.

"We'll talk about this later," he said. "But we will talk about it."

CHAPTER THREE

The officer guarding the gate gave Raven a clipboard with a sign-in sheet. Raven lifted her chin in greeting and wrote down her name and badge number. She checked her phone and then wrote the time – 1:45 a.m. Without looking at Billy Ray, she took several pairs of the shoe covers the uniformed officer was shoving toward her.

"Jumpsuits?" Billy Ray asked with a raised eyebrow as she started to walk into the backyard. He was referring to the personal protection equipment that the chief was trying to get everyone to wear at crime scenes no matter the location. The protective clothing was supposed to keep BLPD personnel from transferring hair or fibers onto the crime scene.

Raven shook her head. She felt the jumpsuits were too restricting, and not needed at every single crime scene. "Shoe covers should be enough."

She continued through the back gate and Billy Ray followed. She could see the white crime scene lamps and a glimpse of shimmering cloth out of the corner of her eye. *That must be the body*, she thought. But she ignored it, as did Billy Ray. The body was the least important thing at the moment – only part of the story. What was and wasn't around Hazel Westcott's corpse would complete it.

She took in the enormous backyard as Billy Ray continued the walk-through, pointing out where the responding officer had marked off the crime scene. Tennis courts, a saltwater swimming pool, and a short pier leading to a boathouse on the lake advertised unabashed wealth. She saw the trees that she remembered rising from Big Bayou, the Spanish moss hanging wraithlike from the cypress.

The trees in the backyard had been strung with white lights still twinkling but of little use in lighting a crime scene. But still, there was enough light to illuminate a sign in red and blue foil letters hanging over the patio doors. 'Happy Fourth!' the sign proclaimed. She could see what looked like the interlocking squares of a portable dance floor stacked near the patio's double French doors. Beer bottles and paper plates burst from the outdoor trash cans.

"I put another officer on the boathouse," Billy Ray was saying, pointing to an officer standing by a short iron gate. "That's where she lived, and I think that's a secondary scene in there."

"What makes you say that?" she asked.

He pointed to several broken branches on azalea bushes near the front door, and more disturbed shrubbery just outside the gate and along the path to the body. "He must have carried her out here," he said.

She nodded and started toward the body. Though CSI hadn't managed to put up tarps yet, two crime scene lamps illuminated Hazel Westcott. She was laid out on a patch of grass surrounded by more azaleas, loose pink petals all around her. Starting at the feet, which were bare, Raven began a slow scan of the body, noting both the position and condition of the hands, the curve of the hip, the tilt of the head. A white satin gown more fitting for a bride clung to Hazel's body, the bell sleeves fluttering lightly in the warm breeze. Raven gave herself permission to turn away for a couple of seconds. She felt sucker punched all over again. What a night to dream about a serial killer.

It wasn't the fact that she was staring at a dead body, or that she had known the victim. She had seen plenty of dead bodies, and investigating the homicides of people she had known was an on-the-job hazard in a small town like Byrd's Landing. It was the way this particular dead body was laid out, together with this particular acquaintance, that had shaken her.

Aside from dressing Hazel, the killer had posed her as if she had been waiting for a lover. One cheek lay against a folded arm. The other arm had been bent so her fingertips touched the parted lips in a come-hither gesture, while her glossy hair lay shining beneath the white light.

And the eyes.

Raven contemplated Hazel's fawn-colored eyes staring up at a Louisiana sky crazy with stars. Raven felt Floyd's ghost as she gazed into those eyes. She felt his presence so strongly that she could smell the Irish Spring soap he had always used.

Raven knew in her bones that this was the work of a serial killer. She wasn't sure if this was his first death or fiftieth, but she knew without a doubt that there would be more, and it was going to be a long morning, perhaps even a long next several weeks depending on when they caught him. *And I will be with you every step of the way, Birdy Girl*, said Floyd's voice in her head. That's what had her gut-punched, the idea of Floyd taking up residence in her head.

She considered Hazel's almost tranquil expression. It was far different from the face that had once stood in the middle of the Blue Heron restaurant and cocktail lounge screaming that Raven was a murdering whore just like her father was a murdering bastard – the only difference being that Floyd Burns got what he deserved.

She stopped and nodded at Hazel. "Has the coroner's office finished with the body?"

"No," Billy Ray answered. "Rita's been back and forth since she got here about twenty minutes before you." He was referring to Rita Sandbourne, the medical examiner Raven had seen peering into the open back doors of the coroner's van. He paused for a long moment before speaking again.

"Things like this make me want to get on back to New Orleans," he sighed.

Raven knew by his voice that like her, he was thinking that this was no ordinary murder, nor would it be an ordinary investigation. She didn't say anything because it was an old story between them. Billy Ray was burned out of homicide, out of all cop work. He was a tough guy, but had seen one too many teenagers with their heads blown off, arrested one too many husbands for killing the mother of their children, and was witness to one too many corruption battles back in New Orleans to remain a cop. He was saving every cent he had so he could quit the force and open his own creole restaurant in New Orleans. And he was ready to quit when she asked him to come to Byrd's Landing to help the city's new police department. A small twinge of guilt ran through her at having delayed what he thought of as his escape from police work.

"Billy Ray," she said now, the serious tone of her voice surprising her. "If you're going to make it to New Orleans, you better do like the song says and start walking. Byrd's Landing has a way of tying people down."

CHAPTER FOUR

"It doesn't even look like a homicide," Raven said briskly as she pulled on a pair of latex gloves, hoping her tone and decisive action would change the subject and help them get back to the matter at hand, which was a homicide she was responsible for solving.

"Well, trust me, it is," said a woman walking toward them from the direction of the back gate. She had on a pair of black jeans, work boots, and a windbreaker that crunched loudly every time she moved. The words 'Medical Examiner' were stenciled in tall white letters on the back. Rita Sandbourne grabbed a pair of blue latex gloves from the pocket of her windbreaker and snapped them over her bony fingers.

She flicked a glance at Raven and Billy Ray. "No jumpsuits?" she said, and shook her head. "What's the old grandma going to say?"

"Old habits are hard to break, Rita," Raven answered, kneeling down. "Besides, we're outside. And I can deal with the chief. Where's yours?"

Rita snorted and knelt next to Raven. "I've been doing this job more years than I can count. And I've done it without dressing up in clown clothes every time I need to touch a body. Too bad if the chief doesn't like it." She stopped and took a breath. "So, you two already know what I know. Death at the hands of another. I know I don't like fancy clothes, but I can't imagine anybody who'd dress up to the nines and lie in a bed of flowers before having a heart attack."

"Any chance it could be a suicide?" Billy Ray asked in a voice that said he already knew the answer.

Raven twisted around to get a three-sixty of the scene surrounding the body.

"Not a suicide," Raven reasoned. "If it was, she would have simply walked out the front door without trampling the bushes. She knew the place." She considered the body. "And why in the heck would she pose herself like this?"

Rita nodded in agreement before pointing to the body with a long blue index finger. "One other odd thing. I think she had a bath either before or after she was killed."

Raven didn't need the faint scent of fresh meat combined with the musty smell of sandalwood to tell her that Hazel had recently bathed. Maybe someone had forced her, or bathed her after she died. It was too early to know. She remembered Billy Ray's comment about the boathouse being the secondary scene. The bath would have had to have happened there along with the killing.

Raven curled her fingers around Hazel's and pulled them closer so she could take a good look at them. Just an old-fashioned manicure.

"No broken nails, can't see anything under them," Raven said.

As Hazel's fingers slipped from Raven's hand, Rita began bagging them.

Raven watched her for a second or two before asking, "Where's Crimes?"

"Where do you think you are, sugar?" Rita asked Raven. "Back in New Orleans? We only have two CSIs, remember? The other one is at a domestic homicide on the south side. We only have Tim, here," she said, indicating a tiny man struggling with a tarp and set of poles near the back gate. Raven noticed that he hadn't donned the jumpsuit either.

"He hasn't gotten as far," Billy Ray said dryly. "At least he has the lights up, and he's already taken pictures of the body."

The body. Raven turned back to Hazel Westcott lying dead in a satin dress. "Had to be someone strong to carry her way out here," she said. "I'm thinking male."

"Why male?" Rita said. "Kind of sexist if you ask me. The perp could have very well been a female."

Billy Ray said, "Had to be somebody strong, Rita."

"And women aren't strong?" she said, looking past him at Raven. "All it takes is a little weight lifting and some determination, right, Raven?" Rita looked over the body. "What do you think she weighs? One hundred? One ten? I betcha Raven could have carried her with all the time she's been spending in the gym lately."

Raven ignored her. She took a pencil from her jacket pocket. Using the pencil, she gently lifted a price tag from the neckline of the satin gown. She laid down the black ribbon attached to the tag around Hazel's neck with the same gentle motion.

"Brand new. I figured it would be," she said. "Expensive too."

She couldn't quite make out the light pen marks on the fancy price tag but didn't need to read it to know that the dress cost a mint. She turned the tag toward her so she could see the faint writing under the white crime scene lamps. "Miss Anne Marie's Place of Fine Clothes." She squinted. "One five zero zero," she read.

"One five zero zero?" Billy Ray said. "You mean fifteen hundred dollars? Scamming poor folks must be profitable."

"Never heard of Miss Anne Marie's," Rita said. Raven looked pointedly at Rita's work boots. Rita snorted. "Have you?"

"Nope," Raven lied. "But I think the bastard who bought her funeral clothes has. It means we're looking for someone who doesn't mind throwing down a lot of cash."

"Could be her dress," Billy Ray answered.

"It's not her dress," Raven and Rita said in unison.

"Why not?"

"Trust me, lover boy, it's just not," Rita said. "No self-respecting woman would buy a fifteen-hundred-dollar white satin gown to wear to a Fourth of July barbecue. Even I know that."

"Look how good it fits," Billy Ray said. "Maybe she bought it for something else."

The dress did fit well, a glowing white sheath harmonizing with the contours of Hazel Westcott's body.

Raven shrugged. "It must be someone who knows her well, like a boyfriend who would know what size she wears."

"I wouldn't be jumping to any conclusions," Billy Ray said.

"I jump all the time," Raven answered. "And what usually happens?"

"Shit." He chuckled. "Sometimes you get lucky, Raven."

"That's not luck," Raven said as she stood up. "That's skill. What do you think killed her?" she asked Rita.

"Hell if I know just by looking at her," Rita answered. And then pensively biting her lip, "Hard to tell."

"You got any hunches?" Raven pressed.

Rita sighed as if in surrender. "I hate to speculate on so little, but he could have smothered her, used a plastic bag after rendering her unconscious. I say 'rendering' because I don't know how the hell he did it without leaving one goddamn mark. But he could have used the bag for asphyxiation even though there's no discoloration around the nose and mouth."

Rita stood up suddenly. Raven noticed that she was chewing her lower lip bloody, a habit of hers that became worse when she was bothered.

"What else are you thinking, Rita?"

"Poison," she said. "God help me, I don't want to go all Hollywood but the only other thing I can think of is poison."

"But...." Raven began.

Rita held out her hands. "I know, I know. It still looks a little too pretty even for that. But I'll figure it out. Don't you worry."

Just as she said this there were startled yells coming from the entrance into the backyard. The uniformed officer who had been guarding the crime scene's entrance was now running after a determined woman wearing a tight black skirt, white jacket and sky-high black heels. She had a microphone in one hand and a small battered notebook in the other. Raven groaned.

Imogene Tucker, Byrd's Landing's intrepid news anchor, was running over the grass toward them, her spiked heels aerating the lawn as she went. Another uniform officer pushed a cameraman back through the fence and thankfully out of the crime scene.

"Oh, what fresh hell is this?" Raven muttered as the woman kept coming, no doubt destroying evidence along the way.

★   ★   ★

Raven knew the woman running as fast as she could on the soft lawn. Imogene Tucker was one of the most persistent reporters Raven had known during one of the most horrid episodes in her life. She was always sticking a microphone in her face asking in her nasal voice for an 'exclusive', only barely giving up when the public started losing interest in the story that she was after.

"Detective, Detective," Tucker said now with an excited edge to her voice. "Can you confirm the death of Hazel Westcott? Was foul play involved?"

Raven held both palms out to stop her. "You can't be here," she said. "Seriously. This is a crime scene that you're about to screw up. Officer...?" she called.

Tucker did her best to get around Raven's block. She came so close that Raven could smell the Wrigley's gum that the woman constantly chewed. When she couldn't get around Raven she stopped and gave her a pugnacious look. "I'm the press," she said and popped the gum in her mouth several times before continuing. "We still have freedom of the press in this town, don't we? Y'all didn't change that, did you?"

"Yes, we do have freedom of the press," Raven answered. "But not at an unprocessed crime scene. Sorry."

"Okay," Tucker said. "Just confirm the victim as Hazel Westcott, and I'll leave. I promise."

Raven was about to answer when someone grabbed Imogene Tucker's elbow. It was Lamont Lovelle, the department's media relations coordinator. Lovelle was an ugly black man made of short, hard muscle that he perfected at the gym. No indentations for a waist, hardly any neck separating his head from his shoulders. His nickname was SpongeBob, but it was a nickname he never heard because no one would dare say it within his hearing. With his broad face peppered with black freckles, he had to be the homeliest media relations coordinator that Raven had ever seen. He was not a police officer, but had been brought in after doing some freelance work for Internal Affairs.

"I don't think you have a lot of room to bargain," Lovelle said smoothly while maintaining the grip on Tucker's elbow. "The detective is correct. You should not be here."

"Oh, come on, Lamont," Tucker said. "Sweetie. Give me a break, will you?"

"I would if I could," Lovelle said.

He flicked a look at the body of Hazel Westcott. His eyes lingered for a while before turning to Raven. A sad smile crossed his face, making him seem beautiful for a moment, like a brief patron saint for all things damaged and suffering. He turned back to Tucker. "It would do no good for anyone if you get into trouble, and believe me, you don't want to see what's behind the good detectives. Why don't you come with me and we can work something out?"

"Whatever you work out," Raven said, "work it on out far away from here."

Tucker flashed a look over her shoulder at Raven while being forcibly but delicately guided away, her tiny red mouth in a full pout.

"What a freak show," Rita muttered, staring after them.

"How did they even know about this?" Billy Ray asked.

"Everybody's got a police scanner," Raven said. "And nowadays with the internet, everybody's got an app."

CHAPTER FIVE

Raven knew that it wasn't protocol to survey a crime scene before CSI, not in Byrd's Landing, but she didn't trust the crime scene investigators. They operated too much by the book, sanitized a crime scene so much with their rules and procedures that she had a hard time feeling what had happened. Besides, there was only one CSI on-site. They would be waiting all night if they had to wait for him.

Billy Ray and Raven walked around the saltwater pool toward the pier. On a wooden sign held by hooks to a black iron gate, the words 'The Boathouse' were printed in cursive letters.

A sidewalk of uneven red brick led to the pier and the boathouse. Timber pilings rose from the lake to support the small building. The murky water of Big Bayou Lake lapped against the supports. The exterior of the house was dark, so dark that its flat roof and exterior walls were no more than a collection of shadows.

Raven and Billy Ray paused by the front door to slip on the shoe covers so they wouldn't transfer any forensic evidence from the outside scene into the boathouse. Raven noted that there were no signs of forced entry, and while CSI may not have been inside the boathouse yet, they had at least dusted the doorknob and jamb for prints. Billy Ray grinned when he saw her noticing the fingerprint dust.

"I had the CSI guy do that earlier. Figured it would take him a while to get inside the boathouse. Didn't want to have to wait on him to lift prints from the front door."

They opened the door onto a large living room decorated with jars of seashells and light blue pillows with red anchors appliquéd on them. Raven noted that there was not a picture out of place on the room's red walls. The maple hardwood floor was freshly swept and polished – no signs of a struggle anywhere.

But Hazel Westcott's room was a different story. Clothes were strewn over the bedroom floor as if someone had been desperately searching for something fresh to wear amid the extravagant mess. On the bed itself, clothes with the tags still on them were stacked in various places. Shopping bags from Dillard's, Macy's, and Neiman Marcus took up more space. Shoes were strewn across the floor in a tangle of dyed pink alligator skin, oiled black leather, spiked heels, and strappy fringed sandals made of suede. The floor was a minefield of shoes.

A fecund smell of unwashed body exuded from the dirty clothes spilling out of a white straw hamper. Several pairs of running shorts were thrown down next to it on the floor. On top of that scent was another, the warm and musky smell of sandalwood.

"You think somebody tore this place up?" Billy Ray asked her.

Raven shook her head. Hazel Westcott was a girl who cared about appearances. It would make sense that the living room where she had guests would be clean while her bedroom, her own private space, would reflect her life. She had a full social life, probably always in a hurry. She just happened to be killed at a time when a spending spree collided with laundry day.

Raven swept away the jangle of nerves that came along with even the slightest hint of domestic disorder. It had taken two therapists engaged by her foster parents to tame the OCD that these days manifested itself in an apartment as sanitized as a hospital ward. She wondered how Hazel could have stood it.

She pulled on a fresh pair of blue latex gloves. In the Dillard's shopping bag, she fished out the receipt and made a mental note of when the purchase was made. She examined the receipt from the Macy's bag.

"What is it?" Billy Ray asked.

"Looks like these purchases were made the same day."

"Recently?"

"Yeah," Raven said. "This past weekend. Don't know what it means."

Billy Ray grinned. "It means the dress she's wearing out there is hers."

"I don't think so," Raven said. She could find no Miss Anne Marie's shopping bag with its velvet black and gold handles. She didn't see a long box that an evening gown would have come in.

"I'm going to hit the bathroom," Billy Ray said. "And get Tim from Crimes in here."

She nodded but didn't respond. She didn't need to go into the bathroom. Instinct told her what he would find. There would be open lotion from Hazel's private stash, toilet water spilled all over the place, maybe some white powder of the same scent. The tub would be glossy with moisture, maybe even wet depending on what time she bathed or was bathed. Splashes of water would be on the floor around the bathtub. They'd find some hairs, too, but those hairs would mostly be glossy black. The killer would have worn gloves. He would have taken pains to ensure nothing of himself remained at the crime scene.

"It happened on the bed," Raven said to Billy Ray, who had returned to the room.

"How do you figure?" Billy Ray asked.

"Well," she said, "the sheets are coming off, like someone was wrestling on it."

"But she didn't have any bruises," Billy Ray said. "She would have had bruises if she were fighting somebody off."

Raven grinned. "Who said anything about fighting?"

The corners of Billy Ray's mouth pulled up in a slight smile. "Okay. So they were having sex. How did he overpower her?"

"A sleeper hold?" Raven ventured.

But Billy Ray was already shaking his head. "No," he said. "It would have taken some time before she went to sleep, and even after that she would have woken up fast. Not enough time to get her in the tub."

"What if he forced her to bathe before he killed her?" Raven speculated.

Billy Ray shrugged. "Could have, but I think she'd still have some marks no matter when he overpowered her."

Raven nodded in agreement. Hazel Westcott would have fought like hell before she went under. There would have been at least one bruise, maybe a broken fingernail or two. Instead her body was perfect.

You could be right about the bed, girly, a voice said in her head. Floyd's voice. She had been living with him occupying a corner of her mind for so long that his voice had merged with hers. Sometimes, she believed that his thoughts were just her own instincts speaking. *I still would have done it on the bed. Maybe pretended like I was taking her for a good ole roll in the hay. If I didn't want to scar her up none but wanted her dead just the same, I would have found me some poison, but not one of them poisons that caused a lot of muscle tensing and frothing at the mouth and carrying on. It wouldn't be no ugly poison.*

She thought about this for a long time, ticking off poisons in her head and dismissing them. Antifreeze would be too slow. There would be signs. Cyanide would be faster, but still, there would be symptoms. Arsenic, no. None of the common poisons would do.

"There was this case, Billy Ray," she said, "before you came up here."

She told him that the wife had murdered her husband over a period of time with antifreeze. It was a long death that caused much pain to the man she had been married to for over twenty years. When Raven finally caught her she asked her why she used antifreeze, something that took weeks and wreaked much more havoc than needed in order to simply kill. The woman shrugged and answered that she had nothing against her husband. She killed him for the insurance money. But she just couldn't think of any other way.

"So, what are you trying to say?" Billy Ray asked. "What has that got to do with this case?"

"I'm getting to that," she said. "What did you find in the bathroom?"

"Probably what you already figured. A mess that smells much better than the stink in here. There're some hairs, hers most likely. I've got CSI in there now."

"Perfume hers?"

"Seems so," he said. "But hard to tell."

"Did you see any clothes in there, clothes she may have been wearing earlier tonight?"

"No," he said. "Nothing like that. Just bath stuff, and lots of makeup. Almost an entire department store of makeup."

She nodded, only half listening.

"That bothered me for a long time," Raven continued the story. "That the only thing the woman could think of was antifreeze. It's like she never heard of Google, or better, talked to a librarian. So I did some research for poisons that killed quickly and effectively. Talked to a few doctors about stuff that wouldn't show up in autopsy reports."

"And what did you find?" Billy Ray asked.

"Well," she said, "what I found wasn't exactly poison, depending on your perspective."

"Perspective?"

"Yep," Raven said. "Perspective."

Raven had finished her examination on top of the bed. She then searched on both sides of the headboard and behind it. Nothing. She knelt down to look beneath. She didn't find the syringe that she only half expected. He had of course taken it with him. He didn't want to be caught. Not just yet. She knew that the only thing that would stop a killer so in love with the beauty of death was another death – either his or someone else's.

She was about to stand up when something caught her eye, a quick flash of blue. She put a penlight into her mouth and squirmed beneath the bed. The object lay on its side, leaning against the bottom of the bedpost. Raven felt as if she was about to faint. The only thing that stopped her was her pride. She didn't want to have to explain why she passed out in the middle of a crime scene.

Being on the job as long as she had, Raven carried things. The penlight she had in her mouth now, the extra weapon strapped to her ankle, tissue paper and evidence bags for retrieving evidence when someone from Crimes wasn't around. She grabbed the object with a pair of disposable tweezers and placed it in one of the plastic bags. It was as light and delicate as a breath. When it and the tweezers were securely in her pocket, she used her elbows to squirm from beneath the bed and was caught by a flash of white light in her eyes.

"Jeez Louise, Billy Ray!" she said.

Billy Ray, holding a flashlight, pulled her up by her arm.

"You were under there for a long time. You find anything?"

As she smoothed her T-shirt back into her jeans and blinked the light from her eyes, she said, "No, not a blooming thing."

But, of course, it was a lie. She had found something beneath Hazel Westcott's bed. She had found a link to the past. Hidden in her pocket was a link to Floyd 'Fire' Burns, the man who was and always would be her father.

CHAPTER SIX

Many years after he left home, Floyd walked out of the mirage glimmering along the newly tarred road as if he were walking up from hell. He wasn't that young, maybe thirty-four or thirty-five at that time in 1983. But he was handsome in a pure country kind of way, with a crooked smile and a beige fedora sporting a blue-and-green peacock feather in the hatband.

Instead of the polyester and angel-wing shirt he used to favor, he wore a pair of overalls with one strap hanging and a beige Henley long-sleeved shirt beneath. He carried a green canvas bag slung over his shoulder, the kind that they give you in the army. But he had cut it in half and had a cobbler sew the bag along the bottom so that it was much shorter and funnier looking than any soldier's duffle bag that a body probably ever seen.

It was hot, and he was sweating some, but the man he saw standing over the open hood of a red-and-white 1960 Ford F-100 that had seen better days was sweating more. The engine sent a whistle of steam into the still, hot air. The man, who would later introduce himself as Mr. Love, looked country from the tips of his thrice-repaired brogans to the broke-down hat on top of his head. His country almost outdid Floyd's, but his country wasn't faked.

Floyd walked up to him as if he already knew him. They stood beside each other, looking at the exposed engine as if just by staring at it they could get it to stop acting a fool and start doing what engines are supposed to do.

"Whew, boy," Floyd said, letting his words end in a long whistle. "She's looking hotter than I feel."

The stranger didn't say anything, just looked at the engine with both thumbs hanging from his front pant loops. Finally, he said in an accent thick with Louisiana, "Figurin' you can help me with it?"

Floyd knew who this man was the minute the man opened his

mouth. That is, he knew where he had come from even if he didn't know his name. And if not him personally, he knew where the man's people had come from. Floyd had heard the story plenty of times since leaving his own family. On the road when he happened to stop here and there for a room or a bite to eat, Floyd ran into blacks from the south. They told him as they gave him a place to sleep and a fried chicken dinner for a few dollars how their mammas and daddies had gotten tired of Jim Crow keeping everybody separate, tired of eating a poor man's feast of beans and rice, and especially tired of learning in one-room schoolhouses while paying taxes just as pretty as you please and just like everybody else. So when they or their people finally got the chance in the 1940s and 1950s, they hopped the trains out of that hellhole called Louisiana as quick as they could.

Most of 'em ended up in California. And now Floyd knew that some of 'em, like this man, ended up right here so as to be standing on a small-town California dirt road in a broke-down truck waiting on ole Floyd to show up and rescue him.

"I'd be willing to help you get it going. Yes sir," Floyd said. "If you give me a ride after."

The man turned to look at him then. For a second or two, it seemed as if he knew exactly what kind of man Floyd Burns was and the knowing sent a sliver of ice right straight to his heart. But like most people, Mr. Love sent the feeling packing in the face of Floyd's made-up country charm.

He told Floyd his name and Floyd let the shortened duffle bag drop to the ground. He tilted his hat back and then he pumped Mr. Love's hand like he was the first person he had seen after forty days in the desert.

"Floyd Burns."

"Floyd?" Mr. Love said only because he was hot and uncomfortable and wanted his hand back.

"Fire, really," Burns said. "They call me Fire."

"Well, you sure brought the fire," he said. "You live around here? I ain't never seed you."

"That's because I've been traveling some," Floyd said. "I just got into town right at this very moment. Born and raised north of here. Looking for work."

"And what is it that you do?"

"I'm a preachin' man," Floyd said.

And that's how it started. He made it up right then and there. He mixed up all of the preachers he had seen while growing up on his family's farm, in all of his going-to-church Sundays, in all of the evangelists selling prayers on television. He was Oral Roberts. He was Swaggart and Graham all rolled into one. His photographic memory flashed on a piece of trivia he read in an abandoned *Reader's Digest* at a Mariposa bus depot and he added the 1930s preacher Aimee McPherson to the mix before topping the entire preacher sundae off with Jim Bakker and his always-bawling wife, Tammy Faye. Floyd – now Fire – Burns had turned himself into a preachin' man.

"Preachin' man?" Mr. Love asked.

"Yes sir," Floyd said, his voice as expansive as the flat white-hot day surrounding them. "Heard the calling when I was sixteen. Kissed the tears from my cryin' mamma's cheeks and took up preachin' the word of God. Ten years and I ain't seen her since."

The other man grunted. He said, "I ain't got religion like that myself. And even if I did, I don't think that praying is going to start this piece of shit up."

Floyd put a serious look on his face and nodded in agreement. He cast a sidelong glance at Mr. Love. Floyd did then what Floyd did best. He sized him up. He needed to know what he could use him for later. Right away he knew that Mr. Love was probably a well-respected man in this no-name hellhole. He didn't flinch when Floyd told him that he was a preacher, even told this preaching man that he didn't care too much for religion. Then he cursed. And he had questioned Floyd about his past as if he had a right to do it. Floyd turned back to the engine and stroked his chin, pretending to look for reasons why it wasn't turning.

"Well, Preachin' Man," Mr. Love said. "Do you know anything about truck engines?"

"Hotwired a few in my time," Floyd said without thinking. The minute it was out of his mouth, Floyd knew it was a dangerous thing to say. But he had been so carried away and tickled with himself for coming up with his new profession as a preacher that he had slipped up.

Before the other man could really think on what Floyd had just said, Floyd laughed and clapped him on the back. "That was before I found the Lord, of course."

Mr. Love looked at him hard and for a long time. Then he laughed, not seeing Floyd let out the breath that he had been holding. "You ain't said nothing but a thang, brotha."

And as they used the glue and supplies Mr. Love had in the bed of the old Ford, they talked of the town, what kind of place it was, what the people were like.

After they got the truck running with a lot of shouts and good-natured ribbing, Floyd went home with the man he had helped on the side of the road. His wife made chicken and dumplings and a peach custard pie for dessert. Floyd ate every bite while making her feel like the most beautiful woman on earth. Unfortunately, that night her daughter, young Maylene Love, felt like the second most beautiful woman on earth, a close and good enough second to her mother.

Later on in a jailhouse interview, Floyd would call the daughter a one-legged diabetic who was ugly to boot. But that night he smiled at her. He winked and helped her with the dishes while her father leaned against the kitchen counter praising the town. How much he loved it, how a man could really make a living here though the land liked to hold things back every once in a while and the sky was sometimes stingy with rain. But it was the best place to be if a man was willing to work and in need of a family. And as he jawboned on and on, Floyd thought that though he might be well-respected, Mr. Love sure wasn't nary as smart as he should have been.

CHAPTER SEVEN

The family told Floyd that Maylene lost her left leg below the knee when she was seven years old. It was around that time that the Loves discovered that their daughter had a chronic condition. But after thinking on it some, Floyd took back the part about her being ugly. She wasn't fat, but plump in a young gal's pleasing sort of way and had a habit of brushing her light brown hair straight back from her broad forehead. She was just a nice churchgoing gal with good manners and fine brown eyes even though all that Jesus praying got kinda tiresome sometimes.

She believed the gospel from her outsides all the way back into her insides. The Old Testament and the New. If it was between the covers of a Bible it had happened. She behaved as if she witnessed Noah's ark being built on Main Street, John the Baptist's head on a silver platter at the local diner, and Jesus dying for our sins on a cross erected for the occasion in the high school football stadium.

Maylene had told her father from the time she was twelve that she was going to marry a preacher. When Floyd came along, it seemed only natural that they'd get together. So Mr. Love went on and let it happen.

The wedding was scheduled for noon on a hot June day out at the lake. The lake had been so clear the day before that those preparing for the wedding joked about scooping out some fish with their bare hands and doing a quick roast over an open flame for lunch.

But when they got there the next morning all the fish were dead. They had died in the water and then floated until they collected along the banks like pressed silver dollars. A stench something awful hovered in a fine dust just above the dead fish before settling on the congregation's Sunday best.

Mrs. Love backed away from the dead water with a gloved white hand covering her mouth and nose. Maylene's father demanded that they call the whole thing off. He may not have had a lot of religion, he said, but he damned well knew an omen when he saw one.

Floyd, like Maylene's mother, was backing away, an uneasy look on his face. For once he was plumb out of things to say. He couldn't think of one mumbling word in the face of all this death on the day he was supposed to get married. Maylene, though, with a wreath of red and white carnations in her light brown hair, seemed peaceful. Almost a head taller than Floyd and twice as wide, she was able somehow to keep him from cutting and running.

Everybody was waiting for Floyd to say something, but it was Maylene who spoke first. She said, "My, my, my, I see the devil was quite busy last night."

A low murmur flowed over the congregation. But the voices were so low it was hard to tell if there was about to be a wedding or if the witnesses were about to get in their Chevys and Ramblers with their fried chicken and homemade biscuits and head home.

Maylene looked at the crowd with her fine eyes and said even louder, "I say, the devil was quite busy last night."

"Amen, sister," a couple of the brave said.

She nodded. "But we are not going to let this foolishness stop this wedding, are we?"

"Maylene," her father said, "I ain't never seed anything as terrible as this as long as I have been on this earth. And I've been around longer than most. Ain't no weddin' goin' on here today."

She gave him a look that made him step back. There was the fire of determination in her eyes, a determination of the foolhardy, but determination nonetheless. She said, "We ain't gone let 'im win. We gone tell Satan not today, right? Not today!"

There were a few louder mumbles behind the hands they pressed to their mouths to keep the smell from getting down too deep inside of them. Then Floyd freed himself from Maylene's arm. He held both of his hands up to a sky hanging clear and blue over the dead fish.

"We must have faith in the Lord," he said. "This is the place he has chosen for us to wed, and this shall be it. We are not going to let the de-*vel*, the *e-vil Lu-ci-ferrrr* run us out with our tails between our legs? Are we?"

"No sir, brotha," they all said, louder now.

Floyd remembered his preaching mojo then. He swirled, he danced, he turned and pointed to one faithful and then another. He waved his arm in fury at the lake, calling it an abomination but not a victory.

People who thought they were going to a wedding then found themselves at a revival. Pretty soon when Floyd shouted something, they repeated it. Then he shouted something else and they repeated that. He said 'amen' and they said 'amen' louder and stronger than anybody ever heard 'em do before. One woman started shaking and convulsing and she fell to the ground speaking in tongues. Her husband knelt beside her and told her to hush but she wouldn't, so he left her be.

In no time at all two brawny farm boys picked up the wedding arch and moved it away from the water. They then picked up the tables, the red and white balloons, and the folding chairs that had been set out the day before and moved them farther away. The women went to the cars and brought out coolers of fried chicken, sweet ice tea, strawberry pies, and foil pan after pan of peach cobbler as if they were trying to feed the multitudes rather than a congregation of less than thirty.

Later, Floyd knew not one of 'em would have remembered what he had said even if God had asked them. They would have thought about it for a long time, but in the end they would laugh that uneasy laugh of the dumb. They wouldn't remember any of it.

Mr. Love watched. The women talked and laughed in over-loud voices. They fussed over Maylene's dress and hair while holding bodies and heads in such a way that they didn't have to look at the lake. Then someone started singing a cappella, and someone else started tugging at Mr. Love's arm. Before he knew what was happening he was walking down the aisle to deliver his daughter into the hands of Floyd 'Fire' Burns, the smell of death at his back.

CHAPTER EIGHT

On the day before the Fourth of July and five years after his daughter Raven was born, Floyd walked into the Lentland Bank and Trust just before closing and cleaned out the church's bank account. He walked away with upward of 30,000 dollars, the money the church was aiming to use for a bigger parking lot, which had been needed to accommodate all the folk who started coming to the once near-empty church because of Floyd's preaching.

While Maylene cooked dinner he packed a suitcase. He folded his jeans and two starched shirts into it before trying to figure out what to pack for Raven. He finally settled on two dresses, one of them denim with ruffles at the sleeves, and a pair of pink tights. On top of that he threw a couple pairs of corduroys and a yellow T-shirt with 'Groovy' written across it in black balloon letters. Nothing matched. And he didn't quite know what he was doing. That made him think for a minute and he almost changed his mind.

But then Maylene started singing at the top of her lungs, some come-to-me-Jesus song that Floyd couldn't place but drove him crazy all the same. He thought as she hollered that maybe he didn't know a thing about bringing up a child, but neither did Maylene know a thing about singing or keeping a husband happy, or for that matter raising someone special like his little Birdy. And he'd be damned if he left a part of himself with someone who would turn it into a mindless Bible-thumping lump of flesh.

He finished packing by putting his straight razor in his shaving bag along with a can of Barbasol shaving cream and a bar of Irish Spring soap still in its wrapping. The straight razor was the only kind of razor he ever used. And Barbasol was the only kind of shaving cream that could give his whiskers a decent run for their money. Floyd liked the commercial, the mindless jingle that went something like 'Barbasol, most modern shaving cream of all'. It tickled him every time it came across the TV screen.

He put the suitcase down in full sight along the right wall leading to the front door. He went to the bathroom and washed his hands for a long time with the Irish Spring from the dish. He listened to the water falling against the porcelain as he rubbed his palms together briskly thinking of nothing in particular, just whistling the Barbasol jingle before getting bored with that one and starting on another. When he finished, he dried his hands on a rag and walked into the kitchen. He sat down to dinner without saying a thing.

He killed Maylene as she dried the dinner dishes. He balled the five fingers of his right hand into a tight fist and socked her in the side of the head. He hit her so hard that the bone in her forearm cracked when she fell against the stove.

She tried to say something but he hit her again, this time in the stomach. He did so with high style and good form while thinking about his daddy the boxer. She fell to the linoleum and curled herself up like a baby in the womb. Maybe by then she just gave up and waited for the Jesus she so truly believed in to come and take her on home.

But Floyd tortured her for hours well into the night as a fog rolled in and settled around the house and the church. Finally, as Maylene lay broken and bleeding on the kitchen floor, he sank a butcher knife into her flesh right where he figured the heart should have been. The shattered ribs moved easily aside to let the blade in. He leaned close to her face and studied her. He wondered if there was really a little light in people's eyes that meant they were alive and if that light really did go out when they died. He waited and nothing happened. He was just about to decide that everybody was wrong when the light flickered and dimmed before fading into nothing. "Well, I'll be. Hot damn if they ain't right," he muttered before pulling the knife from her chest and wiping the blood on a dish towel.

He dug a hole in the backyard. He figured that digging a hole in her zinnia bed next to the tomatoes was something he should do because that's how husbands usually buried their wives – and sometimes wives buried their husbands – in the movies. They buried them in the back garden where no one would find them for years, even when the tomatoes fattened until their red skins were as tight as blisters. He leaned on the shovel and looked his work over and smiled at how well he had covered Maylene over. He stood there a minute or two, not knowing what to do next. Finally, he looked over at Raven, who was sitting on the back porch step sucking her thumb like she used to do when she was two years old.

"Why," he said, "I feel like I should say a few words. Don't you?"

Raven said nothing, just worked on her thumb as if it were the only thing that mattered to her in the world right then.

"How about this, Birdy Girl?" He took the peacock feather tucked into the hatband of his fedora and made a show of laying it on Maylene's grave while saying, "So long, so long, so long, my darling," in a high sweet voice. And then, "Be sure to tell Jesus 'hi' and put in a good word for your ole man."

And they probably wouldn't have found Maylene for a long time, but Floyd set fire to the house and the church. He knew it would probably get him caught but by God, he couldn't help himself. He poured kerosene over the yard and the porch in such an intricate pattern that the flames looked like jumbled-up writing as they slithered yellow and blue through the low white fog before finding the porch steps. Floyd lifted his hands as he stepped back from the heat of the flames, and said, "God let a pestilence loose among ye sinners to spread his wrath. Fire does *burn!*"

Later Floyd read in the newspaper about how a fireman found Maylene's body by poking with an axe at something that just didn't look right in the zinnia bed. He wondered if it was the peacock feather on top of Maylene's shallow grave.

No one questioned who would do such a thing or why they would do it. Everyone knew it was Floyd. With all that preaching about fire this and fire that, he was bound to go over the fence one of these days.

Floyd knew that the sheriff would think he would be an easy man to find, especially with his one blue eye and one green eye, drifting around with a small girl. But Floyd didn't plan on being caught. It took years to find him, long enough for him to kill and kill again. He did so as he rambled with his daughter away from California, leaving his mark in Arizona, New Mexico, Texas, and finally Louisiana. He stayed free and killing long enough for him to take on one of them crazy nicknames. The papers called him the Fourth of July Killer because of that awful killing of his first wife. Even though Floyd wasn't partial to any particular day – any day was good enough for killing – that nickname made him right proud.

CHAPTER NINE

Raven didn't know if the memory belonged to her or if it was one she created by reading the police reports from her mother's crime scene. But she kept seeing the green-and-blue peacock feather flicker in the back porch light of her childhood home as Floyd placed it on her mother's grave. And she could hear him singing *So long, so long, so long, my darling* in a voice that sounded like an angel's.

The memory always played in her mind when she had to meet a victim's family. Now she was meeting with another father – Hazel Westcott's – in an attempt to find out who killed his daughter. And, once again, she had to forcefully will that awful song out of her head as she sat facing Antwone Westcott in the library of his large mansion. Having dismissed the officer who had been chaperoning Hazel's family since the murder, Billy Ray had taken a seat in another leather armchair beside Raven.

She had only been on scene a little over an hour, but with the memories of Floyd on her mind, she felt that days had passed since she received Billy Ray's call telling her of the homicide. Floyd always had a way of slowing time.

Westcott sat behind a cherrywood desk polished so furiously that it reflected the low light emanating from the lamp next to him. He was rubbing one large hand slowly back and forth across the surface. He frowned down at the desk as if he could find answers about his daughter's death there in the reflected light.

Unlike his wife and daughter, who sat on opposite ends of a button-backed leather couch, he was not in pajamas and robe, but fully dressed in a Ralph Lauren navy polo shirt. Raven couldn't see his legs but guessed that he probably wore a pressed pair of coordinating slacks. His face was meticulously shaved, his bald scalp oiled to a shine. Raven wondered about a man who would shower and dress so soon after discovering his daughter dead in the back garden.

She knew that he had been a linebacker at LSU, a position that required strength and mass and relentless resolve. His teammates called him the Wall; his professors called him good enough to pass. He was able to graduate with a NFL contract with the Oakland Raiders under one arm and a New Orleans high society bride hanging on the other. He played for five seasons, even managing to escape into enemy territory by playing several seasons for the 49ers. The savvy move netted him three Super Bowl rings during his five-year career. Once back in his hometown of Byrd's Landing he started what Billy Ray described earlier as nothing more than a legalized loan sharking business. He sold cash to the poor. The interest rate was so high that pretty soon his customers were paying five and six times the meager amount that they borrowed.

Now that look of strength and the muscled mass that supported him through college and his stint in the NFL had transformed into hard rolls of flesh. His jowls hung low on his large face, giving his eyes a droopy look. The only evidence that he was upset that his daughter lay dead in the flower bed was that massive hand sweeping back and forth, back and forth over the smooth surface of the cherrywood.

Aside from senseless killings, Raven knew that this was another part of the job weighing on Billy Ray's soul. He let the grief of the family eat at him. While Raven empathized, she tried not to let it distract her. Death was inevitable, whether a person was hit by a bus, died of old age, or was murdered. It happened to the old and young, the rich and poor, saints and sinners. This wouldn't be the only time Antwone Westcott would be frowning down at his desk wondering how was it that death had claimed something he had thought of as exclusively his. In this case, she and Billy Ray just happened to be the ones who confirmed the news. She could feel Billy Ray shift in his seat. Raven simply let the silence stretch around them.

Finally, Westcott spoke. "Do you have any idea who may have done this?" His voice was what she expected, heavy and deep as if it came from a long way down inside his immense body.

Raven was about to respond when Hazel Westcott's mother stood up. The look on the woman's face froze the words on Raven's lips. She searched Raven's eyes and then Billy Ray's, her body beneath the blue chiffon wrap flexed and tense. Raven thought for a moment that Billy

Ray would stand in case Hazel's mother needed support, and then she sensed rather than saw him lean back. Raven erased all emotion from her face. She knew what Hazel's mother was looking for, what she was waiting for them to say. She had seen those looks all too many times and there was no way that she could give Shelia Westcott, Hazel's mother, what she wanted. She gave Raven one more look before a heavy sigh escaped her lips. Her entire body seemed to deflate.

"I was waiting for you to tell me that it was all a mistake," Shelia Westcott said. She had an accent colored with all things New Orleans, but her voice was high and light almost like a child's. "I was waiting for you to tell me..." she stopped and closed her eyes, turning her head to the side as if it were the most painful thing she had done in her life, "...that she was playing a prank, you know, like she did when she was little."

The room was silent, an empty quiet that Raven knew Billy Ray wanted to fill with anything other than the waves of grief coming from Hazel's mother. The woman had a drink in her hand, whiskey probably, and Raven could hear the ice slide against the glass as her hand wavered. She continued, "Lord, Hazel and those pranks. Lord, Lord, Lord."

"Shelia," Westcott said. "That's enough."

Westcott's eyes flickered toward his wife. He only looked at her for a second or two, but his expression and tone said that he had always been a man who thought he had a right to tell women what to do just as he had a right to plenty of money and a just God.

"Sit down," he said in clipped tones.

Shelia Westcott sat back down next to her remaining daughter, who looked like she was high on something. Angel Westcott was a dark brown girl almost as tall as her sister. Her eyes were red and she swayed as if the ground beneath her moved.

"My wife, Shelia. My daughter, Angel, Detectives." Westcott stopped moving his hand long enough to slowly point to each one of them with his palm cupped as if he would have gladly offered them both in trade for his dead daughter.

Raven acknowledged them with a nod and said, "I'm sorry about Hazel."

Westcott looked her full in the face for a long time. "You are?"

She didn't answer him, only nodded once.

"Even after all the hell she caused you?" he asked. "You sorry?"

She didn't drop her gaze. "Believe it or not, I am, Mr. Westcott," she said. "And we are going to figure out who did this."

He dropped his eyes back to the surface of his desk. His hand started going again. Raven let the silence play. It was broken only by Shelia with a shaking hand putting the drink down on the coffee table. She reached into the pocket of her robe and pulled out a pack of Marlboros and a pink lighter. She shook a cigarette out of the packet onto the palm of her thin hand, put it to her lips and flicked the lighter. She began sucking on the filter long before the tobacco caught flame.

"Mamma, please," Angel said as if she were protesting in a dream. "Nobody wants to be smelling that shit right now."

Tresses of smoke curled in front of Shelia's eyes. "Sorry, Detectives. Please excuse my daughter's language. She really does know how to speak English, though you wouldn't know it when she opens her mouth."

"Get the detectives some tea," Westcott said without looking at her. "Both of you."

Shelia rose and walked past Raven, Angel walking so closely behind her that she stepped on the heels of Shelia Westcott's house slippers. The smell of Jack Daniel's whiskey drifted over to Raven. Not straight, but what Raven and her friends in high school used to call two-dollar Jack after they cut the pint in half with water and dumped sugar into it.

"We'll need witness statements from them both, eventually," Raven said.

"They're in no condition to talk to anybody," Westcott said.

"And when will they be?"

He looked at her a long time. She fought to keep her eyes steady on his. He said, "You and I both know that that'll be 'round 'bout the twelfth of never."

"We'll need to talk to them sometime," she said. "Them and everyone who attended the party. You know that, don't you?"

He shrugged. "Talk to anybody you want. My wife is a mess right now. You can see that. My daughter, the live one, is afraid of her own shadow. I saw her run away from a sneeze the other day."

"They shouldn't be alone right now," Billy Ray broke in. "Let me get one of the officers back—"

He stopped speaking when Westcott rose and walked from behind the desk. Raven had been right. He was wearing khaki slacks pressed to a crease so sharp it could cut. His great belly swinging over his belt, he grabbed a chair identical to Raven's and sat down in it. It rocked under his weight.

"If you think they need a babysitter, Detective," Westcott said, "why don't you join them? Go help the women with the tea if you so worried about them being alone." He never took his eyes off Raven.

She avoided Billy Ray's eyes, not because she was embarrassed for him but because she couldn't afford to take her eyes from Westcott's. She could feel Billy Ray looking at the big man, but she also knew that her partner was a good cop. It would take much more than this to wound his pride. He would not only be able to chaperon the mother and daughter, who were now witnesses, he would be able to pump them for information beyond the shadow of the controlling father.

"Yes sir," he said with a slight smile. "I will go help the women with the tea. After all, tea is my thang."

Westcott didn't acknowledge Billy Ray as he left. Instead, he leaned forward in his chair and placed an elbow on top of his thigh. His other hand dangled between his legs. If it weren't for the chair he would look like he was getting in position to block on the football field. His back was arched, his ass pinned to the back of the chair. Raven surmised that it was on the football field that he had felt invincible. He needed to feel invincible now. He locked eyes with Raven.

Raven leaned over in her chair as well, met his gaze with a focused one of her own.

"Do you know of anyone who wanted to hurt your daughter, Mr. Westcott?"

"Aside from you?" he asked.

She laughed then, but without amusement. She sat back. "I never wanted to hurt her," she said. "She drove me crazy, but I never wanted to hurt her."

"Sounds like we have something in common, then," he said, his voice dry. And then, "My daughter hated your bloody guts, Detective."

"I know that," she said.

He sighed and broke eye contact. "She wasn't too fond of me either, especially lately. All of a sudden she develops a conscience. Went around the house criticizing me for the business, holding it against me for breathing her air."

She waited, letting him talk.

"Still, she didn't have a conscience enough not to take my money, I'll tell you that," he added.

He reached into his pants pocket and removed a handkerchief. He blew his nose hard before stuffing it back in the pocket. His eyes now rimmed in red, he continued talking. He told her that during his first year at LSU, someone murdered a friend of his, stabbed him underneath a bridge on a summer's night before dragging his body behind the pillar on the north side.

"He lay there all curled up for a long time," Westcott said. "A homeless man found him and when the cops found out about it we were all under suspicion. Every single one of his friends. He and I had been feuding a few days before he died. Over some fast-tail girl, I think it was, so the cops were particularly interested in me. I could understand that. But what I couldn't understand is that they were also interested in his mother. And his father. They questioned the hell out of his little brother too. I didn't understand it then, but later I found out through watching TV shows and reading that y'all always focus on those who are close."

He paused then, adjusted his hand flat against his thigh before continuing. "So, I'll save you some breath. Like I said, my daughter and I haven't been getting along lately. She started hating how I made my money. And she didn't like the fact that I just didn't hand it over to her and her sister. Now how ironic is that?"

Raven remained silent.

"They had to work a little for what they got. Angel works down at corporate after school in the mailroom, and I made Hazel work in marketing. She did some copywriting for ads and such." His voice was getting wetter as he went along. "She's always been creative. When you ask around down there, you'll find out we got into some pretty bad arguments."

"But you still made her work? Even though she hated it?"

"She had to do something," he said. "I didn't want her to be a spoiled little rich girl. Anyway, the last time that I saw her was at the party, and then only for a short time. There were so many people here and so many people I had to get around to that I didn't have a lot of time to fool with Shelia and the girls."

"What was Hazel wearing?" Raven asked.

"That's the thing," he said. "I saw that she was all dressed up out there in a silk dress I've never seen before." He stopped and ran his hand across his mouth. His lips trembled. "I know I should have stayed out there, maybe checked her. But I couldn't... not my little girl...." He swallowed.

"Did you or your daughter touch Hazel?" she asked. "Or move anything?"

He shook his head and repeated, "I couldn't. I reached my hand out, but I could tell by the way she was staring up at the sky that she had to be dead."

He stopped and sat quietly for a long moment. And then getting himself together, he said, "The party was casual, Detective. A barbecue. I think she had on a pair of white pants and some paisley-looking silk thing for a shirt."

Raven nodded, reminding herself to tell Crimes to look for that outfit.

"And after the party last night you...."

"Saw the stragglers out and went to bed," he said. "It was late, at least for us old folks. I wanted everyone out."

"Can anyone vouch for you?"

"My wife." He shrugged. "But she'll vouch for anything I tell her, as you've probably guessed by now."

"You or your family see anything or anybody suspicious?"

He looked down at the hand on his thigh and frowned. Then he slowly shook his head.

"No," he said. "Everybody was just having a good time. The music was playing, old school, you know, the Temptations, Smokey, everybody was having fun dancing and running off at the mouth. I even caught Shelia smiling like in the old days." His laugh was short and rough. "Like I was still irresistible."

He touched his face and stopped. There was a faraway look in his eye as if he were remembering a moment and wishing he had reacted differently about it when it happened.

"What is it?" Raven asked.

"It was the damnedest thing," he said. "I had just finished acting a fool with her mother on the dance floor, doing the mashed potato and making everyone at the party laugh like crazy. As we were coming off the floor, Hazel came by and kissed me on the cheek like she used to do when she was a little girl." He paused again for a second or two. "I didn't pay a lot of attention to it then. We had been fighting like cats and dogs earlier that day, so I should have said something to her after she did it. But I was a little drunk and still high off of 'Papa Was a Rolling Stone'. I didn't think anything of it."

He stood up and walked back behind his desk. "There is something else," he said, his voice all business. He opened the desk drawer and took out a notepad. He tore off the top page and handed it to Raven.

"What's this?" she asked opening the note to see a list of names. Male names. Almost a dozen.

He didn't take his eyes from her. "Something else I learned from TV shows. After Mommy and Daddy, check out the boyfriends. My daughter was very popular. She got around."

CHAPTER TEN

Raven convinced Billy Ray that the best thing to do was to regroup at his place before meeting with the chief at seven a.m. No telling when they would have a decent meal again given the work ahead of them, and they had a better chance of getting food at Billy Ray's place than from her usually bare refrigerator. Besides, before they could continue any further with the investigation there were things Billy Ray needed to know, things that went beyond what he already knew about Floyd.

She arranged for an officer she knew to get her Mustang back to her apartment and rode with Billy Ray to his place in the '67 Buick Skylark. Raven stared at Billy Ray's house as he parked. She and Floyd lived in a house like Billy Ray's after Floyd had fled to Louisiana. The house had three rooms stacked one right after the other with a space carved out for a bathroom near the kitchen. First there was the front door, then the living room, followed by the bedroom, next the kitchen and finally the back door – the classic southern shotgun house. She remembered Floyd telling her that they called them shotguns because a person could stand on the porch and shoot a shotgun through the front door and the blast would come clean out through the back. *And that's right fittin' for me, Birdy Girl*, he had told her.

Billy Ray's house was among several clusters of shotguns built sometime after the Civil War, later becoming homes for factory workers and then the poor, the really poor, the Floyd Burns poor after he ran out of Jesus's money and had to rent one for seventy-five bucks a month. That was before marrying Raven's stepmother.

Since Billy Ray's was a duplex, natives referred to it as a double-barrel shotgun. Only a few holdouts, most in their eighties and nineties, still lived in shotgun houses in the poorest parts of town. Most on the city council were waiting for them to die so they could tear down the shacks in these blighted areas. There were several areas where owners turned the houses into mini-showcases as a nod to the past.

They moved the houses to more acceptable parts of town, restored the cypress siding and lovingly recreated the porch spindles. Some lived in them. Others turned them into artist studios and novelty craft stores.

But city leaders had an initiative on the table to destroy the remaining ones as soon as they could. In fact, one city council member made it his personal mission to annihilate every single shotgun left in Byrd's Landing. *Destroy them or die trying* – that was his rallying cry.

This particular council member didn't think they were quaint or historical. He dismissed the fact that they were energy-efficient with their high walls and narrow rooms allowing cool breezes to flow straight through on scorching summer days. The councilman called them roach motels for the poor, a way to shove black people to one corner of the city and forget about them. And for those who wanted to restore them? The investors in these places were peddlers from out of town and the would-be occupants were meddlers from just as far away. They didn't have a clue what it was like to be black and poor and living in a shotgun house in Byrd's Landing, Louisiana.

Raven remembered the councilman's rant in the city council meeting shortly after Billy Ray moved to Byrd's Landing. Billy Ray had insisted she take him to a council meeting so he could get to know who was who in the city. When she asked him why, he replied that he needed to prime his asshole detector.

After the councilman finished talking, his eyes were wet with rage and his lips still moved as if his mouth hadn't gotten the message that the words had dried up. Billy Ray turned to Raven, gave her one of his gleaming, handsome smiles and winked.

The next thing she knew, he had rented one half of a double-barrel shotgun on Peabody in a part of town that was practically abandoned. With the exception of his landlord, who occupied the other half of the double-barrel, no one lived in the surrounding houses, which were crumbling and ready to fall off the bricks holding them up. When Raven asked him why he wanted to live in a shotgun house, Billy Ray just shrugged, tilted back his pork pie hat, and said, "A man's gotta have his roach motel, right?"

Shortly after moving in he painted the entire house white, except for the shutters. For those he chose a bright red. He strung Christmas lights around the front door and hung colored bottles on the naked limbs of a dead tree. Raven was surprised that the tree was strong enough to hold the bottles up. He told her that it didn't matter if the tree was living or not. As long as the bottles were there, the noise they would make in the wind would keep away evil spirits.

"What happened this time?" Raven asked, pointing at a ladder propped against the opposite side of the house with two buckets beside it.

Billy Ray grinned, his white teeth flashing. "My landlord shot a hole in the roof."

"You kidding me. Why would he do that?"

"He said he was cleaning his gun. I say he was drunker than a monkey and the damn thing went off while he was playing soldier in the living room."

"You run into a lot of drunk monkeys who like to play soldier?"

He snorted a laugh but didn't say anything.

"Why didn't you bring him in?" Raven asked.

Billy Ray shrugged. "Guy's old, crazy. I think Vietnam screwed with the clockworks. He didn't mean anything by it."

"How can you be so sure about that, Billy Ray?"

"Who was he shooting at up there, Raven? God?"

He got out of the car before she could answer. As the door slammed, Raven checked that her weapons were still in place. Pretending as if she were tucking in her shirt, she brushed the grip of the Glock 19 with her fingers to make sure it was still there. Next she lightly touched the Smith & Wesson service revolver in the holster at the small of her back, and mentally pictured the blade strapped to her calf.

"Strapped and ready for war, soldier?" Billy Ray teased.

"Always," she said, but she didn't smile back.

"Why aren't you carrying that bazooka you have locked in your desk drawer?" he said, referring to the weapon she no longer carried. "You could strap that Beretta to your waist, and then you'd be all set for the zombie apocalypse."

"You're a riot sometimes, Billy Ray," she answered.

"You need to get rid of that thing," he said. "Every time you open that drawer, I want to put my hands up."

She said nothing. It was a phobia of hers, being caught in public without a weapon. The thought of walking unarmed in the world, especially a world inhabited by the likes of Floyd Burns, made her feel naked.

She waited while he unlocked the front door that opened onto the long front room.

"Every time I walk into one of these things, I'm reminded," she said.

"Yeah," Billy Ray said, removing his jacket and throwing it onto a blue tweed couch. "No hallways."

Raven nodded. "When I was a kid living in one of these dumps, all I could think of was what I wouldn't give for a darn hallway."

"You calling my place a dump?"

Raven looked around the living room. An eclectic mix of books and magazines were stacked to falling on a wooden coffee table. Every possible space was covered with some type of strange knick-knack. Lots of owls. Billy Ray had a thing for owls.

"A little cluttered, Chastain," was all she said. "When it's time for you to go, you'll have a lot to take with you."

"Ain't none of it new," he said. "Garage sales. Refuse new. Reuse. Reuse. Reuse. Save the planet. Before I go, I'll sell the good stuff and leave the rest to the next proud renter of my roach motel."

"Yeah," she said. "If they want it. And save the planet? This is almost as big of a mess as Hazel Westcott's room. You think she was trying to save the planet?"

"Bite your tongue," he said. "Did you see how many pairs of shoes that woman had?"

She followed him straight through the second room. It had a large four-poster bed and a chifforobe, both covered in a dark stain.

"Found them at a garage sale too," he said. "Don't know if you noticed them the last time you were here. Refinished them and now they're good as new."

He flicked on the lights in the third room of the house, the kitchen. This was filled with all new and upscale appliances including a Viking stove and a heavy-duty KitchenAid stand mixer. His fondness for high-end kitchen appliances and good food was the only decadence she ever witnessed in Billy Ray.

He took a cast-iron skillet from one of the cupboards. Soon the coffeepot bubbled in the corner and the heavy smell of chicory filled the air. Pots clanged and cupboard doors swung open and banged shut again so loudly that the landlord who lived next door pummeled the adjoining wall. Without missing a beat, Billy Ray pummeled back while butter and olive oil sizzled in the cast-iron skillet.

"Your sister ready to have that baby yet?" she asked, still standing with her hands shoved into her pockets.

Billy Ray's twin sister was still back in New Orleans with their mother. He carried a cigar wrapped in cellophane in his shirt pocket and had already warned Raven that when it was time, no matter who was dead or dying or running away from the murder, he would be at his sister's side at the birth.

"She's fine. Nothing yet. She got some weeks to go," he said. And waited.

"Aren't you going to sit down?" she asked, still standing herself.

"No, I ain't," he said. "I can see all over your face that I'm not going to like what's about to come out of your mouth. Cooking relaxes me. Why don't you sit down?"

She knew that it did. While sports connected some sons to their fathers, Billy Ray found a connection to his through cooking. Billy Ray's father had always wanted to be a chef, and Billy Ray often spoke of the hours he spent with him over steaming pots of gumbo, or skillets bubbling with frying perch. She made a show of taking a seat at the Formica table, trying to put off until the last possible moment what she had to tell him.

"Spit it out, Raven," Billy Ray insisted.

She folded her hands together on the table, and said slowly, "Hazel Westcott..." and then stopped.

"You told me you knew her and weren't exactly friends."

"No," Raven said. "We weren't friends at all."

"Why is that?"

She looked at him. He was cracking an egg against the side of an orange porcelain bowl and had just picked up a wire whisk when she answered him. "You telling me you don't know?" she asked. "You really don't know, Billy Ray?"

She asked the question already knowing the answer. He didn't know because she didn't want him to know. She thought about how he came to be a homicide detective. He fell into cop work. After his father committed suicide when Billy Ray was a teenager, he vowed to become a psychologist. He wanted to understand his father, but most of all, he wanted to help those with mental illness. He soon realized an undergrad in psychology wouldn't take him far, and he was short of both money and time to go for his master's. A professor told him the NOPD was hiring, and that they needed more people on the force with Billy Ray's background. First, he was a patrol officer and then in a gang unit, putting the skills he learned at the university to good use. He was finally promoted to homicide detective after he went after and caught the killer of a kid he was trying to help. That's how he and Raven met.

As close as they were, when she was going through the worst crisis of her life and he was still back in New Orleans, she was too ashamed to call him and wouldn't call him – not even for comfort. Against all logic, she convinced herself that if he knew what she had done, he would have no choice but to look at her through the lens of her father's past. She didn't want that. He had already absorbed the information that her father was a serial killer and didn't think that it had anything to do with her. What would he think if he found out what happened, and that she herself was also a killer?

But still. "No one in the department said anything to you?" she asked.

Billy Ray kept his head down as he whipped the eggs into a froth. "Y'all aren't the chummiest police department. Everybody walks around like they got a jock full of ice." He looked at her and winked. "Present company excepted," he said.

A smile flickered then died on her face. She nodded. That wasn't surprising. Several layoffs and new hires since the chief was called in didn't make for a close-knit group. She watched as Billy Ray put the bowl down and lit the fire on the stove.

"But if you think I don't know something about what went on, then you don't know me as well as I thought you did," he said. "I've heard a thing or two, some rumors. I almost checked them out myself, but I thought I'd let you tell me when you were ready."

She nodded. She stared at the blue flame on the Viking stove for a moment or two and then said, "I shot somebody."

"It was on the job," he said without any tone whatsoever in his voice.

"Yes," she agreed. "On the job."

"And they died."

"Yes, he died."

He didn't reply. When she could stand it no longer, she said, "Well?"

"Well, what?" he answered. "You shot somebody. They died. You lived. What has that got to do with Hazel Westcott, exactly? That's one of the details I don't have."

"It's a long story," she said.

He flipped his wrist over and looked at his watch before placing a cup of coffee in front of her. "We got a little time," he said.

She gripped the coffee with both hands, the mug so hot that she almost pulled away. She said, "I wish I could say that it happened in a dark alley in the middle of the night, or that the sun was in my eyes. I wish I could say that there were a lot of officers, a lot of confusion and somebody who didn't want to go to jail that day. But I can't say that. I don't have any excuses. It was just the two of us and I shot him in the parking lot of Boones & Sons Grocery Market in the middle of a clear afternoon. I thought about it before I did it. I had a long time to make up my mind. Then I shot him."

She looked into the coffee cup. The warmth swirled over her face, bringing the heat of that afternoon back. She and Quincy Trueblood stood facing each other on a diagonal in front of Boones & Sons. A .22 dangled from his hand. She had the Beretta pointed at his chest. He was a skinny kid with carefully cultivated blond dreadlocks and smooth, tanned skin. He had a backstory, a family who loved him. She knew that, like she knew that he had a tattoo of a star on the inside of his left wrist, another of a paint brush on his upper arm. He had been in trouble a couple of times before – once for smoking dope in the empty back parking lot of this very store, the other for punching a kid in the face at school so hard that he broke his nose and fractured the orbital bone of his right eye. The kid had called Quincy Trueblood a faggot. Raven had always thought it was one of the nastiest words one person could call another, aside from nigger. Quincy got a ticket for the first offense, but for the second, it was three months at the juvenile facility on Cypress.

Raven also knew that he was a scared kid who didn't do well in juvenile. He fought the other kids. He had fits of claustrophobia so bad that they prescribed him Xanax. He had gotten out of juvenile a year earlier, and spent his spare time painting unasked-for murals of ten-foot-tall saints and sad, darkly robed women on the cinderblock sides of liquor stores and cafes. No one complained, especially not the owners of the stores, because to be graced with a Trueblood mural meant more attention and more customers. Stories appeared in the *Byrd's Landing Review* about the painter who was using spray paint to beautify the city instead of vandalizing it.

She knew all of this because she had read Quincy Trueblood's file before leaving to pick him up for questioning on a robbery homicide that she didn't believe for a minute that he had committed. She had seen his murals around town, the red glowing robes of St. Ignatius rising unexpectedly from the walls of the veterans' hall. He even had a patron. Hazel Westcott had taken a special interest in Quincy. At first it was because of the art, but pretty soon, word spread that they were close as a loving brother and sister. No one, not even the chief, believed the two goons who fingered Quincy in a liquor store robbery. But a clerk was shot and left to die on the dirty linoleum floor. They needed to talk to Quincy just the same. He might at least be a witness.

Raven had volunteered to pick him up because she didn't want some trigger-happy, inexperienced uniform going after a scared, claustrophobic kid who didn't want to go back to jail. She thought about calling the kid's mother or Hazel for a brief moment, but pride got in the way. If she couldn't handle one scared boy, what kind of a cop did that make her? She convinced herself that she didn't need any help, especially not from a wealthy bubble-headed socialite.

Later she would admit to herself how wrong she had been. Quincy Trueblood took one look at her waiting for him in the principal's office, pushed past the counselor who had brought him from class, and ran. He ran through the double doors of Liberty High and out into the burning afternoon. Raven ran after him, her long legs stretching into graceful strides, well-practiced from running before work every morning. She knew that it would be only minutes before she caught him. She was already looking for a soft patch of grass where she could tackle him so neither one of them would be hurt too badly.

But it didn't come to that. He stopped outside Boones & Sons and turned toward her with what looked like a .22 shaking in his hand. She looked for the bright orange tip that would tell her the gun was a fake. There was none. She asked him in her best cop's voice to drop the weapon but he didn't. Instead he talked. He said, "I ain't done nothing,"

She held her palm up in a placating gesture while keeping her weapon trained on him. "I know that you didn't, Quincy. Put the gun down so we can talk about it."

"I can't go back to juvenile."

"Juvenile?" she said. "That's a lot better than dead."

She knew that it was a mistake the minute she said it. A shadow of uncertainty passed across his face as if he was actually comparing the two – being dead or locked up.

"I know that you haven't had anything to do with that robbery. But we have to ask you about it just the same," she tried again.

She was breaking protocol and she knew it. She should have warned him again to drop the weapon. Once more, maybe twice. And if he didn't she should have shot him. Hesitation could get you killed. That was one thing Raven did not want to be. In spite of all the things that had happened to her, Raven Burns wanted to live. She thought about the way her lungs used the air during the fourth mile of a five-mile run. She thought about her foster mother and father who would be devastated if anything happened to her.

She had been around death plenty. Maylene and Floyd's other victims. The deliberate death of her father that the state had tried to organize like an army drill but instead turned out to be more like a tragic opera. Her heart thumped, the rhythm like a broken motor in her chest. The gun still hung from his hand but he wasn't pointing it at her. Instinct and the weight of the weapon as it dangled there told her that it was real. But was it loaded?

Shoot, shoot it, Raven. It was Floyd's voice in her head, the one she had always hated. And it pressed her. *Only an idiot would run around waving an unloaded gun.* But there was a competing voice that told her that Quincy Trueblood was only a scared kid. It told her to drop her own weapon, and then dare him to take her life.

But, of course, she couldn't be sure.

"Quincy," she said again. "Put it down. If you don't put down the weapon I'm going to have to shoot you. You know that, don't you?"

He didn't respond. His face just went quiet and flat like he had suddenly become a part of one of his paintings. The look on his face told Raven that of course he knew that she would have to shoot if he didn't drop the weapon. But he had already been arrested twice and was about to be arrested again. He might be locked up for a little or a long time.

But he would be locked up.

The gun stopped dangling. He raised it with both hands aiming at the center of Raven's chest. Raven shot. It wasn't what should have been a kill shot, no double-tap. She aimed for the shoulder, but at the last minute her hand jerked and the bullet hit him in the neck.

A long arc of blood jetted into the bright afternoon air. He spun around and his body slammed against the asphalt. Raven ran over to him. She kicked the weapon aside and it skittered against the curb like some living thing. She pressed her fingers into the hole but it was like trying to press back high tide with her fingertips. Blood, warm and alive, pulsed out of his body until it surrounded his head like a halo. He tried to talk but Raven told him not to. She could see the fear in his eyes so she told him that everything would be okay. She knew it was a lie. He knew it too. She stared into his eyes while she held his now-useless hand against her own useless one, and she watched the twin lights dim to nothing.

She didn't know how long she knelt holding his dead hands in hers but it felt like a long time. She stood up when she felt the man who had been her partner at the time grab her shoulders. She heard a voice of another officer coming from a long way off through the blood pulsing in her own head. The voice said very quietly, "Goddamnit. This piece of shit ain't even loaded."

"Of course all hell broke loose," she continued to Billy Ray, all the feelings during that time coming back to her. "There was an IA investigation. I was cleared, but the community—" She paused for a moment, cleared her throat, and started again. "They weren't satisfied. They wanted heads to roll, my head. And they dug up everything they could on me. All the craziness about Floyd came out in the news again, and Hazel Westcott, she was the ringleader of the whole circus. I remember her crying on the news about how he was like the brother she never had. How everything would have been different if the police had just involved her from the beginning – if I had just called her. At first, I thought it was all drama, but...." She stopped.

"But what?" Billy Ray prompted.

She shook her head. "She confronted me at my apartment after I got home from work one day. It was late. I don't remember anyone else around. I mean, she just flew at me, Billy Ray, like she was trying to kill me with her bare hands." Raven lifted her own hands up and stared at them, lost in the memories. "But I grabbed her wrists and just held them, and the next thing I know she's sobbing against me as if her entire heart was breaking." She let her hands fall against the Formica table.

"And then what happened?"

Raven wiped her face and shrugged. "I held her until she stopped crying, stayed with her until she pulled herself together enough to drive. And I said I'm sorry about a hundred times. Lord knows I was, my God, I still am. I think about Quincy Trueblood every day. But I could still see that she hated me, blamed me for everything. From then on, she's done everything she can to ruin my life."

"You seem all right now," Billy Ray said. "Everybody suddenly just shut up?"

She shook her head. "The chief, a lot of the cops I worked with went to bat for me. And we hired Lamont Lovelle to help us deal with the public. He called us saying he could help. They dug up some crap on Quincy and leaked it to the media a little at a time until he wasn't such a golden boy anymore. I didn't want them to, but they did. And somehow, that made it all right. All the talk just died down."

She waited, thinking that Quincy Trueblood's death was another tragic story the town just absorbed. The air in the room was now heavy with the smell of the cooked breakfast heaped on a serving platter shaped like a chicken, another one of Billy Ray's garage sale finds. Raven's stomach grumbled. The thought of Quincy Trueblood lying with the white sidewalk glittering beneath him while he was choking in his own blood made her ashamed to be hungry. She ate anyway, and soon Billy Ray sat beside her. They didn't talk about anything for a long time. Then he said, "It's a shame that boy had to die," his face unreadable. "I hate it and I know you hate it too."

She nodded.

"You shoot anybody else?" he asked.

"No," she said. "Not like that, not to death, anyway."

"We've been through a lot together, Raven," he said.

"I know."

"How many times have you saved my ass and vice versa?"

She thought about that. There had been a lot of mutual ass-savings back in New Orleans – not only from perps, but from some in the brass who wanted to cut corners or lie to make arrests stick.

"You need to trust me," was all he said. "No matter what. Is there anything else you aren't telling me?"

"No."

"No?" he pressed. "You sure?"

She was about to answer in the negative again, but then there was the peacock feather. She swallowed, trying not to think about it. She thought about telling him everything but didn't want to confuse the investigation. She wanted to wait until she knew for herself what was going on. If it had something to do with Floyd, it was her problem. He was her father, after all.

She waited for a beat or two, and then said, "I swear. No more surprises."

It surprised her when he put his arm around her and kissed her on the side of her head. He said, "That wasn't your fault. You don't have anything to be guilty about."

She wanted to cry in relief that the shooting hadn't affected their relationship. She wanted to turn her face into his chest and cry until the memory of that day was once again safely buried away. Instead, wanting to break the spell, she took a deep breath and said in a firm voice, "So, we square?"

He waited for a moment or two before removing his arm and nodding. "As long as you're telling the truth about surprises," he said. "We're square."

CHAPTER ELEVEN

Raven stared at the low, squat building of the Byrd's Landing police station with hard eyes and thought about what waited for her inside – an accusatory Presley Holloway, the department's only internal affairs investigator, and his staff of one, Lamont Lovelle, the media relations co-ordinator who saved her behind during the Quincy Trueblood shooting aftermath.

At least, she thought as the windows glittered busily in the morning light, she had come clean with her partner about the shooting. That would be one less worry for her as she faced down Presley Holloway. She took a deep breath and started for the double doors.

But before she made it inside, she noticed someone she could have gone all day without seeing, maybe all year. Worried more about what he would say to her than about what any investigation would do to her career, Raven had been avoiding Percival Oral Justice since the Trueblood shooting. She had known Oral since she was twelve years old. People knew him in the community because he ran an afterschool center for kids and took a special interest in helping troubled teenagers. The type of trouble didn't matter. It could be drugs, or crime, or just plain teenage angst, Oral Justice was always fighting to make growing up in Byrd's Landing a little easier for them, their transition into adulthood not so painful.

He was a big bear of a man with a wiry short gray beard that grew high on his brown cheeks. His short hair sprung straight up from his large head as if he had just been suddenly surprised. He wore cheap blue suits badly constructed with large pieces of square cloth to fit his massive shoulders and tree-trunk legs. She remembered him visiting the home of her foster parents with arms full of books and toys and music. Jazz a lot of the times, blues at others, and Zydeco if he was in a mood to move his feet. Over the years his health had deteriorated. He had developed a limp and walked with a cane, which he now leaned heavily on.

When he saw her, he stopped by a fountain of bronze pelicans sculpted to look as if they were about to take flight and waited for her. She focused on the clearness of the water in the fountain, how the sunlight turned his gray hair into a landscape of bright and dark spikes, how he leaned with both hands on the wolf's head of his cane as if it were the only thing holding him up.

And he didn't look directly at her either. He just gazed toward the rushing water for a long time as if he had come down to the police station just to stare into the fountain. Even though it was morning and police and staff hurried by them, it was as if she and Oral were hidden in a bubble of morning light, invisible to everyone not trapped in there with them.

He started with one word. "Well."

She folded her arms over her chest and also found refuge in the fountain that seemed to so fascinate him. She only nodded. "Oral."

Then he lifted his massive head and said, "It's been a very long time, Raven. How are you holding up?"

She lifted her own head and squinted into the middle distance. She couldn't bring herself to face him, even after all this time. She shrugged, and promised herself that she wouldn't cry.

It was his turn to nod. "I figured."

"What brings you here, Oral?" she asked.

"I had coffee with the chief and some of his administrative staff this morning. He asked me down here for some advice about how to prepare the community for Hazel's death. Lord, Lord," he said, while taking out a handkerchief and swiping it across his forehead, "What a thing. First Quincy and now Hazel."

"You know, Oral," Raven started, "I really have to get to work."

"Just give me a moment, Raven. You've been running from me like the hounds of hell were after you just because you don't want to hear what I've got to say about Quincy." His voice was deep and, always a careful man, he enunciated as if he was painting a masterpiece with each sound he uttered. "I can't believe you've managed to avoid me all this time. You'd be surprised to know that I understand about Quincy," he said quietly. "Or I'm trying real hard to. These things happen." He sighed and waited. "Unfortunate, but this line of work you chose has these sorts of hazards...."

She could see how he struggled for the right words, discarding and selecting according to some prescribed rules as he went along. She didn't know that the tears she had tried to hold back were falling until he thrust a handkerchief toward her.

She took it and blew her nose, thinking that it was just as well. She could barely think of the shooting without tears. Someone was dead because of her. Not because of her father, but because of a decision she made. "After all that's happened in my life you think I chose this?"

"You have to admit that if you weren't a cop, you would not have shot that boy," he said gravely. "You had so much talent. Too much to be involved in the nasty business of shootings like Quincy's and murders like Hazel's. You could have been anything."

"I didn't get into this work because I wanted to shoot teenage boys," she said. "But I did go into this line of work exactly because of what happened to Hazel, because I need to stop the bastards who do things like this, bastards like my father."

The silence hung between them for a long time. Raven could see by his face that he still struggled with words, or perhaps, struggled with the need to stay silent. She decided to let him off the hook.

"Go ahead, say it," she said.

"But you stopped Quincy," he said.

"That's not fair, Oral," she responded, even while thinking that it might not have been fair, but it was indeed true. "I didn't want to see Quincy hurt. You know that."

He nodded once. "I do know that," he said. "But what I don't know is if you accepted the consequences of your decision to become a cop when you made it. And in that acceptance, you realized that you may be solely responsible for the death or the prolonged incarceration of an innocent."

She had no problem looking at him now. So it was going back to that. When she told him all those years ago what she wanted to do, what college she had selected and her major, he looked as if he had just been slapped. He tried to talk her out of it. She was talented; she had a story that could make a difference in so many lives. Why not a journalist or a lawyer? A motivational speaker, an author, a profession that would do some good, one where she could make the baggage she carried useful and inspiring.

"Did you stop me, Oral," she asked, "to make a speech?"

He shook his head, then looked up at the blue sky and sighed. "I really stopped with the intention of seeing how you were," he said. "But when I think of that boy lying in the grave...."

He chopped his hand toward the direction of the cemetery. He tried to say something again. His mouth worked but nothing came out. For the first time, she realized the hero she had known during childhood was human like everyone else. She realized that what she was seeing was real grief, not grief brought on by moral outrage, but grief manifested because of the realization of an irrevocable loss. He was feeling the same grief that had driven Hazel Westcott to cling in search of solace to Raven, the woman ultimately responsible for the cause of all of her pain.

"I'm sorry," he said, wiping his eyes with his meaty fingers. "I'm afraid I knew Quincy Trueblood quite well. I know it's been a while, but it still gets to me."

"You have to know," Raven said in a quiet voice, telling him the same thing she had told herself repeatedly since the shooting, "that the same thing would have happened no matter who the cop was on the other side of the gun, right? I could have become a regular Johnny Cochran or Maya Angelou, but Quincy Trueblood would still be dead."

"Yes," he said. "But you would not have been the one to send him to the grave."

She turned away from him. "Do me a favor," she said, hearing the pure meanness in her words but wanting to lash out, unable to stop them. "Keep your bleeding heart to yourself. Maybe if you would have spent more time helping Quincy rather than making speeches, he wouldn't be dead."

His shoulders slumped. "Tell me something, Raven," he said. "Just tell me one thing. Will you give me that?"

She waited with her hand on the cool metal handle of the door to the station, ready to step from the bubble containing him and her, the fountain with its rushing water, and back into the real world.

"Did you become a cop to stop men like your father," he said, "or did you go into this business to prevent yourself from becoming like him?"

She said nothing.

"He's there all the time," he said, not looking at her. "I see him just beneath the surface. You even kept his last name. You could have easily changed it."

"It's not just his name," she spat. "Burns is my name too. He took a lot from me. He wasn't going to take that too."

He continued as if she hadn't spoken. "He's there in that hurtful thing you just said about me and my speeches. You sure he's not deep down in you, guiding you in such a way that not even you are aware of it?"

He looked at her then. They stared at each other for a long time. She willed her face to stay still, willed it until he looked away back toward the fountain. Instead of answering him she walked into the station, leaving him standing there. She knew that if she looked back, she would see him leaning on the silver wolf's head cane with both hands as if it hurt his body much too much to move.

CHAPTER TWELVE

She splashed cold water on her face in the department's women's restroom and tried to make her mind empty, clear of Oral Justice and the memories he brought to the surface. She focused all of her mental energy on the Hazel Westcott murder. As she made her way to the chief's office, Oral was gone from her mind, replaced by the blue peacock feather she had found beneath Hazel's bed.

"Don't just stand there, Detective," Chief Early Sawyer said. "Come in and have a seat."

She didn't realize until he had spoken that she had been hovering in the doorway of the office like the ghoul Hazel had thought she was.

She looked Chief Sawyer full in the face and smiled before walking into the room. He was almost three decades a cop, and had worked almost every position one could imagine on a police force – patrol officer, which was what he was when she first met him, narcotics, major crimes and homicide. Thoroughly dedicated to the work, he was a cop's cop without a political bone in his body. The only reason he sat behind his desk now, he would say, was because of the bullet that tore through his knee at the scene of a triple murder during his long and successful ride in homicide. The knee in question was now swollen to the size of a boxing glove and propped across the corner of his desk.

His office was not an elected one but appointed by the mayor. The chief was as far from a politician that Raven thought a person in his position could ever be. He grudgingly took the job after the mayor promised him freedom to do what he wanted and a bottle of Pappy Van Winkle's bourbon payable on New Year's Day for every year he stayed. There were four unopened bottles lined up as neat as soldiers on parade atop his desk. No one wanted his job and he hardly ever had to remind the mayor of that fact when the mayor started acting too much like a boss.

He waited until Raven was in the room before resuming throwing a baseball in the air, letting it slide off his fingertips before it whirled into the air. For a moment, he didn't say anything. The only sound in the room was the baseball slapping against his palm after descending and Presley Holloway clearing his throat. She ignored him. Presley had hated her on sight when the chief hired her on, and had done all he could to make her life miserable ever since then. He had a field day with the Quincy Trueblood shooting.

Presley's media relations coordinator, Lamont Lovelle, flashed a quick smile and winked at her. She nodded back. Arranging his face into a mask of seriousness, he looked away. She was grateful to Lovelle because he'd fended off the press so deftly during the Quincy Trueblood episode, but he and Raven didn't exactly become friends. She never agreed with how Lovelle systematically destroyed Quincy Trueblood's character after the shooting. The fact that Quincy smoked weed and got into trouble in school didn't have anything to do with why he was shot.

But Lovelle insisted that the character assassination was necessary if she wanted to stay out of jail. They had worked closely together during the frenzy after Trueblood's death, but his methods disquieted her and they never became more than nodding acquaintances. She would say hello to him in the hallway, spend a moment or two in conversation about the weather, and nod to him when she happened to see him at the firing range where she was practicing becoming a better shot. But invite Lovelle for a drink after work or to a weekend barbecue? Unlikely.

"Lamont," she said in acknowledgment before taking a seat next to Billy Ray. "You look none the worse for wear after your late night."

He smiled. "Don't you mean early morning? I just happened to be listening to the police scanners when the call came in and decided to swing by. Glad I could keep Tucker from completely contaminating your crime scene."

"See, Detective," Presley Holloway said. "We're good for more than just saving your ass."

She didn't acknowledge Holloway, a small, fit man who was such a fanatic about following the rules – any rules – that he even counted the amount of water he drank each day. Holloway was never far from his stainless-steel BPA-free water bottle that he now clutched so tightly his knuckles were even whiter than the rest of him.

She hated him. He was a pestilence that was trying its damnedest to turn her into what Floyd Burns wanted her to be. Holloway made no secret when she joined the force that he opposed her position. When she shot Quincy Trueblood, he pressured the DA by at first trying downright lies and then half truths that had only a passing acquaintance with the facts.

Regardless, the DA told Holloway, the kid had a weapon. It didn't matter who Raven's father was or whether the gun was loaded or unloaded, the kid had a gun that he pointed at her. There was no way she could know if he was trying to kill her or commit suicide by cop. She was justified in protecting her life.

Shortly after that Raven had seen Holloway at a local bar having a drink with Hazel Westcott. At the time, Hazel was leading the community protest regarding the shooting. His spiky blond head was next to her black glossy one. Fear shot into his eyes when he saw Raven staring at the both of them. But then he smiled, a sheepish grin that said *caught me*, and lifted his glass to her.

Now she could feel him waiting for her to react to his last statement, but reacting would be the quickest way for the chief to send her packing from the case. She kept her mouth shut.

The chief flashed Holloway a warning look. Holloway returned it with a conciliatory glance of his own before flipping up the valve of his water bottle and taking a delicate sip.

"Better," the chief said before slowly turning away. He threw the ball into the air, again letting it slide off the tips of his fingers. When he caught it, he said, "What do you have?"

Raven hesitated, not wanting to talk with Holloway there. The chief put the baseball back in a gold-colored holder shaped like a catcher's mitt on his desk.

"Look, Detective," he said. "Don't be coy. I can't stand coy."

"Chief Sawyer," Holloway said.

Raven winced at the cadence of Holloway's voice. He had a way of speaking all in a rush as if afraid someone would cut him off in impatience.

"I must renew my objections to allowing Detective Burns

anywhere near this case," Holloway said. "The conflict of interest is astronomical."

The chief gave him a look that caused Holloway to sit back in his chair. "You are here," he said, "because I am in a good mood. And I am being courteous…"

Holloway opened his mouth to say something else.

The chief lifted his hand, cutting him off. "…and co-operative. I am being very co-operative. See? This is my co-operative face." He stopped and stared at Holloway for several seconds. "But co-operative doesn't mean that you are going to run me, Holloway."

Raven said nothing, just drummed her fingers lightly on the wooden armrest of her chair. She crossed her legs and leaned back, listening to some music in her head as Holloway answered. She tried to look relaxed. Inside her heart was beating fast and she had to count up to ten and then back down again to keep from screaming. The case was about to be snatched from underneath her. She knew it as sure as she knew that Presley Holloway lived with his mother.

"I understand and appreciate that, sir," Holloway said. "But I respectfully submit to you that you are willingly walking into quicksand if you let her anywhere near this case."

Grimacing in pain, the chief used both hands to move his leg from the top of his desk. He leaned over and laced his fingers together. "So what do you suggest I do?" he said. "She's the best I have right now, the most experienced in this area. We aren't exactly lousy with homicide detectives, Holloway. Why in the hell do you think I convinced her to come back here? We need to find this perp. This is personal for me."

Holloway nodded. "I do see your dilemma," he said. "May I suggest we start with some questions before making a final decision?"

The chief glanced at Raven. He said, "Go ahead."

"Where were you last night, Detective Burns?" Holloway asked.

"At a crime scene," she answered. "With a lady in a beautiful white dress."

"You know what I mean, at the time of the murder."

She looked at him for a minute and then slowly nodded as his meaning became clear. Here he was again, trying to set her up with anything that he could.

"You are trying to interrogate me?" she said. "You were a math teacher, for Christ's sake. You've been riding desk since you joined the force. The only reason you're in Internal Affairs is that the chief didn't want to put you anyplace where you could accidentally blow your foot off."

Holloway stood up, trembling with anger, ignoring the water bottle as it tumbled to the floor. "She's being impossible as usual," he said. "Impossible and disrespectful."

"All right, all right," the chief said, waving his hands. "Just answer the question, Raven. We do need to clear this up."

"I was in bed," she said.

Somewhat mollified, Holloway retrieved the bottle and sat it on the table next to him before continuing. "Alone?" he challenged.

"No, with the fleet," she said. "They are in, you know. I have about five hundred sailors waiting to give me an alibi."

"That's enough, Detective," the chief broke in. "We need to know if you were anywhere near Big Bayou Lake when Hazel was killed. Answer his question."

"I was in bed when I got the call," she said.

"All night?"

"Yes."

Holloway wrote in his pad. "Alone?"

"Yep." She nodded, "Don't know anyone out there who would put up with me."

Billy Ray laughed shortly. "Amen to that," he breathed with a slight laugh.

She gave him a warning look, and watched the laugh fade.

"And the last time you saw Hazel Westcott?" Holloway said, ignoring him.

She thought about that for a long time not because she couldn't remember, but because the scene lived in her memory like a burn scar. She felt her entire body go stiff as that memory and another one she was not about to share with Holloway and the room crowded into her mind. She breathed deeply and focused on the question. When was the last time she had *seen* Hazel Westcott? She could feel Billy Ray watching her. She studiously ignored him.

She had seen Hazel at an upscale downtown restaurant, a new place that she didn't want to go to but her date did. It was the first time she had gone out with this man and she really wanted to please him. The Blue Heron, it was called. The place had a long marble bar and vases of magnolias and hydrangeas with blooms as large as severed heads. She and her foster mother shopped all day for a new dress, and Greta would not let her leave the house without forcing lipstick on her. Even with that the evening hadn't turned out half bad. She found herself enjoying being on a date and imagined herself finally finding a steady boyfriend and the normal life she craved.

But as they were leaving, Hazel Westcott, in a black cocktail dress with a trio of diamond bracelets dangling from her wrist, blocked their way. Hazel got close to Raven as if she were trying to entice a punch to the face. Raven wanted to oblige her, but her date stopped Raven from doing so with a horrified look on his face. Needless to say she never saw the guy again.

"You know good and well the last time I saw her," she said.

"Yes, yes," Holloway said quickly as he flipped through pages in a brown file folder. "That was at the Blue Heron. What did you call her? Ah, yes, here it is – a spoiled little rich girl who sniffed too much nail polish." He looked up from the file he was holding. "Or that is what the complaint said." He looked at the chief. "One of many, I might add."

Raven leaned toward him, her voice quiet and deceptively calm. "Does it say anywhere in your complaint file how she blocked my way out of that restaurant and called me a murdering bitch whore just inches away from a much-deserved needle?"

He smirked. "Missed that part."

She leaned back. "I thought you did."

The chief sighed. "He's got a point, Raven," he said.

"You can't be serious, Chief!"

"I'm not taking you off the case," he said. "But I'm making Billy Ray a co-lead."

Raven swiveled toward Billy Ray. He had been quiet up to this point but she could see that he wasn't about to protest. "What in the heck is that supposed to mean?" Raven said.

Holloway's face indicated that he was not crazy about the idea either. He wanted her off the case, completely off. Holloway was about to disagree but this time he wasn't quick enough. Before he could get the words out of his mouth, the chief leaned back in his chair. "It can mean anything you want it to mean, but I will tell you what it means for me. It means that you work the case, but anything that has to do with the public, anything that needs a public face aside from Lamont's, I want Billy Ray out there. You work this behind the scenes."

"What," Raven said, "you ashamed of me now, Chief?"

"Of course not, but that doesn't mean that I'm not going to be practical about this." He stopped and turned to Billy Ray. "I also expect you to keep me informed about what's going on, let me know if things start to get away from your partner."

"I hope you don't expect me to be a snitch," Billy Ray answered.

The chief sighed and looked down at his desk. He looked up at Billy Ray. "No, I don't expect you to be a snitch, but I expect you to do what's right. This could be a tough one for Raven. You know that."

"Presley," the chief said, turning toward Holloway, "you okay with this?"

Holloway crossed his arms over his skinny chest. "I guess I have to be."

The chief lifted his fingers in concession. "For now, yes. I will keep you in the loop. Now that that's over, Raven and Billy Ray, tell me what you have."

She let Billy Ray speak first. He told him about the scene and what had been found in the bathroom, the few hairs, the spilled sandalwood toilet water and bath powder.

"Doesn't sound like you have anything good," the chief sighed.

"A new dress," he said.

The chief picked up the baseball once again from its holder. He curled his fingers around it and kept it there as he stared at Billy Ray. "New dress?" he asked.

"How many phone calls about Hazel's murder did you get from the mayor and city council this morning, Chief?" Raven asked before Billy Ray could elaborate. "And how well do you know Antwone Westcott, Hazel's father?"

He shrugged. "About five million phone calls from the mayor and five million from the council. And a meeting with a few of them on top of that. I'm sure you already know that Hazel's father and I are acquainted. Antwone Westcott and I go back a little ways, and he still supports a couple of charities of mine. We even hung out together a few times. He's a fun guy to be around but recently we've lost touch. I'll tell you this. I know him enough to make me sorry that he lost his daughter and that she suffered. Talk to me about this new dress," he said, swiftly changing the subject.

Billy Ray was about to answer when Raven cut him off again. "What makes you think she suffered?"

"Didn't she?" the chief asked.

She didn't answer him.

"How do you think she died?" the chief pressed. "Somebody just showed up and sprinkled a little fairy dust on her and she fell asleep?"

"Frankly, Chief," Raven answered, "that's what it looks like. But I'm not sure what killed her. I have my suspicions. They are just that, though. Suspicions."

"So let me get this straight," he said. "You have a new dress." He pointed at Billy Ray. "And you have suspicions?" He pointed at Raven. "That it?"

"We've got a kiss on a cheek," Raven said with a slight smile to her lips. "A new dress, a kiss on a cheek, and suspicions as to the cause of death. I think we're doing quite fine."

The chief grunted. "I think you're both in a hell of a lot of trouble. You want to know what else I think, Raven?"

"What's that?"

"That you're not telling me everything."

Raven kept her eyes on his. "You'd be right about that," she said. "I'm worried about those ten million phone calls from the mayor and council. I want you to have some plausible deniability when they start grilling you for information."

The chief nodded. "How long you need before I whip out the microscope?" he asked.

"Two days," Billy Ray answered.

The chief laughed. "I like you, Billy Ray. And that surprises me. I knew you were good but I didn't think I'd like you."

Billy Ray grinned. "Then we have two days?"

"I don't like you that much," he said. "You are not getting two days, Detective."

"Then give us at least twenty-four hours before you start giving the mayor any details," Raven said. "He'll just go straight to the press and we'll have more mess to deal with. You know that, Chief."

The chief stared at her and then nodded. "That sounds like a good idea," he said. "I can buy you twenty-four."

"If I may make a suggestion." It was Lovelle.

For a minute Raven had forgotten he was in the room. He now smiled in that disarming way of his, dimples appearing fleetingly on his two huge cheeks. "We don't have to give him everything, of course, but if we want to keep the press under control, as well as the mayor, we need to throw them a bone. A little something that they can gnaw on for a while and that'll keep them out of our way."

"What did you have in mind?" the chief asked.

"I'll write a press release saying that Hazel Westcott was found dead in her home yesterday and that we are still investigating. Rather than say anything about the dress – don't want to sensationalize any of this, not yet anyway – I'll say that we suspect foul play is involved. That sound okay to you, Chief? Presley?"

The chief thought about it for a moment or two and then sighed in agreement.

"And if I'm not being too forward, may I make another suggestion?"

"Lamont," the chief said, "stop bullshitting me and spit it out, okay?"

Lovelle smiled. "Okay. Tell Marcus about the dress, confidentially of course. But nothing else. He'll feel like he's in the loop."

"Sounds like a good idea. That will buy us some time," the chief agreed. He turned to Billy Ray.

"I can keep the mayor off your backs for twenty-four hours, and maybe the press. But I expect an update in twelve hours," he said. "Not thirteen, or fourteen, but in eleven hours, fifty-nine seconds you'd better be in my office with a warrant or I'll be up your asses with a microscope."

He put the baseball back into its holder and looked away from them. Lovelle, Holloway, and Billy Ray stood to leave. When Raven rose to do the same, the chief said, "Raven, hang on a minute."

Once the door closed behind them, the chief asked, "I'm hoping you filled Billy Ray in on the Trueblood thing?" he asked.

She took a deep breath and nodded. "I thought it was about time," she said. "Especially since it involved a connection with the victim."

"Did he take it okay?"

She looked toward the shut door. "I don't know," she said. "He seemed to take it pretty well. Didn't ask a lot of questions."

The chief didn't say anything for almost a minute. When he did speak, he said, "You aren't going to have this guy caught in the next couple of days, are you?"

"I'm going to try my best."

He gave her a pointed look. "With Billy Ray's help?"

"With his help."

"Make sure you listen to him," he said. "He may be a little green here, but he's a good cop with a lot of common sense."

His phone rang and he let it ring. When it stopped, silence enveloped the room. "What's your gut telling you?"

"Not telling me much," she lied. In fact, her gut was telling her a lot. It was screaming the name Floyd Burns. But if she told the chief that, he would most certainly take her off the case.

He stood up and hopped to the coatrack. Making no offer to help, she watched as he shrugged into a beige suit jacket made of linen. A man too stubborn to use a cane would not appreciate an offer of help. "Got an appointment with the doc today to see about this knee. Then I'm going over to the Tipped Cow for dinner with the mayor," he explained. "Lucky me. Doctor's appointment and then a dinner watching the mayor pick meat from between his teeth. I expect a call from you tonight, Raven."

She nodded. "We'll let you know what we find." And then she said, "You should get that knee replaced, Chief."

"So say you and my wife. Now even my kid's getting in on the act." He walked stiff-legged past her, stopping while she smoothed the collar of his coat around his broad shoulders.

"When are you going to share a bottle of that bourbon with me, Chief?" she asked him with a nod to the four unopened bottles of Pappy Van Winkle on his desk.

He looked at them and then back at her. "When we're ready to celebrate something," he said. "When I retire, you and me are going to have a drink. And I hope by that time you'd be ready to take the reins. Full circle, Raven. And the department will be in good hands."

She said nothing. He held the open door for her so she could go through. "You're a good detective, Raven," he said as she passed him.

"And a good person. I don't care what your pops did. You'll catch this guy."

"Thank you, Chief," she said quietly.

"One more thing," he said.

"What's that?"

"I got a call this morning," he said. "Get to your shrink."

Raven thought about it. Her shrink, fresh out of school, was almost as afraid of her as her old partner was. "It's not helping," she said. "Where does the department get these bozos anyway??"

"I don't know and I don't care," he answered. "It's mandatory. Until he checks you out on the Trueblood shoot, keep the appointments. Think about juke joints, barbecue, your morning run, whatever when you're there. But keep the appointments."

CHAPTER THIRTEEN

Billy Ray's sense of family was good for Raven because when she made an excuse about a meeting at the school with the principal and one of her foster brothers, Billy Ray didn't blink. He just said that he'd get started and catch up with her later.

Instead of making her way to Liberty High she drove to a storage shed in Bossier City. She used the back roads so she could spot anyone following her. She didn't think they would be, but then again, she didn't think that someone would throw her past into her face by placing a peacock feather at one of her crime scenes.

She entered the code at the gate and parked at unit 446. The master lock slipped out of her hands three times before she could open it. She put the lock into her jacket pocket and using both hands, she lifted the metal door of the shed.

She stood there for a moment holding the door over her head even though it would have stayed up by itself without her help. She imagined Floyd's eyes on her as she stood there with her hands raised above her head facing what remained of him.

After Floyd's execution in California for the murder of Raven's mother, San Quentin officials gave Raven everything that Floyd had claimed as his and even some things that he hadn't. There was an inventory, but the boxes were so hastily packed that she found many things that weren't on the list. It was as if someone had gone into Floyd's cell, hastily swept his belongings into boxes, and taped the lids shut before any more of him could escape. Maybe that's why she rented an entire storage shed for just a few boxes. She could have kept his belongings in her apartment. But she shuddered at the thought of that. She could have burned them, but she wasn't ready for burning either.

Raven let go of the door and walked into the shed. The boxes were lined up on the white concrete floor. Long ago she had unpacked them and reorganized the contents according to category. She had packed copies of all the official documents surrounding Floyd's arrest and execution all in one box – the visitor logs, the logbook kept during the deathwatch, trial transcripts, California extradition papers, even the death warrant.

Letters were carefully lifted from envelopes and stapled together and laid in neat stacks in another box. There were a lot of them, many of them from repeat senders, but she had read every single one. Most of them were from death row groupies, and to her, they made no sense. The rest were official correspondence between Floyd and his lawyer whom Floyd was fond of calling his 'NO-good-PUB-lic-DE-fend-er'.

The remaining box contained the few toiletries and other items he kept in his cell – shavings of the Irish Spring soap he so loved, the graphic novels he read, and the meandering sermons of fire and brimstone he wrote even in prison. And there were the items he had carried with him as he drifted around the country – the shortened duffle bag and his fedoras decorated with peacock feathers. There was also another item that Raven didn't like to think too much about – his Sheffield steel straight razor.

A few days before his execution, he made a request of her.

He said, "Birdy Girl, do you still have my straight razor?"

She told him that she did.

He then leaned toward her. He looked into her eyes and said, "Then I want you to bury it with me. Open and lying across my chest. It'll be like a secret between you and me."

After Floyd killed her stepmother, and it was soon revealed that he had killed her mother, and many others who had the misfortune to cross his path, she had tried to decide if what she felt for him was pure hate. Hate for the very essence of his being or just hate for the things he had done. At that moment, she realized it was the former. She hated Floyd so much that if she could have gotten at him, she would have wrapped her hands around his old throat and done what the state promised to do two days from then.

Instead she did the next best thing. She looked into his eyes and without effort smiled back at him. She said, "Yes, I will. You can count on me, Daddy." The lie in her voice made her sound as silky as Floyd used to in the pulpit.

Floyd shrank back with an uneasy and knowing light in his eyes. She kept her eyes on him. She knew he could read well what was in them. *In two days*, they said, *the state is going to gas you just like you asked. You are going to die choking and sputtering and begging for clean air. And you will have no more control, old man. None. So don't give me orders about what to do with your blessed straight razor. You are done, Floyd Burns.*

"Okay then," he said bobbing his head. "Thank you, Birdy Girl."

"You're welcome."

Now she walked over to the metal shelf that contained Floyd's neatly washed and pressed clothes and a white fedora that he never got a chance to wear. The hat still had the tag hanging from it and a blue peacock feather in the black hatband. She picked it up and held it for a long time before placing it back on the shelf.

The shelf also held Floyd's thick and worn leather Bible. She remembered Floyd sitting in his underwear on the side of the bed reading the Bible out loud in a low humming voice. His mouth would move rhythmically as if he were reciting catechism and not catching the true meaning of the words.

Floyd Burns was convicted and given the death penalty for killing Maylene, his first wife And if it were physically possible, the district attorney in Byrd's Landing said that he'd wake him up and kill him again for the murder of Jean Rinehart, since the jury in that case also thought he deserved death. But Floyd was responsible for many other murders, some she knew without a doubt had happened. She knew because she'd been there. Raven tried to turn him in when she was a child, but they didn't believe her at the time. Floyd, at that time using the name of Floyd Baxter, charmed the responding officers. He apologized to them, gave them sweet tea and insisted that they were the victims of a little bird with an overactive imagination and a hankering for too much TV. Floyd closed the door behind them when they left and said, *It wan't just me, Birdy Girl, who done all them things. It was we, 'member? Your pretty lil' face was a great help. Best if you stay quiet.* And then he told her what happened to little girls who told on their daddies.

After he killed her stepmother, the police questioned Raven about other possible victims but, heeding Floyd's warning, she kept quiet. They still investigated and linked him to murders in Texas, New

Mexico and even more in his adopted home state of Louisiana. By then, he was already on death row in California for the murder of Maylene and the other states didn't pursue. The district attorneys there chose to focus on living perps they could still punish. That and his indefinite kill count and over-the-top personality raised his celebrity status and mystique level among serial killer fans. Some said he only killed the nine or so the cops knew about, others said it was upward of thirty. They delighted in blogging about how they reached various conclusions about the caliber of Floyd's street cred. There was one who had even written a book about him. *Straight Razors and Peacock Feathers*, it was called.

She held it now, running her hands across the book's glossy cover. It had a picture of a peacock with his feathers spread in glorious neon blues and greens. The book claimed that Floyd's daughter had been telling the truth all those years ago when Floyd still called himself Floyd Baxter, and he was responsible for over a dozen murders in towns stretching from California to Louisiana. Most committed on the Fourth of July, and all containing an element of fire whether it was just a body or entire structure burned. The book was a success, and there was talk of a screenplay, and a possible deal with Netflix.

Intrigued, Raven had picked the book up when it was published, thinking that finally someone had been able to find out Floyd's real crimes. But the book was filled with so many lies that she sent a note to the publisher telling them so. They didn't respond, but she remembered about two weeks later reading a short article in the *Byrd's Landing Review* that the author had his book pulled from the shelves and was forced to return a 50,000-dollar advance for fabricating what was supposed to be the true story of one of Byrd's Landing's infamous locals. No more screenplay. No more Netflix.

She sighed when she read the article, getting no satisfaction out of it. She even questioned why she bothered to inform the publisher, despite the voice whispering that Floyd belonged to her, and no other – especially not to someone who clearly didn't know him. She placed the book back in the box, closed the lid and taped it shut again, the tape gun making an ugly ripping sound in the quiet shed.

She retrieved the visitor and deathwatch logs, and then, for good measure, she took the entire box of letters. She would go through the letters later but she would compare the names on the visitor log to the guests at Antwone Westcott's Fourth of July party. If the murder of Hazel Westcott had anything to do with Floyd, then the killer may have been one of Floyd's many fans. If Floyd had come back from hell dragging fire in the form of some death row groupie, she would not rest until she extinguished the flames.

CHAPTER FOURTEEN

When Raven first saw her, Jean Rinehart had on spiked high-heeled shoes in a red so shiny it looked like she had just pulled her feet out of a pool of blood. Her uniform was pink and looked soft as powder and as clean as sunshine. It lay across her body without one wrinkle or fold, as neat as a soldier on inspection day. Raven kept asking for more syrup or milk or anything that she could in order to see those high heels click over to their table, her hips swaying in time with the rhythm of her shoes.

At that time Raven was almost eight years old. Floyd had been on the run a long time after killing his wife. The sheriff had thought that he would be an easy man to find with his hair and funny-colored eyes, dragging a little girl along with him. But the sheriff hadn't counted on number two dark brown hair dye or the big glasses Floyd took to wearing, or the fact that Floyd would drift two thousand miles away from the place of his wife's killing. How Floyd would cackle when he told Raven that he'd been able to fool them.

The 30,000 dollars of Jesus's money Floyd had stolen had long since run out, and he had been running out of ideas on how to keep himself in Camels unfiltered and Raven in milk and pancakes. Sometimes she would catch him looking at her. He'd complain about how she never smiled anymore and how her face always looked quiet and pinched. He'd tell her that she had to stop clenching her teeth. And then he would say, "Why, Birdy, you always look like you hurtin', even when you sleep?"

"My," the waitress said. "You certainly do like milk. How many glasses does that make?"

Raven held up four fingers and kept her eyes on the waitress as she chugged the latest glass down. The waitress's nametag had black and white rhinestones glued along all four edges and proclaimed that the woman it belonged to was named Jean Rinehart.

Floyd looked from the waitress to Raven and back to the waitress again before a big grin took over his face. He cocked his head to one side and said, "I don't think it's the milk so much as the pretty lady serving it."

There was no ring on her finger saying that she was married. Raven put her glass on the table. She wiped away the milk from her mouth with the back of her hand, still looking at the woman as if she wanted to gobble her up from her red shoes all the way up to her perfect eyes, both of the same light brown color.

"Listen," Floyd now said with that same wide smile on his face. "Will you marry me?"

"I beg your pardon?" the waitress said.

"You see," he said, "I'm a widower. My wife died some years ago right in front of our girl."

The waitress started to say something, but he cut her off. "Murdered, actually. It's almost more than a full-grown man could bear, but poor Raven saw the entire thing as little as she was."

He waited. Jean Rinehart didn't say anything, just stood there in a silence that made the people sitting at the table next to them stare at their hands and clear their throats. Raven felt the breath gather in her chest and knew it was happening again. She wanted to tell the woman to run away but couldn't get the words unstuck from inside her throat. It was hard enough for her to just keep breathing.

"I can see that you are a little speechless," Floyd said to the waitress. He twisted in the booth so he could face her. Sweat glazed his forehead and his words came faster than sounded natural. "My girl hasn't said more than two words since you walked in the room. She ain't looked at a woman the way she's looking at you since my wife died." He stopped and then corrected. "I mean since she was killed."

He waited for her to ask him more about what had happened to his wife but she didn't, so he went on as if she had asked him anyway. "Ma'am, she was killed by some Baptist preacher who couldn't hide the evil inside even beneath the shield of God. He couldn't hold it in no longer and one night while she and Raven were bringing him his supper, he just plain simple up and killed her."

He looked down at the floor and swallowed hard just one time.

He was waiting for the woman to stroke Raven's hair and call her poor thing. That's what usually happened.

But Jean Rinehart didn't do that. Instead, she put the pitcher on the table and one hand on her hip. "What's your name?" she asked Floyd.

"Fire. I mean Floyd Baxter."

"And you, young lady?"

"Raven Baxter," she said, just like Floyd had drilled into her.

Raven heard the breathless sound in her voice and her body felt so full of energy that she had to sit on her hands and press her bottom hard against the chair to keep from springing up. She wanted to scream at Jean that she had just missed a clue the size of a twelve-foot alligator, the kind she heard about that swished around in the swamps of Louisiana. But she didn't want her to go away either. So Raven did a thing that she would regret for the rest of her life. She kept her mouth shut.

Jean turned back to Floyd. "Is this story your way of telling me you don't have enough money to pay the check?"

"No'em," he said. "It's the truth."

"Are you telling me this so I will go out with you?"

"No'em," he said. "I'm telling you this so you will marry me and help me raise my daughter. You are the first woman she's been interested in."

"You don't even know me," she said.

"I know that you are a good woman."

"And how do you know that?"

"Because you're clean," he said, still looking at the floor with a shyness that was as put on as the pants he stepped into this morning. "And because you listened."

"You'll marry any woman that your daughter is interested in?"

Floyd stared at her for a moment or two without blinking. "I would do anything for my daughter, Miss...?" He paused and asked her name even though it was right there on her nametag surrounded by rhinestones. He paused because he knew it would have more of an effect on her that way. He always told Raven how important it was to stop for a little bit right before the big parts.

"Rinehart. Jean Rinehart."

"Jean Rinehart. Anything. I'd pluck the stars from the sky if it'd make her happy."

Jean Rinehart looked at Floyd for a long time. Then she turned to

Raven and stared at her a long time too. After a minute or two she picked up the check and put it in her apron pocket. She then took the pitcher in her arms and cradled it against her flat belly.

"I'll tell you what," she said. "I'm not looking for anybody to marry, and frankly, you don't look like a prize. I can tell you've just blown into town and don't have much in the way of money. I can still see the smoke coming from the Chevy that you drove here in and you've been sitting down for the good part of an hour. The girl has grime around her neck and probably hasn't had a bath in days. Do you even have a job?"

"I can get a job."

"A place to stay?"

"I'll be able to scrounge something up," he said. "I always do."

"Something you can afford?"

"I get by, ma'am."

She turned away, carrying the check in her apron pocket and the now-warmed milk in her brown hands. She sat the milk on the soda board and Raven Burns – for the moment Baxter – held her breath wondering if Jean would come back to the table, half wishing that she wouldn't, half wishing that she would. She closed her eyes so tight that they hurt. She thought about that for a long time – how she could wish for two things that were the exact opposite and still wish for them while knowing all along that there was no way she could ever have both.

She remembered a time in another town when another waitress didn't miss the clues. And she not only didn't return, she also called the cook, who emerged from the kitchen greasy and angry and kicked both Raven and Floyd out.

Floyd removed two five-dollar bills from his wallet and laid them on the table. Then he took two ancient-looking one-dollar bills out of his wallet and laid them across the damp fives so the money looked like a cross. It was the way he always left the tip.

When Jean Rinehart did come back, she looked into Raven's eyes and studied the set of her mouth. Raven had no idea what she was looking for, but wondered if she could see the picture of her mother being beaten to death by the hammer-like fist of a crazed Baptist preacher.

She herself had gazed many times in the mirror, sometimes holding her one eye open with her fingers to see if she could catch one or two pictures maybe of blood dripping and a body dying.

But she never saw anything. And it looked like Jean didn't see anything either. Jean turned back to Floyd. "Look, there is no way I'm going to marry you. I don't think you're serious anyway. I think you're either trying to get out of paying the check or to get a date. Regardless, I can tell that the two of you have been on the road and could use a friend in town. I don't know if you plan on settling here, but I know a guy in Byrd's Landing who rents shotgun houses to people down on their luck. Seventy-five bucks a month plus utilities. I can give you directions if you like."

"I'd appreciate that, Miss Jean Rinehart."

"I know he's looking for someone to help with his other places. A handyman." She looked at Floyd. "No drinking or drugs. Someone trustworthy and dependable. Are you handy around the house? Dependable?"

"I am very handy around the house," Floyd said solemnly. "I am dependable as death."

She wrote out the address on the back of a blank order slip. When she put the cap back on the pen and pushed the paper across the table toward him, he touched her wrist. "If you won't marry me," he said, "would you at least let me take you to a movie?"

She moved her hand away. "I'm sure you can't afford a movie," she said.

When Jean Rinehart left the table he turned to Raven.

"Don't worry," he said. "I ain't gonna hurt her none. She is the one, the one I'm gonna marry, Birdy Girl. It's just gonna take me a little longer than I thought, that's all."

And it did. It took him almost a full year.

CHAPTER FIFTEEN

Floyd Baxter *né* Burns and Jean Rinehart were married in the Old Union Baptist Church in Coushatta in the fall of '92. The building was infirm with age and loomed out of the earth as if it had been grown there, the dingy gray siding stained with grime and streaked with orange rust. Floyd held Raven tightly by the hand as he led her up the crumbling cement steps that someone in another time had dared to paint red. The steps were now faded and peeling, their color almost gone.

Raven had heard Jean Rinehart tell Floyd that it was a poor church. The small congregation didn't have a lot of money to keep things fixed up, but every one of them, down to the very last Sunday-best-hat-wearing one of them, believed that the Lord would provide a way.

But the Lord hadn't quite gotten around to that yet. Dusty, crunched plastic was used in the place of glass for the front doors. The front windows had the glass broken out and the ones not boarded up by plywood were stuffed with the same type of dirty plastic covering the front doors.

The groom's dressing room had an old countertop with a rusted sink that let out a trickle of water that Floyd used to shave. He didn't use a safety razor or even need a good mirror. He quite capably twirled an old-fashioned straight razor made of Sheffield steel in his hand while occasionally glancing into a cracked hand mirror nailed upside-down from a wire on the wall next to the sink. The glass distorted his face. It divided it in two so that one side looked normal while the other looked like it was behind the mirror coming from far away.

As Raven watched him she knew that he didn't even need the mirror. It was no more than a prop like they had in the plays at her school and in the movies. Floyd could handle that straight razor in his sleep. He could handle it without a scratch or a nick, even around the curves of his face, that slim spot under his nose and that soft place next to his earlobe.

Raven wore white gloves and held a basket of rose petals. Jean Rinehart told her that she was to scatter the rose petals over the floor as she walked to the altar. She and Floyd would then be able to walk down the aisle floating on a river of rose petals after Raven. That's how Jean talked, fancy like from a book. She said things like floating on rose petals and singing like a white-robed angel. Raven smiled as she thought about what that was going to be like – living with Jean all the time. It would be like living in a storybook. Then she frowned again thinking about a speck in her eye that really wasn't a speck at all, but a full picture of what Floyd had done to the last woman he married and so many others since.

"Put that basket down and come help your old man with his tie."

She put the basket down on the table next to a destroyed T-bone steak and eggs Floyd had ordered from the diner that morning. Floyd had taken the steak knife and stuck it upright in a biscuit. She stared at the leftover meal for a long time thinking about something but not quite sure what.

"Come on, girl," he said. "We ain't got all day. We got no less than two appointments. One with God and the other with an angel at the altar."

As he stooped down to expose his neck she smelled the Irish Spring he had used to bathe. Even as young as she was she knew that it was a smell even hell would never let her forget.

In that ritualistic way of his he placed his hands on both of her shoulders as she tied the bow tie. "You are about to get a mommy, my little bird. How do you feel about that?"

She said, "All right, I guess."

"All right?" he asked, almost jerking the tie from her small hands. "What do you mean all right? I thought you loved Miss Jean?"

She shrugged. "I guess I like her some," she said.

"You couldn't take your eyes off of her when you first met her. Why, I bet you'd marry her yourself if you could."

She didn't answer him. He stood up and went to the cracked mirror. He smiled at the part of the reflection that was most like him.

He walked over to the table and opened a travel bag. He removed a bottle of Stetson cologne. She watched him walk back over to the mirror and slap the cologne on his cheeks and neck.

"I just want it to be us again, Daddy," she said.

The slapping sounds stopped. She didn't look at him, but was forced to when the silence drew out so long that she thought she would lose every ounce of food she had put into her body that morning.

They looked each other in the eyes, his blue to her green and her green to his blue. They looked at each other for a long time. Then he said, "That's a lie."

"It's not," she said.

He picked up his brown plaid wedding coat and shrugged into it. He adjusted his pearl-buttoned white shirt until all the buttons aligned perfectly with his belt and the waistband of his pants. Then he said, "I ain't gonna hurt her, if that's what you thinkin'."

"I'm not thinking that," she said.

"Your mamma was an accident," he said. "In fact, it may have just been a dream that you had. You ever thought of that, Birdy Girl? Just like the other stuff. Remember what the doctor said and the police said that time you called 'em? They couldn't find nothing to it, not on old Floyd Baxter with his big black glasses. Ain't none of it real."

She knew enough to stay quiet. He poured more cologne in his hand and spread it across his hair before brushing it with a silver-toned paddle brush.

"But let's say for a minute that it was real. Let's just pretend. No telling what would have happened if she hadn't slipped in all that blood. Hadn't cracked her arm. All that hollering and carrying on. That was liable to drive anybody crazy. Maybe if she just hadda shut up." He laughed in a quiet way and started humming 'The Battle Hymn of the Republic'.

Raven's hand brushed the handle of the steak knife as she reached for the basket of rose petals she had set down to help him. He had taken the jacket off and was retying the yellow bow tie. He bent a little so he could see what he was doing in the low mirror, exposing the back of his neck as he did so.

She looked at his neck, then back at the knife and then at his neck again before returning to the knife. She pulled it out of the biscuit and turned it over and over in her hands looking at it as if all of her life depended upon it. The knife's blade was sharp and ragged like teeth on a beggar. The handle was made of faded black wood with three silver round dots holding it all together.

Floyd had switched songs. Now he sang in a tuneless voice about a lamb being lost in the woods, someone needing to follow his lead, the words trailing off into a whistle.

Raven thought of beautiful Jean Rinehart with her clear brown skin, her painted nails, her shoes that were always high-heeled and red no matter what she wore. She thought about the Miss Jean who walked her to school, helped her pick out dresses – not just jeans and T-shirts – but dresses with frilly collars and ribbons for special occasions. She thought about how she brushed her hair with hemp oil and braided it and tied red ribbons around her ponytails.

Floyd's whistling slowed a little before lapsing into a thick silence. He turned suddenly and grinned at her standing there. There must have been a flat look in her eyes that Floyd couldn't help but recognize.

"Them things are dangerous," he said. "You shouldn't be playin' with knives, little Birdy."

She didn't drop it. Raven thought that she still had a chance. Instead of the neck it would have to be the heart. It would just have to be a quick lunge, a hard jab like she had seen in those sword-fighting movies.

Floyd walked over to her, his chest in the white shirt stretched wide as he once again shrugged into his jacket. She tried to say something but nothing came out. She told her body to move but it didn't listen to her. It was as if Floyd was inside her head commanding her little body, telling her what to do.

And he was telling her to be still.

He took the knife from her and kissed her on the forehead. "I love you, Birdy Girl," he said. "And you make me proud." He whispered it as if it was a special secret only between the two of them. "Now take that plate over to the sink. I'll meet you by the door."

She picked up the plate, the knife now teetering harmlessly on the side. She scraped the leftovers into the trash and set the plate in the bottom of the rusted sink. She was about to turn away but then she froze. Sitting right there on the countertop was Floyd's straight razor, open so that its Sheffield blade gleamed like a column of light.

She knew that he knew that she saw it. She knew that he knew what she was thinking. The straight razor was much sharper than she could have ever wished for in a knife. She was a little girl, but all she had to do was have it in her hand in order to go after him. After all, she was one of Queen Mab's fairies. That's what Miss Jean called her sometimes. She was full of color and light and strong, and perhaps a little crazy like her father, except Jean never said that last part. She might not kill him but she could hurt him – she could hurt him good. Maybe good enough so they would call off the wedding. Maybe good enough to save Jean Rinehart.

"I ain't gonna hurt her none." His voice was as soft as vapor, but loud enough to freeze her small hand hovering over the straight razor. "And remember what I told you after that time you called the cops. There is a special place in hell for girls who hurt their daddies and even a specialer place in hell for girls who tell on their daddies. And for them little girls they send their mammas down there with 'em so as they can take care of 'em. Is that what you want, Birdy Girl? Do you want to call your mamma out of heaven so that she can take care of you in hell?"

He had told her what hell was like – a hot place where they beat you with switches from noon to midnight, where they branded you with hot irons until your skin blistered and ran with water, and where they fed you nothing but flying water bugs and live rattlesnake teeth that could bite the insides of your throat on the way down to your belly.

He was still talking, but Raven didn't even need to hear the words anymore for her to feel something click in her head like a key in a lock.

Her hand fell to her side. She turned away from the sink. She left the straight razor with its blade swirling with light next to the sink like some demon sleeping.

CHAPTER SIXTEEN

Floyd hung on for as long as he could before he decided that it was Jean Rinehart's turn. The struggle up until that moment was written all over his face. It didn't help that Jean didn't talk or smile or laugh as much as she used to. And when she did talk, it was mostly to Raven. Jean and Floyd hardly talked at all. As the days that year got hotter and longer, Floyd got jumpier and Raven could see fear starting to drive his urge. She could see that flat, speculating look he got in his eyes when he was considering a kill. Worse, Raven wondered if he suspected that maybe Jean had begun doubting Floyd's lies about who he was and where he came from.

On that Fourth of July, Raven stood next to Floyd on the front porch of the townhouse where they lived as he fiddled with the keys. They had just returned from getting ice cream. Raven sensed something was wrong because Floyd took longer than usual to find the right key for the door. These days Raven was feeling everything twice as hard as usual. It was like that every Fourth. The jangle of the keys sounded like trombones in her ear. She jumped almost a mile as a group of blackbirds folded like a blanket in the sky before swooping away back up again straight toward heaven.

The front hall was empty and as clean as a hospital ward. They found Jean sitting on the couch in the living room, a copy of *Ebony* on her lap. The smell of her bourbon barbecue ribs slow baking in the oven filled the house. She was wearing a pair of white shorts and a crisp red shirt that matched a pair of red sandals, silly-looking things with a line of silver studs running along the back of a spiked heel. She set the magazine aside and stood up, aiming to give Raven a hug.

"Ribs will be done in about twenty minutes and then we'll be ready to go. I've already made the potato salad."

She was smiling as she said this and Raven noticed how much she was looking forward to getting out of the house. Before Raven could answer, Floyd knocked Jean Rinehart back down on the couch.

He didn't give her a chance to scream. She tried to sit up but he punched her full in the face. He snatched a red sandal from her right foot and drove the heel home into her belly. When he pulled the heel out, Jean Rinehart opened her mouth and stood up, clutching her stomach. Raven thought that she would finally scream. But she didn't. Instead she said as she teetered there, "Raven, run," the words coming out with a stream of blood now flowing from her flattened nose.

As Jean went down, Raven saw them all fall as only Floyd could make a body fall. She saw Suzy Freedman of Mesa, Arizona, an artist who sold crooked pottery in town. Floyd slashed Suzy with a straight razor in 1988 and lit fire to her tiny adobe house while Raven sat in the old pickup with their bags packed and engine running.

Before Jean hit the ground, she saw Tammy Buckley of Deming, New Mexico, a rich lady Floyd and Raven had followed home from the grocery store in 1989 to a red brick house in a fancy neighborhood. Floyd made Tammy change into white linen before taking her behind the train depot to open her up with the razor. And when he was done, he dumped kerosene on the body, lit it, and breathed in the smell of burning flesh as Tammy lay there smoldering.

She no longer saw Jean, but Jimmy St. Paul in San Antonio, a homeless man who dared to give Raven a dollar in 1991. Jean Rinehart became both Lucille and Miguel Rodriguez in Vidor, Texas. A year after Jimmy, Floyd shot Miguel in the head so he could have his peace as he went to work on Lucille. That's what he told Raven, anyway. He had to shoot Miguel so he could have peace. And she saw the face of one of her babysitters, Felicia Harris. Floyd had told Raven that Felicia stuck her nose in all the wrong places. She suspected Floyd was not who he said he was. She had to go.

As Jean Rinehart's body finally hit the floor, she turned into Floyd's last victim. She became Ruth Jefferson, a big black woman who lived in a shotgun in town. Ruth Jefferson had screamed so loud and took such a long time to die she almost got Floyd caught. He wanted to set the house on fire, but he had simply run out of time.

Jean was all of those people and none of them. When her body stopped twitching, she was only Miss Jean, the woman who wore only red shoes and had been her stepmother for the last three years.

Raven couldn't move.

She just stood there as if her feet were nailed to the floor. But then Floyd laughed and drove the spiked heel into Jean's eye, drove it right down to its shiny black sole.

Raven ran then.

She bolted out the front door and ran in a zigzag pattern down the sidewalk with Floyd chasing after her telling her to wait, wait, wait, they had to go together just like they always did. But Raven just ran. She ran to the only place she had felt safe in Byrd's Landing, the place where she found and spent so much time since moving into the townhouse. She ran screaming from Floyd and all that he had made her watch while threatening her with snakes and hell if she told.

She only stopped when she smelled charcoal burning and meat cooking. She looked up to find herself surrounded by red, white, and blue balloons, picnic tables covered with chips and fruit salads, streamers and people. Lots and lots of people with their mouths open. The same ones who had been waiting for Jean to bring her special slow-baked barbecue ribs and potato salad to complete their feast at the park.

Raven fell to her knees and dared a look over her shoulder. Floyd was still chasing her but had slowed to a trot. The look on his face was confused, as if he were asking himself if it were fitting for him to be here in the middle of a holiday barbecue covered in blood. His right hand slowly rose and he pointed at Raven. He kept coming and soon he was immediately behind her. She remembered the moment when he placed a bloody hand on her shoulder as the moment when her life truly started. As he did so, two men separated from the crowd and tackled him hard to the sidewalk.

One of them happened to be a cop patrolling the park for Fourth of July troublemakers. The other was an off-duty cop in civilian clothes. Raven never forgot how brave they both were, especially the cop in uniform. She never forgot how strong and competent, how he didn't seem afraid of anybody or anything, and she especially remembered how his nametag, black letters on a field of gold, gleamed in the Fourth of July sun. Sawyer. She would later learn that it was a patrol officer named Early William Sawyer who had saved her from her father.

CHAPTER SEVENTEEN

After Raven secured her father's boxes at her apartment, she went back to the Byrd's Landing Police Department. Her Android bleated along the way and she answered without looking at the caller ID. Before she could even get a greeting out of her mouth, she heard the strident voice of the news reporter who had crashed the Hazel Westcott crime scene.

"Don't hang up," Imogene Tucker said. "I just want an interview, just one, an exclusive about Quincy Trueblood and Hazel. It's gold, Detective Burns. Especially now. All I need is an hour. And I promise I'll leave you alone." Raven sighed in exasperation before moving the phone from her ear and pressing the end button. That woman never gave up, she thought.

She walked into the conference room Billy Ray had set up as the investigation's command center to find him leaning back in a chair with his gleaming black shoes propped on the conference room table. He wore a whiskey-colored pork pie that she knew was from his favorite hattery, a place in Chicago called HooDoo. Raven thought how strange it was that the two men in her life had a thing for hats.

But unlike Floyd's, Billy Ray's hats sported no feather. No flash or flair aside from the cut and shape of them. Floyd would never wear such a hat. "There is no hat, Birdy Girl," Floyd would tell her as he smoothed the brim with his thumb and forefinger, "that's complete without a feather. Preferably peacock."

She imagined Floyd adjusting his hat to just the right angle in the afternoon light falling through the slatted blinds covering the room's two big windows. She heard his cackle breaking the silence of the conference room, and saw his small wiry body in mid-twirl. At that moment, he was as real to her as Billy Ray leaning back in his chair with his feet propped on the conference room table. *Get out of my head, old man*, Raven thought, *or I'll have my partner squash your little body like a bug.*

"You say something?" Billy Ray asked.

"Not a thing," Raven answered.

Floyd was gone from her head with the sound of Billy Ray's voice, disappeared in a wink of light. She flung the messenger bag she used as a briefcase on the table, knocking several file folders to the floor. The table was covered with evidence. Billy Ray, who always said he needed to touch things, already had some of the photos from the crime scene printed in eight by ten. They were scattered all over the table, some stacked on top of each other. Raven reached down and started sorting them.

"Would you, please," Billy Ray said, reaching down for the files that had fallen to the floor, "watch what you doing? You are seriously messing with my mojo."

"Well hello to you too," she said, as she tapped a stack of photos against the table to make sure their edges were straight. "What's got you so cranky?"

He waved a hand to where a magnetic whiteboard stood with more photos of both a dead and living Hazel Westcott attached to it. She saw that Billy Ray had also started a timeline depicting Hazel's movements from the moment she woke up on the morning of her death until the time her body was discovered. There were a lot of blank spots.

"I see," she said, laying the photos down and pushing them aside. "Sorry your mojo got messed with. Looks like you got a lot done."

"I did," he said with his eyes on the whiteboard. "I haven't stopped working on this. I read all the witness statements we got so far, started looking into her movements for that day, guest lists from the party. But none of it's falling into place. Still don't tell us why she was all dressed up and dead in the flowers." He stopped and looked over at her. "What's your take on this?"

She took her time pulling a chair out from the table and sitting across from him. He had already resumed his position, leaning back in his chair with his feet up, his deep tan and perfectly pressed bowling shirt clinging softly to his broad chest, making his skin appear more charcoal than it was.

She made sure her face was still before she answered. "What do I make of this? Well, it's curious."

"Curious like this is going to keep us up all night and take over our lives for a while, but we're going to figure it out? Or curious like this town – us included – is in for some serious shit?"

"I don't think the murder is personal," she said. "And that's what scares me."

He grunted. "You'd think that would make you feel better given how you two got along."

She looked at him. "What's that supposed to mean?"

"If it's not personal," he said, "then there's no reason to be looking at you."

She gave him her best blank look and said, "No one's got any reason to be looking at me in the first place. Even though Hazel and I weren't friends, I'm going to do my job. And I certainly didn't kill her."

He looked at her for a long moment. She held his stare until he broke it by taking his feet off the table. "I know you didn't kill her, Raven. That's stupid," he said. "But you're holding something back."

Holding something back. The words reverberated in her head as she thought of how she should answer him. She had pushed him far in the kitchen of his house earlier. He had asked her if there were any more surprises, and she had looked in his face and lied. How much further had she to go before he snapped? She decided stalling was the best tactic.

"I don't know what you mean, Billy Ray," she said, her voice flat.

He sat back. "The hell you say."

"I already told you everything back at your place," she said. "Why would I leave anything out?"

But he was shaking his head even before the words left her mouth. "No, Raven," he said, "I may be a lot of things but stupid isn't one of them. You told me what people already know around here. You're not telling me all of it. When Holloway asked you when the last time you saw Hazel, you hesitated. And you stiffened up. Your whole face went cold. And you got that look." He waved his hand over his face. "Tight around the mouth and eyes."

"I hesitated because he knew exactly when I saw her last," she said, allowing a hint of exasperation in her voice. "He was with her, remember?"

"No," he said again, shaking his head. "You're holding onto something else. Tell the truth and shame the devil."

"Billy Ray," she said, "this is serious."

"Don't worry about it," he said. "I know how to do serious."

"If I tell you, it could put you in jeopardy, your career—"

"I don't give two shits about my career," he interrupted. "You know my long-term plan."

She sighed. He'd find out anyway. It would be in the phone records. She wondered if he had already pulled them and was just waiting to hear it from her own lips. She said, "I told Holloway the truth. The last time I saw Hazel was at the Blue Heron. But that wasn't the last time I heard from her."

He raised an eyebrow and waited.

"I don't think it means anything," she said in a rush. "As a matter of fact, I didn't think anything of it when I got the call." She shrugged. "I thought it was just Hazel being Hazel."

"Call?" he questioned.

She sighed heavily and put her hands up. Without looking at him, she said, "I did something really stupid. Against all my instincts, I did something really jackass stupid."

"Raven," he said with an impatient edge to his voice. "Stop pussyfooting and tell me."

"Okay," she relented. "She called me about a week and a half ago. It was very early in the morning and I had just been running. I had wanted to do eight miles but could only make just under six. It was hot and the humidity was thick as syrup even that early in the morning. And the smell, Jesus, honeysuckle and magnolia. My allergies were going crazy. I was sweating, tired, and irritable as hell."

"Not a good time to get a call from your nemesis," Billy Ray said.

Raven nodded, not looking at him, "Not at all. I told you that the Quincy Trueblood situation had passed. When Pam Jones, the DA, decided not to prosecute, and most everyone agreed that I really didn't have a choice in the shooting, it all just started to die down. But Hazel, for the love of all that's holy, hadn't given up yet. That call proved it."

"How do you mean?"

"She said that she had proof that the weapon found at the Quincy Trueblood crime scene was a throw-down."

She looked at him then, trying to read his expression. He said nothing. He just sat there waiting. She knew enough about him to know he wouldn't react until he had the entire story.

"And Hazel said that she had proof," Raven went on. "A signed and notarized witness statement and the only copy of a video from the surveillance camera at Boones & Sons, the grocery store parking lot where Quincy was shot."

His eyebrow went up at her choice of words – *Quincy was shot*, not *I shot Quincy*. She had used the passive voice, the voice of no fault, no blame. Mercifully, he didn't comment on it. All he said was, "What else?"

"Like I was saying, I was tired and irritated and frankly had had enough of Miss Hazel Westcott. And I told her so. I told her that there was no video and no witness statement because there was no throw-down. I told her that Boones & Sons didn't have a surveillance camera, and even if they did Holloway would have been all over it. I told her to stop messing with my life and leave me the hell alone."

"You didn't believe her?"

"Of course I didn't believe her, Billy Ray!" Raven said. "Because it wasn't true. I mean, if it were true, why would she be calling me? Why not slip the video and the witness statement in an envelope and mail it to the *Byrd's Landing Review*? Put it on Facebook or YouTube? Or better yet, give it to the chief or Holloway so they could arrest my behind immediately? She just needed a reason to continue torturing me. I told her that."

"And what she say?" Billy Ray asked.

Raven slumped back in her seat. "She said that she was calling me because of how I helped her that night when she came over to my apartment," Raven said in a quiet voice. "She said that she had been thinking about it a lot and the fact that I comforted her proved I wasn't all bad. She wanted to give me a chance, which I thought was crap and told her so. But she insisted that all she wanted me to do was resign and leave town. For good. She gave me a week to make up my mind, or she was going to go public."

"And what'd you do that was so stupid?"

Raven looked down at her hands then back up at him. "I told her to stop tormenting me for something that I didn't do on purpose, called her a blessed fool, and I hung up on her."

"You didn't check it out?" Billy Ray asked, incredulous.

"As if you don't already know." Raven shook her head. "Do you think that I wanted to rehash all that confusion again? After it was over? To have everybody out there again looking at me and questioning me like that for some madness Hazel cooked up?"

He let out a long breath that he must have been holding for some time. Reaching up, he palmed the HooDoo pork pie and removed it from his head with one immaculately manicured hand. He sat the hat on the table between them. He didn't say anything for a long while. Finally, fingering the brim of the hat, he said, "This could be big, Raven. Hell, it is big. She tries to blackmail you and ends up catching a ride with Jesus a little over a week later?"

"I know it's big, Billy Ray. And that's why I'm kicking myself. I should have checked it out or called it in or something."

"Chief know?"

"No, you going to tell him?" she asked. "He'd take me off the case. You'd be doing this by yourself, or with someone from Major Crimes. You know how green they are over there. You need me on this one."

"You don't have to convince me," he said.

She propped her face on her hands, covering her eyes until she couldn't see his face anymore. Part of the reason she couldn't look at him was that she was ashamed for allowing herself to ignore Hazel. But the real reason was that she wanted to give him time to think about what to do next. She owed him that.

"I've subpoenaed her phone records but they aren't in yet," Billy Ray said after a while. "When I do, your number is gonna be on there. You know that, don't you?"

"I know that," she agreed through her fingers.

"We don't have to tell anybody that, though, not for awhile. And if it's just the one time she called, it won't stick out right away. But when Hazel's death hits the papers, that witness might come forward, that is if Hazel was telling the truth and there is some jive-turkey out there saying some mess about a throw-down. You know that, too, don't you?"

Raven nodded.

"How'd she get your number anyway?" Billy Ray asked.

"I don't know," Raven said. "I surely didn't give it to her. And it's not public."

"You think she's working with anybody who could have given it to her?"

"I don't know, Billy Ray," she said, knowing that she sounded a little helpless and hating herself for it.

He nodded. "I'll keep it quiet for as long as I can. But what you do in the dark is going to come out in the light. You can't hide this forever."

She looked at him. "Thank you, Billy Ray."

"Don't thank me," he said. "Because that means we'll have to find out who killed Hazel before then."

Relief washed over Raven in a wave and she sat up. She wondered if this was what a reprieve felt like to a death row inmate.

"That's another thing that's on my mind," she said. "I think we are looking at a serial."

He was nodding before the words left her mouth. "That's what's scaring the shit out of me too."

Raven looked back down at the whiteboard at the other end of the room, the one with Hazel's pictures all over it. God, she had been beautiful, Raven thought, even with all that venom.

She turned back to Billy Ray. "You said you had the guest list from the party. Do you know if there were any gate crashers?"

"We don't know yet," he said. He ran his fingers along the brim of his pork pie. "I told a couple of officers from Patrol to talk to all the guests to find out if they noticed anything unusual. They're still interviewing. I don't expect them to be done for a while."

"It had to be someone who Hazel Westcott felt comfortable enough with to invite into her bedroom. I can't imagine that the person she took by the hand and led to the boathouse would be someone the family didn't know well."

"How do you figure?" Billy Ray asked.

"Because," she said, "that bedroom was a complete, smelly disaster. She wouldn't want someone she barely knew to see her room like that."

"Well," Billy Ray agreed. "Yeah, it was a mess. And I'll give you that it was probably someone she knew. No signs of forced entry. The front door faces the backyard. If the killer was breaking in and she made a fuss, someone in the house probably would have heard. But I'm not sure I'm buying that she gave a shit about who saw her room."

"She did. This woman cared very much about appearances. I knew her, remember? I think she started most of the mess about Quincy Trueblood because she wanted people to notice her, to think that she was a solid, capable person. And besides, you saw how clean the living room was. It was someone she knew well, maybe one of her boyfriends."

"That what Daddy Warbucks told you?" Billy Ray asked.

She thought back to the conversation with Antwone Westcott, Hazel's father. "Not in so many words. He just spent the entire time staring balefully into my eyes before giving me this."

She took the scrap of paper out of her jacket pocket, went to the other end of the room and pinned the note to the whiteboard.

"What's that?"

"A list Westcott gave me. Says these are all of Hazel's boyfriends."

Billy Ray let out a low whistle. "Man," he said. "Where did she find the time or energy? I get tired just looking at that."

"I can imagine," Raven answered wryly. "We'll cross-reference with the guest list and see if anything shakes out. See if we can get some more officers to run these boys down too."

"Yeah, about that," he said, and lifted his hand to scratch the side of his temple. "I not only went ahead with setting Patrol up with the guest interviews, I pulled in the Westcotts for formal statements."

She lifted an eyebrow. "Oh?" She was a little bothered that he didn't wait for her, but it wasn't his fault that she went AWOL during a critical part of the investigation. Billy Ray had a job to do, and he didn't need to wait on her to do it.

He didn't look at her as he continued. "Yeah," he said. "Just Mamma Westcott and Angel, Hazel's sister. Figured you already talked to Daddy Warbucks. And since me and the Westcott ladies got so close while making the tea…."

"I'm sorry about that, Billy Ray," Raven said.

He waved his hand at her. "It's nothing. Didn't get a lot out of them in the kitchen. They were too upset. So I told them to get some sleep and come in early this morning. Still a waste of time. Of course, Daddy Warbucks insisted on being in the same room with his daughter. Angel kept looking over at him every time I asked her a question. And even though I talked to Mamma Westcott alone, she kept looking at the door like he was going to bust through it any minute. We recorded both interviews in case you want to look at them later."

"Should I?" she asked.

"If you want to waste your time," he answered. "Nothing to what they said. I did ask Westcott to give a formal statement, anyway, but he lawyered up."

Raven nodded. She wasn't surprised. Westcott didn't strike her as the type of man who would keep subjecting himself to more questioning after saying what he thought he needed to say. Raven also remembered Westcott telling her that the police wouldn't get anything out of the remaining Westcott ladies. What had he said about Angel? That she was so scared of her own shadow that he saw her run away from a sneeze once.

She let it go and asked, "How is Rita doing on the body?"

"She said she's processing late this afternoon."

"This afternoon?" Raven said. "You mean now?"

He looked at the time on his cell phone. "More than likely," he said. "I didn't realize it was so late. I guess we better get going."

"I guess we better," she agreed.

"And Raven," he said, stopping her at the door.

She looked up at him. "Yes?"

"You aren't hiding nothing else from me, right?"

When she looked into his face, she saw that she had pushed him just as far as she could by not trusting him enough to tell him all. The dark light in his brown eyes told her that it wouldn't take much to send him over the edge as far as their relationship as partners went. She thought about the peacock feather she had found under Hazel's bed, but she couldn't tell him. Not yet. Not after all she had laid on him. Her first thought was to lie to him again, but she couldn't bring herself to do that. Instead, she said, "I need you to hold on, Billy Ray. Hold on and trust me for a little while longer with this case. I'm asking you for that."

She could see the wheels turning behind his eyes, but she couldn't read him, not completely. Finally, he nodded slowly, his mouth tight and his eyes a little wary. He would give her time, but she knew that sooner rather than later, she would have to come clean.

CHAPTER EIGHTEEN

Raven and Billy Ray left the police station through a metal exit door in the back of the building. The medical examiner, Rita Sandbourne, referred to the location as having an office in the outhouse instead of being near the hospital, which was her preference. "Brand new building," Rita would joke to Raven, "and they still managed to put me in the outhouse with the dead bodies."

The landscapers had turned the space separating the morgue from the station into a small garden. A sidewalk meandered through plumes of deer grass and fuchsia bushes. Honeysuckle grew tightly against a cinderblock fence painted a sage-green. Nearer the station sat two cement picnic tables with umbrellas to protect smokers from the sun.

Today the tables sat empty. If the morgue didn't deter the smokers from becoming part of the still life, then the July sun certainly did. The heat created a damp warm haze that wrapped around Raven's body. She could feel waves of humidity running through her hair and down her back like fingers. She looked at Billy Ray, who always remained unperturbed no matter how hot or how cold it was. His tan bowling shirt looked just ironed, still crisp even in the humidity.

"Aren't you hot?" Raven asked him.

He unwrapped a piece of cinnamon Trident and shoved the gum in his mouth before thrusting the package toward her. "So they tell me," he said. "But I think they just might be jivin'."

Raven laughed a little as she waved the gum away and smoothed moisture into her hairline.

"I don't think you're human, Billy Ray," she said. "It's burning up and you aren't sweating. You just worked a graveyard shift, did all that work this morning, and you look like you just woke up from hours of sleep."

She pressed open the double-glass door of the morgue and they found themselves in a small, cool room with textured carpet the color of cement. A love seat striped in gray and blue sat in front of an oak coffee table stacked with brochures on coping with death and advertising local funeral homes.

"I fucking hate autopsies," Billy Ray muttered as they walked farther into the room.

Raven handled the dismantling of the human body as a necessity. The victim was no longer a person but evidence that needed to be dissected, evaluated, and tagged. The person on the table had nothing in common with her. In fact, the body was no longer a person. To her it was a locked chest that needed to be pried open.

Not so for Billy Ray. Not anymore, and it was getting worse with every autopsy he saw, and the closer he got to leaving police work. "I just see myself lying on that table," he had finally confessed to her.

The wall to the right of them had a door that led to another similarly decorated room. It had a viewing glass so that families of the dead could look through it and identify their loved ones.

Raven strode to the door on the wall to the left. Punching a code on the locking mechanism, Raven grinned and said, "Morpheus, I choose the red pill."

Billy Ray said something about understanding why she scared the shit out of her old partner as the door opened onto a large expanse of a room with blinding white walls covered in murals of beach scenes from around the world, a couple as far away as Thailand. Some of the murals had a checkmark in black sharpie in the right corner. Rita told her that those were the places she had been, the posters without the checkmark, the places she had yet to go.

Everything in the room except for the white sand and blue water murals thrummed with cold efficiency. Rita had two morgue tables made of steel with raised sides to drain away the bodily fluids. The floor was made of tiny white tiles that dipped toward a drain between the two metal tables, and hooks on the walls held the instruments she used during autopsies.

Rita sat on a stool next to the table occupied by the body of Hazel Westcott. Showing beneath Rita's white lab coat was a black Grateful Dead T-shirt and a pair of old faded jeans, the only two unserious things about her at the moment. Hazel's head was propped on a block, a blue blanket folded neatly to her chest, but not high enough to hide the whipped stitching that made her chest look like a repaired quilt. Her glossy black hair was brushed back from her still face, and if it weren't for the blue beneath her eyes and the stitching on her chest, Raven would have sworn she was sleeping.

"I see you couldn't wait for us," Raven said.

Rita pulled a pair of ear buds out of her ears and cocked her head at them. "Say again?"

"I see you got anxious," Raven said.

"Not anxious. Bored. I was bored," she said. "Finished up about an hour ago." She gave Billy Ray a mischievous grin but Raven could see that the grin didn't reach her eyes. "I bet you're sorry you missed it."

"You'd guess wrong," Billy Ray grunted at her.

Raven sat on the stool on the other side of Hazel's body.

"What did you find, Rita?" she asked.

Rita looked at her, then she laughed. "What did I find? What did I find? Why, I found absolutely nothing. I don't understand why she just doesn't get up from that table and go get her hair done."

Billy Ray looked at Rita as if he hadn't heard her correctly. "Wait, what? You saying that she wasn't murdered?"

"Who knows?" Rita said. "Maybe I was wrong at the scene. Maybe she was sick or something and knew she was about to die and decided to kill herself before the Lord decided to take her. Maybe she had the time and inclination to get all dolled up before arranging herself in the flower bed. What do you think, lover?"

"That's crazy," Billy Ray said, "I've never heard of a suicide acting like that."

"Me neither," Rita agreed. "But guess what? I can't get my hands on her medical records to even check out the possibility that she was dealing with some terminal illness that might lead to suicide. The family won't release them."

"What do you mean the family won't release them?" Raven asked. "She's dead. And you're conducting an investigation. They can't keep them from you."

"So you say," Rita said. "But Papa filed an injunction probably before the meat wagon pulled out of the driveway. We'll get them, all right. But he's not making it easy. Still, if she overdosed on something, I should be seeing some signs of that in the body. But our Hazel is as perfect as a summer's day."

"You find anything in the medicine cabinets?" Billy Ray asked.

Rita shook her head. "My guess is that one of the family members cleaned it out before we got there. Can't prove it, though."

"So what happened, somebody bore her to death?" Raven asked.

"For all I know, yes," Rita said. "Heart beautiful. Someone should bronze it and put it on display. Liver, kidneys, fine. A better-looking pair of lungs da Vinci couldn't paint…and the brain."

"Smaller than normal, I bet," Raven said dryly.

Rita gave her a look. "Be nice. But actually, no. I couldn't tell what her IQ was, mind you, but her brain was also spectacular. All in all, a beautiful specimen of human flesh."

Raven stood up to look into Hazel's face. "So, what happened to you, lady?" she asked her.

Rita walked over to Raven. "She did have one tiny imperfection," she said, tilting her head to one side.

"What was that?" Raven asked.

"Her ass."

"Her ass?"

Billy Ray laughed. "I seriously doubt that."

"Do either one of you have any reverence for the dead?" Rita asked. "Can I please get a little respect for my patient?" She waited for several seconds before continuing. "Yes, in spite of what you believe, Mr. Tall, Dark, and Squeamish, the beautiful Hazel Westcott's ass was not perfect."

"What was wrong with it?" he asked.

Rita picked up a manila file folder on a rolling tray next to the autopsy table. She took out a photograph and handed it to Billy Ray.

"It looks pretty much perfect to me," was all he said.

Raven snatched it from him. What she saw didn't surprise her.

"That puncture mark," Rita was saying, "is recent. Delivered before she died. It's from a syringe."

"Of course, you don't have the toxicology results," Raven said.

"No," Rita agreed. "But I did send out for them already. Had Sandy take them to the lab in Shreveport and told her to use her gorgeous lips to sweet-talk anyone she knew over there so we can get the results before the Second Coming."

"What could have done this, Rita?" Billy Ray asked.

Raven and Rita looked at one another for a long time, but it was Raven who spoke.

"Succinylcholine, or Sux," Raven said slowly, her voice barely above a whisper.

"Wait, what?" Billy Ray asked.

"Sux, it's a muscle relaxant used in conjunction with anesthesia for surgeries. It makes it easier for the dream weaver to tube the patient," Rita explained.

"You mean the doc who puts her under? In conjunction with anesthesia?" Billy Ray asked. "But...."

Raven nodded. "It doesn't reduce pain or make the patient unconscious. They have other stuff for that. This relaxes all of your muscles, starting with those in your face and neck and continuing on until even your diaphragm becomes useless. So you...."

"Stop breathing," Billy Ray said. "You stop breathing and no one watching can see that you're in trouble."

"Except for maybe your eyes, if they're open," Raven finished for him.

Rita studied her for a moment. "Raven," she said. "You after my job? How do you know about all of this?"

Raven shifted on her feet. "I did some research for a case I was working," she said quietly. "I had a case a while back where a woman poisoned her husband with antifreeze."

"Now that's a painful way to go," Rita said. "Throwing up and shitting all the way to the graveyard."

"That's what I thought too," Raven said. "How painful and cruel is something like that? I asked the wife why she would use antifreeze on the father of her children and a man she had been married to for so long."

"Did she say the bastard deserved it?"

Raven shook her head. "Come on, Rita. Nobody deserves something like that. Anyway, I did a little research. Looked into some poisons that wouldn't be quite so...."

"Messy?" Rita asked. "Messy, Raven?"

"No," Raven answered. "Not messy. Though that's a bonus. So painful. I was looking for something that wouldn't be so painful. That's when I ran across Sux."

No one said anything. Billy Ray waited in the silence for a while, then he said, "But still, if this is what killed her, then she was feeling everything that was happening to her the entire time?"

Raven nodded. "That's the one drawback."

Everything. She had felt everything, the warmth or stinging cold of the bath if the killer bathed her after incapacitating her, and the silk dress falling over her helpless body. She had probably smelled the sandalwood cologne the killer sprinkled over her while she lay dying. She probably felt all of this, all the while unable to plead for her life or beg for an end to her suffering. The drug even robbed Hazel Westcott of the ability to release a final, primal scream.

Rita stood looking at Hazel with a fist knotted on her skinny hip.

"You're looking for someone who worked in or knows someone who works in or around hospitals," she said. "You're looking for some bastard who's supposed to be helping people but who's killing them instead."

"How sure are you?" Billy Ray said. "Shouldn't you wait for the tox results?"

"I'm sure as you are standing there," she said. "A lot of people are getting a kick out of using Sux as a murder weapon lately. It was only a matter of time before it showed up here."

Just then Raven heard a Buckwheat Zydeco ring tone coming from Billy Ray's phone. The waltzing accordion rhythms of Buckwheat's 'Mon Papa' broke through the morbid silence that had been enveloping the three of them. Billy Ray held up his finger as he pulled his iPhone from the pocket of his loose black slacks. He looked at the screen and stepped away from them.

"What about the standard stuff, Rita?" Raven asked after Billy Ray had left. "Time of death and all that jazz?"

"You probably know this from the temperature. I saw you holding her hand before I bagged them." She stopped and turned to Raven. "And by the way, nothing under the nails, and no defensive wounds. That body was pretty fresh."

Raven nodded, remembering how she pulled Hazel's free hand to hers at the scene to look under her nails. She hadn't been in rigor yet.

"Probably killed forty-five minutes to an hour before she was found," Rita was saying. "And you know that despite what they put on the CSI crime shows, it's not an exact science, but my best guess is she died between eleven and eleven thirty that night."

"Food in the belly?"

"Yep," Rita said. "Some undigested barbecue chicken and potato salad. Confirms that she hadn't been dead long."

"What about signs of sexual assault?" Raven asked. "Any seminal fluid?"

Rita shook her head. "No."

Raven thought about that for a minute. She remembered telling Billy Ray at the scene that the actual crime probably happened in Hazel's bed. The killer pretended he wanted to have sex with her but ended up injecting Sux into her bare bottom instead. The perp had to be male.

"I've been working with you long enough to know what you're thinking," Rita said. "And I'm well acquainted with that nasty habit of yours to overthink. Don't do it. Your perp could have been either male or female. A gun to the head would make me drop my drawers in a minute if I thought it was the only thing I could do to save my life."

Raven laughed and was about to respond to Rita when Billy Ray walked back over. He had a serious look on his face.

"We got to roll," he said.

"What's going on?" Raven asked.

"Angel Westcott, Hazel's sister," he said. "She wants to meet us at Big Bayou Lake."

Raven didn't move. "Bring her in and get her statement."

"We tried that, Raven," Billy Ray said.

"So why is she calling now?" Raven countered.

Billy Ray nodded. "She has some info she wants to pass to us away from her father."

"Why is she calling you? Why now?" Raven asked, and Billy Ray smiled.

Rita snorted at the puzzled look on Raven's face. "Don't you get it?" she said. "Lover boy used his good looks and his beautiful black skin to talk that girl into a crush." She shook her head. "Never stood a chance."

Raven looked from Rita and back to Billy Ray. He shrugged. "I could see she was holding back this morning, so I slipped her my card when Daddy Warbucks wasn't looking. I did what I had to. Anybody could have done it. It's easy for a teenager to fall for the big strong cop, especially after her sister just died."

"And you say I'm the one full of surprises, Billy Ray," Raven said as she started for the door. "Looks like you have a few surprises of your own."

CHAPTER NINETEEN

Raven cut the Mustang's ignition in the parking lot of Big Bayou Lake and watched Angel Westcott sitting at one of the faded green picnic tables. Raven contemplated the blue haze settling over the lake. It didn't look real to her, none of it did. Not the lines of trees stacked in shadow one behind the other, not the lake, not the fact that everywhere she turned lately she saw reminders of her father.

Hunched over a cell phone, Angel sat sideways on the bench. Her long brown legs were stretched out before her like a model in some 1940s pinup calendar. Angel Westcott was a tall girl, at least five ten, and her legs betrayed what must have been an awkward height for a girl her age. Raven knew from the investigation that Hazel's little sister was only sixteen. And she looked every bit her age sitting there in a pair of denim short-short cutoffs and a bright orange tank top while focused on the tiny screen of her cell phone.

Raven knew how it would probably be for Angel from now on, and it was not fair. She knew from working with families of other homicide victims and from her own experiences. Some of Angel's classmates, most maybe, would look at her pretty heart-shaped face and not see Angel at all. They would see instead the dead sister – no, not just the dead sister – the murdered sister. And they wouldn't know what to say to her.

Angel's new experiences would be similar to those Raven had after her father was exposed as a killer. After Floyd was caught, Raven's classmates looked at her and saw not the preteen girl, but instead the murdering father. Unlike Angel, Raven had a lot to clean up. She spent a good part of her life erasing that image from her classmates' eyes and later from the eyes of the good citizens of Byrd's Landing. She had almost succeeded. But now the sister of the girl sitting at the picnic table had threatened to blow all of her hard work to hell. Raven chuckled to herself. Even she was doing it – looking at Angel but seeing Hazel. Even in death Hazel was still able to subsume her sister. Even in death Hazel might still have a chance to ruin Raven.

"You sure you don't want to do this in an interrogation room, maybe pull her in again?" Raven asked Billy Ray, who was sitting in the passenger seat of the Mustang.

"No," he said. "If we did that we'd get Daddy Westcott *and* Angel." He pointed toward the picnic table. "We need this one alone. No Mamma or Daddy."

"Billy Ray," Raven said, "you know without a guardian present anything she says may not be admissible. They'll fight it."

He looked at her. "You in one all-fired bad box right now, Raven. You really want to recite the rules to me? I'm not looking for anything for court. I'm looking for something that's going to help us find out who killed Hazel Westcott before that phone call comes out. And before the sonofabitch who killed her starts laying out more of Byrd's Landing's finest in their flower beds."

"I know it," she said in a low voice and with a bob of her head just like Floyd used to do.

She and Billy Ray only had an hour or so before they would have to update the chief. And he was right, so far, they didn't have much – a guest list two officers were trudging through, a long list of boyfriends that would take days to track down, a time of death, and only a guess at the murder weapon. The state of Hazel's bedroom made it difficult for CSI. They had a lot of items to process. On the drive over to meet Angel, Raven had told CSI to concentrate on the bedding and the dress. Even though they found a few fibers on the dress, and hairs on the sheets, the final results could take weeks.

She itched to find time alone to compare Floyd's visitor logs to the guest list, but things were moving so fast that the time just wasn't there. They had no choice but to take advantage of the situation Angel presented to them. Raven and Billy Ray climbed out of the car and made their way over to Angel.

"Hey Angel, how are you doing?" Billy Ray said when they reached the bench, his voice both grim and caring.

Angel placed her cell phone facedown on the picnic table, rubbed her hands together and looked at him.

"I'm okay," she said, sounding as if she were half asleep.

"You remember Detective Burns?" he asked.

Angel nodded and Raven gave her what she hoped was an encouraging smile.

"Anybody know you here?" Billy Ray asked gently.

Angel shook her head. "No, I did like you said, slipped out, but it wouldn't have mattered. They all too busy to be worried about me." She stopped and a wan smile crossed her lips. "Almost like before Hazel died. They never been too worried about me nohow. But especially not now. Everybody at the house, and Mamma and Daddy running around planning the funeral. I could set myself on fire and nobody'd know the difference."

"You have something for us, Angel?" Raven asked. She knew that Billy Ray was the one Angel trusted. He should be the one leading the interrogation, but Raven couldn't help it.

Angel looked at Billy Ray, who smiled back at her. "She's okay," he said. "Go on, Angel," he said, her name sounding like an endearment.

Raven shuddered. Billy Ray's voice and the cajoling way he said Angel's name reminded Raven of her father every time he tried to get her to do something that she didn't want to do.

Be good to your ole daddy and stand here like you lost or *Be my sweet little Birdy Girl and peek out around the corner in case anybody come. And don't pay attention to any hootin' and hollerin'*. She took a deep breath and blew the memories out on the exhale. She wasn't being fair to Billy Ray. He cared about Angel, but right now he was more interested in the information she had promised him.

Angel didn't speak, just sat picking the green paint from the surface of the table, her head down as if she didn't even know why they were there. Or maybe she hoped that they would forget why they came.

Raven felt the heat of the late afternoon slide across her face with another breeze coming in just behind it. She looked out over the water in the same direction that Angel Westcott stared. Billy Ray followed her gaze.

"Now that's not something you see every day," he said, pointing at the water. Raven knew he was giving Angel time to find enough strength to tell them why she had asked to meet.

A brown pelican with a broken wing lumbered atop the water. Park rangers in a silver canoe kept close. One had what looked like a tranquilizer gun; another appeared as if she was trying to coax the bird into a crate sitting on the stern of the canoe.

"They trying to rescue it," Angel said in that same dreamy voice. "They think she worth it. She just a brown bird like a thousand other brown birds. She ain't nothing special."

"You're special, Angel," Billy Ray said. "Don't let anyone tell you that you're not. And your sister was special too."

Angel laughed. "I ain't talking about her," she said. She looked down at her hands. "And, no, I ain't that special. Never been. Not with Hazel in the house. Besides, I'm just talking about a bird about to die." She turned away from the water fast and said, "Do you know who she named after?"

Raven shook her head.

"Hazel Scott. She was a big jazz piano player in the 40s and 50s. Ma'dear loved her. She had brass, that's what she'd say. Hazel West had brass and she wanted a granddaughter who had brass. So she made Mamma name the first granddaughter after her. They wanted her to be some big-time singer. Gave her all kinds of lessons, but she never could sing good. Sounded like a bunch of frogs in a glass cage. So they switched it up and gave her piano lessons. But the reason she couldn't really sing, not even in choir, was that she couldn't keep a tune. Even as dumb as I am, I knew that."

"You shouldn't talk about yourself like that," Raven said.

But Angel went on as if she hadn't heard her. "And do you know what they said about her?"

"No, what?" Raven asked.

"The other kids in high school said that a light-skinned black girl who couldn't sing or act was like a blind man who couldn't play the piano."

Billy Ray whistled and took off his hat. "Man, that's rough," he said. "Sorrowful. That'd bring a tear to a glass eye."

Angel giggled, a small one, but a giggle nonetheless. And then probably remembering why they were there, she clamped a hand over her mouth as if she was afraid that a full-throated laugh would escape.

"What did you say about her?" Raven asked.

Angel shrugged as if she didn't care but Raven knew that she did. The compulsive need to eulogize her sister like she just did, the quiver to her lower lip betrayed her. Raven could see that she was trying to be tough.

"She was a good person," Angel said in a casual voice she had successfully cleansed of grief. "A little mixed-up. She partied too much, was a little dumb."

"Angel," Raven said. "Do you remember seeing your sister with anyone that night, anyone suspicious?"

Billy Ray waved a hand at Raven, a signal she knew meant to hold on. "When I saw you that night, Angel," Billy Ray said, "had you taken any drugs or done any drinking before we got there?"

She gave him a blank look.

"You just didn't seem all there, that's all," Billy Ray explained.

"I don't take no drugs," she said, only a bit more animated than she had been before.

"Yeah, I hear you," Billy Ray said. "But you were moving pretty slow. What was that all about?"

"I smoked some weed but didn't take no drugs. I don't do drugs."

Raven dropped her head trying to stifle a laugh.

"That's how I found her. I couldn't sleep so I thought I'd smoke a bowl...."

"Never mind," Billy Ray was saying briskly, but Angel wouldn't stop.

"I smoked like four bowls. That was my mistake. I just wanted a lil' somethin' to take the edge off and let me sleep, but I smoked too much. I stumbled around the house to throw up, and that's when I found her. That was some strong stuff...."

Billy Ray put up his hand to stop her.

"Really strong," she said. "I hadn't smoked anything in a minute, and that 'bout did me in."

"Okay," Billy Ray said. "Okay."

"Weed," she said. "No drugs. Never. I may be dumb, but I'm a mile from stupid."

"Thank you, Angel," Raven said, hoping to put an end to the subject. "Before then, at the party, did you see Hazel with anybody suspicious?"

Angel shook her head. "No," she said. Then she shrugged. "She said something about meeting a jack-off in the boathouse to take care of some business."

Billy Ray, recovered, sat up straighter. "She say who it was?"

Angel looked toward the water watching the drama being played out there with a weary look on her face. Her voice had returned to that same slow pace. "Just some dude who wanted to talk to her. Said he wanted to go out with her, but she told him that she wasn't interested. She told me that she might have to anyway."

"Did she say why?" Raven asked, unable to keep the eagerness out of her voice. "Was someone blackmailing her? Trying to get Hazel to sleep with them?"

Angel shrugged. "Kinda."

"Kinda?'" Raven repeated, prompting for more.

"Said something about nobody could know about it or we'd all be in big trouble. But that girl was always doing shit," Angel said, uninterested. "Things that she kept away from Daddy. I think she was afraid that he'd snitch her out."

"Snitch her out?" Billy Ray asked. "About what?"

"I dunno," Angel said. "It could be anything. Like I said, she was always doing something. And she slept with a lot of guys. Way too many guys. But the only reason she did that was to make Daddy mad."

"Was she any good at that?" Raven asked. "Making Daddy mad?"

A grin passed over Angel's face. "She was a beast at it," she said. "Nasty beasty."

"Was he ever violent toward her?" Billy Ray asked.

"You mean did he whoop her?" she asked, grinning again. "Where you from with that pork pie hat? We from Louisiana. He whooped us when he thought we needed it."

"He ever have to be restrained?" Raven followed up, having been witness to her friends' Louisiana 'whoopings' while in high school.

Angel turned her face back to the water and considered. Raven didn't say anything in an attempt to wait Angel out. When it became clear that Angel could sit there until sunset without saying anything, Raven reached across the table and covered Angel's hand. "Look at me, Angel."

Angel's head slowly turned back to Raven. Her face was calm as if indeed she had been drugged. Her eyes held no urgency, and Raven wondered if she had been smoking before meeting them.

"I know that your sister and I didn't get along. I hurt her by taking Quincy Trueblood away from her even if I didn't mean it. And she hurt me by dredging up every painful part of my past."

"Raven," Billy Ray warned.

He was about to say something else, but Raven held up a palm for him to stop.

"I wish I could have given her what she wanted. I wish I could have gone back and given Quincy Trueblood back to her. But I couldn't change what happened. But now I have a chance to make it up to her. I can find out who killed her and bring them to justice. Don't you want us to do that?" she asked.

Raven expected Angel's stare to turn baleful. But it didn't. She just gazed at Raven as if she were trapped in a dream. Then she breathed, "Yeah, I want you to do that."

"Then tell us what happened," Raven said.

The girl sighed. "Daddy made both of us work down at the office for our allowances. I went when I was supposed to but Hazel always cut out."

"And that's why your father hit her?" Raven asked.

"Not at first. He took her car away," she said. "The 'vette. He said if she didn't know how to work for her money, she'd never be no good in the world."

"What happened when he took the car away?" Raven asked.

"She went ballistic. She got mad real easy. Any little thing could set her off. She ran all over the house pulling things off shelves, throwing pillows off couches and chairs, breaking everything she could get her hands on. When Daddy got hold of her, he had her by the shoulders. At first he just shook her for a while, shook her like a rag doll, head snapping back and forth. Mamma was screaming like she was being stabbed." She looked off into the distance and continued on.

Westcott, Angel told them, slapped his daughter across the face with the front of his hand and then the back of his hand just like they used to do in the movies. At first he was just trying to calm her down, then he kept looking at the broken things all over the house

– the curio cabinets lying on the floor with his Super Bowl rings, his trophies, his awards spilled all around them. She'd broken mostly his things and he started to hit her harder and harder and faster and faster.

"And watching it," Angel said, "I kept wondering if somebody could get a broken neck just from a slap. He was completely messing up her face. That was the weirdest part of the whole thing."

"How so?" Raven asked.

"Daddy loved Hazel's face. He used to say Hazel Scott be damned. They should have named her Lena."

"What made him stop?" Billy Ray asked.

"Molly called the cops."

"Molly?"

"The housekeeper," Angel said, and then let out a bitter laugh. "We may have to work for a living, but Daddy draws the line at cleaning up after our own shit."

Raven's mind raced. Billy Ray had pulled out the little notebook he always carried and was furiously flicking the pages back and forth.

"Did you check police calls to the house?" Raven asked him.

"We did," Billy Ray confirmed, but said that they came up with nothing. Angel watched them with something new in her eyes – a twinkle of laughter that said she was a thousand years old and they the babes in the wood.

"You people so funny," she said. "Ain't no way my daddy gone let a police report be written about some mess like that."

"You don't understand," Billy Ray said. "Your daddy didn't have a choice. That's the way we do things. It's standard."

"Not when you know the police chief, it ain't."

Raven slowly nodded. A favor, maybe the beginning half of a favor friends trade back and forth, or maybe the ending half. "The chief made it disappear," Raven said.

She thought about the chief of Byrd's Landing Police Department. The chief was the man responsible for saving her life, the reason that she had chosen to become a cop. He was the reason she came back to Byrd's Landing even though her career had taken off in New Orleans. And he had protected her, stood by her during the Quincy Trueblood shooting aftermath. She thought that he'd place his own head on the chopping block if he needed to do so in order to save his integrity.

And here he was, covering up police calls to the Westcotts' estate. The question was, why?

"Your father been to the doctor lately?" Billy Ray asked. "Or a friend in the hospital he went to see recently?"

Angel shook her head, confused. Then she screwed up her pretty brown face and said, "He had surgery some months back. Gallstones."

"Was that before or after he beat your sister senseless?" Raven said dryly.

"I don't see how it got to do with anything, but it was right around that time," she said. "But that ain't why I called you out here."

She reached into the back pocket of her shorts and pulled out a slip of yellow paper. "That list my daddy gave to y'all," she said. "Well, there's one name ain't on it."

"Jabo Kersey," Raven read aloud. "Who's he?"

"That's Hazel's ex-husband," she said. "Nobody know about him except me. Daddy don't know a damn thing. Mamma don't either. But he used to be married to my sister."

"Uh-uh, no, I'm not buying that," Billy Ray said. "He knew all about her other boyfriends. Kept pretty close tabs on the both of you. How could he miss an entire husband?"

Angel did laugh then. She said, "He knew about who she wanted him to know about. She let him find out what she wanted him to know, and hid real good what she didn't."

"What does Mr. Kersey look like?" Raven asked.

"He old," she said. "Real old. At least forty. Has nappy hair with some gray up top in the front and a big belly. And he real black too. Black like a cast-iron skillet."

"Do you know where we can find him?" Raven asked.

Angel was shaking her head. "I only met him the one time."

"Doesn't sound like Hazel's type," Billy Ray said.

Angel smiled. "He was the perfect type," she said. "The type that could piss my daddy off. She hadn't told him yet because she was waiting for the right time to whip him out. But then Jabo got kinda weird, and the next thing I know she telling me they were breaking up and she wasn't planning on telling Daddy at all."

"Kind of weird how?" Raven asked.

"She wouldn't tell me," she said. "She just said it wasn't funny no more."

"Is there anything else you can tell us about him?" Billy Ray asked. Angel frowned. She shook her head.

"What does Mr. Kersey do?" Raven persisted.

"Mostly he a no 'count. Hazel said family got money and he don't have to do much. I think that might be one reason she married him. 'Cause he had money and she wouldn't have to rely on Daddy no more. But she told me that he claim he a nurse," she said, picking up her cell phone as if to say the conversation was over.

Raven watched her for a long time before saying, "You said Hazel's specialty was pissing Daddy off. What was your specialty?"

Angel smiled. "Pissing Mamma off," she said. "Daddy belonged to Hazel. He didn't even know I was alive. Mamma so drunk most of the time that's the only way I can get her attention."

They stared at each other a long time; Angel's smile was bitter and a little lost. Angel had turned her gaze back to the park rangers now sitting unmoving in the silver canoe. The bird was nowhere in sight.

Without saying anything, Raven swung her legs over the bench and strode toward the Mustang. Billy Ray was saying something to Angel in a low voice that Raven couldn't quite hear – probably something about not hesitating to call him if she remembered or needed anything. Eventually, she heard Billy Ray's footsteps crunch behind her but didn't turn around.

She and Billy Ray had risked the interview with Angel without a guardian present hoping for, if not expecting, a major break in the case. And the risk paid off big time. Instead of zero suspects, they were walking away from Angel's slow, dreamy voice and complicated grief with no less than three – a 'jack-off' who might have been trying to blackmail Hazel; Westcott, who had beat his daughter senseless a month before she was killed and who might have learned of a secret husband in spite of Hazel's best efforts to hide him; and Jabo Kersey, the mysterious ex-husband who had been getting 'kinda weird'. Weird enough to kill? Raven wondered.

She should have been happy, but then there was a cackle in her head. A cackle and a lot of crazy talk about not really knowing a person until you knew him. The chief. How deep he was into this she didn't know. Part of her didn't want to.

"You all right?" Billy Ray asked as he folded himself into the Mustang's passenger seat.

"No," she said, thinking how in hell the chief that she knew could be the same man who helped Westcott cover up the fact that he beat his daughter.

CHAPTER TWENTY

The Tipped Cow restaurant was located in a renovated barn in a cleared field surrounded by thick cypress and live oaks just outside the city limits. It was the kind of place with a flapping screen door leading out back to where the pits sat smoking with cooking meat swathed in creole spices and smelling sweet like molasses. Any other early evening there would be cars parked in the low grass beside Raven's Mustang, and a line of people out the door praying to whatever God they believed in that T-Bone, the owner, wouldn't run out of brisket before they got to the counter to place their order.

But T-Bone closed once a week for a private party. It usually consisted of the chief, the mayor, a couple of his aides, and the city council member who wanted to level every single shotgun house in Byrd's Landing, because it reminded him of the times when Jim Crow ruled in Louisiana.

Raven could see the chief in the dining room from the entryway. He was at home with everyone at his table, a true son of Byrd's Landing. He wore a white shirt under a beige jacket made of stiff linen, the same jacket Raven had watched him put on just that morning. *He look sharp as a tack, don't he?* Floyd whispered in Raven's ear, ending his words with a triumphant giggle. *A re-AL cri-min-AL just like them he puts in the poky.* She shook her head in an effort to will the voice away. Floyd was strong in her these days. She could not only hear him, she could smell him – all Irish Spring and Barbasol emanating from a ghost who had the nerve to provide commentary on events long after his death.

The mayor, shaped like a beach ball with legs, hunched over the remains of a rack of beef ribs, his hands and mouth working so furiously that it looked as if the effort might give him a heart attack. The councilman frowned down at his plate, waiting for the mayor to finish chewing.

Raven turned to see T-Bone making a beeline toward her and

Billy Ray. He was a tall man, a deep black with a glistening handlebar mustache and a wiry black beard that hung down to his chest. He wore a clean white T-shirt and apron, black jeans, and a pair of black leather boots almost as shiny as his beard. He and his family had been fixtures in Byrd's Landing for generations, opening restaurants in odd places before closing them, only to reopen them again someplace else and under some other name. When people came to their restaurants, wherever that place might be, the family required that they came only to eat. No drama. No tears. Even laughter was sometimes called into question. T-Bone had even posted a sign outside the barn door. It said, 'Eat, praise and then leave.' Only his new customers thought it was a joke.

"T-Bone," Raven said at the look on his face. "We're not here to start a mess. We need to talk to the chief."

"I don't have talk on the menu, Raven," T-Bone said. "Y'all need to get on up out of here. Do yo' talking at your jobs, let me do the cooking at mine."

She looked over at the table where the mayor, who seemed to be the only one still eating, wrestling with the ribs and winning, if the gray bone appearing under the torn meat was any indication. The chief was smiling at the mayor, who continued to slurp on the rib bone. He looked as if he was about to say something when Raven saw him finally notice her and Billy Ray with T-Bone at the door of the restaurant.

"Now I ain't playin' with you, Raven," T-Bone said as Raven tried to cut around him. "We closed."

"You don't look closed," Billy Ray answered and pointed at the table where the chief and the city council were seated.

"Private party," T-Bone said, wagging his head at Billy Ray. "We closed."

The chief wiped his hands on a cloth napkin and stood up. The mayor stopped chewing. He looked from the chief to the detectives and back to the chief again as if he expected one of them to explode. He tried to speak but the chief clapped him on the back and said something to the mayor in a low voice. Whatever it was seemed to calm him because the mayor waved his hand dismissively and said, "Just get back here when your update is over and let me know what the hell's going on."

Raven remembered thinking in the chief's office this morning that he wasn't a politician. If anyone were to ask her, she would say that

Chief Early Sawyer was the best man she had ever known. Now, as he patted the mayor's back a couple of more times she wondered how she could have been so mistaken. After all Floyd had taught her about how to read people, how could she have misread the chief so badly?

"There's a room around the corner," T-Bone said. "Y'all go on in there and he'll be along directly. You giving me a stomachache."

They didn't have to wait long. By the time Billy Ray had sat in one of the dining room chairs and tossed his pork pie hat onto the table, the chief opened the louvered door.

"Make it quick before the mayor gets in his head that he needs to come in here," the chief said.

He was about to say something else but then stopped when he saw their faces. Billy Ray was now rubbing both hands over his eyes as if he hadn't slept in months, the first crack in his usually unflappable façade. Raven leaned against a window with her arms folded. She stared at the chief while Floyd chattered on in the back of her mind. She was still trying to decide what kind of man the chief really was. Floyd was trying to tell her.

The chief didn't say anything for a few seconds. Then he said, "Oh I see. You mad? Isn't that what the young folk say? You mad? That's why you busted in here like Jason Bourne ready to stick it to the man?"

He sighed and pulled an empty chair from the dining room table and sat opposite Billy Ray.

"I've seen that look," he said more to Raven than Billy Ray. "It's called righteous indignation. I know. I've seen it staring back at me in the mirror many times when I was a young homicide detective. So, let's have it, Raven. It's me you mad at, right. What did I do?"

"Antwone Westcott beats the snot out of his daughter," she said. "You make it go away."

"He didn't beat the snot out of her," he said tiredly and not at all surprised that they knew. "He slapped her. That's it."

"And you used your mojo to cover it up?" Billy Ray asked. "Why?"

The chief stared at Billy Ray. A long silence stretched around them, and the room became so tense that Raven found herself letting out a breath when the chief finally spoke.

"Don't push me, Chastain," he said. "And let's get one thing straight – there was no beating."

"Then what happened?" Raven asked.

"Things got out of hand," the chief said. "The 911 dispatcher went to school with my wife and is a good friend of the family. Instead of sending an officer, she called me because she knew that Antwone Westcott and I went way back. So I went over there…"

"…to cover things up," Billy Ray said.

"No," the chief said smoothly. "To calm things down. There was nothing to cover up."

Billy Ray started to speak, but Raven cut him off. "And you didn't care that he beat his daughter?" she asked.

"He didn't beat her," the chief repeated. "Who have you been talking to, Detective?"

"He slapped her until the housekeeper called the cops. She had bruises."

He let out a short burst of laughter. "Shit. Who told you that?"

"Her sister told me that, that's who," Raven said.

He waved his fingers in a dismissive gesture much like the mayor had a few minutes ago.

"Her perception is off, Detective," he replied. "She's either downright lying or exaggerating."

"You still made it go away," Billy Ray said. "No police report. And even when Hazel died you kept it to yourself."

The chief sighed then. "You know," he said, looking at Billy Ray, "ten years ago, I wouldn't have even thought about doing anything like that. Friend or no friend. But times have changed. Let's say we would have had a police report, whatever." He waved his hand. "The way Imogene Tucker monitors police reports? That rabid high-heeled, weave-wearing Tasmanian devil reporter? She would have smelled career-maker and had a field day. She and the rest of those bloodhounds would have not only tortured that poor girl, but they would have tortured Antwone as well. It was a private family matter."

Raven thought about Imogene Tucker. The chief was right. The woman was tenacious. Tucker made no secret that she hoped her local position as a news anchor would someday lead to a big job at one of the national networks. Remembering the phone call from Imogene Tucker earlier, Raven couldn't help but admire her persistence. She was tempted to take Tucker up on her offer for an interview just so she could verify her suspicion that the woman had a framed photograph of Barbara Walters on her desk, a woman intent on making her subjects cry as she was being 'kind' to them.

"That doesn't matter, Chief," Raven said. "Westcott assaulted his daughter."

"He lost his temper. She was out of control. He hit her once across the face to try to get her to calm down."

"You mean that's his story," Raven said.

The chief shrugged.

"You could have told us this morning when we met," Raven said.

"Look," the chief said. "I'm not stupid, okay? I thought about telling you, but the entire thing would have just been a distraction. We don't have a lot of time to waste on distractions."

"That's a load," Billy Ray said. "I can't listen to any more of this." He stood up and positioned his hat on his head. He headed for the door, but stopped short when Raven spoke again.

"Why did you do it, Chief?"

The chief grinned and looked down at the table. He picked up a coaster with a picture of a cow's head etched on it and started tapping it against the dark wood. Then he said, "The proverbial 'why' question." He shook his head. "Man, I used to ask a lot of why questions and you know what? In the end the answers meant nothing. The answers didn't keep people from killing or being killed. That goes on no matter the answers to all of those why questions. I'm through with whys, Raven."

"Chief," Raven pressed.

"If you must have a reason, I did it for her as much as I did it for him. Hazel was way too fragile to take the onslaught of what would happen if she were exposed."

"Exposed? What do you mean?" Raven asked.

He lifted an eyebrow. "You don't know?"

"Know what?"

"Hazel Westcott was bipolar," he said. "From what Antwone told me she was in a constant state of chaos, in and out of hospitals. Highs so high she'd be missing for days, lows so low that they had to lock her in one of the guest rooms so she wouldn't hurt herself."

"Chief," Raven said. "How well do you know the Westcotts?"

He laughed. "That I didn't keep from you," he said. "Antwone told me all of this when I went there that night. We hadn't talked for years. You think I would have covered up something like that without some convincing?"

"So, Antwone Westcott had access to hospitals in more ways than one," Billy Ray said in a musing voice.

"What does that have to do with anything?" the chief asked.

Raven told him what she and Rita had suspected. Someone poisoned Hazel Westcott with succinylcholine. The chief agreed with her that it was a possibility but dismissed out of hand that Antwone Westcott had anything to do with it.

"Come on, Raven," he was saying, laughing. "You don't think he's good for this, do you?"

"Why didn't he tell us himself about this incident and why would he block access to Hazel's medical records? And someone in the house cleared out Hazel's medicine cabinet."

"He's a private man, Raven," the chief said. "He's still trying to protect his daughter."

"Not too private to give us a list of her men friends," Billy Ray said dryly.

"Maybe that's the distraction," Raven added. "Give us a list of boyfriends so we won't look at him."

"He's not that smart," the chief said. "And why the ritual, why the dress and pose?"

"He thought his daughter was beautiful. According to Angel, he loved Hazel's face. Maybe he did that as a tribute to her," she answered.

Laughing harder, the chief threw the coaster on the slick surface of the table and it skidded to the floor. "He's not that smart," he said again. "Or sophisticated."

"He keeps things to himself, is not that smart or sophisticated, and he slaps his daughter around. How did you become friends again? Doesn't sound like somebody you'd hang out with," Raven said.

"Circumstances and proximity," he answered. "I met him at some national fraternity meetings and we just hit it off. I saw him every time I went to one of those conferences. I hadn't talked to him, really talked to him, for ten years before I got that call. I told you that."

"Were you at the party?" Billy Ray asked.

"What, you looking for even more distractions? Haven't you got enough?" the chief countered. "Besides, did you see my name on the guest list?"

"No."

"Then that means I wasn't there, wouldn't you say, Detective Chastain?"

"No, I wouldn't say," Raven pushed. "Were you there, Chief?"

The chief let out a sigh of exasperation. "I don't see how that's got anything to do with anything, but okay, yes, I was there. It was in an official capacity, though. I showed up when it started, shook a few hands, and left."

Raven rolled her eyes so hard that she was surprised that they didn't roll right out of her head.

"I swear, Raven," the chief said with a little laugh. "It's me you talking to. I didn't even think about it when we talked this morning. I was only there about ten minutes, and I have to make the rounds at parties like that because I'm the chief. The fact I was there has nothing to do with Hazel's murder."

Billy Ray threw her a look that told her to push harder, but Raven let it go. Instead, she said, "I still don't get why you covered up for him."

"Let's say that I had an attack of loyalty," he said. "You know how that is, don't you, Detective Burns?" He said the last quietly.

She didn't answer him, but she didn't have to. Even after all her father had done, she had visited him on death row. It was only once or twice, but she went with a nagging sense of guilt because he was, no matter how bad, her father. He was, no matter how much she feared and hated what he had done, a part of her. At his request, and because of her loyalty to him, she attended his execution, the only family member to do so. Raven lowered her eyes. She understood.

"Chief," Billy Ray said. "He had access to the drug that killed her. He was in the hospital a month before she died. Gallbladder surgery. And frankly, Hazel's mental illness provides motive. No telling what a man like Westcott really thought about a daughter who didn't live up to his expectations."

"Yes, maybe he did have access and motive," the chief said. "But how would a man like that know how Sux works? And how would he have managed stealing it? That hospital missing any drugs?"

"We don't know yet," Billy Ray said.

"Don't know," he said. "You don't know, but you come in here with fire in your belly ready to accuse me. I expected more, Chastain. And I'm telling you that no way Antwone Westcott could have done such a thing to his own daughter. So, who else you got?"

They told him about the ex-husband, Jabo Kersey. Raven saw the gleam come into the chief's eyes, but to his credit, he didn't immediately pounce on Kersey as a suspect. Instead he laced his fingers together, and index finger to index finger, he touched them to his lips three quick times.

"Have you run down the dress yet?" he asked.

Raven could see he asked from instinct. It was one of the many things that made him such a good homicide detective, working the instincts that occurred in a place beyond the boundaries of his understanding. He told her that there was a time he seldom trusted instinct and hunches, despised them in fact. But as he worked more homicides his instinct became a valuable tool, one that he never went to a crime scene without.

"No," she said. "We haven't run down the dress yet."

"Haven't run down the dress or the drugs." He stopped, looked at her and said, "What in the hell are you waiting for?"

CHAPTER TWENTY-ONE

The following morning, Raven looked at Billy Ray standing next to her at the front door of Miss Anne Marie's Place of Fine Clothing, the shop where Hazel's shroud had come from. The store was located in one of the many renovated warehouses in Byrd's Landing's arts district just beneath the deck truss of the Texas Street Bridge. The traffic over their heads hummed rhythmically. Raven thought about staying in the protection of the shadowed coolness created by the bridge's thick cement columns if not for the rest of her life at least for the remainder of the case.

"Well," Billy Ray said. "What are you waiting on?"

"You know," she said. "I am more than capable of taking care of this myself, Billy Ray."

"So you've been saying the entire drive over here."

"I just didn't think you had such an interest in ladies' garments," Raven answered. "Something you not telling me?"

Billy Ray laughed and looked around him. "No, I'm an open book, Burns. Something you not telling me?"

There was certainly something Raven wasn't telling him. A job as a homicide detective was grueling. But Billy Ray knew that. What he didn't know was that Raven had planned a long time ago not to let it eat her alive. She vowed to keep one thing for herself.

And that one thing was beyond the door of Miss Anne Marie's. And she could go the rest of her life without Billy Ray and the rest of the Byrd's Landing Police Department finding out. She had tried to come by herself, but Billy Ray, probably sensing she had something to hide, stuck to her like gum on the bottom of her running shoe.

The other vendors in the warehouse stores had set up some of their merchandise on the sidewalk. A woman with skin like copper, wearing a bright blue sequined turban and a patterned maxi dress, waited until Billy Ray noticed her before winking at him. Billy Ray smiled his beautiful smile and winked back. She removed a long turquoise necklace and held it up in the air with both hands so that the blue stones dripped from her long fingers.

"For the lady, no?" she said with just the hint of a Haitian accent.

"I know it's an old joke," Billy Ray said, laughing. "But trust me, she's not a lady."

"Oh, hey now," she said. "She beautiful lady. Beautiful lady need beautiful things. Mine cheaper than that store you 'bout to go in. They rob you blind. Take you money and leave you with junk. So for the lady, no?"

Raven stared at the woman, who then shrugged, obviously giving up the sale. She dropped the necklace back on the hanger, the bright smile disappearing as the blue stones clattered against the metal rack.

"For the lady, *no*." Billy Ray laughed. "Damn, girl, you're mean."

"I don't have time for antics," Raven said. "Why don't you let me go in and ask about the dress? I'll probably get more out of them because I'm a woman."

Billy Ray looked at her for a long time. Raven struggled to keep her face straight. Finally he shook his head. "That's all right," he said, "I don't mind helping out."

A bell tinkled as Billy Ray opened the door. Raven followed him inside. The place was air-conditioned and smelled of cinnamon. Funnels of sunlight fell through an enormous skylight cut into the warehouse's roof.

"I'm coming, I'm coming," said a voice accompanied by high heels clicking across a floor made of shimmering bamboo. The woman who belonged to those high heels looked like a throwback to the 1950s. Her hair, more gray than blond, was caught up in a glistening and perfectly made chignon. She had on a square-neck gray dress nipped by a thin belt at her waist, and she wore a shade of coral-pink lipstick that Raven remembered seeing in the old movies she used to watch with her stepmother Jean Rinehart.

"Ah," the woman said. "My dear, yes."

She came over to Raven and took both of her hands in hers. The woman's hands were small and cold, her French manicure cut low and perfect.

"I was wondering when you would pick up your order," the

woman said. "Is this your young man? Has he come to help you pick out something even more to his liking?"

Raven tried to stop Miss Anne Marie from talking, but the woman could not be interrupted. Billy Ray, who had been about to say something about the price of a pair of red silk panties that now hung from his large hands, looked from Raven to the woman and back to Raven again.

"He is not my young man, Miss Anne Marie," Raven said. "He's my partner."

Anne Marie clasped her hands together and said, "Ah I don't care what you call each other. Partner, lover, boyfriend. He has come to help you pick out the lingerie, yes?" She stopped and fluttered her fingers toward her chest. "Perhaps a nice little brassiere with lace on the bottom and a nice dangling rhinestone right in the middle? Hmm...."

"Miss Anne Marie," Raven tried again.

But the woman couldn't be stopped. "You go ahead and browse around to see if you can find anything," she said to Billy Ray. "I will go and pick up Mademoiselle's order."

She started out of the room, heels clicking against the floor with such rhythm that Raven wondered if Miss Anne Marie had a song playing in her head. When she was gone, Billy Ray turned to Raven with a raised eyebrow.

"Not one word," Raven said.

"Your order?" he asked.

"Not one," she said again. "And if you ever tell anybody about this, I will gut you like a fish."

"Did you see how much this shit cost?" he asked, gesturing at her with the red panties hanging from his hand.

"I know how much they cost, Billy Ray."

"For some damn panties," he said. "A hundred bucks."

"Matching panties and camisole," she countered.

"Shit," he said, hanging them back up. "I would be embarrassed paying that much for panties too. Don't worry about me. My lips are sealed."

Anne Marie returned with a small black bag, which she handed to Raven.

"Billy Ray," Raven said. "Why don't you look around while Miss Anne Marie and I talk?"

"Yes," said Anne Marie. "Pick out something sexy for her."

Grinning, Billy Ray started to move deeper into the underwear section, but Raven grabbed him by the shoulders and pointed him toward the bath soaps.

"We will only be a moment," Raven said. "Behave."

As Miss Anne Marie walked to the register, Raven said, "I'm not just here for the order."

Anne Marie stopped. "My dear, what is it? Everything all right? Do you have a return? You know I can't take returns."

"No," Raven said. "I don't have a return. I'm here on an investigation. You know, Miss Anne Marie, for my job with the police."

Anne Marie leaned over the counter, her eyes skating left and right. She needn't have bothered because the store was still empty except for Billy Ray, who had his handsome nose buried in a pot of cream. "Oh yes," she said. "I almost forgot that you were a detective. An investigation?" Anne Marie whispered. "Here?"

"No," Raven said, smiling. "Not here, but perhaps one of your customers."

Raven removed her cell phone from her coat pocket and showed Miss Anne Marie a picture of the dress. It was actually a picture of Hazel Westcott's corpse wearing the dress, but without the face in the frame, Raven hoped that Anne Marie wouldn't notice that she was actually looking at a picture of a dead body.

She bit her lip and looked at Raven. "Yes, that's one of mine," she said. "It's actually a Vera Wang wedding dress."

Raven was taken aback. "Wedding dress?"

"Yes," she said while reaching under the counter and bringing up a large binder. "One of the more simple styles, very elegant and flattering." She flipped through the pages, then stopped before turning the book around so Raven could see the model wearing an exact copy of the dress.

Miss Anne Marie said, "I ordered five because they were so cheap." She looked pointedly at Raven. "I would rather talk about it looking at this picture instead of the one you have on your phone, Raven."

Raven nodded. "I understand," she said, and put her phone back in the inside pocket of her jacket. "Did you know Hazel Westcott? Did she shop here?"

Miss Anne Marie shook her head. "No," she said. "I didn't know her, but she stopped by once or twice. She has one of those faces, one of those it would be hard to forget. But she wasn't a regular like you. Lord knows I tried to get her in here more. Personal invitations. Flyers. I heard she spent a lot of money in boutiques," she said and sighed. "But I don't think the girl was interested in quality things. She was interested in pretty things." She shook her head sadly. "But not quality."

"This dress was new," Raven said. "It was bought here and still had the tags on it. You're saying that Hazel didn't purchase it? That's odd for a wedding dress, isn't it?"

"Why yes, of course it is," Anne Marie agreed. "It reminds me of that time a man came in here and bought one of these. Said it was a gift for his bride. I advised him that it would be better if he brought her in for a fitting, but he said he wanted it to be a surprise."

"That's strange," Raven said. "When was this?"

"I'm not quite sure, maybe eight or nine months ago." Anne Marie frowned. "Do you think the dress Hazel Westcott was wearing in the picture on your phone was this—?"

"Eight months?" Raven cut her off, wanting her not to get distracted.

She nodded. "Yes, around that time, the holidays. The dress was on sale because it was cut so low with those little split bell sleeves. Hardly a thing to wear in winter."

"Do you remember what this man looked like?"

Anne Marie laughed. "Of course, I do. It's not every day a groom comes in to buy his bride's wedding dress. And I would have remembered him anyway because of that ridiculous Hawaiian shirt he was wearing in the middle of the cold. Even though we don't get the weather too much down here, it was still too cold for that nonsense."

"Do you remember his name?"

But Miss Anne Marie was still lost in the memory. "And the way he carried his money," she continued. "Like a child."

"Money?"

"He paid cash. Had all kinds of money balled up in his pocket like trash. Kept pulling hundred dollar bills from his pants pocket one at a time, counting real slow as if he had some type of mental disability. He may have been a little drunk, now that I think about it."

"Did he happen to give a name?" Raven tried again.

She laughed, a short laugh with real amusement. "Would you believe that he did? That was the other odd thing. I asked him if he would like to join our newsletter. It was automatic. I have asked that question so many times that I don't even think about it anymore. Why, I believe I even asked the delivery man that same question the other day."

"What did he say?"

"He mumbled yes before I think he knew what he was agreeing to. By then, it was too late for me to take the question back. I mean, I didn't want to offend him. We were both pretty embarrassed about the entire thing. I gave him a pen and he wrote his name and email address on a slip of paper."

"Do you have it...?"

But Anne Marie was already shaking her head. "I threw it in the garbage the minute he headed for the door. And I asked myself what was I thinking inviting him to join the newsletter."

"Do you remember his name?" Raven asked.

"Yes. It was *J* something," she said slowly. She stopped and twisted her head, "Jaro, something like that."

"Jabo?" Raven asked.

The woman snapped her fingers. "Yes. Jabo, Jabo Kersey. I remember the Kersey because I have some people by that name up in Shreveport."

Miss Anne Marie rang up Raven's purchase and as she was taking her bankcard from her, she said, "No relation."

Billy Ray was already in the car when Raven left the store. She climbed into the driver's seat and sat staring out of the window at the wide empty street beneath the bridge. So Jabo Kersey had bought the dress for Hazel Westcott. But he had bought it eight months ago and it was never worn.

She turned to Billy Ray to say something but then noticed the smell.

"What?" he said, looking at her.

"You smell like you've been attacked by every perfume girl in Macy's," she said on the beginnings of a sneeze.

"You're the one who told me to check out the scents," he said. "All your fault, Raven."

They sat in silence for a few minutes before he turned to her. She thought he was going to ask what she found out from Anne Marie.

"So," he said instead. "What's in the bag?"

"Shut up," she said.

"Only if you promise to model it for me later."

She ignored him. It was looking like Jabo Kersey killed his wife. Two days, and their case was all but solved. The chief would be pleased. And Raven herself was pleased that the phone call between her and Hazel the week before the murder would never have to come out. Never mind that her pleasure was overlaid with a slight sheen of unease. Nevertheless, she looked at Billy Ray and smiled.

"Kersey bought the dress Hazel was found in, Billy Ray," she said.

He let out a long, slow whistle. "So it's looking like it's all over but the shouting."

"Yes, it indeed is," she said, feeling a sense of relief. All she had to do was hand Jabo Kersey over and her life would be back to normal.

But then, her mind went back to the peacock feather. There was a part of her that knew it was not over. It didn't help that she heard Floyd's cackle in her head. He was laughing so hard that Raven was sure that if he were real and if he were alive, he would be peeing his pants.

CHAPTER TWENTY-TWO

Billy Ray sat across the table from Raven in the Hazel Westcott investigation command center. It was the day after their visit to Miss Anne Marie's dress and lingerie shop. They had been looking for evidence to shore up their case against Jabo Kersey ever since. The conference room table was now strewn with photographs the uniforms had been able to collect from the cell phones and digital cameras of the guests at the Westcotts' Fourth of July party. Surveillance camera footage played without audio on a Samsung display screen that Billy Ray had found somewhere and rolled in earlier that morning. The Samsung contained a high-definition illustration of about a hundred boozy people wearing expensive summer clothes and good moods.

Rita Sandbourne, the medical examiner, was with Billy Ray and Raven in the conference room. She wasn't saying much because she was too busy pounding down the red velvet cupcakes Billy Ray had brought in that morning.

Raven and Billy Ray had been working on the case practically all night, only stopping to get a few hours of sleep before starting everything up again. She didn't know how Billy Ray found the time to bake cupcakes.

"I just can't believe he did these," Rita said, picking up another cupcake. It was the perfect color red topped by a handmade strawberry of red and green sugar paste. "Let me see your hands again, Billy Ray?"

Without looking up from a file folder he was perusing, Billy Ray held up his left hand and waved it around for Rita.

"You did all of this with your big hands?" she said. "How?"

"It's what I do," he said.

She took a big bite. "And just the right amount of sweetness," she said. "You are in the wrong profession, Billy Ray."

"Don't I know it," Billy Ray agreed.

"Rita," Raven said. "That's your second cupcake in five minutes. Can you please leave them alone and tell us why you're here?"

Rita walked over to the table while wiping the red crumbs from her face with the back of her hand.

"Does he bring you food all the time?" she asked.

Raven slapped the remote she had been holding onto the table and started searching through the photographs for someone who looked like the man Angel had described as Jabo Kersey. If he was the killer, it wasn't enough that he bought the dress. They needed to place him at the scene.

Rita sat down next to Raven and waited until Raven looked at her again. With her huge limpid eyes ringed in black eyeliner, Rita's face appeared as innocent as a puppy's. "You are not happy right now, Raven," she said. "How can cupcakes not make you happy?"

"Because I'm a little busy right now. We all are a little busy. Did you ever get a hold of Hazel's medical records?"

Rita looked at her indignantly. "Moi? Why, of course. That's why I'm here."

Raven raised an eyebrow.

"And the cupcakes," Rita admitted. "When I saw handsome coming in with his little covered tray this morning, I beat it over here as soon as I could get away to tell you in person. Anyway, got a little tired of waiting for a judge, so I called in a few favors at some of the medical facilities nearby that would treat her condition. Struck out at the first two, but the third time really is the charm."

"What did you find?"

"That the chief pretty much had it right," she said. "Acute bipolar disorder. She's been in treatment for the last four years or so."

"What about missing drugs?" Billy Ray asked. "The Sux that killed her?"

"Nothing," Rita said. "Not at Memorial and not at Doctor's. Besides, they don't lock Sux up like they do the controlled substances. If you know what you're looking for, you can find that stuff pretty easy in any emergency room."

Raven stood up and closed the blinds on the sunlight streaming through the room's big windows. What a day for the precinct's air-conditioning to be on the fritz. Hot and bright yellow since sunrise, the sun had conspired with the clouds to wrap all of Byrd's Landing in a damp haze of heat. Raven's jacket was off for once and sweat rimmed her underarms, the dampness making the white cotton shirt stick uncomfortably to her well-toned torso.

Hazel's ex-husband was also a nurse, or that was what Angel had told them. He would have had access to emergency rooms, and he would know what he was looking for. Raven rubbed the back of her neck, thinking he had to be the killer. But then she remembered the peacock feather, her father's marker found beneath Hazel's bed. And she heard Floyd's soft cackle in her head.

"You okay, Raven?" Rita asked, while pawing another cupcake. "You look like someone just pissed in your whiskey."

"I'm fine," Raven said, trying to sound annoyed at Rita instead of frightened of how easily Floyd could slip into her thoughts. "Don't you have a body to cut up or something?"

Rita just licked frosting from her fingers and shrugged.

Raven turned her attention back to the surveillance video playing on the Samsung. She could see the light bouncing off the gleaming head of Antwone Westcott, Hazel's father. He was smiling as he did the mashed potato with his wife. Raven's foster parents used to dance like that to songs that were older than she was. She remembered Otis Redding, The Temptations, even Junior Walker belting 'Shotgun' in a house full of dancing old folk.

As she watched Westcott slide his huge body across the makeshift dance floor in his brightly lit backyard, she thought he certainly didn't have the demeanor of a man about to commit the ritualized murder of his daughter. It had to be the ex-husband, Jabo Kersey. Had to be, she thought again, wondering if it was more of a wish than a fact.

Beautiful Haze, as her family called her, came under the stationary gaze of the camera more than once. She was wearing what Westcott said she would be wearing, a paisley off-the-shoulder top with a pair of stretch white capri pants and silver sandals with thin high heels. Her glossy hair was swept into a large ivory clip at the back of her head.

But she wasn't smiling like Westcott. Or dancing. Instead, she was walking in a straight line toward her father as he and his wife left the dance floor holding hands and laughing.

Raven picked up the remote and walked through the video frame by frame. Westcott's wife had left him at the edge of the dance floor. Before he could follow her, Hazel intercepted her father. He frowned at her serious face with a wary, questioning look in his eyes, maybe thinking she was about to resurrect the verbal altercation they had earlier that day.

Raven said, "Here it comes," as the two figures faced each other on the screen. Before Westcott could say anything, Hazel placed both hands on his shoulders, stood on tiptoes and kissed him on the cheek.

"So what?" Billy Ray asked. "She kisses him on the cheek. Who cares?"

"I don't know," Raven said. "Westcott said that they were arguing like cats and dogs all day long."

"Do you think it was her way of trying to say she was sorry?" Rita asked.

Raven leaned close to the display. "I'd think she'd be looking a little shamefaced if she were trying to make up to him," she said. "But no, she puts her hands on his shoulders like she's made her mind up about something, then they share that touching father-daughter kiss."

"Maybe it's like all young women," Rita interjected while leaning back and licking cream cheese from her fingers. "Maybe she's starting to realize that Daddy isn't such a bastard after all, and that he won't be around forever."

Raven rewound and played what they were calling 'the kiss' two more times in slow motion. She was about to press rewind again, but then saw something that made her stop with her finger hovering off the button. Raven watched for a moment and then said, "Billy Ray may have a point. I think that we're paying too much attention to the kiss."

"Well, hallelujah," Billy Ray said.

Raven ignored him. She pressed rewind to the point just after Hazel kissed her father on the cheek. "Look," she said. "We should have been more focused on what happened after."

They all stared at the LCD screen. They watched as Westcott wiped the sweat from the corner of his eyes with his bare fingers. While he was rubbing the sweat off his head, Hazel suddenly tensed as something, or someone, off-camera caught her eye. There was almost an imperceptible shake of her head. Then she put a protecting arm around Westcott's waist and turned him away from the person she had just signaled to. Westcott appeared to be too preoccupied with cleaning up after the dance, or perhaps too buzzed to notice any of this. Hazel then guided him around until they were out of camera range and walking away from whomever or whatever Hazel had seen off-camera.

Billy Ray, who had been leaning back in his chair, sat straight up, "What in the hell was that all about?" he said.

"She signaled someone off-camera with that headshake," Raven said. "Remember what Angel said about some dude blackmailing Hazel into a date at the party? Could that have been Jabo Kersey?"

"No," Billy Ray said. "Angel would have said so. She met him, remember? Maybe it was the man blackmailing her into a trip to the boathouse."

Raven said, "But if it wasn't Jabo, who was it? It's obviously someone that she doesn't want Westcott to see, as if she's trying to protect him."

"I don't know if I buy that she was trying to protect her father from anything," Billy Ray said. "She just didn't want to be snitched on, that's all. And that was probably Jabo about to walk over there and start calling Westcott daddy-in-law. Besides, the girl was really sick. You heard Rita. She had *acute* bipolar disorder. Someone with an illness like that would have a hard time taking care of themselves, let alone protecting a man like Westcott."

"I would say the same thing," Raven said. "But to me the way she acted just then seemed all about him, not herself. She didn't have to be that chummy with Westcott to keep Jabo from going over there."

Raven stopped and turned in her seat to Billy Ray. She gestured toward the file Billy Ray had been reading when Rita barged in with cupcakes on her mind. "You find anything in Westcott's background check?"

Billy Ray threw the manila file folder to her. Raven opened it, skimmed a few of the documents, and whistled.

"Yeah," Billy Ray said, nodding. "After reading that, even I would believe that his shit doesn't stink."

"Not even a speeding ticket. Gives money away like it's water," Raven went on. "Lots of money to Oral Justice's organization and the

Gospel Mission. Man sure is not afraid to spread his money around to the local charities."

"Even his business," Billy Ray said. "Those payday loan stores are almost philanthropy. Don't look like he's feeding off his customers either. Calls them 'patrons', gives them credit counseling, micro loans to businesses in the 'hood, finance classes. He's a good guy on paper. So even if she could protect Daddy Warbucks, what would she be protecting him from?"

Raven threw the file back on the table. She sighed. "The chief is right. Westcott as the killer is turning into a dead end."

"Raven," Rita groaned. "That pun is not worthy of you."

Raven ignored her. "He looks like a superhero, on paper anyway," she said. "CSI come back with anything yet?"

Billy Ray shook his head. "Way too soon for that. Called over there this morning. They're still trying to find a match to the hairs and DNA they found in the sheets, but they think they figured out the fibers on Hazel's dress."

"Well?" Raven asked, when he paused.

He tapped his long fingers on the table and said as if he were humming a tune, "Gray po-ly-pro-py-lene."

The way he drew the words out and half sang them reminded her of Floyd. He lifted his HooDoo pork pie at her and flashed a smile, a perfect, straight, white-toothed and handsome Billy Ray smile. At first, she had the disquieting feeling that he was mocking her with Floyd on purpose. But then he said with a twinkle in his eyes, "See, who says I can't do the big words?"

She let out a breath that she didn't know she was holding. He wasn't mocking her and never would. She was losing it. "Carpet?" she said in an overloud voice. "Someone was around carpet? Maybe carpet in the house?"

He shook his head. "Ruled the house out, boathouse too. Could be carpet from someplace else."

"Or the jumpsuits," Rita put in. They looked at her. "Just trying to pay for the cupcakes." She laughed a little. "I had this case before I started working here. Some idiot got all excited about some fibers that turned out to be from the jumpsuits one of my team was wearing when she picked up the body."

"Do you think that's what happened here?" Raven asked. "An accidental transfer?"

Rita shrugged.

"Was CSI wearing the jumpsuits?" Raven asked.

"Should've been." Rita grinned. "They're not as loose with the rules as you and Billy Ray."

"I don't remember seeing you in a jumpsuit either, Rita," Raven responded.

"I told you," Rita said, laughing. "I'm a pro."

Raven thought back to the crime scene. She remembered seeing one of the CSIs struggle with tarp poles and later taking pictures. He hadn't been wearing the jumpsuit then. He could have put it on later and accidentally transferred the fibers to Hazel's dress. But Raven didn't think so. The jumpsuits were a new rule of the chief's. He hadn't made it mandatory yet.

"I see your mind going a hundred miles an hour over there, Raven," Billy Ray said.

She shook her head, trying to slow her thoughts enough to articulate. She said, "Forensics didn't find anything in the bathroom that they couldn't identify as belonging to Hazel, right?"

"No," Billy Ray said. "The hairs in there looked like they were all from her, long and black. CSI doesn't seem to have anything else, not yet anyway."

"What if the killer wore a jumpsuit and booties to keep from leaving evidence at the scene?" Raven asked. "After he drugged her?"

"That doesn't sound likely," Billy Ray said. "What, he waltz into her room with a jumpsuit in shrink wrap, talking about a roll in the hay? How would he explain it?"

Raven shrugged. "Maybe he didn't have it when he met her. Could have brought the jumpsuit with him, hid it somewhere near the boathouse before meeting her and retrieving it after drugging her."

Rita looked from one to the other. "That doesn't sound like a civilian," she said. "That sounds like a cop."

Billy Ray stood up and stretched. He said, "That's why it doesn't make no sense. I can't see Kersey doing that. Those fibers could have come from anywhere. Hell, they could have come from the dress shop."

"Miss Anne Marie's has bamboo floors, Billy Ray," Raven said in a quiet voice.

"Well," Rita said. "Even if those fibers came from a cop in an accidental transfer, or if there are any accidental transfers at the scene, we'll find out when the results from the elimination samples come in. At least that's a new protocol the chief has been able to make work."

Raven agreed. The chief had not only insisted on his staff wearing the jumpsuits and booties at crime scenes, he had instituted a new protocol where every staff member at a crime scene involving forensics had to submit elimination samples. Most of the BLPD police force had samples on file.

"We don't have time to be worrying about some stray fibers," Billy Ray said with annoyance. He was clearly done with the subject. "Too much stuff going on. And those damn fibers coulda come from Jabo Kersey's carpet. Or Miss Anne Marie's stockroom. You think of that?"

She sat there looking at him for a long moment. Then she said pensively, thinking about the peacock feather, "So, we're still liking Jabo for this? Even after thinking it might be the start of a string of serial murders?"

He started rearranging some of the photographs beneath his fingers.

"Why, I'm just riding the horse in the direction it's going – following the evidence," he said, his tone steady and even. Still not looking at her, he counted off on his fingers. "He bought the dress she was killed in, we can prove that he was obsessed with Hazel from Angel's testimony, and Hazel dumped him. He was mad as hell at that girl and he killed her. Or maybe he's just a sex freak, and he killed her."

"But it doesn't look like a rage killing," Raven said. "Or a sexual sadist killing. It was too perfect."

"So you say," he said. "Maybe Kersey isn't stupid and he's just making it look like a serial killer to throw us off the scent."

She said nothing, just nodded, hoping Billy Ray was right. Maybe Hazel's murder had nothing to do with her past. She thought about Floyd's murders – the ones the cops knew about and the ones that were still being debated. Not one of them was ritualized. Death to him wasn't beautiful. Death was messy, dying a curious state of the human condition that he only wanted to pay tribute to and observe.

It was an experiment when it wasn't a necessity. Though he buried her mother in the flower bed, he did so in jest, not as part of a ritual. Dead bodies held no interest to him. It was the dying that caught all of his attention. If it was a copycat who killed Hazel, it was a poor one.

"Just yesterday you were telling me that you liked Jabo for this because he bought the dress," he said. "Now you having doubts?"

Raven grunted and leaned back in her chair. She folded her hands over her flat belly and said, "It's all just starting to feel too convenient. And Westcott is bothering me," she admitted. "Something's not right there, Billy Ray, in spite of all the money he's giving away. My gut tells me that he's hiding something. We still need to talk to Kersey, though. Have you had any luck in finding him yet?"

"Memorial or Doctor's wouldn't cop to a Jabo Kersey working there. Memorial acted like their feelings were hurt just from me asking. Said no nurse named Jabo Kersey worked there. Ever. The woman in HR just kept repeating that same line. Sounded like a damned parrot. What the hell kind of a name is Jabo, anyway?"

"It's a tribe in Africa," Rita said. "Liberia, I think. They named themselves after the liberation."

They stared at her. She had left the table and was lying on the sofa against the wall of the conference room, holding her cell phone over her face. Raven surmised that she had been busy searching the internet while they were talking.

"What?" she said. "White girls can't know about African culture? Knowledge is free, lady and gentleman. Just ask the Google. Like I said—" Rita gestured at them with the phone "—I have to earn my cupcakes."

Raven ignored her. "So, you haven't been able to find an address? Anything?" she asked Billy Ray.

He shook his head. "So far, he's a ghost."

"Do you have any idea where he and Hazel may have gotten married?" Raven asked him. "What about marriage records for Westcott?"

"Nothing," Billy Ray said. "Only one for Mamma and Daddy."

"State nursing licensing board?" Rita put in, still staring up at the face of her phone.

He shook his head. "No Jabo Kersey."

Raven looked at Rita, who was momentarily sans cupcakes, thinking about what she had said regarding Jabo's name.

"Either one of you ever consider that Jabo is not his real name? Maybe it's a street name? How many parents out there name their kids after an African tribe in Liberia?" Raven asked.

Billy Ray grunted a laugh. "Do you not remember the names we ran into down in NOLA?"

"Vegas," Raven said absently.

Billy Ray looked at her, his face intent with interest. "Bipolar disorder," he said. "During manic episodes she'd require a lot of stimuli."

"The chief said she used to disappear for days at a time," Raven said.

"And people with bipolar disorder in a manic state think they are as lucky as hell. Invincible," Billy Ray rejoined.

"Don't worry about the first name. It's probably a nickname," Raven said.

"Vegas?" Rita asked. "You sure?"

"As sure as death. Lots of stimuli plus manic episode plus hasty marriage equals Vegas," Billy Ray said. "We need to check marriage records for Hazel Westcott and anybody by the last name of Kersey in Vegas."

CHAPTER TWENTY-THREE

Raven was exhausted with the marathon that had been the aftermath of Hazel's death. And Billy Ray could use some down time the same as her even if he didn't say so. They had continued working for so long that the state offices to research marriage licenses had closed, anyway. Jabo Kersey could keep. The case could keep. Hazel would be just as dead in the morning when the work to find her killer would still be waiting for them. Besides, they had a good suspect. The case appeared to be winding down, or at least that was what the chief said after they updated him before leaving.

Billy Ray chose to retire to his double-barrel shotgun and his secondhand four-poster on Peabody. He told her that after catfish and a side of gumbo from the Snack Shack downtown, he had planned on sleeping until Tuesday, or until they found Jabo – whichever came first.

They were saying goodbye next to the pelican fountain in front of the police station, the same place where Oral Justice had told her that she had wasted her life by becoming a cop. That seemed like years ago, but it had only been a couple of days.

"I'll see you in the morning," she said as she headed for her car.

"Bright-eyed," Billy Ray answered.

The solemnity in his voice made her stop. She turned back to him. And indeed, his face had that edgy intensity that sometimes made her uncomfortable. When she cocked her head curiously at him, he tilted the whiskey-colored pork pie back on his head and a slow grin moved across his lips. She nodded slowly before turning and resuming her course to the parking lot.

But halfway there she couldn't resist another look over her shoulder. He was standing there with his pork pie hat pushed back on his head and his hands in the pockets of his slacks. He was looking at her, his face once again grave. She didn't want to know what was on his mind. She was afraid that it might be her – and not in a good way. Maybe Billy Ray was finally seeing her father in her eyes. Maybe he knew that she was hiding something. When he saw her watching he slowly took one of his hands out of his pocket and waved it. She waved in answer before resolutely turning her back to him and starting toward her Mustang.

Once in the driver's seat guilt washed over her. She just sat there gripping the black leather wheel until both shoulders knotted from the strain. After all she and Billy Ray had been through together, and here she was betraying both his friendship and trust by continuing to lie to him. She'd snapped her fingers and he had put off his retirement to come help her in Byrd's Landing. She told him about the phone call with Hazel, and he was ready to put himself in jeopardy by questioning Angel without a guardian. Even now, he was working quickly to pin the murder on Jabo Kersey. There was certainly plenty of evidence against Hazel's mysterious ex. But Billy Ray knew she was holding something back, and the thought of it made her feel horrible.

Floyd's voice protested in her head as she thought about Jabo Kersey as the killer. *Ain't no way it's a boyfriend who did that there*, it said. *And ain't no ex-hus-BAND either.* The voice paused for a minute. The resulting silence was almost as painful as the sound. And then he started up again. *I can buy a daddy. But can't buy no boyfriend.*

"I know," she breathed back to him.

My God, she thought. She had actually said that aloud.

She knew that her head would burst with the force of Floyd if she didn't clear it. Memories of him were causing her to miss something. No telling how badly she would screw this case up with the voice of Floyd fighting with the life she had been trying to build for herself since his capture.

She started the engine and put the car in gear. She knew what she had to do.

At her apartment she dressed in a pair of running capris and an old worn pair of trail running shoes. As she did so, Imogene Tucker was on the news, her tiny features working in her round brown face as she asked the audience what was the BLPD not telling them about the murder of Hazel Westcott.

Raven shrugged a light jacket over her holster, and fastened the

Velcro straps of the hunting knife around her ankle as she watched Imogene Tucker. She was reporting on location, and the camera panned away to reveal Tucker in a tight red dress, her bare legs in a pair of sky-high pumps. Tucker moved her streaked blond extensions out of her face before pointing to the sign on the red brick building behind her. Raven saw that she was standing in front of Boones & Sons Grocery, the place where Raven shot Quincy Trueblood.

"How vigorously," Tucker asked in her best news reporter voice, "is the BLPD investigating this case when the victim was not exactly a friend of the department? If you recall, Hazel Westcott was highly critical of Raven Burns' shooting of Quincy Trueblood, which happened right behind me." She looked over her shoulder, paused for a dramatic second, and turned back to the camera.

Raven snatched the remote from the table, looking for the off button. But before she could find it, the camera moved close in on Tucker's face. She said, "We've tried multiple times to contact the BLPD and Raven Burns for this and other stories, but they have not returned our calls."

The TV blinked off and Raven threw the remote at it. She stood there a few moments, her chest heaving, thinking that she needed this run more than ever now.

She took the back steps down two at a time to the parking lot and her waiting Mustang. She steered the car toward the highway and Ronald Gold State Park, which had an eleven-mile looping trail that the locals affectionately called the Scorpion's Tail. She glanced in the rearview mirror as she drove. Though not quite dark, the sky was turning a hazy red from the glow of the orange-yellow sun sinking low and slow behind her. After the thirty-minute drive and another hour run, it would be full pitch before she got back home. Maybe even dark during the run itself. She was okay with that. Raven had never been afraid of the dark.

The trail was closed when she got there but she paid that no mind. She simply parked the car outside the entrance and climbed over the low chain stretched between two steel posts, kicking the sign that said 'Park Closed' in big black letters as she did so. The sign flapped with the chain, making an uneasy rattling sound in the dusk. Halfway to the trailhead she stopped and considered.

The place was deserted. Not a car was in the gravel parking lot. In this moment any enemies that she might have had existed only inside her head. A silo, round and hulking, appeared sinister in the dying light as if to deny her the comfort of that thought. She turned from it to the young beech trees marking the entrance to the trailhead. She hopped on one of three tree stumps just outside the entrance to the trail. She peered between the long stand of beech trees on either side, remembering steep climbs and switchbacks. Primarily a bike trail, Scorpion's Tail could be torture on runners. She thought about the shoulder holster clamped to her side beneath her light jacket. It would rub like hell as she climbed the hills and maneuvered over the downed trees she knew to be there. And the knife still strapped to her ankle would feel like a ball and chain at the end of the run.

Ignoring the soft voice of warning in her head, Raven flipped around and climbed back over the chain. She popped the trunk of the Mustang. Off came the light jacket, next the shoulder holster. Both went into the trunk along with the knife that she had unstrapped from her ankle. She rummaged around until she found a headlamp that she pulled tight over her curls. She ignored the ethereal pull of the weapons as she trudged back toward the trailhead, and told herself that she could do this, that she didn't always need to be protected. Floyd was dead.

And she thought the same thing before taking off on a run, especially a challenging one like Scorpion's Tail. This, she thought, this was living.

Back at the trailhead she stepped onto the stump nearest to the entrance and dove into the forest, Floyd's voice along with others in pursuit. There were Holloway and Hazel telling her she was no better than her father. The whispers of all of Byrd's Landing skeptics after the Quincy Trueblood shooting became a stinging mist crowding around her head and shoulders with Imogene Tucker leading the way. How hard are they really working? Tucker had asked.

The trail felt soft, the clay damp and a little spongy beneath the leaves dropped from the beech and twisted pine trees overhead. She lengthened her stride. The faster and louder the voices became, the faster her feet flew, and the greater her confidence increased. And pretty soon the voices dissipated until she was left with only the sounds of her own footfalls. She had slipped Floyd and the critics of Byrd's Landing like a second skin.

She ran fast, but cautiously, reading the ground so a misstep wouldn't send her sprawling into the patches of blackberry vines off the trail. She barely noticed the last of the light filtering through the trees as she leapt over a flat rock with strands of rust, and only became fully aware of the darkness when she noticed that the only light guiding her feet radiated from her headlamp.

The earthy, sweet smell of the forest made her feel as if she were running in a place a thousand years old. She listened for her breath until she found and caught hold of it. She regulated her breathing until she was evenly exhaling after every third step. About another mile or so the trees gave way to a wide opening. Her headlamp picked out a flash of the lake to the left, its surface flat and smooth with the reflected light. What looked like a blue heron stood ankle-deep in the water along its banks.

Her run was feeling like music to her at that point, her body adapting to the twists, steep climbs, and sudden downward slopes of Scorpion's Tail as it always had. They would arrest Jabo Kersey, she thought. Her nightmare would be over. And all her critics would be silenced. She was feeling good, as if she had finally beaten Floyd, when she heard a sound that made her heart skip.

It started with a hiss, a low raspy sound unwinding like smoke in the darkness. Her feet stopped as if they had a mind of their own, and she stumbled with the sudden loss of momentum. She began a plunge face-first onto the forest floor. Somehow she had the presence of mind to twist her face away as the ground rushed toward her. Both hands shot out to break her fall as she came down with a thump.

The hiss came again, this time with a low rattle. She lay there a long moment with her eyes squeezed shut. She didn't want to open them. She was too afraid of what she might see. Floyd seemed to come back then in a thousand coarse whispers from somewhere just below her consciousness. She screamed for him to shut up, and hearing the sound of her own voice gave her the courage to open her eyes.

A tangle of what looked like slender tongues confronted her in the bright white light of her headlamp. Black beetles climbed under and over them, scurried between and through them. She screamed and sat up, scrambling backward, mud and dirt coating her legs and backside. Her body itched all over as she thought of those busy, fine feet navigating through those coiling tongues.

Her breath, that she had so earlier easily regulated, came out in short spurts and gasps. *Holy shit, holy shit, holy shit,* she thought repeatedly as she remembered what Floyd had told her would happen to little girls who told on their daddies. She thought about the Glock and hunting knife in her trunk and then thought how ridiculous she was being by wishing for them. There was nothing here she could shoot, no danger she could slash into oblivion. She clutched the front of her shirt, telling herself to calm down, willing her heart to slow.

She concentrated on what she was physically feeling, the mud along her bare calves, the leaves cooling her scraped and stinging hands. The sound came again, and there was something almost mechanical about the rattle, the clicks and clacks, and familiar.

Still shaking, she stood up. She rubbed the mud and dirt from her hands onto her running capris. She took a couple of breaths, big ones that went all the way down to the base of her belly. The first order of business was finding out what in the heck she had been looking at. She turned to the tangle again and followed it until a tree trunk lying on the ground glowed silver beneath her headlamp.

A shaky laugh escaped her. Tree roots, an uprooted beech. *That was Thing Two,* she thought. *Now what about Thing One?* As if being called, the hiss and rattle came again. She pointed the headlamp skyward. Two perfectly round eyes in a heart-shaped face of snow-white feathers stared back at her from trees above. She laughed almost fully now. It blinked at her, unmoving, before letting out another long warning hiss and cackle.

Relief washed over her as her confidence came back. She thought about giving the barn owl the finger but didn't want to push her luck. Still shaky but ready to finish the run, she dusted as much dirt and mud from her backside as she could. She did a mental scan of her body and didn't start running again until she was satisfied that she was still in one piece.

In about a mile and a half she had recaptured the mood she had earlier in the run – one of confidence as her body picked up the chaotic but familiar rhythm of the trail. She finished the second half of the run in the circle of light from her headlamp, telling herself that she was still here. Floyd, in spite of occasional flashes in her head, was only as powerful as her imagination allowed. Who was he to still haunt her? He was gone, as helpless as only the dead could be. And she would not let people like Holloway define her because of what Floyd had done. She would find out who killed Hazel without worrying about the threat of the past hanging over her head. If it was Jabo, then so be it. If it was someone else, like Westcott, then that was just as well. She knew that it wasn't her, and she would take a cue from Billy Ray and follow the evidence wherever it led her.

The trail had done its work, and she finished with a clear head and Floyd swept clean from the corners of her mind. She was at peace the entire drive back to her apartment. Just as she came down them before driving out to Scorpion's Tail, she took the stairs two at a time, but this time she glided up.

The brown envelope tilted against the white of her apartment door stopped her. She stood there for several long seconds with her keys still in her hands, the headlamp dangling from her crooked arm. The knife was back at her ankle, and the holster carelessly thrown over her shoulder. She looked up and down the long hallway. No surveillance cameras and no way to know who had left her this lone gift.

She bent down and scooped up the envelope, holding it against her chest before opening the door to her apartment. She flicked on the lights and laid her holster down on the entrance table along with her keys.

After she stripped out of her muddy clothes and donned a robe, she plopped down on the couch, staring at the envelope now back in her hands and thinking about the times her father used to send her letters from death row. With a sinking heart she slit it open and took out a single sheet of paper. Written in large and beautiful cursive were these words: *She told me what you did. Come after me, and the world will know it. They will see for themselves who you really are. You can't hide your nature. You are a murderer, just like him.*

The letter was signed E.J.K. Raven sat for a few minutes staring at the signature. She didn't know what the E stood for, but had no doubt about the J.K. Jabo Kersey.

Floyd's voice rose up again. *See, Birdy Girl, you always gone need me. I ain't gonna let you come to no harm. All you have to do is listen.*

She laid her head back on the couch and closed her eyes before letting out a long breath. With the note dangling from her fingers, all the confidence and determination she had found during the run of Scorpion's Tail was gone like smoke. This is the real world, she thought, one that she would never be able to outrun no matter how hard she tried.

CHAPTER TWENTY-FOUR

She came early into the office after spending a restless night dreaming about the black beetles busily climbing in and out of the tangled roots she had tripped over during the Scorpion's Tail run. The warning hiss from the barn owl clicked and rattled in her nightmares.

She knew that she couldn't tell Billy Ray about the threat from Jabo Kersey. She had made up her mind that to involve him even further than she already had would only put him in jeopardy. He hadn't quite saved enough for his restaurant, not yet anyway. And if she compromised him too badly, the chief would fire him. He still needed his job and his reputation for a little while longer before he began that long walk to New Orleans.

Someone was torturing her, she was sure – Hazel from the grave with a manufactured piece of evidence, along with her ex-husband most likely. Raven wouldn't at all be surprised if Presley Holloway, Hazel's ally in the days after the Trueblood shooting, was also in on it. The department's internal affairs supervisor had hated her on sight. He had been receiving the same updates about the case the chief had, and it would've been easy for him to leave that note outside her door just to play with her.

Whoever it was, Raven planned on making them more than sorry. She would find a way to get Jabo Kersey alone to learn who he was working with before he was officially questioned for Hazel's death. *And why else*, Floyd insidiously hissed in her head, reminding her of the barn owl's warning, *why else do you need him all by his lonesome?*

She ignored the voice and his question. There was one thing she needed to do before moving on – she needed to make sure there was nothing out there that could incriminate her in the Trueblood shooting. And there was only one person who could set her mind at ease on that point – Lamont Lovelle.

Lovelle shared a windowless office with Presley Holloway in

the far reaches of the Byrd's Landing Police Department, next to a janitor's closet and kitty corner to IT. The message was loud and clear that the BLPD wanted them out of sight and out of mind. Holloway complained to the chief but it did no good. The ignominy of being regulated to the same place as the mop buckets wound the little man even tighter than he already was.

Raven knew Holloway wouldn't be at work yet. He usually spent the mornings taking care of his mother, whom he had taken care of ever since a car accident left her paralyzed from the neck down. But Lovelle, ever the early bird, sat behind his desk when she walked in, as if expecting her.

"Good morning, Lamont," she said almost tentatively.

"Ah, Raven," he said, his voice as pleasant as the smile on his face, but frosted with the politeness he tended to use with her.

She had always thought that Lovelle had an odd way of mirroring the personalities of those in his company. When with the chief, Lovelle spoke in that slow, plodding way the chief had. While with Holloway, Lovelle's back would be a little straighter, the corners of his full lips pinched and a ready frown on his face. Once she saw him joking with a group of BLPD janitors. He was laughing with his head thrown back and his white teeth flashing, responding to their jokes with ones of his own, using words of slang and belonging. Floyd would call Lovelle an empty vessel – ready to fill up with whoever happened to be around him.

"Please, please, sit," Lovelle said as he swiped away a stack of magazines from the chair in front of his desk. He sat the stack on the edge of his desk. They would have teetered to the floor if Raven hadn't reached out a hand and steadied them. His desk was covered with coffee cups, books, magazines, and crumpled pieces of yellow paper. Behind him was a bookshelf crammed to overflowing with books.

She looked over at Holloway's desk on the opposite side of the room and facing Lovelle's. A computer monitor, a desk blotter, Scotch Tape, and a stapler were its only occupants. Behind the desk was a wall covered with Holloway's degrees, training certificates, and awards, all in identical black frames and lined up in neat rows. If Lovelle's way of charming people reminded Raven of Floyd's, Holloway's apparent need for order was quintessentially Floyd 'Fire' Burns – and herself, for that matter.

Lovelle noticed her looking at Holloway's desk and said, "Yes, yes, I know. He gets on me about my desk all the time, but I require my space to be slightly more creative."

She went to sit down but saw that he had missed a magazine on the chair. She picked it up and handed it to him after looking at it briefly. "You like wine," she said, handing the *Food and Wine* magazine back to him. "I can see why you'd need a drink after working with that." She jabbed a finger behind her at Holloway's desk.

"Now, Raven," he chastised, "you're too hard on Presley. What can I do for you?"

She searched his face for a minute, wondering if she could trust him, even though his eyes appeared open and friendly.

She began slowly as she eased into the chair. "How far would you have gone, Lamont," she said, "to save my ass in the Quincy Trueblood shooting?"

He stared at her. "My, my. You don't waste any time getting to the point," he said. "Where is this coming from, my dear?"

She tried to meet his eyes but couldn't.

"You are among friends," he said in a gentle voice.

She let her gaze sweep over Holloway's desk. "Am I?" she asked.

"I wouldn't worry about him," he said. "He's about three Froot Loops short of a full bowl. He's so stressed taking care of his poor mother that I'd be surprised if he lasts another year on this job. All you have to do is wait him out. Tell me why you're asking about the Trueblood shooting?"

"Did anyone tell you that the weapon found at the scene was a throw-down?"

He looked at her as if she were joking. Then he laughed shortly. "Absolutely not."

"And that there was video?"

He laughed even harder now. "Video?" he said. "At Boone's & Sons? Are you kidding, Raven? Old man Boone was still using a flip phone when you shot Quincy Trueblood. His idea of security was leaving his Scottish terrier in the store at night." He shook his head now, chuckling. "Video."

"What about the surrounding businesses?"

He stopped and looked at her seriously. "No, nothing," he said. "You know that, Raven. I have no idea what you're talking about."

Raven sighed with some relief. She pulled her fingers through her tight hair. "I think someone is trying to set me up," she breathed.

"Now?" he said, a smooth black eyebrow lifting.

She nodded.

"A little late, wouldn't you say? And an asinine way to go about it by threatening you with evidence of a throw-down and a video. I mean, there are witnesses who would contradict that a weapon was planted at the scene by the police. And *you* saw Quincy Trueblood point a weapon at you, didn't you? That's why you shot him. And I can guarantee you that Boones & Sons didn't have a video. No one around them did either."

"And if they did?" she asked him. "Or if someone came to you saying that the weapon was a plant?"

Lovelle shrugged and looked down at his desk. He said without looking at her, "I like winning, as I'm sure you do, Raven."

"I wouldn't have let it go that far, Lamont," she said. "If someone said that there was contradictory evidence, I'd want to see it played out. I wouldn't want it covered up."

He looked at her. "So you say now," he said. "But I'm a bit older than you, and I know you have had some life experiences, but so have I. Not as intense, but I've been around. And I do know one thing."

"What's that?"

"There is no telling what the body will demand from the soul when one is in mortal peril, Detective," he said.

She laughed. "That's a little dramatic, Lamont. And a little creepy."

He gave a rueful smile. "Sorry," he said. "I'm afraid I read too much noir. But I'm telling you that one doesn't know what they will do in a situation until they are in it – especially one where the stakes are life, death, or a reputation they tried so hard to build. Still, there is no evidence of a throw-down because you know as well as I do that there was none. And there is no video, not that I know of anyway."

She jerked her head over her shoulder. "What about him?"

Before he answered, she stood up and walked over to Holloway's desk. She could feel Lovelle's eyes on her back as she strolled over with her hands in the pocket of her jeans.

"Nothing that he wouldn't have shared with me, I assure you," he said. "And he wouldn't have waited until now."

She noticed how Holloway had lined up his Scotch Tape holder, his stapler, and blotter so that the edges matched. She stared at the blank face of his computer, wishing she could dive through and see what Holloway had been up to since before and after Hazel's death. Would she find any research on poisons? Ties to Jabo Kersey?

"He'll be in any minute," Lovelle said in a warning voice. "He mentioned that he would be coming in early today. I'm sure you wouldn't want to ruin your breakfast with an unplanned meeting with him."

She sighed. "You got that right," she said.

She was about to turn away when she noticed that Holloway also had a bookshelf, this one waist-high to the left of his desk. The books were lined up, arranged by subject, and in alphabetical order. One of the books caught her eye. She thought she recognized the neon greens and blues along the book's spine. Almost in slow motion she reached in with her index finger and pulled it out. She stared at the cover for several long heartbeats. She then turned the slick cover over in her hands and saw the picture of the author on the back of the book – Michael Gorman.

"What's this?" she asked Lovelle in wonder.

He gave her a blank look. "I wouldn't be disturbing his things. He doesn't like that."

"No, seriously," she said. "This is my father's book."

"I didn't realize that your father wrote," he answered in a bland voice.

"No, no," she said, walking slowly over to him. "*Straight Razors and Peacock Feathers*. It's a book about my father. Why would Holloway have it?"

"Maybe he's a fan."

With both hands she held the face of the book in front of him. "No, not a fan," she said. "Because a real fan would have known that this book was full of garbage, lies. They wouldn't be reading this trash."

He cocked his head at her. "I don't understand, Raven," he said. "Why would this get you so upset?"

"Upset? Upset? The truth is horrible enough without having to deal with lies on top of it. And this guy, this guy," she said, turning the picture of the author back around to face him, "thought he was going to use lies about my father to get famous — even had a screenplay and a deal with Netflix all lined up before I told the publishers what a fraud he was. Not by lying about my pain will he make it. He won't profit from my tears."

She finished, panting, realized that she had been yelling almost at the top of her voice. She blinked until Lovelle's face was once again in focus. He looked at her as if he pitied her, and a feeling of shame spiraled through her.

"I'm sorry," she said. "I shouldn't be yelling at you. It's not your fault."

He simply nodded as a quiet smile touched his lips. "I don't know why this man did what he did, Raven," he said. "But you shouldn't let it get you so upset. Maybe he just likes winning too. Now if you'd excuse me, I have work to do, and I really don't feel like explaining your presence to Holloway once he arrives."

CHAPTER TWENTY-FIVE

She left Lovelle's office still shaking. She had tried to leave with the Michael Gorman book, but Lovelle took it away from her, saying, "I don't think this belongs to you." As she leaned against the door with her eyes closed, the doorknob felt as warm as human flesh against her palm. She let her hand drop and opened her eyes. When she did, she saw the door of the IT office located diagonally from Lovelle and Holloway's office. It wasn't until she blinked the haze away from her eyes that she realized what it fully meant.

She swallowed, took a deep breath, and waited for her heart to slow. She counted up to ten and back down again until the sound of her own shouting in her head quieted. She couldn't believe she let herself lose it like that. Lovelle must have thought her a complete fruitcake. When she felt in control she walked across the hall and through the door of the IT department.

A man a few years younger than Raven sat behind a desk piled with all kinds of electronic equipment in various states of repair – computer monitors, desk phones, hard drives, and CPUs, some with their circuit boards exposed. He hadn't heard her come in because a pair of Beats headphones bisected his giant afro and was clamped over both ears. He was repeating every other phrase of Wu-Tang Clan song. When it became apparent that she might have to stand there until the entire brain-beating song was over, she said, "Cam."

Nothing. He started swinging his fingers and shoulders and bobbing his head to the beat pounding in both ears. She walked over to him until she was standing behind him, unclamped the Beats from his ears, and held them over his head.

"Hey, hey," he protested, his chair thumping to the ground and his feet leaving the cluttered desk. "Ain't you ever heard not to mess with a black man and his music?"

He twisted until he could see her face. Grinning, he said, "Hey, Big

Sis, how lovely to see you and your pretty blue eyes...." He stopped and squinted at her. "I mean pretty blue *eye*."

"Cameron," she said again with all the authority she could muster though she knew it would do no good.

"So," he said as he swiveled around to face her. "What are you today?" He cocked his head in speculation. "Are you meanie greenie or blissful and blue?"

"Cameron," she warned, "I don't feel like playing with you right now."

"Oh, I see," he said, yawning. "It's meanie greenie. What brings you and your bad 'tude up in here this fine morning, Big Sis?"

"Stop calling me that." She spotted another chair on the other side of the room next to a cabinet of blinking servers and switches. She wheeled it over next to him and plopped down.

"What am I supposed to call you?" he said. "Big foster sister? How would that work? Let me see." He stopped and said, "Hey, Big Fo' Sis." He shook his head. "No, that doesn't sound right."

"Cameron."

"Too much of a mouthful. I'll stick with Big Sis."

"How about Detective when we're at work?"

He laughed shortly before reaching over and answering a prompt on the monitor by typing a few keys on the keyboard in front of him. "When you start calling me Mr. IT, I'll start calling you Detective."

"Why so early this morning?" she asked.

"Server maintenance," he said. "I would do it during the day, but don't want thi police with guns after me for taking down email. What are you doing here?"

"I need your help."

He looked from the monitor to her. "You? Need my help? Oh happy day! Can I name my price?"

"Cam," she said. "Who got you this job?"

"I'd like to think my sparkling personality and incredible genius," he said, smiling.

She didn't answer him.

"No?" he asked.

Still nothing.

"Okay," he conceded. "Is this the point where I ask the big meanie greenie what kind of payback she's looking for? What she wants?"

"I need a big favor."

"So you say," he said.

"Holloway has a virus."

His face went serious. He let out a puff of air. "Man, he can't have a virus. That dude *is* a virus."

"Cameron," she said. "Can you please focus?"

He spread his arms out and swiveled in his chair from right to left, taking in the racks of servers, switches, and computers humming in the small room. "Do you not see all that I am master of? I focus just fine."

"Holloway's got a virus and I need to get some evidence off his computer."

"Since when you run errands for Holloway? Tell that mo' fo' to put in a work order and I'll get to it when I get to it."

"We need the evidence today."

"Then why he ain't in here?" Cameron challenged.

"He asked me to do him a favor."

He looked at her a long time. "Shit, Raven. Why did he ask you?"

She sighed. "Look, that's what you should know – that Holloway asked me to report it. I don't want to get you into any trouble. I just need access to his computer."

"So let me get this straight. I go get his computer, bring it back to the castle that is IT and walk away while you have your way with his hard drive?"

She grinned. "Good-looking and smart. I now know why you were my partner in crime all those years in foster care."

"What if he catches me?"

"You say you were doing your job."

He thought for what seemed like a long time. "What DEFCON is this?"

She smiled. That was their signal to each other when talking about how much trouble they were in. DEFCON three meant that they might be grounded for a day or so, a two meant it was a lecture from their foster mother, Greta, that made you wish she simply believed in a butt whipping, and a one meant that you were about to blow out yet another foster home. They got themselves into plenty of threes and twos, but never managed a one, especially with their ever-patient and loving foster mother.

"It's a Floyd Burns DEFCON, Cameron," she said, her voice serious. "It's a DEFCON that could mean my career if I don't figure out what the hell is going on."

He said nothing for a long while, and then, "And I can't know about it?"

"Not yet."

He took a deep breath and turned around. "Okay, you got it, but we don't have to go and get his computer."

She looked at him questioningly.

"I only bring computers in here when they have a hardware problem," he said, "when I can't get to them remotely. I'll just log into Mr. Stuckup's computer and see what's going on. We can get to it from here."

"Doesn't he have to answer yes when you remote connect?" Raven asked, remembering a time when Cameron had to take over her computer when helping with a printer problem.

He grinned. "I can get around the remote connect."

He had switched to another display, his fingers flying over the keys.

"But when I was over there a minute ago, his computer wasn't on," Raven was saying.

"Oh, yeah, it was on. Probably just in sleep mode," he said, eyes flashing between the keyboard and screen. And then, "I'm in."

She scooted closer to him until they were shoulder to shoulder. "What you need?" he asked.

"Search history, first," she said.

A few more clicks and they were looking at Holloway's recent internet searches.

"Can you go back further?" she asked.

Cameron scrolled up and down a few times before saying absently, "I should be able to, but...."

"But what?"

"Wait, let me check something out."

He typed in a few more things and then opened an application on another display. After a few commands he said, "Yeah, thought so."

"Thought what?" Raven said. "Why can't we go back further?"

"Because," Cameron said, "your friend Holloway's computer got reimaged – erased and built back up again."

"What, when?" Raven asked. "And why? Was something the matter with it?"

"Uh-uh," he said, shaking his head, and pointing to an application he had brought up on another screen. "See this work order on the screen? Looks like it was assigned to Danny on the night shift to reimage his computer. It was a user request. Holloway told him to do it."

"Why would he do that?" she asked.

Cameron shrugged. "Some people like to do a reimage every couple of years just to clean up memory and the system's registry. I erase my computer and start over every once in a while."

"Was Holloway's computer due?" she asked.

"That's what's so freakin' weird," he said. "No, his computer ain't even three months old. It's practically brand new."

She sat back and thought about what reason Holloway would have for reimaging his computer. And the answer came rather quickly. He reimaged his computer to cover something up – most likely his research on how to kill someone without leaving overt signs of violence.

CHAPTER TWENTY-SIX

Raven called Memorial Hospital while sitting at one of the stone picnic tables in the garden between the back door of the BLPD and the morgue. She had taken her jacket off and folded it next to her on the bench, hoping that fewer clothes would provide some relief from air that had grown more humid with the progress of the morning. The cloying scent from the honeysuckle growing close against the cinderblock fence, together with the heat, made Raven feel claustrophobic.

Add to that the black fear rising in her that whoever was trying to bring her down would succeed before she could find out who killed Hazel. And with every passing moment, she believed that the person behind her impending demise was Presley Holloway. Why else would he erase his computer after Hazel's death? To hide any incriminating evidence. She would get him one way or the other, but first she had to find out how Jabo Kersey was involved in Hazel's killing.

She had indeed found a copy of a wedding license for Kersey in Las Vegas. Jabo Kersey – no, Emmanuel Jacob Kersey – married Hazel Westcott in Las Vegas in October of last year. When Raven learned Kersey's full name, she thought about what Billy Ray had said yesterday – Memorial kept repeating like a mantra that no Jabo Kersey had ever worked there. She tapped a pen against a copy of a marriage license, willing someone to answer the ringing phone so she could retreat to the cool of the conference room now that the air-conditioner was working again.

When a crisp female voice finally answered the phone, Raven insisted on speaking to the chief of staff. It only took the mention of the name Kersey to get him on the phone. Hot and impatient, Raven had barely let the drawling voice introduce himself before peppering him with questions. What about anyone with the last name of Kersey? What about contract employees? Temps? They hired temps, didn't they? Did they check all of their files? The next thing she knew, the drawl on the other end of the phone was inviting her to a sit-down at Memorial Hospital so they could discuss the matter while looking each other in the face, like, he told her, decent people.

When she pressed the end button on her Android, she turned to reach for her jacket and stopped short. Billy Ray was standing there, his pork pie hat pushed back on his head, and his arms folded across his broad chest. He had an expression on his face like he had never seen her before. And he said very quietly, "I guess you found something, partner. Where to?"

She told him as she shrugged into her jacket and they headed off to Memorial.

★   ★   ★

When Raven was a little girl living in Byrd's Landing, the official name of Memorial had been the Confederate Hospital. Ever since the name had been changed to comply with the country's political sensitivities, it had come to be known by the good citizens of Byrd's Landing as the old Confederate Hospital. Only newcomers called it Memorial. The building was wide, but just seven stories high with an exterior the color of vomit and an interior filled with long hallways tiled in white and high walls painted a soft green.

Four people were waiting for them in a conference room at a large table, the top a deep glassy brown. Three of them stood when Raven and Billy Ray walked into the room. They lined up stair-step style, reminding Raven of Russian nesting dolls – two males in almost identical gray suits, one several heads taller than the other, and a small woman in a sleeveless top with a wide white skirt and black flowers stitched along the hem in a style reminiscent of the TV show *Mad Men*. Her bright blond hair was pulled back in a severe bun, and a dry red shade of lipstick defined her large lips, making them appear chiseled in her white face. She seemed young to Raven, trying everything she could to look like an accomplished adult.

The woman introduced herself as Mavis Butterman, the hospital's risk manager, and Raven caught a whiff of breath laced with stale cigarettes. Butterman smoothed her skirt over her bottom like a schoolgirl before sitting down in an enormous black leather chair. The taller man, whose suit was hopelessly rumpled, pointed to the man standing next to him. "This is Dr. Ewing," he said, as if the man had no tongue in his head to introduce himself. Before Dr. Ewing could speak, he continued, "All you need to know about me is that I'm his lawyer. He's my sole interest in this matter. I represent Dr. Ewing." He shoved a meaty hand toward Raven and Billy Ray. His palm was cool, but slightly wet with sweat.

The man sitting at the other end of the table appeared to be even taller than Dr. Ewing's lawyer. He occupied his big leather chair in what appeared to be a painful formation of crossed legs and arms. Raven thought that he could have easily passed for a spider, had that spider been close to seven feet tall and white as chalk. He unfurled when he saw her looking at him. He introduced himself as Dr. Fabian Long before sitting back down.

"We spoke on the phone," he said, his Byrd's Landing accent slow but careful. "You and I did, Detective Burns," he added as if she might have forgotten. He waved his fingers at her. "I'm the hospital's chief of staff. I never liked phones. They make me feel like I'm throwing my words away, down to some dark place where they get all mixed up before finally reaching the person on the other end. I like face-to-face. I like looking people in the eye."

He leaned back in the chair and picked up a glass of water. He swirled the glass around a couple of times before looking away from her.

Raven watched him for several long seconds as he took a drink, then she said, "And I see you also like stalling."

"My, my," Billy Ray said before Long could answer. "If I'd known all of you would be here, I would have baked a cake."

Raven sent a quick glance her partner's way. This would not be a good meeting for him, she could tell. He was already in a foul mood because on the drive over she had deftly avoided or deflected his questions about why she had come in so early and what she was hiding.

But that was not the only reason his temper would be short with Dr. Fabian Long and his merry trio of lawyers and doctors. Billy Ray didn't care for authority. A dislike of authority was the reason he took the shotgun house he now lived in for a rental. He did it so he could deny the city councilman who was so adamant about tearing them down. Billy Ray was letting the councilman know wealth or power didn't mean a person automatically got their way – not all the time.

"All of this for one contract employee, Dr. Long?" Raven said.

"I'm sorry if this appears to be overkill, Detective," Long answered, as a smile that was no smile flickered over his face. "This is a sensitive situation for the hospital."

Raven leaned back and returned the now-retreated smile with a broad grin of her own.

"Someone merely mentions the name of Emmanuel Jacob Kersey to you and it becomes a sensitive situation? How's that?"

"I'm not sure I understand your question," Long said, with his hands now laced in front of him.

"The question is," Billy Ray followed up, "how did he screw you?"

"Don't answer that," Butterman said, her white teeth flashing beneath her dry red lips. "Raven, how may we assist you and your partner? Billy Ray, is it?" She didn't wait for Billy Ray to answer. "We'd like to be specific so we don't waste your time, and as the hospital's risk manager, I'm here to make sure we don't violate our patients' privacy."

"And so that we leave here with our mouths shut and your rep still good enough to keep you in the running for hospital of the year award, isn't that right, Mavis?" Billy Ray said.

"You may," Butterman said, her face turning scarlet, "call me Counselor."

Long cleared his throat. "Kersey betrayed this hospital and put patients and our doctors in danger. We ended his contract to ensure our patients' safety, as we should have. That's nothing to be ashamed about, Mavis," he finished in a drawl, waving his fingers at his risk manager in a dismissive gesture.

He stopped, leaned back and sighed. He shoved his hands into his thick black hair and hung onto it before letting go. His hand fell back on the table. "But even though he isn't here anymore, that doesn't mean the danger has passed. We have to protect ourselves from certain liabilities, Detective Burns. Of course, you understand. That's why I asked Mavis to join us."

"It's about the fentanyl, isn't it?" Dr. Ewing said, his voice shaking and high. "I thought it was all settled, Dr. Long. I don't understand why the police have been brought here."

Dr. Ewing's lawyer placed a puffy hand on his client's shoulder. He probably wished he could have placed it over his mouth. "Please, Doc," he said. "You need to hush."

Raven reached for one of the heavy crystal glasses on the table. She turned it right side up and poured water into it from one of the two glass pitchers. No one said anything. They simply watched her while water and ice gurgled in a twirling crystal stream into the open glass. She leaned back and noticed how all of their images shimmered up from the table's polished surface, an upside-down world where nothing was clear or sure. The hospital thought they were here about fentanyl. They were here about the Sux. Dr. Ewing, for some reason, thought they were after him. They were after Jacob Kersey.

"What does Kersey have to do with you, Dr. Ewing?" Billy Ray asked, with a New Orleans drawl that was both slow and dangerous. "You make some kind of deal about the drugs? He steals fentanyl for you and you steal Sux for him?"

Dr. Ewing looked at him, confusion driving the fear out of his face. He said, "What? Succinylcholine? What has that got to do with anything?"

Raven drank. The water was cold and tasted bitter.

"We are investigating a murder," Raven said, wanting to slow Billy Ray down. "Hazel Westcott. Perhaps you heard about it?"

Long frowned and stood up. He opened his blazer and stuck two fingers in the pocket of a white vest. "I'm afraid I'm not following," he said. "What does Jabo Kersey's working at this hospital have to do with Hazel Westcott? Did the woman overdose?"

"How well do you know Jabo Kersey, Dr. Ewing?" Raven asked, ignoring Long's question.

He shrugged. "Well enough, I suppose. For a while I thought we were friends."

"Not just drug buddies?" Billy Ray said. "Friends? You went to basketball games, hung with the fam? Go to church together? Help each other move? That type of friend?"

"Okay, Detective, settle down. I know what you're getting at. They weren't really close friends, they just happened to have something in common, that's all," Long said. "But Kersey used him. Plain and simple."

"Can you be more specific?" Raven asked. The question was directed at Dr. Ewing, but Long answered with a question to Butterman. "Can we be more specific, Mavis?" he asked. "I know your job as risk manager makes you a little overprotective of the hospital, but can we just put this matter to rest by answering these folks' questions?"

Butterman thought for a minute, and then nodded. Long waved his fingers at Dr. Ewing. "Go on ahead then, son," he said. "Tell it."

"Okay, you're right," Dr. Ewing explained. "We weren't friends. Could never be, perhaps. But I fooled myself into thinking that we were. I was an addict. Kersey knew. He caught me pocketing some fentanyl and...."

"And what?" Raven prompted.

"He didn't report me," Dr. Ewing answered. "He said that he understood, and even started helping me with acquiring—"

"You mean stealing," Billy Ray said.

"Okay, yes, stealing the fentanyl. He was an addict too. Or pretended to be. And we talked all the time about getting clean. We swore every time we..." he gulped, "...injected, it would be the last time."

"So let me get this straight," Billy Ray said. "Kersey gets caught and gets the boot. Dr. Ewing gets caught and what, he gets promoted? A blue ribbon for the best pig at the fair?"

"Dr. Ewing," his lawyer said, "is one of the most renowned anesthesiologists in the state. He has an addiction and he's in treatment with this hospital's full support. Am I right, Mavis?"

Butterman sent a nod Billy Ray's way before smoothing the slick side of her head with a hand that shook. She said. "Our full support."

"Oh, excuse me, Counselor Mavis," Billy Ray said. "I wasn't thinking clearly. I forgot that there are a whole bunch of people out there who would pay good money to have the most renowned anesthesiologist in the state putting them under. Never mind that he's as high as Pluto. Stupid me."

"Detective," Long said. "Of course Dr. Ewing is not in the operating room while he's going through his treatment."

"Then why not give Kersey the same consideration?" Raven asked.

Long looked at Mavis. She nodded, her dark red lips pursed into a grimace.

Dr. Long began to pace. "Mr. Kersey is a different matter," he said. "He isn't an addict. I mean not really. He did the drugs, but I don't think the man was addicted. He's just a liar and a thief. We have the ability to treat addicts but I don't know of any cure for lying and thievery."

"I don't follow," Raven said.

Dr. Ewing ran his hands over his anguished face and answered Raven before Long could continue. "I know you don't believe me when I tell you that I thought we were friends, if not good friends," he said. "I thought we were going through what we were going through together. He even came over to my house a couple of times."

"To shoot up," Billy Ray said, his tone somewhat mocking.

Dr. Ewing nodded. "That too," he said. "But we hung out as friends, shared things about ourselves. It was only later on I realized that it was me doing most of the talking."

"How did it end?" Raven asked.

"Things stopped adding up," Butterman put in. "Luckily the hospital has processes in place to make sure controlled substances are properly stored and handled."

"You sure it was luck? Maybe it's because those processes are mandated by the state," Billy Ray countered.

"So they are," Mavis said, her eyes sparking. "But sometimes the processes work, and sometimes they don't. Ours did. I take my job very seriously, Billy Ray."

Billy Ray picked his hat up off the table and tipped it toward her.

"So," Dr. Ewing continued. "I told Jabo about it. I told him, I said, 'Jabo, they know.' And do you know what he said?" he asked, looking around the room.

"No, what?" Raven said.

"He said, 'Don't worry, I got you,' just like that," Dr. Ewing said in a voice that suggested he still found the statement incredulous. "'Don't worry, I got you.' Can you believe it?"

"I don't understand," Raven said. "He was going to back you up?"

But Dr. Ewing was shaking his head. "No, that's not at all what he meant. That's the way he tried to say it. But there was something in his eyes, something laughing at me. When I asked him what in the hell that was supposed to mean, he tried to clean it up. He said he had all kinds of connections, saw all kinds of people come through the emergency room, people from the police department."

Raven looked at Long, who was staring out of a window, clearly done with them and the conversation. He explained with a small lift of his hand, "Kersey sometimes filled in for shortages in the emergency room."

Raven sat up. "Did he say who his connections were?" she asked Dr. Ewing.

But he didn't seem to hear her. He appeared to be lost in the day when he realized what a fool he had been. She asked him again.

He replied in an uninterested way, "He said something about taking care of somebody's mother, that the son was a big deal with the Byrd's Landing Police Department. Jabo said he sometimes sat with the mother when the cop couldn't. And he got to know lots of other people who worked at the police department who sat with the cop's mother too."

"You talking about Presley Holloway's mother?" Raven asked. "The guy who runs Internal Affairs at the department?"

"I don't remember any names, and frankly don't really give a damn about what they did," Dr. Ewing answered. "All I know is he just kept saying he had connections, grabbing at my sleeve trying to get me to believe him." Dr. Ewing cupped his elbow when he said the last, still not seeing them. "I think the man would have gotten on his knees had he thought it'd do any good. But I had seen his eyes. The mask had slipped. He was lying to me like any trashy person would, trying to make me believe that he had my best interest at heart."

"Dr. Ewing is the one who turned him in," Dr. Ewing's lawyer said, his florid face running with sweat. "That's a big point we all need to remember."

Raven looked at Long. He had once again sat down and was watching the shadows glisten in the upside-down world of the table's surface. He began drumming his lengthy fingers on top of the table.

"Dr. Long...." Raven started.

He sighed. "Yes," he said. "That doesn't sound like that'd do it, does it? All this foolish talk. I said the same thing when Dr. Ewing told me all of this."

"So there's more."

"Of course there's more. Dr. Ewing, tell her so we can all get on with our day."

"Like I said, he knew people because he worked intake in the emergency room sometimes. And I found out that he was not only giving me the fentanyl, but providing it to civilians," Dr. Ewing said.

Dr. Ewing's lawyer told him to stop talking. He appraised Raven and Billy Ray. "I'm sure that's enough, and that there won't be any criminal charges for my client?"

Raven leaned forward. "That depends," she said. "Who was he giving the drugs to?"

"I'm afraid—" Dr. Ewing's lawyer began.

Raven stood up to leave. "Billy Ray," she said. "Grab your hat. Looks like we're going to have to get a subpoena."

He grinned and winked at Mavis. "Good. I love subpoenas. And this will be a good one. It'll expose drugs, race, cover-up. Say," he said, turning to Raven, "should we stop off at Lamont's and see if he can do a press release? You know how ole Lamont loves those press releases."

"Okay, enough, enough," Dr. Long said. "Sit down."

"Dr. Long," Dr. Ewing's lawyer warned. "We have co-operated enough."

"Look," Raven said. "We're not after anyone. Not you, Dr. Ewing, or the hospital, Dr. Long." She looked at each of them in turn. "We're here because we're investigating a murder. A woman is dead and we want to know why. You said that Kersey knew a lot of people, Dr. Ewing. Do you know of his relationship with Hazel Westcott?"

Dr. Ewing looked up at her. "Why yes," he said, surprised. "He was giving her fentanyl too. Maybe he was dealing more, but I knew for sure he was giving it to her."

"How do you know that?"

"She came over to my place looking for him one night. She was acting as crazy as a trapped alligator screaming and crying that she had been waiting for him all day but he never showed up. She acted like she didn't have any sense at all."

Raven made an effort to keep her face very still. No one said anything for a while. That answered the question of what Hazel Westcott was doing with the likes of Jabo Kersey. It wasn't that she was trying to get away from Daddy's money by finding some of her own. She needed the drugs. But Raven didn't remember Rita saying anything about fentanyl at the autopsy. Did Hazel get cleaned up and no longer need Kersey? Was that why he killed her?

"When was this?" Raven asked Dr. Ewing.

"Why, months ago," he answered.

Raven turned to Mavis. "Any other drugs missing?" she asked her.

Mavis Butterman laughed for the first time, and said, "Well, isn't that enough?"

Raven waited.

"No, really, I don't know what you mean," she insisted with a little smile on her lips.

"Sux," Billy Ray explained. "Or, let me see if I can say it right, succinylcholine."

"No, you butchered it, Detective," Butterman said dryly. "And if it is missing, it's probably in a patient."

"Probably?" Raven asked.

"It's not locked up or logged if that's what you're getting at," Butterman said. "We don't treat it like fentanyl."

"How would you control access?" Raven asked, remembering what Rita had said back at the police station earlier, suspecting that she already knew the answer.

Butterman shrugged. "We don't. Why would we want to?"

"So everyone in the hospital has access to it?"

"We keep it in the emergency room, yes," she said. "It's not addictive, and we need it close just in case we have to intubate someone quickly."

"So Jabo Kersey would have access to it?"

"Kersey, nurses, doctors," she said. "Anybody really. Patients if they knew what they were looking for and had a few minutes alone. But I couldn't imagine what in the world anybody would want it for. It's not an addict's drug of choice."

Raven sat back in her chair. She looked at Billy Ray and he returned her gaze. Mavis sat staring at them both with a thoroughly confused look on her face. Raven gave her a comforting smile. "No," she said. "I couldn't imagine why anyone would want it either. Thank you for your time. You've been a great help."

CHAPTER TWENTY-SEVEN

The chief summoned Billy Ray and Raven to his office a few hours after their return from Memorial. The office was quiet even though everyone was there – Lovelle, the chief, and Presley Holloway, who sat off to the side of the chief's desk, clutching his ubiquitous water bottle but too wound up to drink, his body tightly coiled as if he was fighting to stay controlled. It was a repeat of the meeting in the chief's office after Hazel Westcott died. But this time, they weren't talking about a victim, but a killer.

Lovelle's intent stare felt as hot as a branding iron as Raven read the press release the chief had shoved toward her after Billy Ray had read it and handed it back without a word. She could actually feel Lovelle's look. She knew that he took his writing seriously, labored over it for so long that specks of blood seemed to appear in the tortured sentences. He had once told her that he *would* write in blood if it could get him published. She remembered coming upon him in his office as he was putting what he called the final touches on a press release. Wads of paper were balled on his desk, torn pieces scattered at his feet. He was muttering to himself and at the same time shuffling papers in his trembling hands while sweat glazed his broad forehead. When he noticed her standing in the doorway, his face changed. He smiled as he stood to greet her. He explained away the wads of paper and broken pencils as a touch of writer's block. She took care, since then, when responding to anything he had written.

Billy Ray stood in the corner of the chief's office leaning against the window with his arms folded. Billy Ray was staring too, but not at her, thank God. She could only take one stare at a time, especially if one of them was from Lovelle awaiting a critique of something he had written. Instead Billy Ray looked out of the window as if he were trying to read some sense in the July sun, now dying with the coming dusk. The arrest warrant in his hand was folded double.

Raven reread the press release, more slowly than the first time. It read how most of Lovelle's press releases read – clichéd embellishments full of sentiment about closure and justice and stating that the Byrd's Landing Police Department had made an arrest in the Hazel Westcott murder, one Emmanuel Jacob Kersey, also known as Jabo Kersey, the only suspect in the case. Raven placed the press release carefully on the chief's desk right next to the unopened bottles of Pappy's Van Winkle bourbon. She didn't say anything for a long time.

"Good detective work in finding him," the chief said in the heavy silence. "It took some skill to come up with the Vegas angle."

Raven didn't answer.

"Well," Lovelle finally said, looking at Billy Ray in his corner, then back to Raven again. "What do you think?"

Billy Ray said, "It's your best work, Lamont. It'll probably be a best seller."

Lovelle blew out a breath of air as if he had been holding it for some time. "Are you saying that it's good or are you saying that it's fiction?" he asked, his voice both low and dangerous.

"What I'm saying is that it's not right," Billy Ray responded. "Not yet. We need some more time on this."

"Explain," the chief said.

"You know how when you frying something in cast iron with the grease too hot? And it gets all golden and crispy on the outside?"

"Chastain," the chief responded, sounding tired.

"And you think it's done and pull the whole mess out ready to dig in?"

"Don't talk to me in parables, Billy Ray," the chief said.

But Billy Ray continued as if he hadn't spoken. "Then when you cut it open you find out that it's raw on the inside – no good to anybody. Not for eating, not even for a doorstop."

"Billy Ray, cut it out," the chief said. "I thought you were favoring Kersey."

"I do favor him," Billy Ray said. "That's why I want it to stick. We need some more time on this. To make sure we have a good solid case to back up the evidence, Chief. And Memorial, that hospital needs to be held accountable. They're involved in this too."

The chief stood up with all his weight on one leg because of his bad knee. He reached toward the edge of the desk and pulled a pen from the penholder before sitting back down with a heavy sigh into a black leather chair. He scribbled something on the hard copy of the press release draft. Raven watched as he did so, thinking that he didn't look like the Early Sawyer she had first met all those years ago. Back then he looked strong, sure, and ready for anything. Now he looked old as if he had already let go of youthful ideas about right and wrong and hypocrisy, as if the journey closer to retirement and old age made it all about expediency.

"It's right. Very right. All the evidence points to Kersey," the chief said in a voice that sounded grimly satisfied. "We don't have time to make sure you have all your *T*'s crossed and your *I*'s dotted, Billy Ray. You heard Tucker on the tube last night. She's wondering if we're sitting here with our thumbs in our asses. And if I read one more editorial in the *Byrd's Landing Review* about how we're bound to screw this case up, I'll puke in my soup."

"I don't like it," Raven said.

"What's not to like?" the chief asked. "He bought the dress she died in."

"It feels…" Raven said, "…I don't know. Wrong. I'd like to watch him for a while, like Billy Ray said. We need more evidence to lock it up tight. We need to treat this like any other case."

The chief held up his hand. "He was a nurse and a drug abuser if not a straight-out dopehead," he said. "And besides, we have the Sux."

Raven nodded. The Sux. The toxicology screen had come back. Evidence of Sux was found in Hazel Westcott's body. When Hazel learned that she wouldn't be able to escape her controlling father because Kersey didn't have any money left to keep her in Gucci, she annulled the marriage. Kersey had then stolen the Sux and killed her out of grief and revenge. Or so the story would go.

"And Billy Ray's right about Memorial. Kersey was Hazel's fentanyl supplier and the hospital made that possible," Raven said. "What if he was also supplying others? We should follow that angle up before we go pulling him in."

But the chief was already shaking his head. "If we can help it, I don't want that to get out about Hazel. It's too damaging and doesn't mean anything to the case. You're homicide detectives, not DEA agents."

Raven took a deep breath. It was time to go all in. She didn't want the case to end before knowing to what extent, if any, Holloway was involved. Hell, if he wasn't directly involved, maybe he was Jabo Kersey's accomplice after the fact. And she wanted a little more time to follow up on that threatening note left at her door.

"Chief," Raven finally said, "Dr. Ewing said that he had friends in this department." She stopped and looked at Presley Holloway, sitting coiled like a rattlesnake in the corner next to Lovelle. "Friends in positions of authority."

No one said anything for a beat or two. Finally, the chief said, "We could still bring him in and let Pam Jones worry about that. You have the warrant. She's on board with pulling his ass in tonight."

Pam Jones was the DA. She had a reputation for obtaining convictions on the slimmest of evidence. If she was on board with it, then Jabo Kersey was going to jail regardless of how neat and contrived it looked. And no matter who else was involved.

Raven pushed. "Pam's good, but she won't be happy with all these loose ends. No one saw Kersey at the party. And he was never accused of stealing Sux. Only fentanyl. It's all too circumstantial."

"We have enough to bring him in now," the chief said. "She's on board with it."

"Don't you like easy?" Lovelle's voice rumbled in the room. He was trying to be casual but she could tell he was still troubled by Billy Ray's response to the press release. "I thought you would be glad to have this behind you."

"I echo that sentiment," Presley Holloway said with his lips pursed like a nun's. "I thought you'd be running to arrest Jabo Kersey."

She turned to look at Holloway, his bright pink shirt perfectly pressed, collar stiff and his undershirt a pristine white. Even his black leather belt had a high polish that perfectly matched the gloss on his shoes. Her eyes moved back to his face. His small features were tight and controlled, but his eyes glittered with a frenetic energy he was trying hard to keep, as Floyd would say, a hold of. She thought about what Dr. Ewing said about Kersey's connections, and she could imagine what was going on in the back of Holloway's mind. If Holloway had befriended Kersey on one of his many trips to the emergency room with his paraplegic mother, then the reputation Holloway had so carefully cultivated would be questioned.

She also thought about Holloway's grudge against her, his probable connection to Kersey and his sure one to Hazel. Raven knew that Hazel did not come up with the angle to blackmail her into resigning all by herself. She had to have help. And that help most likely came from Holloway. He was obsessed with Raven, as evidenced by the Gorman book Raven found in his office. And the fact that he had his computer erased made Raven think that he was trying to hide his research on Sux, or other digital exhaust of his and Hazel's blackmail plans.

"And why would I be running to arrest Kersey, Holloway?" she asked.

Holloway carefully sat the bottle down on the chief's desk. He removed a gold ink pen from his shirt pocket and tapped the top of a clean manila folder he had on his lap. His grip was so tight on the ink pen that it was almost as if he were trying to break it. "I have always followed the rules," he said in a low, strained voice. "Tried to do what was right."

"Presley," the chief warned. "This is not the time."

Raven nodded as if she understood Holloway. She wanted to keep him talking, thinking that maybe he would let something slip about his relationship with Kersey. "I like to think of right as a matter of perspective, Holloway," she said.

His eyes met hers, blue and filled with hatred. "That's what makes you and me different, Detective."

"There is a lot that makes me different from you, Holloway," she answered.

"Presley," the chief said. "You've had it in for Detective Burns since the Quincy Trueblood thing. Even before that. Exactly what is it that you want?"

"I want justice," he said. "I tried getting it for Quincy Trueblood and I failed."

She could see that outrage threatened to swallow him whole. Raven leaned forward, "What's got you so mad, Holloway?" she asked, hoping to goad him further.

"You got away with Trueblood," he said. "Now you're about to get away with Hazel's murder."

He threw the manila folder he had been holding toward the chief, who stopped it in mid skid. He glanced at Raven before opening it.

Presley Holloway had been following her. She could see upside-down on the chief's desk photos of her at the storage shed in Bossier City, among some other documents.

Finally the chief looked over at Holloway. "You following my detectives around, Holloway? Looking at their phone records?" His voice was mild, but troubled.

Raven didn't have time to be nervous though she could feel her breath quicken. She was too busy watching Holloway. He had stood up and now paced the chief's office.

"I went to school, I studied. Didn't party like my friends," he said. "Got a job teaching at a private high school only to get fired because I didn't fix grades for Mamma and Daddy's little angels." He stopped in the middle of the room and looked at all of them in turn.

Along with his meticulous pink shirt and gray slacks, he wore a Browning 9 millimeter semiautomatic in a shoulder holster. The holster's catch was not fastened. The chief closed the file. Raven sat up straighter as Billy Ray released his lean against the window and sauntered over to them.

"So I became a cop," Holloway continued. "I thought that it couldn't get any blacker and whiter than a cop, right? The law is the law. What is correct is correct."

He was snapping. He was like a fence being destroyed in a hurricane, each picket unhinged and flung up by the wind one at a time. For the first time in days Raven looked at the chief not as a boss, but as the man who saved her from the bloody hands of her father and the one for whom she wanted to become a cop. She started to say something but the chief once again motioned for silence. She stayed quiet.

"Point, Presley?" he said in a mild tone.

"And then what did I find? My first partner taking bribes and half the cops I worked with dirty. That was a long time ago, before you took the job, Chief Sawyer. So I convinced the sheriff to form IA. Do you know how many cases I broke since my department formed?" When no one said anything, he said, "Zero. Not one. And now my staff and I sit tucked away next to the janitor's closet like a bucket of shit."

He sat back down and crossed his legs again. His head down and tilted to the side, he said with a small sob in his voice, "And do you know what happened in the meantime?"

The chief nodded, looking down at his desk. "Your mother, Presley," he said, his voice edged with sympathy.

Without looking at him, Presley nodded. "My mother. Never a parking ticket. Doesn't even smell alcohol and drive. And what happens? Hit by some drunk-on-speed Bubba driving a truckload of dead cows. Maybe she would have been okay if she hadn't unfastened her seatbelt to pick up the cell phone she had dropped. And maybe she would've still been all right save for that damn idiot intern at the hospital."

"Look, Holloway," Billy Ray said. "That's tough, man, but what has that got to do with this case?"

Holloway snatched the water bottle off the desk and took a long drink as if he were a man dying of thirst. When he wiped his mouth with the sleeve of his shirt, Raven knew that he was truly about to lose it.

"It has everything to do with this case!" he said. "Everything. Because she's about to do it again. She is about to get away with murder." He pointed at Raven, and for one crazy moment she remembered her father's bloody hand raised toward her after he had killed her stepmother. "You and your boyfriend bringing in Jabo Kersey when you both know he had nothing to do with Hazel's death."

"And you're saying that I did?" Raven asked.

"Yes, I am!" he said. "I know it, but I just can't prove it. It has something to do with your father, doesn't it?"

"Why would you say that?" Raven asked with so much righteous indignation in her voice that she thought this had to be the best performance since the last Oscar-winning movie.

But it was the chief who answered, his large hand resting on top of the now-closed manila folder. His voice was quiet when he spoke. "Because the morning right after Hazel was found, instead of working the case like you should have been, you were at a storage shed. What's in there, Raven?"

She looked at Holloway, knowing that he knew. He stood up. Without a word he slid the folder from beneath the chief's hand and opened it again. He pulled out one of the photographs and laid it on top of the desk. It was of the metal shelf with Floyd's clothes neatly folded and the new white fedora he never got to wear. She wondered where Holloway was when he took the picture. It was obvious that he had used a long range lens. How could she have been so distracted that she didn't see him? This case was making her careless. Holloway slid the photograph back toward the chief.

"If I killed Hazel," Raven asked in a reasonable voice while the chief studied the picture, "what reason would I have had to go through Floyd's things?"

A torrent of emotion poured over Holloway's face — despair, helplessness, and more anger than Raven had ever encountered in anyone aside from her father. He was having a hard time figuring it out. There was no reasonable explanation in the reach of his closed mind.

He said, "You must have found something at the murder scene to make you think of Floyd. Crimes said you and Chastain were at the secondary in the boathouse a long time before they came on scene."

"But I killed her, right, Holloway?" she continued levelly. "What could I have found in Hazel's bedroom that would have made me want to seek Floyd's effects?"

Of course, there were many things. She could have gone to celebrate with what was left of her father, perhaps to commune with his spirit. Maybe even hide the murder weapon there. But it was as if Holloway's imagination couldn't stretch that far.

But the chief's did. He asked, "Just what were you doing there, Detective?"

Raven looked at him and said nothing for a long time. She thought about lying, but in the end decided it wasn't worth it. At least not about that.

"It was stupid," she finally said apologetically. She looked at Billy Ray. "I just thought that this might be a serial killer starting up, the way the body was laid out and everything. The ritual."

They all waited. She gazed at them, finally letting her gaze rest on Holloway. He seemed both exhausted and wound down. She swallowed hard, and said, "You're right. I found something that reminded me of Floyd under Hazel's bed."

"You have got to be kidding me, Raven," Billy Ray said in a voice dangerous and low.

"I didn't tell you, Billy Ray," she said, "because I didn't want to confuse things if it turned out to be nothing."

"What did you find, Detective?" Lovelle asked.

"A peacock feather," she answered. "Peacock feathers are all Floyd. He loved those things. I went to the shed to see if there were any connections between those at the party and Floyd. I wanted to check his visitor logs and his old mail."

Billy Ray was shaking his head. He let out a small laugh. "I wish you would have told me," he said.

"I had to see for myself first," she said.

"Raven," Billy Ray explained. "You never went into the bathroom. You let me do that, remember? She had this vase thing on the counter filled with peacock feathers, like flowers. Didn't you see it in the crime scene photos? You got yourself all worked up over some stupid decoration." He shook his head again. "I could have saved you a lot of trouble. And time."

No, she hadn't noticed. She was not interested in what they found in the bathroom. She was too focused on the scene in the garden and Hazel's cluttered room.

She noticed the chief still staring at her. He said, "That's not all that's in here, Raven. There are phone records. And I'm guessing since it's your name on the file that those records are yours." Raven's heart began hammering in her chest as he continued in a measured voice, "You want to tell me what I'll find when I look at them?"

Trying not to look at Billy Ray, she shrugged. Holloway jumped in. "I'll tell you what's in there, a phone call between you and Hazel a little over a week before she died."

Raven arranged her features into a mask of mild annoyance. "You get your hands on my bank records too, Holloway?" she said. "My credit cards? You know how often I buy meat and deodorant? What kind of mouthwash I use?"

"Don't try to deflect," Holloway all but snarled, but sat back at the chief's warning glance.

"Explain yourself, Detective," the chief said.

Thinking fast while trying to look unperturbed, Raven said, "I don't know what he's talking about, Chief," she said. "I hadn't talked to Hazel Westcott for months before she died."

"Liar," Holloway said. "The call lasted six and a half minutes at five in the morning."

"Five in the morning?" Raven repeated. "I run in the mornings at that time. If she called me, there's a chance that I didn't even hear the phone ring."

Holloway started to say something, but the chief stopped him and said, "You didn't hear the phone ringing through your headphones?"

"Chief," she said, "I don't listen to music when I run. It messes with my concentration and my rhythm. If she did call me, there's a chance I accidentally answered it with all the bumping around."

"What, you're not human?" Holloway said derisively. "You don't wonder where your missed calls come from like the rest of us? Unbelievable."

She looked at him, pity on her face. "Look, Holloway," she said. "I'm so tired after a run that sometimes I don't think right. I may have punched some buttons and dismissed the call notifications. I'm telling you that I don't remember any call from Hazel, or talking to her for that matter."

It surprised her how easily she was able to lie. She hadn't known that about herself. It both surprised and scared her.

"You have an answer for everything," he said, his voice high with frustration. "But that call lasted six minutes!"

"She wasn't talking to me, Holloway," Raven said. "I told you that I could have answered it accidentally."

"Then why didn't she hang up!"

"You want me to tell you why that girl did anything?"

"You're a liar!"

"Holloway," the chief said. "Shut up."

The chief's eyes pierced her own for several seconds. She had seen the look before. It was the same one he used during the aftermath of the Trueblood shooting, one that said he would protect his detectives, especially her, at all costs.

"If you think this is not going to come out, you're crazy," the chief said. "And when the press gets ahold of it, they are going to crucify you." He pointed to his chest. "And me, and the department. All of us. I'm having a hard enough time keeping the mayor and that reporter, Imogene Tucker, away from this clusterfuck."

He let the silence play for longer than comfortable to let his last comment sink in. Raven didn't know if he believed her, but for now, he had chosen to leave it alone. She held her breath so she wouldn't sigh with the relief she felt coursing through her.

Finally, the chief said, "You and Billy Ray go pick Jabo Kersey up before this thing gets ugly, not to mention public, for all of us. That includes you too, Holloway. You leak this thing and you'd be in the shit with us. You are part of this team. And I'll fire your ass." He turned to Raven. "No more fooling around. It's starting to get out of hand, and I don't like the effect it's having on the department. Pick him up tonight."

CHAPTER TWENTY-EIGHT

It was growing dark as Raven and Billy Ray drove away from the BLPD to pick up Jabo Kersey. Streaks of red rimmed in gold overcame the daylight, and soon dusk gave way to full darkness. The only thing Billy Ray could manage from the motor pool was an old Crown Victoria with a broken air conditioner. Billy Ray hadn't chastised her about the peacock feather or visiting the storage shed or lying to him. Instead, he just said quietly once they were inside the car with the doors closed, "Your daddy's dead and there is no reason for you to always be thinking about him like you do. Only when you believe that will you be ready to let him go, Raven. And let all the lying and deceit go too. I thought you thought more about me than to look in my face and lie."

She glanced over at him and tried to apologize, but he waved the words off. She could see by the set of his face that he wasn't having any of it. But Billy Ray had his own reasons for not wanting things to get too complicated. His twin sister had called earlier and said she had been having contractions. "Time to get rambling, Raven," he had told her. He was supposed to leave within the next couple of days, and had already purchased his ticket. It would be good if he could leave with the case wrapped up.

Raven rolled down the window as Billy Ray steered the Crown onto Main in the direction of Jabo Kersey's last known address. The smell of both heat and rain hanging in the humid air drifted into the car window. She thought about Kersey and what he would say about Hazel's attempt to blackmail her once he was arrested. The threat left at her door when she got back from her Scorpion Tail's run proved that he knew about it.

Even without all of that, there would still be questions. Those good citizens the chief would convince that he had found his killer during his morning press conference would take one look at the accused and wonder aloud. They would ask how could a man like Kersey, a drug addict, have both the imagination and will to murder Hazel Westcott in the way that he was accused of doing? *Who cares?* Floyd answered for her. *Just let it all be. By tomorrow afternoon, we will be as right as an army of ants at a picnic. Besides, I think you be giving the good citizens of Byrd's Landing too much credit.*

Maybe. But what about the jury? A smart jury would ask questions. They would ask what motive Kersey could have for killing a woman he was only married to for such a short time. *She was his wife, wasn't she?* Floyd spoke up again in her head. *What other motive does a man need?* Raven was convinced that bringing Kersey in wasn't safe for her.

Kersey lived in a small one-story house made of faded red brick. Among the sparse blades of grass, dandelions, some still with yellow petals and others gone to seed, moved in the warm wind. A group of three pine trees spiraled into the black Louisiana sky. Cicadas made discordant music in the quiet neighborhood as Billy Ray and Raven approached the front door.

"It looks like we're in luck," Billy Ray said. "He's home."

Yellow light blazed from the two front windows while faint jazz played just beyond the arched entrance. This would be easier than she thought. But she was also thinking how in her previous job this would have been a carefully orchestrated pickup. It would have happened at three in the morning when the suspect would have been most likely to be at home. Depending on how dangerous the situation was, they probably would have had SWAT involved. There definitely would've been uniformed backup.

But the chief dismissed that idea. Pick him up now, he said. And as far as having backup, this was Jabo Kersey, a probable drug addict and a loser. The pickup should be a cakewalk. When Raven reminded him that Kersey was also responsible for a murder and that a cakewalk was an intricate and competitive dance, the chief waved her away. Luck. She and Billy Ray could handle a man who had only gotten lucky one time in his life with the almost-perfect murder of his wife.

A woman with smooth brown skin answered the door. Her hair was dyed a reddish-blond and twisted into dreadlocks that hung all around her face like tiny bells. She wore a blue halter top that exposed her midriff and a pair of spandex-infused blue jeans that stretched around her wide hips and heavy thighs. Though she dressed like a young woman, Raven could see by the few lines around her eyes that she had to be at least in her mid-forties. She held a spatula in one hand and stared at them as the smell of catfish frying slipped out onto the porch.

"Well, don't that beat all," she said as she crossed her arms over her ample chest. "We got a black mayor, a black police chief, and now we finally got what matters, black cops. You know it only starts counting when they let you carry guns away from the office. Ain't it funny you can tell a cop's a cop just by the look of 'em? Even black ones?" She cocked her head at Raven. "Except maybe you, sweetheart. What are you with them funny-looking eyes? Albino?"

"Do I look like an albino?" Raven asked as she flashed her badge. "I'm Detective Burns and that's Detective Chastain."

The woman shrugged and shifted on her feet, the toe nails appearing a bright blue under the splash of the porch light. "What did the bastard do now?"

Billy Ray grinned. He didn't bother to take his badge out of his pocket. "Is the bastard at home?"

"Uh-uh," she said, holding the spatula up in the air to make a point. "I don't know what you think you know, but this ain't his house. This ain't his *home*."

Raven was amazed at the gall of a man who would put the address of his girlfriend on a marriage certificate application between himself and another woman.

"And your name?" Raven asked.

"Nunya, that's my name," she said. "That means 'none of your business' if you need a translation."

"Do you know where we can find him, Ms. Nunya?" Raven asked with a straight face.

The woman stared at Raven for a few moments. "What he do?" she asked again.

Billy Ray smiled his best handsome Billy Ray smile. "Do you mind stepping outside, miss, so we can talk about it some more?"

The woman laughed then, a nasty laugh with little humor in it. "Y'all think I'm stupid?" she asked. "Just 'cause I'm black and live in Louisiana? My brother made that mistake once with a couple of cops, stepping out on the porch after they asked him to. Do you know what they did?"

Billy Ray said nothing, so she continued on. "They 'rested him right on his front porch, in front of God, his neighbors, in front of everybody."

"What did he do?" Raven asked.

She shrugged. "I don't know. The usual. Littering. Living," She stopped for a moment and then she and Billy Ray said in unison, "Being his ole black self."

The woman looked at Billy Ray, surprised. He was still smiling, his eyes as friendly as a dog's. Her entire body relaxed. She laughed and said, "Y'all come on in here before my fish burns. Name is Fonda."

They followed her into a bright kitchen where catfish was bubbling in a large cast-iron skillet filled to the rim with hot grease. She motioned to two bar stools at the island and Raven and Billy Ray sat down.

"Expecting company?" Billy Ray pointed at a plate of fish drying on paper towels next to the stove.

She shook her head. "I own the Snack Shack down on Central. We ran outta fish and the stove over there broke. That's the only reason you caught me at home. Y'all want some?"

"We're not supposed—" Raven started, thinking about the rules with a picture of Holloway flashing in her mind.

"Are you kidding me?" Billy Ray asked. "Fried catfish from the Snack Shack? Right out of the skillet and cooked by the owner herself? Bring it on over."

Fonda did, along with two tall glasses of sweet tea and sweet potato fries. Billy Ray fell on the food as if he hadn't eaten in ages. Raven began more slowly as Fonda busied herself wrapping catfish in brown paper. The smell in the kitchen felt overpoweringly like home. It reminded her of the fish fries she and Jean Rinehart used to attend before Floyd beat her to death with one red high-heel shoe.

Fonda was talking as she worked. "He would usually be here," she admitted. "Drunk or drugged up, slobbering across my couch like a big sick dog. Those are some of his favorite things to do. Drink, sleep, and drool."

"What are his other favorite things?" Raven asked.

"It's just one. And that would be gambling, honey, losing what money his daddy left 'im and trying to get his hands on mine."

"How long you been seeing him?" Billy Ray asked, around a mouthful of sweet potato fries.

She stopped what she was doing and then stared at him a long time with one hand on her hips. Then a light suddenly went on in her eyes and she laughed. "Been seeing him? Why, since the day the little fucker was born. He my uncle. What you thinking, man?"

"Oh right," Billy Ray said shoving two more sweet potato fries into his mouth. "What was I thinking? He's younger than you, lists your address as his. I should have realized he wasn't your boyfriend but your uncle. What's wrong with me?"

Fonda sighed. "Okay, yeah," she said. "I know it sounds weird. But it's like this. After my grandmother got through raising one set of kids, she got to wishing for another set. She got married again – at least this time the mother trucker had money – and had fo' mo' kids. Jabo is one of them. Even though he five years younger than I am, he still my uncle."

"You and Jabo close?" Raven asked.

"Hell no," Fonda said. "Just family. If he wasn't kin to me I wouldn't give him the time of day. But he blood."

"Did you know about Hazel Westcott?" Raven continued.

Fonda pursed her lips and nodded. "Um-hmm. I knew about her. He used to bring her here. I never could fix in my mind what she wanted with a man like Jabo, but he has that way about him. Doesn't have the looks like that one sitting there stuffing his face, but he has the charm and a smooth way of talking girls right outta they panties. He went out with a lot of young girls."

"Do you know where he is now?" Billy Ray said, wiping his hands on a napkin.

Fonda didn't say anything for a while. She scooped the remaining fish up out of the bubbling grease with a mesh spatula. She let the oil drip back into the frying pan for several seconds before placing the fish on brown paper. She turned toward them, rubbed her hands on a dish towel, and leveled a gaze on both of them.

"What he do?" she asked again.

"Fonda," Billy Ray said. "We just need to find him."

She crossed her arms again. "You ain't gone hurt 'im, are you?" she asked. "He may be an asshole, but he still my kin."

"If we don't pick him up he may get hurt," Raven heard herself saying.

She felt Billy Ray looking at her. She didn't know why she said that, but as the words left her mouth it was a thing that she truly believed. If Holloway wanted her to go down for the murder, getting Jabo Kersey in custody would be as much for his own safety as any desire of the chief. And this would be especially true, as Raven was coming to believe, if Holloway had anything to do with Hazel's death.

Fonda's face changed and she nodded gravely as she made up her mind. "Gambling in a building made of gold. That's what he calls it, anyway. A building made of gold as if he could just walk right up and break off a piece and put it in his pocket like Hansel and Gretel. That's what growing up rich will do for you. Make you behave like you livin' in a fucking fairy tale. Excuse my French," she said. "I hate cussing, especially that word, but when it comes to Jabo I can't help it."

"Don't worry about it," Billy Ray said.

"But I've been on this earth long enough to know ain't nobody gone give you nuthin' just from rolling the dice or gettin' the cards right. Where do he think they get all that money to make a building out of gold, anyway? From his stupid ass and from stupid asses like him."

"Is that where he is tonight?" Billy Ray asked.

"When he ain't here, he's there. When he ain't there, he's here. Don't take much to satisfy him, honey," she said.

Brown paper crumpled in the room as she began wrapping up the remaining fish. "Let me finish wrappin' this up and I'll see y'all to the front door," she said, not looking at them.

Raven noticed a heavy sadness had crept into her voice. She stood in the open doorway as she had met them and watched them leave, still holding the mesh spatula with a smell of cooked fish in the air. Raven could feel Fonda's eyes on her as she walked away. She wasn't surprised when she called out, "Detective Burns."

When Raven looked over her shoulder, Fonda said, "If you find him, don't hurt him. You may not know it now, but he used to be a good man, Jabo did. He could play the piano like a dream and had a voice like an angel from heaven. You wouldn't know it by looking at him, but he was a damn fine nurse too. Drink got him, drugs. Then gambling. Everything bad that man see, he like. That's all." Then she said, "Just don't hurt him."

They looked at each other for a long time. Then finally Raven said in a voice as serious as a grave, "I won't. I won't hurt him." And she meant it too. At that moment, she meant it with everything in her that wasn't Floyd 'Fire' Burns.

CHAPTER TWENTY-NINE

Clarence Beauchamp, the head of security at the Four Leaf Casino, met them in the employee parking lot just outside the casino's security offices. Beauchamp, in a navy blue double-breasted suit with large gold buttons and a blue tie, was not a fat man but he was a large one. Raven's hand almost disappeared in his when he held out his meaty palm for a handshake.

The building he guarded did indeed look as if it were made of gold. The twenty-six-story Four Leaf Casino was on the north side of the Texas Street Bridge. The architects had treated the entire façade with gold film and during the day it was the brightest and richest-looking building on the Byrd's Landing skyline. During the night it loomed against the dark, greedily drinking in light from the surrounding buildings so that the Four Leaf appeared to be made of a thousand glittering gold stars. There was a wall inside the casino with a million real American dollars behind Plexiglas. Behind the casino on the wide expanse of the Red River was a party boat full of happy, nearly broke patrons gambling away the little money they had remaining.

Beauchamp turned to Raven. "You have to do this here, Detective?" he asked. "Why can't you wait until he goes home?"

"That's just it, Mr. Beauchamp," Raven said. "He's pissed off his niece and has no more home to go to. The chief wants him on lockdown tonight."

Beauchamp sighed. "I guess there's no way around it. Follow me."

They followed him into a large room that held two walls of monitors with high-definition video of various areas of the casino. The four security guards watching the monitors did not look up when they walked in. Their work surfaces did not hold anything that looked like it shouldn't belong, not a coffee cup, a picture of a loved one, not even a speck of dust.

"Mr. Kersey is a whale," Beauchamp was explaining to Raven and

Billy Ray. "Plays a lot, bets a lot and lucky for us, he loses a lot. We try to keep track of what he's doing. Juney," he said to one of the guards, "bring up the Red Room."

A room with a red patterned carpet and red velvet furniture appeared on one of the monitors. Jabo Kersey, in a hopelessly faded green Hawaiian shirt, sat at a blackjack table all by his lonesome, stacks of poker chips in front of him. Several people stood around his chair watching the contest between Kersey and the dealer.

"Move in closer, Juney," Beauchamp said.

The camera focused on Kersey's face. He was just as Angel, Hazel's sister, described him, exceptionally dark and thick around the middle. He looked troubled, but not the sort of troubled of a man who just killed his ex-wife. He seemed more concerned that more chips were in the middle of the table than were in front of him.

"Is that the man you're looking for?" Beauchamp asked.

"Clarence, my man," Billy Ray said grimly. "You have made my night."

"I will take that as a yes."

"How you want to do this?" Billy Ray asked Raven.

She started to answer, but then Kersey began fumbling with his pants pocket and soon had a cell phone pressed against his ear. As he listened, he looked up and all around him, his eyes skittering over the red room as if in search of someone who was about to hurt him.

"What the hell...." Bill Ray whispered. "Could someone be tipping him off?"

Kersey stuffed the phone back in his pocket and stood up so fast he almost fell from his chair.

"Looks like it," Raven said. "Let's go get him."

Beauchamp motioned for them to wait. He picked up a black phone that was so clean Raven could see lights reflecting from its lacquered surface. In less than a minute, four men in navy blue double-breasted blazers and tan slacks made their way to Kersey, pushing people out of the way as they did so. Kersey kicked out and flailed. But the guards knocked down his arms. They grabbed him by the elbows until he was securely clamped between them. The four men escorted him out of the room while the other gamblers looked at them wide-eyed.

"I told them to bring him around to us here," Beauchamp said.

Raven and Billy Ray followed Beauchamp to the parking lot. After a few minutes, the door to the parking lot opened and the men emerged with Jabo Kersey, holding onto his elbows. Walking right in front of Jabo was another large man wearing a pair of Oakley sunglasses. The one with the sunglasses was bald except for a long ponytail that hung over his thick left shoulder in shiny lines of blond. Though the men were dressed like Beauchamp, Raven was sure that beneath their white shirts were bodies covered with jailhouse tattoos.

When the big man with the ponytail stepped aside, Raven could see Kersey's eyes moving frantically between the men who were holding him. He rocked his shoulders from side to side trying to twist away from them, his lips pulled back from his teeth like an animal's.

The terror redoubled on his face when he saw Raven. In what only could be a burst of adrenalin, he elbowed the men holding him hard. One of them was prepared for it, the other one wasn't. Kersey was able to wrench away from them. He took off running like his shoes were on fire.

Raven heard Billy Ray say, "Shit, shit, shit." Before she could register what was happening, the man with the ponytail had a Glock 9 millimeter pistol in his hand and was firing warning shots into the air. The shots only made Kersey run faster, his arms pumping to propel his body forward, his feet kicking behind him at turbo speed.

"Hey, hey, hey!" Raven shouted at the guard. "Put that damn thing down. Beauchamp!"

Beauchamp yelled something at the man in the ponytail but she couldn't tell what it was. Billy Ray motioned that he would cut Kersey off in case he circled around to the back. She took off behind Kersey as if she herself were being chased.

Jabo Kersey didn't look like someone in the greatest shape but the man could run. Raven followed him, barely keeping up as he sprinted through the open parking lot. But he had nowhere to go but a chain-link fence that divided the lot from the property surrounding the casino. On the other side of the fence was a short embankment of white rock appearing to glow in what was otherwise a dark night. Beyond the rock there was a band of mud, and beyond that, a wide expanse of water, brown and murky, and as thick as table syrup. A haze of blues music drifted toward them from the party boat on the water. To the east of them was a short hill leading to an abandoned railway trestle. Raven shortened her steps, allowing herself to slow. The fence had to be at least eight feet high. Kersey had nowhere to go. He was trapped. She took the Glock 19 out of its holster.

But Kersey didn't stop. He began scaling the chain-link with long crab-like movements. Raven came to a full stop, her Glock dangling from her hand. The fence rattled in the darkness with the weight of Kersey against it.

"Oh, come on," Raven shouted. "You have got to be kidding me."

But he wasn't kidding her. Up the fence he went, faster and faster like Jack climbing his beanstalk.

She stood there for a moment or two before Floyd tuned into her head again. *Slash it all to pieces*, he said, *Pick up that rag-a-muffin in the morning. He ain't going far.* For once, she felt that the ghost of Floyd was right. Kersey had nowhere to go except the banks of the Red. He couldn't escape onto the steamboat. From where they were the only entry was from the catwalk to the passenger deck above their heads.

If he were brave enough, he could run east toward the trestle. Perhaps he could escape by running beneath the trestle and into the woods. He might be able to hide in the semi-wilderness near the river. But from what Raven had learned about him from Memorial and Fonda, he didn't strike her as the bravest or most persistent man in the world. If fear of alligators or diamondbacks didn't drive him out, hunger would. They could certainly pick him up later.

But there was no later. The chief wanted Kersey tonight. And he was the man who helped deliver her from the stench of her father's reputation, and that was *after* he actually saved her life. She owed him and needed to give him what he wanted. She gave the sky a look of exasperation. The clouds had broken down some. Tendrils of what remained scudded past the moon, a yellow fingernail hanging above her. She took a deep breath. She threw the Glock back in its holster but didn't bother to fasten it. She flung her body against the fence.

Kersey had reached the top. He sat on the narrow ledge for a few seconds. His hands gripped the railing on either side of him, the back of his white Keds resting in the openings of the chain-link. His back was rigid with fear as he stared down at the sharp white rock along the bottom of the fence. The riverboat festooned with lights and Fourth of July banners sat far out on the surface of the wide Red River.

When she was almost within touching distance he twisted his body around and began lowering himself to the ground. At first his movements were slow and careful, but no sooner had he gotten started than he lost his grip. He tumbled the last five feet and sprang up running the moment he hit the ground.

Raven whipped her body around the minute she hit the top of the fence. She didn't have to see Kersey to know that he was running along the bank away from the casino and the riverboat.

And he was doing exactly what she thought he might do. He was running toward the trestle.

Before she knew it her own feet were on top of the white rock and she was crunching after him, trying to keep her balance on the uneven surface. Kersey's head was fully visible, then disappeared as he skidded down the embankment. Forgetting to be careful, Raven ran heedlessly after him. Soon she too was falling. She skidded along the rocks, her hands bloodied and stinging as she tried to stop her descent.

When she was back on her feet she could see Kersey limping along the embankment and clutching his left shoulder as his feet flirted with the thick water of the river. Ignoring the stinging scrapes on her own body, she stumbled after him. Kersey kept throwing looks over his shoulder. It slowed him down. As she got closer she could hear him sobbing. His entire body was shaking with them.

"Stop," she shouted. "Just stop."

He threw her one last look before one foot slipped down the bank. She was close enough to touch him now. She grabbed the sleeve of his shirt in an effort to bring him down but he jerked away, knocking her off balance. They both rolled along the mud and into the cool water. They stood facing each other with the water moving languidly around their thighs as if it were waiting for something and could wait all night and into the next day.

Kersey was shouting for her to leave him alone, to get away. He went to shout something else, still moving backward into the water as far away as he could get, when he just disappeared. It was like a magic show. One minute he was there shouting at her, pleading with her, and the next he was gone.

Cries of revelry came from the riverboat along with another burst of music. Brown water foamed and churned as the paddles rotated, but she heard no more from Jabo Kersey.

Without thought she lunged toward the drop-off.

The heavy water closed over her head. It tugged at her, making her clothes feel as if they were made of lead, her shoes dead weights. She opened her eyes and was greeted with a dark so black and foul that for a minute she thought that she had dropped into the throat of hell. A thousand Floyd Burns were inside her head, their tongues wormlike and slithering with words of murder and terror.

In a panic she swam to the surface. She gave herself a second or two to tell her brain that the water was dark beneath because of the darkness above, and the sounds she heard were not whispers but the muffled sounds from the band on the steamboat.

Soon she saw Kersey's hand beating at the water, then the top of his head and then his mouth begging for help before the water took him again. She marked the spot where he had been. Taking a deep breath, she ducked beneath. She waved her hands in the water thinking how hopeless it was. She was never going to find him, especially since she couldn't see anything. But she forced herself to stay down a bit longer.

When she thought her chest would explode, with one final prayer she reached out again. Her hand clutched the fabric of Kersey's shirt. For a moment she was all frantic movement, swimming around him and maneuvering his weight to get him into a rescue hold. Then she heard the whispering again. The whispers in her head were more distinct now. *Hold him,* Floyd said. *Hold him in the water, Birdy Girl. He'll cause too much trouble if you let him up. This jackass wrote that note. He'll tell 'em about you and Hazel, and they'll try to come after you for the killin'. You need to take 'im out.*

She paddled slightly away from Jabo Kersey before lunging suddenly upward. As if something else commanded her body, she stood both hands on his shoulders and held him down. He kicked frantically but she didn't relax her grip. The whispers in her head became a roar. *That's right, that's right, Birdy Girl. Hold 'im! Hold 'im!*

So she held him, she held him and held him until she thought her arms would break. But then another voice broke through the shrill words filling her head. The voice sounded like music, and with it came the smell of pancakes and a double dose of maple syrup. *My, my,* Jean Rinehart said. *You sure do like milk. How many glasses does that make?* And then that other voice, sad and final from his niece Fonda. *Don't hurt him.*

She let go. She swam around Jabo Kersey and maneuvered Kersey's weight until she was able to loop her forearm beneath his chest. They both surfaced at the same time. She gulped the Louisiana air as if she hadn't tasted it in a year. It took all of her strength to drag them both out of a river that seemed to want nothing more than to pull them back in.

When she reached the bank Kersey was not breathing. His face was still and cold. She twisted his head to one side and pressed on his chest to expel water from his lungs. How long had he been underwater? One minute? Two? And how much longer had she held him there? Her rational mind told her that it was only seconds, but another part of her wondered if it were longer. It felt like a thousand years.

When his airway was clear she covered his mouth with her own. The sweet taste of alcohol along with the river appeared to be not only running over him but through him. She pushed away her disgust. She alternately breathed into his mouth and pumped his chest for a long time. It was no use. He was as still as stone. Once again she had let Floyd kill.

But that wasn't quite right, was it? She had killed him. Floyd was dead. It was like in the Eudora Welty short story she had read a long time ago. But instead of both heroine and victim, she had become victim, heroine, and now villain. She was all three in the same body. She sat back on her heels and felt a wail come up from deep in her belly. But before she let it take her, she decided to try once more. Her soul depended upon him waking up. She breathed into his mouth and beat at his chest again and again until the side of her fist ached. When she was about to give up for a final time, he sputtered and vomited. He hunched his body against the mud like an earthworm.

She could see that he remembered immediately where he was and what had happened. He groaned and protested as he rotated his body from side to side, swinging his arms and demanding that she get away from him. Before she could stop him, he stood up and started backing toward the river that they had just come from.

She was sputtering herself, covered in mud from head to toe. She was both exhausted and disgusted and just wanted to go home and forget about the moments she spent in the water allowing Floyd to overtake her.

"Kersey," she said. "Get your ass on the ground now." She reached for her weapon. It was gone. She must have lost it as she fell down the embankment.

"Get away from me," he said. "You tried to kill me."

She reached into the holster at the small of her back where she always kept the Smith & Wesson, her second weapon. That one was gone as well, a likely victim to the Red River. She flopped down on the ground and said to the diseased moon. "I'm not trying to kill you. I saved you, remember? I'm here to take you in." Even to her own ears, her voice sounded flat, a monotone.

He stopped for a moment and tried to focus. He was looking at her quizzically. "You held me down," he said. "You tried to kill me. I felt you holding me down."

"Fuck," she breathed, surprising herself.

She avoided cursing as much as she could, but some situations just demanded a good, solid *Fuck*. That made Raven think of Ms. Nunya Fonda and her French, and she laughed. She laughed until she coughed. River water ran out of her mouth and over her mud-streaked chin. She spat. She reached for her handcuffs and stood up. Thank God the cuffs were still there. Reaching for them hurt like hell and all she wanted to do was sit back down again. Placing her palms against her knees, she bent over at the waist to catch her breath. She only had enough energy to motion for him to turn around.

He shook his head. "You came here to kill me," he said. "He said you'd try to kill me."

"Jabo," she said and took a step toward him. "I don't know who you've been talking to, but I'm here to take you in for the murder of Hazel Westcott. Your wife. You killed your wife. I have a warrant for your arrest."

He continued as if she hadn't spoken. "But I'm telling you just like

I tole him. I bought that dress because I thought if we had a proper wedding wearing proper clothes it would last longer, be realer...."

"Jabo," she said, more intrigued now, "who are you talking about? Who have you been talking to?"

"You know who," he said. "The special investigator. I know him. I got connections. He's gone help me."

"Holloway," she spat at him before she could stop herself. "You and Holloway trying to set me up."

Shaking his head, he walked backward until he was up to his calves in water. A few more steps and he would reach the drop-off again. Raven didn't know if she would have the strength to save him a second time. She looked at him for a long moment. She listened to the sounds coming from the steamboat, a place from a fairy tale, all strung and surrounded by the lights that appeared to embrace both her and Kersey. But he wasn't looking toward the boat, the lights, or at her. He was looking at the trestle, now only a few feet away from them.

She followed his gaze. She studied the trestle, the darkened aperture beneath that led to the woods. What possible reason could Kersey have to run toward it? The answer brought the metallic taste of fear to her mouth. She knew now, the way Kersey stared at the trestle, how he had run straight toward it. The phone call that he had received at the casino was not a warning that they were coming.

"You meeting someone here, Kersey?" she asked. "Is that it? Are they helping you to escape?"

"Yeah," he said. "Helping me to escape you. Come out," he said, "Come out now. She tried to kill—"

Before Kersey could finish, the top of his head peeled off. He was talking to her one minute and the next his scalp just lifted and his face dissolved into a crushed red pulp. He stood there for a moment, his body refusing to realize what his brain had already accepted. Jabo Kersey, the man whose favorite things in the world were to drink, sleep, drool, and gamble, that man was gone.

Another shot rang out. Kersey fell backward into the water with his hands outstretched in a dead man's sprawl. A dark cloud bloomed in the water and the Red River dragged Kersey's body backward until he sank straight down.

Raven flipped onto her belly as the sick feeling of fear like she'd never felt before overtook her. She had only the knife strapped to her ankle, but a lot of good it would do her against a shooter. She crawled on her elbows toward the river. It was her only cover.

She scrambled on her belly toward where Kersey had fallen. He was dead, all right. The river hadn't entirely swallowed him. His body lay only a few inches from the drop-off. As she stared at the part of his head not quite covered by the water, she confirmed that no amount of breath would bring him back.

From the trestle, she saw sparks of neon green and blue flicker in the night. Soon, illuminated by the lights from the riverboat, she realized that she was looking at feathers, thousands of them, fluttering down from the trestle. She was so mesmerized by this seeming greeting from her father that she barely registered the sound of running feet crunching above her on the white rock. She simply watched from her knees as the feathers floated down, seesawing lazily on a night breeze as if they had all the time in the world to get their message across. Peacock feathers littering the muddy banks of the Red River.

CHAPTER THIRTY

Raven didn't go home. She didn't want to be alone. She found herself at Billy Ray's double-barrel shotgun wearing a change of clothes she had hastily gathered at her apartment. Billy Ray insisted she lie down on the couch. She had gotten the worst of it, he said. She immediately contradicted him. Jabo Kersey had gotten the worst of it.

All Raven could hear was Fonda's voice in her head saying *Don't hurt him* and her own solemn promise that she wouldn't. At least she was clean, newly dressed in a white T-shirt and a pair of Levi's. But Raven didn't think she would ever get the taste of river mud and stale alcohol out of her mouth, or the sounds of Floyd's voice out of her head. *Hold 'im!* came his high-pitched squeal, and beneath that Fonda's voice absent of all attitude but rimmed in sadness, *Don't hurt him*. Raven didn't think she would ever see the steamboat the same way again or listen to bayou blues without thinking about the night she almost became her father.

Another storm was gathering in Raven's career. Kersey had been killed with her weapon, the Beretta 92 that she had kept in a locked drawer at the station, the same weapon used in the Trueblood killing. The only witnesses were the passengers on the boat who were so busy gambling away their life savings that they had no desire to look beyond its light-festooned balconies.

Billy Ray said that he found the Beretta lying by the white rock. Those crunching steps she heard as she watched the rain of peacock feathers must have been the killer planting it there. She knew that her office drawer, the previous home of the Beretta, would be empty. The weapon belonged to Ballistics now, but she didn't need their report to tell her that it had recently been fired.

Raven's other weapon, the Glock 19, was nowhere to be found. She assumed that the river had claimed it. And since it was missing, no one would believe that she wasn't carrying the Beretta when she went after Jabo. Who would carry an empty holster to a pickup?

She wasn't exactly suspended. Last night at the Kersey scene, the chief just ordered that she go home after the paramedics checked her out. Holloway was also there, his nose turned up at a fastidious angle as they pulled Kersey's body from the tug of the river.

The bile that rose in her throat at the sight of him almost made her reckless. Floyd's warning whisper in her head stopped her. *Not yet, Birdy Girl,* it said. *We'll get Holloway, but now ain't the time.* And she agreed that it wasn't. She was covered with mud from head to toe, shirt torn and hair full of the stink from the river. Worse, she was surrounded by the trappings of her father. Holloway, on the other hand, had regained the self-control he had lost in the chief's office earlier. He was talking furiously with the chief while plucking nervously at the cap of his water bottle. Raven watched the both of them leave together.

In the intervening hours since Kersey's death and his new knowledge of the peacock feathers, Billy Ray had gathered the murder files connected with Floyd 'Fire' Burns. The peacock feather beneath Hazel's bed might have been a coincidence. But the multitude of peacock feathers at the Kersey scene was another thing. He had swept his collection of owls and magazines from the coffee table, and now the contents from the files covered it from one end to the other in a tablecloth of horrors.

"I still don't know why he just didn't shoot you," Billy Ray said as he stared at the guest list and witness statements from the Westcott party in his dark hands.

"He didn't shoot me," Raven said as she stood up and started pacing as much as she could in the cluttered living room, "because he is as crazy as my father. He's playing with me, Billy Ray, like poking a dying rat with a stick."

"Who? Raven, who?" he challenged as he swapped the witness statements he had been holding with the crime scene photo from the death of Raven's mother – Maylene. Raven kept her face turned away from him so she wouldn't accidentally catch a glimpse of how her mother was found, so she wouldn't have to connect the photos to her father, Floyd Burns, and ultimately to herself.

"What do you mean who?" she railed. "Holloway! The freaking jerk tipped Kersey off and waited for him at the trestle."

"Stop it," Billy Ray said.

"And then when he had his chance, he shot him and framed me for it. That was his goal all along. He's evil."

"Where's your proof?" he asked.

She sat back down on his plaid secondhand couch and stared back up at the ceiling fan whirring above them.

"His connection to Jabo, for one," Raven said. "Have you already forgotten what Dr. Long at Memorial said? Jabo worked in the emergency room where Holloway's mother has been taken on more than one occasion. Hell, that Ewing waste of human flesh, Jabo's drug buddy, said how Jabo kept bragging about his connection to brass at the police department. He even sat with Holloway's mother. Holloway was Jabo's connection."

"You and I know that a lot of people went and sat with Holloway's mother. That doesn't mean anything, Raven. You want to bring in most of the department because of that? You want to question Lamont for sitting with Holloway's mother? The chief for helping that man out?"

"Jabo said on his dying breath that he had been talking to someone in the department who told him to stay away from me," she reminded him.

"Yeah, you said that," Billy Ray agreed. "But he could have been talking about anybody. Even if it was Holloway who tipped him off, that doesn't mean he's the one who killed him."

God, she thought. How would she ever be able to convince him that Holloway was after her? She could tell him about the book she found in Holloway's office, but she would also have to tell him about her reason for being there – the threatening note she found after her run and the subsequent conversation with Lovelle. Then she remembered what he said in the car on the way to pick up Kersey. *How could you look me in the face, Raven, and lie to me?* She didn't have strength to admit to another lie.

Instead, she said, "Come on, Billy Ray."

"You're saying 'Come on, Billy Ray' because you've got nothing on Holloway except for the fact that you two didn't get along. There's more proof against you than that piss pot."

"Like what?" she said, and at his look of incredulity, she pushed ahead. "There's nothing really against me except that Hazel hated my guts. And if you're implying that I shot Kersey, you saw same as I did Jabo get that phone call. Someone warned him while I was with you. My father may have been a serial killer but that doesn't mean I have magical powers. I can't be in two places at once."

"So, let's talk about what you're conveniently forgetting," he said. "The fact that Hazel might've been blackmailing you, the phone call? You have no alibi for the night she was killed and you have been going to the gym like you have some sort of disease? Or maybe a purpose? Getting in shape for something? Maybe to carry a dead body around?" Billy Ray stopped in the ensuing silence, and then broke it by saying, "And don't get me started on Jabo."

Raven whipped to a sitting position. She ignored the shooting pains in her arms and legs.

"Billy Ray," she said again, this time with the memory of her hands pressing down on Kersey's shoulders stark in her mind. *Hold 'im,* Floyd cried. *Don't hurt him,* Fonda countered. "That would be like me saying that you had something to do with Jabo's death."

"What's that supposed to mean?" he snorted. "Now you're talking crazy."

"Am I?" she said. "All I know is that when I went after Kersey, you were nowhere in sight."

Billy Ray didn't say anything for several seconds. He just stared at her with one of the many inscrutable looks he had been in the habit of wearing lately. It was as if the more she lied to him, the harder he was to read, the further away he drifted. Then he said softly, "I told you that I was going to see if I could cut him off around back."

"Sure," Raven said. "Cut him off around back and then conveniently show up to find my weapon – that probably is the murder weapon, mind you – on the rocks. You had access to my office, and you knew where I kept that Beretta."

"Come on, Raven," Billy Ray said. "You don't mean that."

"Of course I don't mean it," Raven said. "I'm just saying that what you're saying about me you could be saying about yourself too."

"Even though you're lashing out because you're hurting and confused right now, and I don't think you're serious, I'm going to answer your question. I thought I could cut him off but couldn't find another opening in the fence. And I wasn't as lucky as you and Jabo. They had some razor wire along the part I would have needed to climb over in order to get to you. By the time I doubled back, you and Jabo were gone."

"Let's just drop it," Raven said.

"I know I let you down."

Raven sighed. "You didn't let me down. Don't worry about it."

"Look," Billy Ray said. "Nobody is focused on me. But Holloway's got you on the brain. He's pushing hard. You heard him. And him finding out about the call from Hazel and springing it like he did isn't going to help you any—" He stopped when he caught the look on her face.

"It's Holloway behind this whole thing!" Raven said. "You saw him in the chief's office. He's a nut bar. And him stalking me? Spying on me? Following me and taking pictures with a zoom lens? What's that all about? He hates me more than the plague. He warned Jabo, stole my weapon, lured him to the trestle and shot him to set me up."

"How would he know that he could put that weapon in your hand?" Billy Ray challenged. "That you would lose the Glock and have to explain an empty holster?"

"I don't know," Raven said. "Maybe it was luck. But I bet his ultimate goal was to not allow Kersey to be taken in alive. Holloway hasn't finished playing games."

"Games? Games?" Billy Ray said. "You listening to yourself right now? Why do you think he's playing games?"

She said nothing, just picked at the piling on the plaid couch. Billy Ray looked at her. "Tight around the mouth and eyes," he said. "Remember what I told you? That's how I know when you're hiding something. Spit it out."

She took a deep breath, knowing that she had to tell him everything. She told him about the threatening note she found, the conversation with Lovelle, and the Michael Gorman book about her father in Holloway's office.

"He's obsessed with me," she finished. "I think Holloway believes that the sins of the father should be borne by the children. That's why he can't stand me. By his twisted logic, I'm threatening the very order of the planet."

She looked at him and found his gaze steady on her. There was hurt and disappointment in his eyes.

"When did you stop trusting me, Raven?" he said. He cursed under his breath and threw the papers he had been holding onto the coffee table. "You make me feel like two kinds of fool by keeping all this shit to yourself."

"I didn't want you involved, Billy Ray!" she shouted at him with a sob of frustration in her voice. "I thought I could handle it myself. And if I'm going to go down, I don't want to take you with me."

He sighed. "Look," he said. "You aren't going down, you aren't going nowhere." He reached up and squeezed her hand. "And I've been taking care of myself for a long time. But you have got to tell me everything. No more secrets." And when she didn't say anything, he said, "Okay? Every step of the way."

"All right," she breathed. "I still say—"

He shook his head and let go of her hand. "No," Billy Ray said. "We need to work on this together. Now let me tell you something that you don't know. Holloway's alibi for last night is solid. He went over to the chief's house to apologize for his behavior. And let's say he did call Jabo. He could say he thought you were unstable, and he was trying to prevent another tragedy. It's not him. And even if it is, you need more proof than just finding a book in his office."

"Then who, me?" she said.

"Look, homegirl," he sighed. "I'm not saying I think you did it."

"What are you saying, then?" she asked him. "Why the third degree?"

"I'm saying that we had better find out what's going on here, and quick before the chief has no choice but to protect his own house."

"By kicking me out of it?"

"He's a politician, baby," he said. "And no matter what you think, he's slicker than owl shit. You saw him yucking it up with the mayor. He isn't loyal to anyone but himself. And that phone call between you and Hazel scared the shit out of him. I saw that all over his face."

She didn't believe for a minute the chief would betray her, but didn't say so. It was no use arguing with Billy Ray when he accepted something as true.

"Speaking of phone records, what about phone records from Jabo?" she asked, changing the subject.

"Yeah, that," he breathed. "That number from the warning call he got in the casino looks like it came from a throwaway phone. No connection to Holloway. In fact, no connection to anyone."

Raven sighed. She knew the killer would not have been dumb enough to use a phone connected to them.

Maybe not Holloway, Raven thought despondently. Maybe Floyd. Maybe it was Floyd doing this to her, his ghost coming back to haunt her for testifying against him during his murder trial. Maybe that was the reason his spirit hung so heavily on the air that she couldn't walk two steps without thinking of him.

She stood up and said, "Maybe it's Floyd Burns risen from the grave to take his revenge."

"Stop talking like a damn fool," Billy Ray said. "Ghosts aren't who you should be worried about right now. Let your daddy go."

There was silence for almost a full minute. For the first time since she was a child wondering how to escape Floyd's grasp, Raven had no idea what to do next. Maybe she should run and take to rambling the country like Floyd did. Maybe as Floyd accepted and Holloway was coming to believe, rules were for suckers. Why should she wait for them to catch her and lock her up?

"Look, Raven," Billy Ray said, interrupting her thoughts. "I know you think Hazel's killing has something to do with Floyd, maybe someone who's obsessed with him knocked her off. But look how Floyd laid out your mother."

"No thank you," she said. "I've looked enough at those photos to last a lifetime."

"That may be right," Billy Ray said. "But not in relation to Hazel's death. Look at it again."

She turned away but he shoved the photograph into her face. "I'm not playing, Raven, look."

"Okay, okay." She snatched the photograph from him. She stared at it for a long time.

"Pretend like it's not your mother," he said.

She gave him a disgusted look, but he ignored it. "Pretend like she's just another vic."

She shut her eyes. Billy Ray was right. She couldn't let emotion cloud her judgment, especially not now.

She looked down onto Maylene's open grave. A fireman leaned on a shovel next to it, his hat pushed back on his head and his face grim and dirty with soot. Maylene's corpse lay exposed in the rich soil that used to be the only nourishment for the tomatoes and the zinnias. It was an ugly scene. Maylene's dress lay in rags over her body. She was still wearing her apron but it was filthy with dirt and tattered by rips that could only have been made by the butcher knife Floyd Burns had wielded. Her head was thrown back in agony, her mouth open as if in screaming prayer. The brown eyes that Raven had only a faint memory of were two black holes in her face. Raven shuddered and thrust the picture back to Billy Ray. He didn't take it. He gently pushed it back to her.

"Look," he said.

"I've seen it," she snapped.

He took it from her and then picked up the crime scene photo of Hazel Westcott's body and handed it to Raven. It couldn't have been more different. Maylene Love's corpse was hideous, the stuff of nightmares. Hazel Westcott's was beautiful and easy to look at. It was something that a romantic could stare at for eons.

Maylene was buried in a shallow grave with little protection from the environment, including the animals and birds that fed on the dead. One glance would be enough to freeze the blood of a strong person. Hazel Westcott was laid out carefully among the azalea bushes, her body very easy to find, her eyes still open, her lips parted and still tantalizing enough to kiss. Raven stared at it for a long time. Then she said, "They're opposite."

Billy Ray nodded. "Not a copycat. You are letting what Floyd did get to you. And whoever is messing with you now knows that. Put it out of your head and let's get this bastard."

"Exactly opposite, but related," Raven said slowly with sinking realization. "They were both murdered. They were both marked with the feather. Maylene was buried in a shallow grave. Hazel was laid out in full view, like someone was getting her ready for a funeral viewing."

"What are you talking about?" Bill Ray said. "You don't know that Hazel's scene was marked. I told you—"

"It's too much of a coincidence," Raven answered. "Hazel's scene is Floyd but not Floyd."

"Now you aren't making any kind of sense."

"It's exactly opposite," she said. "Not only are the scenes opposite, but the killers. My mother was killed by a crazed serial killer, and Hazel supposedly by a cop." She stopped and looked at Billy Ray. "Two things opposite. Like ghost eyes, Billy Ray," she whispered, bringing her hand to her face. "The ability to see evil and good from within the same body."

"Shut up. Stop it."

"But the same results," she went on. "Murder, violence, and evil. I'll never outrun it. I shouldn't even try."

"You need to cut this shit out," Billy Ray said quietly.

Raven stood up. She felt shut in, alone, as if an invisible hand had reached through her chest and started to squeeze her heart. She heard Floyd in her head, the words he dared only to tell her in nightmares. *You should have seen it, Birdy Girl,* he giggled. *Them ribs just moved on aside and let the blade in as if it were a long-lost son returning from the battlefield to the heart of his mamma.* He hadn't passed the fifth grade, but Floyd was all about experiments, empirical evidence. He wanted to kill Maylene to see if the lights really went out of a person's eyes like they did in the movies. And he loved twists, puzzles. Was Holloway patient or smart enough for this? Or could she be underestimating him?

"Raven, what? Tell me."

She took a deep breath, gulped air all the way down to her belly. She let it out slowly and turned to Billy Ray.

"I thought the feathers had to do with Floyd, with 'Fire', you know?" She stopped. Billy Ray nodded. "But they have nothing to do with Floyd. They have everything to do with me."

"I don't—"

She took the Maylene photo from Billy Ray and held it up alongside Hazel Westcott's.

"Yes, like I said—" he was almost shouting in frustration now, "they aren't copycats."

"But it's someone trying to prove that no matter how much I try to make myself the opposite of my father, I will never outrun my true nature. I can dress up like a cop. I can catch killers, but I will always be just like him. His evil will follow me wherever I go…no." She stopped, reconsidering. "Not following me. The killer wants to prove that Floyd's evil is inside of me."

Billy Ray said nothing, so she went on in the space his silence left. "The murders may be opposite, but they are still murders. It's the reason he killed Jabo. If Jabo had been accused, it would have taken the attention away from me and ruined his plans."

"His plans?" Billy Ray asked.

"He's not done," Raven said.

"What you talking about?"

"There will be at least one more murder."

"What?" he groaned. "No, Raven. No. No more killings."

"When I was a kid I had this babysitter. Girl, about sixteen. She disappeared."

"And you telling me you think your daddy killed her."

"Don't think," she said. "I know. I think I was there."

"Think?"

"I mean I dream about it. Him luring her into the truck with us one night. I was with him because it was the only way he could get her in the truck. Fed us first, Burger King. And then drove us down to the levy. They got out and walked a little ways out of sight into the trees. When I saw him again, he was by himself."

"And you think he killed her? He could have—"

"No," she said. "He could have nothing. He came back to the truck. She didn't. And he told me. He said she was getting too nosy, and that she had to go. A few days later it was all over town that she was missing. Her body was found about two weeks after that. Throat slit."

"And you didn't say anything?"

"I couldn't." She swallowed. "But they figured it out anyway. They attributed the murder to Floyd but never tried him for it. He already had been given the death penalty for Maylene, and that trial had been a circus."

"Felicia Harris," she said with wonder in her voice. "He's not going to be able to resist it."

"You are freaking me out," he said quietly. "You need to cut it out."

"Don't you see, Billy Ray?" she said. "It's going to be an old man. Exactly opposite of Felicia Harris. It's going to be brutal."

"Why do you think that murder?" Billy Ray said. "Why not one of his others?"

"Because Felicia was the only one he killed because he had to," Raven said. "He had a good reason. It was a murder that Floyd didn't really want to commit. And it was so clean, like slaughtering an animal. No torture. No fun and games."

She could see Billy Ray's mouth begin to form the word bullshit, but then his cell phone rang. At some point Billy Ray had changed the ringtone from Zydeco to an old-fashioned telephone ring, and the sound took Raven further back into the past. The iPhone rang loud in the silence and vibrated among the papers spread out on the coffee table, causing them to rattle and shake. She thought of Floyd calling from the grave. Raven froze. Billy Ray looked at her as if she were twelve years old and just had her pants scared off from watching a horror movie that she had no business watching.

He snatched up the phone and, still looking at her skeptically, he said, "Chastain." He listened for a few moments before hanging up. He folded his hands together and said, "That was the chief. They're putting together some people to look into the Kersey killing. He wants me in the office. You," he said, pointing to her, "he wants home and resting. A couple of days off, he said. And right now, after this conversation here..." he wagged an accusing finger at her, "...I'm agreeing with him. You are not using the thinking side of your brain, Raven. Get a grip."

CHAPTER THIRTY-ONE

Floyd chose gas. Not many know that you can choose gas over the needle in the state of California, but you can and Floyd did. The state hadn't killed anybody in the big green can since Harris, and he didn't have much of a choice in the matter. The guards he was friendly with told Floyd that San Quentin hadn't used the chamber in so long that they had to practice for weeks like they were rehearsing for some sort of play. The executioner acting out Floyd's part was all calm and solemn in the face. His movements were small and co-operative as they strapped his hands and feet to the arms and legs of the chair where Floyd was to take his last breath. Floyd listened to the guards tell him about the practice with a grave and serious look on his face as if he was listening for his life. He didn't bother telling the damn fools that they were working from the wrong script.

Floyd Burns was not about calm. Fire didn't co-operate. Floyd could imagine the warden, a sure and arrogant man, saying to those who asked, "The coming of death has a way of quieting even the most hardened of men. I've seen it plenty of times." And he had. The warden liked telling Floyd how many executions he had presided over during his time at San Quentin. Ten times total. But he hadn't had his eleventh yet.

He hadn't ever executed a man like Floyd 'Fire' Burns.

★   ★   ★

There was a man on the death team by the name of Gerald Lockhard. His duty was to guard Floyd while Floyd shuffled from one place to the other like the exercise yard or the room where they let Floyd have visitors during his last days. Gerald was the size of a tractor, strong, but he had a weak mind that you could find your way into easy if ever you needed to do it. Floyd told him when he met him that his name should be Smitty and he called him that just to see how far he could go with him. Lockhard didn't tell him to cut it out, so Floyd found he could go pretty damn far. He knew a man that was willing to be renamed probably didn't have a lot of steel in his backbone.

Lockhard wore a ring with a cross carved on top of it on his pinky finger. Knowing that he was a religious man, whenever Floyd got close enough so that only Lockhard could hear, he would start up with the whispering – Bible verses so twisted around with Floyd's own words that they didn't resemble their original form at all. He kept up with the Bible verses for a while, and then he started whispering made-up things with birds and snakes and disloyalty in them like he did when Raven was little. He whispered his dreams to Lockhard. "They'll drop the pellets to start the gas," he would say, "but I don't care nothing about that. It's what happens after the gas gets me. I wake up spread out in a field and black crows circlin' forever and ever in a sky wide and blue and not heaven and I know they ain't never gone stop. Them crows tease me. They dip and swirl and fly around my head pretending to poke out my eye. But they lift them black bodies up just before they touch my eyeballs. The devil divided them up into a thousand little devils and God gone send 'em back to y'all. He's gone have them drag y'all to hell 'cause you know why? 'Cause you killin'. You takin' the power of God and God gone make you pay."

Lockhard would stop and cock his head until Floyd finished or someone came up and interrupted.

But Floyd kept going at him hard and with a purpose. He needed him for the big show. He needed him and he told him like he told Raven, "Them sonsofasumpthin's gone know they killing me."

CHAPTER THIRTY-TWO

They set the execution up for ten p.m. on a summer's night absent of both moon and stars. The sky was just a stretch of black nothing overhead as if it never held anything since it had come into existence. At the execution were Jean Rinehart's parents and some state officials along with five or six people from the media.

Except for Raven, nobody from Floyd's family was there. Floyd told the warden that he was an orphan without any family that would claim him. Maylene Love's parents had died one right after the other about five years after Floyd killed their daughter.

They kept Raven, Floyd's witness of one, separated from Jean Rinehart's parents by two guards who looked harried and stressed as only Floyd could harry and stress a person. Since she was the only one there supporting Floyd, they directed her to the side of the viewing area with the reporters and official witnesses of the state. But she was still in full view of Jean Rinehart's parents. Jean's father was a man with a large belly and legs as skinny as birch trees. Her mother's face was made up so perfectly she looked like an advertisement for cosmetics. And her perfume was strong. It lay over the witnesses, cloying and sweet-smelling, like lilies at a funeral.

Raven had met Jean's parents shortly after she and Floyd were married on that long-ago day in the Union Baptist Church. They swooped down from Baltimore, disapproved of everything in Jean's life from her choice of husband to her footwear, and then left only chaos and hurt feelings behind them. Now they pretended not to know Raven, and that suited her just fine.

They all waited. They waited in a silence so thick and heavy that Raven imagined she could hear the scratching of roach legs against the baseboards of the old prison. She thought about the killing that was about to take place. Everything that happened from here on out would be voluntary – except maybe for Floyd's part. It could be stopped anywhere along the line. Not just with a call of a stay from a judge, or a phone call of clemency from the governor, which wasn't likely to come.

Anybody could stop the killing right here if they had will enough. The guards could refuse to strap him down. The warden could decline to give the signal. And the executioner could refuse to flip the switch that would send the cyanide pellets beneath Floyd's chair into the bucket of the sulfuric acid that would cause clouds of the killing gas to rise up all around him. She chuckled wryly to herself. Maybe it would be Floyd that would stop everything after all. Maybe ole Floyd 'Fire' Burns would refuse to die.

She knew something was wrong when the blinds to the gas chamber opened. Floyd should have been sitting there neatly strapped to the chair about to die whether he was ready or not. But the chair was empty. Raven and a couple of reporters looked at the guards in the witness area. They both looked confused. One of them, a big man with an untrimmed gray mustache working over his mouth, checked his watch than looked back at his partner. He hunched his shoulders like he didn't know what the hell was going on. The other one had caught on, though. He mouthed the words to his partner "Too early," but he didn't seem entirely sure. It would make sense, though. They had let the witnesses in too early, before everything was sanitized and ready to go.

Presently, what sounded like a million footsteps filled the chamber. They came from six men in riot gear, two on either side of Floyd, one man in front of him and the other behind him. When the footsteps stopped, a voice that sounded as if it came from deep inside of Floyd filled the chamber. It was the same voice he used to rain down fire from the pulpit onto the congregation in Lentland.

"Ye, though I walk through the valley of *death*," he shouted in the same voice that once nailed his followers to their seats, "I will fear no e-*vil*. For thou *art* with *mee*...." The guard in front opened the door to the chamber. The others carried Floyd in, his feet bare and the tips of his toes trailing along the floor.

Raven checked her watch. It was five minutes to ten. She had heard that some tie-down teams could get an unwilling inmate strapped into the killing chair in ninety seconds. She didn't think a ninety-second tie-down would be possible with an unwilling Floyd Burns and, of course, it wasn't.

Just when Raven was beginning to think they would never be able to tie him down regardless of how much time they had, Floyd went slack. The guards took that moment to propel him toward the chair. While they did so he worked his eyes around the witness area, searching among the witnesses seated there. Those eyes landed on Jean Rinehart's mother. He wrenched out of the guards' grip and ran to the window. She stood up and started toward the viewing window expecting God knows what – maybe it was something as foolish as an apology. He was still staring at her, the corners of his mouth drawn down into a clown's frown, then he said, "Boo."

Jean Rinehart's mother jerked back like he'd spit into her beautiful face. But that shock didn't last long. She flew at the window to the chamber. She beat her fists against the window until one of the guards caught her around the middle and swung her around back to her seat.

Raven saw Floyd's shoulders shake. He was laughing as if it were the greatest joke in the world. He looked at one of the guards in the bubble helmets and said, "Now, that's almost worth it. Did you see the look on her face? Almost worth dying for."

One of the helmets picked Floyd off his feet and slammed him into the chair. Floyd laughed as he did so, telling him repeatedly to hold it, hold it, he had one more thing to say. They were doing their best to ignore him, but Raven could see that Floyd had flustered them. They'd get one strap fastened and he'd slip out of that one while they went for the other. He kicked at the metal grate covering the bucket of sulfuric acid. The sound was loud and hollow in the room. A couple of reporters stood up. The big guard with the mustache threw an anxious glance at the door leading out of the viewing area.

"How would you like to take a trip to hell with me, boys and girls?" Floyd asked, swinging his elbows at the guards and pounding the metal grate with one loose foot.

"I don't care about my dying," Jean Rinehart's mother screamed. "As long as he dies with me!"

"We should stop this," one of the reporters said.

The guard with the mustache shook his head. "These are trained men. They'll get him strapped down."

"They don't look like trained men," the reporter said. "They look like a couple of rednecks trying to corner a greased pig."

Raven walked over to the glass. Floyd didn't acknowledge her at first. He kept flailing his little body around, trying to get at the bucket and pellets behind his chair. She placed her hand flat against the window. He was swinging his elbows one way and then another, yelling something unintelligible. He threw his head back and let out a whoop. His eyes ricocheted crazily around the viewing area. He was about to let out another victory whoop when he saw Raven standing there with her hand pressed against the window. His breathing slowed and his eyes lost some of that crazy sheen. He watched her for what seemed like a long time and nodded.

"Raven," he said. "All right, my little bird. All right."

He sat there calmly while they finished tying him down. As she returned to her seat, she caught a glimpse of Jean's mother staring at her as if she wanted to rip the flesh from Raven's bones.

Finally, the tie-down team left the chamber and Floyd sat there as he should have been sitting when they first opened the blinds. One of the guards on the death team shut the door and cranked the hand wheel to seal off the chamber. For the first time, Raven noticed the other chair beside Floyd in San Quentin's two-seated gas chamber. There was nobody sitting there waiting to die with him. This final act he was to do alone, without the daughter he'd had at his side for so many years.

Then the warden said, "Any last words?"

What happened next seemed to take a long time but it only took a few seconds. Floyd nodded once. Then all of a sudden, he slipped his scrawny wrists out of the restraints like an escape artist and unbuckled the straps from his legs. He shot up out of his seat. In his hand was a piece of broken mirrored glass. Raven would learn later that Gerald Lockhard had delivered the glass during the commotion of the tie-down. Floyd had gotten to him during those days before his execution, convincing the young man that he would be saving his entire team from 'God's judgment' if Lockhard made sure that they weren't the ones doing the killing. The glass was so sharp that blood flowed from Floyd's palm.

Raven got up and ran to the window, not even realizing she was saying over and over, "*Daddy, Daddy, no, no.*" There was a lot of shouting and whooping and Floyd's voice, like he had trained it to do, broke through all of it. Looking into Raven's eyes for the last time, he said, "Souls. Don't. Die."

And then he drew the piece of glass across his throat. He stood there until the loss of blood forced him down. He was unconscious before the warden gained enough composure to tell the executioner to pull the lever dropping the cyanide into the acid. He was almost entirely bled out before the executioner was able to understand what was wanted of him and complied. It was all too late. Floyd 'Fire' Burns had died before the state could kill him.

CHAPTER THIRTY-THREE

Raven was at the gym when the call came, her mind filled with Floyd's last moments as well as his last warning as her Nikes worked the treadmill. She had been trying to conquer the soreness that had invaded her body since the night of Jabo's death. Panting and exhausted as she climbed from the treadmill to retrieve the Android that had fallen during her run, she saw the message from Billy Ray. It consisted of only two words – Oral Justice – and an address. The address was unnecessary because she already knew where Oral Justice lived, in a white house with a wraparound porch and wisteria spilling over a pergola attached along the side.

She remembered the summers when the blooms created a haze of lavender atop the pergola and along the roof of the white house. She used to think that a fairy princess must live there, not a man going on fifty – which Oral was at that time – who would eventually be forced to use a cane with a silver wolf's head.

"God bless it, God bless it," she said as she stared at the Android that appeared to want to do nothing but bring news of blood and pain and death.

She pulled away from these thoughts and pressed a button on the Android. The screen turned black as it went into standby. In the shower she didn't bother with soap, just rinsed the sweat away, watching the clear water twist over the scratches and bruises on her racked body. She shrugged into her Levi's and a white collared shirt. From the gym locker, she retrieved the Glock 22 she had bought to replace the Glock 19 she lost in the Red River while struggling with Jabo Kersey. The 22 was heavier, more powerful than the 19. It made her feel safer, though she knew in her gut that the feeling of safety was an illusion. She walked back to the gym floor. All of this she did slowly, as if in a trance, as if she had all the time in the world, though a voice kept whispering to her that she didn't. She had hardly any time at all.

Raven drove the speed limit to Oral's house, thinking about and regretting the things she said to him outside the BLPD on the day of Hazel's murder. Lights didn't flash. Sirens didn't cry murder in the still air. Instead of the department sedan with lights and sirens whooping, she took her own car, the red Mustang she bought in honor of another murder victim, her stepmother Jean Rinehart. She drove slowly and carefully, thinking about what she had told Billy Ray in his shotgun after Jabo Kersey was killed. She had said it would be an old man, just the opposite of the clean kill of Felicia Harris. She just never thought it would be Oral Justice.

Oral had a dirt front yard that dipped unevenly with rocks and patches of weeds. His garden was in the back. And if he still kept a garden like he did when she was a young girl, it would be filled with peppers and tall sunflowers, tomatoes so red and juicy that their skin threatened to burst from a simple touch.

Now in the wide front yard, marked and unmarked police cars were parked at odd angles in the dirt as if the drivers ditched the vehicles before the engines had stopped. Someone had swung crime scene tape around the porch, leaving an opening at the steps leading to the screen door. Three uniformed officers milled around, their eyes blank and faces grim. Oral's neighbors pressed against the police tape encircling the yard, some with shocked faces but dry eyes, others wiping away tears.

There were plenty of white jumpsuits pacing from the front door to a crime scene unit van from Shreveport, which was parked alongside the house just beyond the crime scene tape. It had to be really bad, Raven thought, for the chief to call in help from Shreveport.

Billy Ray stood on the front porch with his pencil behind his ear, talking to one of the crime scene technicians. A pair of black Wayfarers covered Billy Ray's eyes. His sunglasses, when he wore them, were usually perched on top of his head or slung around the back of his neck when he had his hat on, but today they covered his eyes. He didn't know Oral, only in passing. And he had seen plenty of murder victims. If his eyes were covered, it must mean that what was inside was just one more horrible scene that affirmed his decision to leave homicide. He waved at her and she signaled with a nod that she would be up shortly.

Along the road sat a bevy of news vehicles with their satellite antennas spiraling high into the humid air. Another sort of garden, she thought, one of repetitive sensationalism and misinformation. All of the local major networks were there. She saw that anchorwoman from Channel Three, Imogene Tucker, the woman who had been all over her during the Quincy Trueblood fiasco and at the Hazel Westcott crime scene. When she noticed Raven standing alongside the red Mustang watching her, Imogene Tucker dropped the microphone she had been talking into and pushed the camera out of her face. *Oh crap*, Raven thought as she made eye contact with Tucker. She wore a tight black skirt, a blue silk blouse, and black pumps that caused her ankles to twist unnaturally as she tried to hurry toward Raven over the uneven dirt. Raven watched her come, thinking how Tucker looked two-dimensional as she sidled between cars, a paper cutout with a round belly and backside. Raven prepared herself for Tucker's arrival and the rhythmic sound of spearmint popping in her puffy cheeks while saying, *Just give me an exclusive, an exclusive and it'll be worth your while.*

Just as Raven was about to put her palm up in a stop signal, Lamont Lovelle smoothly intercepted Tucker. *Way to go, Lamont*, Raven thought. *Your second save in these past two weeks of hell.* He placed both of his hands under Tucker's elbows and guided her back into the direction of the news truck. He turned to Raven, the look on his face catching her off guard. If she hadn't known him, it was a look that would have been disquieting. His smile looked friendly enough, but it reminded her of how a tomcat grinned just after placing a bird with a broken neck at his master's feet. She could see for once that he wasn't dressed as well as he usually was. His pants were old and worn, and he had on a thin blue summer sweater thrown over a dingy white T-shirt. Like everyone, Raven thought, he had dressed in a hurry. The malice in the grin, if she hadn't imagined it, was for Imogene Tucker's quest for an exclusive in the face of Oral Justice's death. She knew that Lovelle and Oral had been friends. He wouldn't appreciate Tucker salivating over his friend's death as a way to further her career.

Tucker safely out of the way, Raven walked toward the chief. He had moved down a ways from the property and was standing on the border of a pecan grove next to Oral's yard. He gazed at the towering green trees undergirded by soft grass while he talked on the cell phone pressed to his right ear. His other hand was on his hip, his bum leg bent so he wouldn't have to put any weight on the knee. He was saying words into the phone like, "We don't know yet, we're on it, don't worry about it, yes." She knew he had to be talking to the mayor.

She knew also that he had to have heard her come up and stand beside him but he didn't acknowledge her. He just kept staring out into the grove of trees, his head cocked like a dog's trying to figure out what new thing just happened, what important thing did he just miss. Unlike Billy Ray's, his face was bare. And he had tears in his eyes.

He dropped the cell phone from his ear and looked at it a long time before putting it into his jacket pocket. She still didn't know what her status was, so she decided to let him start talking first. When he did, he said, "You took a bus over, Detective? The slow train?"

"I got here as soon as I could."

"Well, as soon as you could is not good enough. We are three-quarters through the scene. I'm sure you saw Shreveport CSIs over there. We can't handle this thing by ourselves, not with just our two."

She swallowed, knowing the answer even before asking, and then asked anyway, "Robbery, homicide?"

He sighed. "I don't think robbery had a damn thing to do with it. To tell the truth, even homicide was the last thing on my mind. When the call came in I thought he probably had a heart attack or stroke or something natural. Just unattended. I never thought about homicide." He stopped and stared at her. "But even so I came quickly."

She didn't apologize or explain. Not yet.

He let it go. Shaking his head, he said, "I swear, Raven, sometimes I wonder if this shit doesn't follow me around."

"Who found him?"

He turned slightly and pointed over his shoulder. A skinny kid in a Saints T-shirt leaned against a patrol car. He was still shaking and crying while a female officer rubbed his back in a soothing, circular motion.

"His latest project," he said. "Came to help out in the garden like he does every week."

"Could he have been involved?" she asked.

The chief shook his head. "He doesn't have a drop of blood on his clothes, no cuts on his hands, not a scratch on him. He voluntarily took off every stitch he had on to show us that he had no bruises or anything that could make him good for this. Said he didn't want us to waste our time looking at him. He's ready to go downtown to give a statement, says he'll take a polygraph, DNA, whatever we need. He's not in this, Raven. Just a poor kid Oral was helping out."

"Chief," she reminded him. "I'm suspended, remember? Why am I here?"

He put his hands in his pocket and stared at Oral's house. "You are not suspended."

"If I'm not suspended, then what am I?"

"You were on a thing. That's all. I never officially suspended you."

"So," she said slowly. "I'm on a thing. Can someone on a thing be at this crime scene?"

His head swiveled toward her. "You *were* on a thing," he said. "I said *were*. You are not on a thing anymore. The shit is too deep and you are the best detective I have at the moment. Believe me, if I had someone better than you, less hotheaded than you, less trouble than you, you'd still be on your thing. But since I don't, you're not."

He turned back to the line of trees, the only order at Oral's house that Saturday late afternoon. The sky had darkened considerably. Night was almost with them.

She nodded and then said, "How bad is it?"

"Go see for yourself," he said bitterly.

CHAPTER THIRTY-FOUR

She took the four steps two at a time. Now that she was finally on scene and knew what happened, every vein and sinew in her body yearned to understand who had done this to Oral. Who had killed her childhood hero and the man so many in the community had respected and admired? Who and how and why?

But she knew why, didn't she? She recalled the conversation she and Billy Ray had in the living room of his shotgun. "It'll be an old man," she remembered saying. Oral Justice was killed because of her.

"Raven," she heard Billy Ray call. "Hold up. Careful, careful."

She ignored him. She didn't want protocol, had no patience for a walk-through. She wanted in the house. She wanted to see for herself what made the chief walk as far away from the last moments of Oral Justice's life as he could get. A uniformed officer pushed a clipboard toward her so she could sign in. She shoved it away. She heard a voice telling her that she wasn't allowed to be there, that she was suspended.

It was Holloway, his voice dripping with disgust. She turned to face him. He was about to say something else but took a step back. Fear widened his eyes and his hands fluttered to his face. His response gave her a small amount of satisfaction. She looked at him a long time until she was sure he understood. She watched for a second or two as he backed down the steps before turning and fleeing toward the chief.

Oral's house had a wraparound front porch with wide columns that narrowed at the top. What was left of the sunlight slanted through the spacious windows encircling his living room filled with bright overstuffed furniture and dark hardwood floors.

Oral's door was always open, especially to the neighborhood kids. No knocking required. When she was a teenager, Raven would just burst through the door to find him sitting in a love seat with a huge leather Bible in his lap while light from the big windows fell all around him. If he wasn't inside she would run through the living room and the kitchen to find him in the garden, his meaty arms buried in dirt almost to the elbows. He'd not even raise an eyebrow when he saw her, would just say, "Help me up," as if she were expected at that very moment to do just that.

And she would remember what she would do if the house were empty. She'd spend the first few minutes going from room to room, running her hand over the beige old-fashioned bedspread covering the feather mattress or making faces in his bathroom mirror. Then she'd flop on a rug braided from rags next to the TV and watch *Bewitched* or *I Dream of Jeannie* with her head propped in her hands until he came home. Oral always did that; he always had one kid he adopted as a project, someone he thought needed a little extra help to make up for the crappy start they had in life. Like the kid in the Saints T-shirt. Like Raven.

And now a sick violence had destroyed the house that she had once felt so protected in. The wood and glass coffee table lay on its side, the glass shattered into large, jagged pieces. A CSI agent was putting two broken wineglasses in separate plastic evidence bags. Blood soaked the braided rug she had lain on as a child. He must have been standing there when the killer landed the first blow. She looked up to see cast-off blood on some of the beams crisscrossing the vaulted ceiling. And there were more blood stains improbably high on the bright yellow walls.

Other people were in the room, but it was as if she were there alone with Oral's blood and her memories of him. She felt Billy Ray grab her elbow and she shook him away.

"All right," he said, but she only heard this faintly as she continued deeper inside the house.

She followed the blood splatters. She ignored the careful path their own CSI team and the CSIs from Shreveport had laid out. Oral must have run; at first it looked as if he went for the front door but was blocked. He had no choice but to run out of the room, deeper into the house as that demon hacked away at him, just as she felt now that she had no choice but to move deeper into the house following Oral's last steps. She noticed dimly that Billy Ray was following her.

"They find the murder weapon?" she asked, already knowing the answer.

"Yeah," Billy Ray said. "Next to the back porch. Bastard just threw it in the dirt when he was finished with it."

She nodded. It was no longer of any consequence. For the killer, the weapon had served its purpose. "Pretty darn confident, aren't you?" she asked the man who had killed Oral.

But it was Billy Ray who answered, his voice tired and grim and edged with disgust. "He thinks we're too stupid to catch him even with the murder weapon plain as a tail on a rattler."

"An axe?" she said.

He shook his head. "A scythe. The bastard went all medieval and shit. Like the reaper. You think he brought it with him?"

"No," she said, remembering that Oral collected gardening tools, especially strange ones. "Do you?"

"No," Billy Ray agreed. "Neither does Crimes. They think the killer just grabbed the first thing he saw out back before coming inside."

Like a scythe, Raven thought, knowing the glee the killer felt when he found the scythe on the wall next to Oral's other gardening tools. *I was just coming out here to find a boring ole axe,* a voice, Floyd's voice, echoed in her head. *And look what you done brung me? A scythe.*

She followed the blood trail into the bedroom. She could see in her mind's eye Oral trying to use the walls to stay erect as he fled to the only safe place in his house, or the only place he thought was safe. He must have been able to lock the door because the wood was broken and splintered. She touched the broken door and let her fingers linger there for a long time. She couldn't help herself. Every cop instinct told her to make herself as small as possible as she walked through the crime scene so she wouldn't contaminate anything. But she couldn't think that clinically. Not with Oral. She could feel hot terror emanating from the broken door. She imagined his fear and leaned against the wall, suddenly exhausted beyond all measure.

"God dammit," Billy Ray said as he grabbed her shoulders. "Get a hold of yourself. Are you going to be able to do this?"

Am I going to be able to do this? She repeated the phrase in her mind. And as the thought passed through her, she remembered all that Oral had done for her and the community. And she imagined the fear he must have felt as he ran limping from room to room in his own house away from some bastard with a – what had Billy Ray said? – a scythe of all things. She nodded slowly at first, then more emphatically.

"Damn straight," she said. "You are damn straight I'm going to be able to do this."

She looked at the bed. Blood soaked the knotted fabric, but there was no body.

"This wasn't where the body was found?" she asked Billy Ray.

"No," he said. "Looks like he made it out of here with the fucker chasing him. Made it to the kitchen, almost to the back door."

She nodded and thanked him before turning away, all cop now. She skirted the yellow plastic tags marking the blood spatter as she made her way to the kitchen. Oral lay facedown on the kitchen floor between the kitchen island topped in granite and the ebony cabinets. The body was turned slightly on its side, the right hand twisted faceup.

"He was playing with him," Rita said. "Son of a bitch played with him first."

Raven hadn't even noticed that Rita was in the room. Rita wasn't crying but the tip of her nose was bright red.

"What makes you say that?" Raven asked.

"See that hack across his neck?" she asked. "He did that last. That's what killed him. But all the other wounds are non-lethal, love taps and pokes really."

Billy Ray said, "You have a way with words, Rita."

Rita ran the back of her hand across her nose. "Well, maybe not love taps, but it looks like he kept poking at him just to scare the shit out of him."

"He wanted him to suffer," Raven said.

They stared at Oral, at the fat and muscle exposed by his broken flesh.

"Who would want Oral to suffer, Raven?" Billy Ray challenged.

Raven didn't answer him. She didn't want to get into the Holloway argument with him again, not in front of Rita. Instead, she examined the body from its head to its feet, the span of the massive shoulders, the torso beneath the torn T-shirt. And then something caught her eye beneath Oral's right hand, something that had no business being there.

"Get our CSI team in here," she said.

"They're out back photographing the murder weapon," Billy Ray said. "I saw one of the CSIs from Shreveport in the living room. I'll bring him in."

She grabbed the sleeve of his jacket and held it hard. "No," she insisted. "I want ours. I want one of ours. This is Oral, Billy Ray. Oral."

He didn't ask any more questions but did as she told him. After Byrd's Landing CSI took pictures of Oral's twisted hands, both Rita and Billy Ray watched as Raven used tweezers to grasp what looked like a wet tangle of hair from beneath Oral's right hand. She placed the peacock feather in the plastic bag.

"It's not him they were trying to make suffer," she said. "It's someone close to him. They were trying to make that person suffer, to make them think that Oral's death is all their fault."

She handed the evidence bag with the feather to one of the CSIs and ran out onto the porch to get away from the smell of blood. Raven had to stop short to keep from slamming into Holloway. He was talking, a constant stream of words that made her head throb. They buzzed around her without meaning, a wild, crazy hum that made her want to scream.

But instead of screaming, she drove him backward into the wall beside the screen door with her forearm across his neck. The buzz stopped instantly. Everything stopped. She felt rather than saw or heard the CSIs, uniforms, neighbors, reporters, and other detectives freeze in mid-motion. She could feel their eyes on them. No, not on them. Their eyes were on her. They waited to see what she would do. Holloway's face had gone ash-white. His eyes looked as if they would bulge right out of his head. She could tell by the way he gulped that he had trouble breathing with her arm so tight across his neck.

"It's you, isn't it?" she whispered so low that she knew only he could hear her even in the silence surrounding them. "You did this. You killed Oral. And Hazel? Didn't you? Then you killed Kersey because you just couldn't quite let it end yet, you torturing me. You were having too much fun."

Holloway didn't answer. His eyes grew wide and large in surprise. She wanted to kill him so bad that she suspected that the sound of his neck snapping would bring her physical pleasure. Surprised and dismayed at the thought, she removed her forearm from his neck and took a step back.

"You are not going to get away with this," she said, breathing hard while pain and grief and adrenalin coursed through her body. "I'm going to prove it was you."

"You not only want to prove it was me," Holloway said, smiling. "You want to kill me, don't you? Admit it."

She didn't say anything because he was right. That is exactly what she longed to do.

"When you realize who you are, it will be easier for you, for us all," Holloway said. "Now let me pass."

Raven took a step closer to him, imagining how he would look with her hands around his soft throat. She had no intention of letting him pass, and didn't move aside until she felt Billy Ray place a hand on her forearm.

"It's not him," he said. "The guy who did this is probably cut up all to hell. It's not him, Raven."

Raven jerked away from him, her eyes still on Holloway. She didn't care what Billy Ray was trying to tell her, every instinct in her body told her that it was Holloway who had killed Oral. It wouldn't be the first time a killer was able to slash someone to death without getting cut. All they had to do was prove it.

CHAPTER THIRTY-FIVE

Raven stuck next to the crime scene investigators most of the night. Billy Ray left her there to see what he could find out from Oral's neighbors. Tired and seeing blood behind her eyes every time she closed them, she walked into the Byrd's Landing Police Department's conference room the next morning to find Imogene Tucker in a bright pink tweed skirt-suit seated in the padded chair next to the window. Her legs were crossed at the knees and one high-heeled platform pump dangled from a foot hanging in the air. She looked up when Raven walked in, popped her gum once before winking at her.

Billy Ray was there but he didn't look up. He just sat hunched over the glass-topped table with his head in his hands as if he were recovering from the biggest hangover in his life.

"Sit down, Detective."

It was the chief. She hadn't noticed him because he was standing in the corner of the conference room, out of direct view of the open door. He wore a light blue suit, the jacket held open by both hands lightly planted on his hips, his holster and badge in full view.

"Chief, what the heck—" she started, but he waved the words away.

"Sit," he said. "We need to talk."

She sat down in a chair opposite Billy Ray. The table was still covered with evidence. Two magnetic whiteboards filled with conjectures written in dry ink and more photos were at the end of the table. One of the whiteboards was labeled 'Justice', and the other 'Westcott'. A flip chart with the name 'Kersey' written in black marker sat off to the side of the two whiteboards.

Someone, most likely Billy Ray, had even written a list of potential suspects – including the ex-husband and the supposedly loving father – on the Hazel Westcott board. Of course Oral's board was empty. And so was Jabo Kersey's pathetic flip chart. Billy Ray must have felt Raven looking at him for answers because he just shook his head.

The chief sighed. He limped to the chair beside her. He made a show of sitting down in that way of his – half in pain and half as his way of stalling.

He rubbed his face for what seemed minutes. Then he said, "We got a problem."

"You telling me," Raven said, not taking her eyes from the reporter.

At first, Raven didn't know why the woman's face gave her pause, but after a second or two she realized that it was Tucker's makeup. It was not quite right, not bad but not as perfect as when Tucker was staring at her from a television screen. Her rouge was uneven, and the eyeliner was a crooked black line over her small eyes. Tucker, who must have noticed Raven's appraisal, shrugged as if to say, *So sue me, I was in a hurry.*

"But," Raven said, not taking her eyes from Tucker, "the problem should be easy enough to take care of."

"That's where you're wrong," the chief said. "I've had to make some concessions."

"Concessions? Chief, what are you talking about?"

"Ms. Tucker," the chief said. "Could you give us a moment, please?"

Tucker nodded at them and then at Raven before shutting the door softly behind her.

After she was sure the woman wasn't listening on the other side of the door, Raven started again. "What is this all about? What is she doing here?"

The chief didn't answer. He just stared at her for a long time. Then he said, "Someone's been leaking to her, Raven. I'm sure you heard her on the news the other night questioning our motives. Right there on TV, standing on the same corner where you shot Quincy Trueblood, remember that? Now she's threatening to put on a story about the phone call Hazel made to you and your lack of alibi for her murder."

His words blew her back. "And you know Holloway leaked,

don't you, Chief? You said you'd fire him. Are you going to do it?"

He looked at her as if she'd lost her mind. "Hell no, are you serious? After that stunt you pulled at the crime scene last night? Don't be surprised if that doesn't end up on the ten o'clock news too."

"Me?" Raven said. "Oral's murdered and all you care about is that I pushed the man who did it against the wall?"

"Let's get this straight," the chief said. "Holloway is not a suspect. And he wants you fired, Raven."

"That's where you're wrong," she said. "He doesn't just want me fired. He wants me disgraced and locked away."

The chief sighed and nodded. "Raven," he said. "He wants me to arrest you for assault. I spent an hour talking that man out of pressing charges. But you need to know this – Holloway may have his problems with you, but they are not personal."

She snorted.

He ignored her and continued, "Until you made it personal yesterday. That wasn't one of your shiniest moments, Detective."

"Could you please explain to me what this is all about?"

The chief tried to stand up but then abruptly sat back down. He waved tiredly at Billy Ray.

Billy Ray stood up and walked to the whiteboards standing at the end of the table. Raven watched as he picked up a red Expo marker. On each board in neat, round print, he wrote *Raven Burns* under the suspect list.

It was as if someone, perhaps her father, had pulled a red shade down over her face. The entire room now came to her through a veil of misted blood like she had been seeing all night at the Oral Justice crime scene. She'd swear that the room actually tilted, and when it righted again, she felt that not only the room had changed, but her entire world.

First Billy Ray and now the chief, the man who had saved her from her father, the man she had admired and wanted to be like. He thought she was a murderer like Floyd – a crazy bastard with a straight razor and a desire to study killing. Her stomach roiled, sending a hint of bile to her throat.

Billy Ray was speaking carefully, but his voice sounded like it was coming from another world. He was saying that they had been able to hold Holloway back from the Hazel Westcott murder but Oral's death was a different thing. And Jabo Kersey's.

"I don't get Oral," Raven said, looking from Billy Ray and back to the chief. "It's not even logical to think that I had anything to do with that."

Billy Ray started to say something, but the chief cut him off. He leaned into Raven, so close that she could smell his aftershave along with the chemicals left in his newly cleaned suit.

"Why isn't it logical, Raven?"

"What are you trying to say, Chief?"

"I'm trying to say that your head isn't where it should be in this investigation. Something's going on with you. I don't know what it is but you better put it in a pocket until the investigation is done."

"I don't know what you mean," she said.

"Yes, you do."

Raven took a deep breath. She choked down the bile in her throat. She counted to ten and then backward to one again before she spoke. When she finally did, she started slowly, "Okay, maybe Hazel. I could see Hazel. We argued, but—"

"You couldn't stand her," the chief countered. "You fought with her so much that it even made the style section in the paper, those damn gossip pages."

"Okay, I couldn't stand her," she agreed. "But I didn't kill her. Obviously."

"We aren't there yet," the chief said. "Not to her murder. Back it up."

"So, I may have had motive to shut her mouth because of the Trueblood boy," she said. "But I wasn't anywhere near the Westcotts' place the night Hazel was killed. Plus the entire Trueblood thing had died down considerably by the time of her death. Hell, Billy Ray didn't even know the whole story until I told him."

The chief looked at her squarely. "What about the phone call, Raven?" he said. "And if I know you, I'd lay bets there's more. You may have explained it away in the confines of my office, but do you think you'll be able to explain it away to the press or the public?"

"Hear that sound?" she asked them. "That great ripping sound you're hearing? That's you tearing my world apart." They said nothing so she went on, still carefully and slowly as if she were addressing a class of kindergartners. "Chief, even if I did have an opportunity or a motive, there is no way I could have carried Hazel's dead weight to the bathroom, bathe her, dress her, and then lay her in the garden like a Barbie doll."

The chief nodded in concession. "I believe that, but Holloway is asking a different question."

"A different question?"

"How much do you bench press, Raven? A hundred? Hundred thirty-five?" the chief asked. "You're at the gym every day. You run marathons, how many already this year? Two? Three?"

"And then there's the Sux."

That was Billy Ray. She whipped away from the chief to stare into his face. She couldn't read him.

"Holloway had Forensics take a look·at your computer," Billy Ray said.

"You mean Cameron?" she asked, horrified, thinking why hadn't Cameron, her foster brother in IT who had helped her with Holloway's computer, warned her.

He shook his head. "No," the chief said. "Holloway isn't stupid enough to ask your foster brother to search your computer, Raven. Forensics from Shreveport. We got the results back this morning. They found some searches on Sux."

"Someone should search Holloway's cotton-picking computer," Raven said, using an expression Floyd had often used. "Oh, wait, that wouldn't be possible because Holloway had it erased and reimaged the day after Hazel died."

There was silence in the room. And then the chief said, "I'm not going to even ask how you know about that,."

She ignored him because now it didn't matter how she knew about it, not when her butt was about to go down in flames.

"Let's forget about his computer for a minute," Raven said. "Let's talk about DNA. I bet if you test Holloway's elimination sample like you will the rest of us, you'd find a match to the hairs found in Hazel's bed."

"I can't even picture that in mind," Billy Ray said. "I don't think Holloway was sleeping with that girl."

"Holloway wasn't at the scene, so no need for us to test anything. It'll just throw more confusion on top of this clusterfuck," the chief said. "Don't try to deflect. Why were you researching Sux?"

Raven had had enough. Even though the chief had asked, she stood up and walked over to Billy Ray until she was in his face.

"You know damn well why I did that," she said. "Didn't you tell the chief? It was the antifreeze case. I was just curious. I told you about that, Billy Ray."

"A strange thing to be curious about, Raven," the chief said. "And I heard from Rita that you suspected Sux even before she did, even knew how the stuff worked."

"So how are you making me for Oral?" she asked. "I was at the gym when I got the call."

"Let's get something straight," Billy Ray said. "We aren't making you for shit. We think the entire thing is bullshit. But Oral's a hard one."

She waited for the chief to agree with Billy Ray that they weren't trying to pin the murders on her, but the chief said nothing. Raven stared at the chief until he looked away.

"I don't understand," she said, waving both hands on the side of her head as if the motion would clear her it. "I really, really don't understand why this is happening."

"You argued with him too. Right out here in front of the police station the very day Hazel Westcott died. A lot of people heard," the chief said. "He was also killed late last night or at least that's what Rita is saying. The autopsy isn't done yet."

"I argue with a lot of people," she said. "Maybe I'm just hell with people. That doesn't mean I kill them." She wanted to add that she wasn't like her father. But she didn't have to. The words left unsaid floated all around them. It was the one piece of supposed evidence that both Billy Ray and the chief would have the decency not to mention.

"There's the blood, Raven," Billy Ray said.

"The blood?"

"Whose blood do you think we'll find on the shirt you had on the day Oral was killed if we test it?" the chief said.

"His blood was all over the place!" she said.

"Exactly," the chief answered. "And I hear you weren't very careful at the crime scene. So you may be fucked even more if they test your shirt and find his blood on it. And you wonder why I'm such a freak about the jumpsuits. All the time I tell you guys about the jumpsuits, the booties. And what do you say? Old Grandma. Don't think I haven't heard it."

"Come on, Chief," she said. "This is stupid."

"Even if they don't find his blood on your clothes," Billy Ray said, "they already found your blood type mingled with Oral's near the body."

"You already got the blood analysis back?" she asked incredulously.

"This is Oral we're talking about," the chief said. "Everything's been rushed. The blood came back with your type, Raven. And you have a very rare type, am I right?"

She didn't have to say anything. Of course he was right. Her blood type was O negative. Very rare.

The chief read the answer on her face. "I have told you guys over and over," he said to the rhythm of his hand thumping the table, "to wear the jumpsuits and booties. We have protocols for a reason." He stood up and limped until he was standing behind his chair. He leaned on it for support. Raven thought how much the chief needed to use a cane and his stubborn refusal to do so. For some reason, the thought fascinated her for several seconds. Finally, she nodded.

"How did your blood get there, Raven?" the chief asked.

She pulled back her sleeve to reveal a long cut that stretched from elbow to palm. It had barely sealed since rolling in the gravel on the banks of the Red River. "As you can see by the bruises still on my face, I got quite scraped up with Kersey."

"That could go both ways," the chief said. "And Kersey...." He stopped, shaking his head.

Raven agreed silently. Holloway had plenty to go on there without even trying.

"Okay," she said. "I'm getting it. But there's still something I don't understand."

"What's that?"

"What does this have to do with Imogene Tucker?"

"Two reasons," the chief said. "But first, for the record I'm not convinced that you had anything to do with any of this. And I told Holloway he'd better keep the shit to himself or I'd make sure he was covered in it before the investigation was over."

"Thank you," Raven said. "Thank you, Chief."

"But this damned," he said, waving his fingers at the door, "Imogene Tucker came around asking me about it. She wanted an interview, an exclusive."

"Yeah," Raven breathed, familiar with Tucker's quests for exclusives.

"So, I made a compromise," the chief said.

Raven nodded and said, "Control the leak by promising her an exclusive after we catch the killer?"

"I didn't have a choice, Raven," he said.

He stopped and examined Billy Ray. "You two need to find out who or what the hell is going on here before that platform heel-wearing tornado pulls the whole weight of her news station down on our heads. If you think you went through hell with Quincy Trueblood, Raven," the chief said, "imagine what would happen if Imogene Tucker started making noise about us covering up for a serial killer. This thing could go national."

"And by serial killer, you mean me," Raven whispered, the words scraping against her throat.

"I mean you," the chief confirmed. "But like I said, I'm not convinced yet. Find the killer, Raven," he said, preparing to leave. "Are we clear?"

She nodded, knowing that in order to find who was doing this she would have to allow her father deeper into her head. She would have to start thinking like Floyd.

"One more thing," Raven said with determination in her voice as she watched the chief limp to the door.

"What's that?"

"Oral's cane," she said. "Anybody find Oral's cane, the black one with the silver wolf's head?"

No one replied. She sat back in her seat and thought. Maybe the killer had taken it with him for some reason.

"You start looking at hospitals yet?" Raven asked. "For people with cuts on their arms and hands or stab wounds?"

Billy Ray sighed. "Got some officers working on it."

"Any other leads from the scene?" the chief asked. "You been there all night, right?"

Raven shook her head. "But we do have the peacock feathers. Find out where the bastard is getting his feathers. Maybe that will lead us to him."

CHAPTER THIRTY-SIX

She looked at Billy Ray for a long time after the chief left. Billy Ray returned her gaze steadily. When she didn't speak, he said, "Go ahead, Raven. We've come too far for you not to say what's on your mind."

She opened her mouth to speak, and then closed it. She wondered how well she really knew him, and if she had been right to trust him. But it was much too late. If he was starting to turn against her, she was screwed. And after all the lies she had told him, she would have deserved it. She would have to take a leap of faith, and hope their friendship still meant something to him.

"Nothing," she said. "Let's get to work."

Billy Ray quickly learned that anyone could buy peacock feathers from just about anywhere online if they were willing to wait and pay the shipping fees, or at any craft store in Byrd's Landing if waiting wasn't in their game plan. The lab had examined the peacock feathers found at the Westcott and Kersey scenes. Preliminary results revealed that there was nothing particularly special about them. The lab still had the one that had been retrieved from beneath Oral's hand at the crime scene. Raven briefly wondered if they would discover the feather had both her and Oral's blood on it – another set-up gift from Holloway.

Raven had been going over the crime scene photos and rereading the file on Westcott. Her eyes were so tired and grainy that the words started to blur together. Nothing was jumping out, which wasn't good for her. She could almost hear the cell door banging shut. She threw the pen she had been holding down on the table, leaned back and rubbed both her eyes until they hurt.

Billy Ray sighed. "What you want me to do, Raven?" he asked.

"It's Holloway, I know it."

"You don't have any proof of that," he said.

"We've got to find proof."

She leaned forward, looking at him. "The chief did say that Holloway had a DNA sample on file?"

Billy Ray looked at her and lifted an eyebrow.

"Do you think you can talk someone from our CSI to compare it to the hairs found in Hazel's sheets?"

"You are seriously overestimating my charm, Raven. I don't know anyone in Forensics who would do me a solid like that."

Raven folded her arms across her chest.

"I'm guessing that's ditto for you?" he asked.

She nodded. "I don't know anyone like that. Rita does," she said. "That woman seems to be popular with both the living and dead. She hangs out with the people over there a lot."

"You want me to see if I can get her to run some interference for us?" Billy Ray asked. "Make Holloway's sample part of the comparisons, and maybe speed them up?"

"Yes," Raven said.

"How am I supposed to do that?"

Raven shrugged. "I don't know. Promise her cupcakes?"

Billy Ray smiled ruefully and sat back. "I'll see what I can do."

Raven let out a breath of relief. "That would be awesome. I just have to know or it will drive me crazy."

He nodded. "I'll do that," he said. "But let's say that it's not Holloway. Who's your second favorite?"

She thought for a long moment. "I don't know," she said. "I'd still like to take another good look at Westcott, though. Something is just not adding up there."

"All right," he said.

She picked up the manila file on Westcott and gestured toward him with it. "You know he and Oral had a connection financially, right?" she said. "Westcott gave him thousands and thousands of dollars for his charity on a regular basis. And let's just say for argument's sake that Hazel was really trying to protect her father before she was killed."

"Okay," Billy Ray answered slowly.

"I'm thinking that maybe Oral had something on him too," she said. "Not blackmailing him – Oral wasn't like that, but maybe Oral knew something that made Westcott uncomfortable enough to kill him."

"So no serial killer," Billy Ray said. "And no one trying to persecute the shit out of you because of what your daddy did?"

She looked at him. "I know I sound like a narcissist," she said. "But I still think this has a lot to do with my past. And I'm not sure Westcott is involved. I'd just like to know what he's hiding so we can eliminate him."

"So what are you thinking?" Billy Ray asked.

"I need to talk to him again."

"But he lawyered up," Billy Ray said.

"I know," she answered. "Maybe I can get around that."

"How?"

She sat back. "I don't know. I guess I'll have to make it up as I go along."

Billy Ray said, "This is something you need to do without me. You two got along so fine the last time. He'd just ask me to go and help the women with the tea."

CHAPTER THIRTY-SEVEN

Raven strolled out of the conference room, leaving Billy Ray on the phone to sweet-talk Rita into helping them light a fire under CSI and do something that the chief didn't want done. She climbed into her red Mustang in the BLPD parking lot racking her brains for how she was going to convince Westcott from throwing her out on her ear.

As the engine rolled to a start, she heard someone call her name through the slightly cracked window. Imogene Tucker ran toward her, a bright pink purse dangling from one arm, a laptop bag from the other. As Raven looked on in amazement, Tucker opened the passenger door and sat noisily in the passenger seat. She smelled of sweat and perfume.

"Good," she breathed heavily. "I thought I missed you." She twisted around and threw her purse and laptop bag into the back seat. A memo pad was in her hand, and a ballpoint pen was clipped to the front of the ivory top she wore beneath the pink suit.

"Ms. Tucker," Raven said patiently.

"Please, Raven," she said. "Call me Imogene. I feel like we know each other."

"Detective, Ms. Tucker," she said. "You may call me Detective. And we do not know each other."

Tucker sighed. "Oh hell," she said. "I knew it was going to be like this with y'all, but I was hoping against hope."

She twisted in her seat again until she was in a position to loosen both platform pumps. She kicked them off in front of her. It didn't take a genius to understand that Ms. Imogene Tucker had no intention of getting out of Raven's red Mustang.

"I hate those damn things," Tucker said. "But hey, they make me wear high-heel shoes because that's the uniform, right?" She turned to smile brightly at Raven. "The high-heel shoes, the short skirts, the hair extensions, and the makeup. That's what I have to wear to do the job. Would you believe they even let me write that shit off my taxes?"

Raven cut the engine. "I don't know where you're going with this, Ms. Tucker, but this car's not going anywhere until you are out of it."

"Just hear me out," she said. "I wear the uniform just like you, you know? You have to be all tough, all cop-like, not trusting anybody, especially a reporter. But I know you're not like that on the inside."

Raven stared at her. "And how would you presume to know that?"

Tucker shrugged. "This morning for one," she said. "A little of it slipped through. But of course that didn't surprise me. I knew what you were like from the Quincy Trueblood case." She reached into the back seat and grabbed her pink purse. She snapped it open and took out a stick of spearmint. She shoved it into her mouth while she was still talking. "I did a lot of research on you. I know a lot about you. You would be amazed."

Raven nodded. Yes, she would indeed be amazed.

"I called you a million times to try and get an exclusive on Trueblood," Tucker said, looking at her. "But you didn't return any of my calls."

"You stalked the hell out of me," Raven said. "And you slandered me on the news the other night."

Tucker was shaking her head. "Just doing my job," she said. "And you forced me. If you had just answered my calls, I would have had your side of the story. I'm not one of those reporters who replay YouTube videos for the audience and call it research. I'm a journalist, Detective. I got the leaks like everybody else on the Quincy Trueblood case, but I didn't just report them. I made sure I had facts to back them up or dispel the bullshit. I was more than fair to you when the rest of the town wanted to tear you apart. You have to give me that. You have to know I didn't score any points."

Raven nodded. Yes, Imogene Tucker was fair, almost positive, or as positive as she could be given the situation.

"So," Tucker said, and Raven could see that the woman sensed her about to give. "Can you at least call me Imogene and let me call you Raven?"

Raven eyed her. She was beginning to like Tucker if not altogether trust her. "I can do that," Raven finally said.

Tucker smiled. "Great. Where are we off to?"

Raven looked at her in amazement. "*We* are not off to anywhere," she said. "I'm going to interview a witness."

"Who, Westcott?"

"How could you know that?" Raven asked before she could stop herself.

Tucker shrugged. "Guessed," she said, smiling. "New wrinkle in the case, have to go back to the beginning. I watch the cop shows like everyone else."

"Please get out."

"I heard Westcott lawyered up," she said. "How are you going to talk to him?"

"Now," Raven insisted. "Get out now."

"I could help."

"No, you can't."

"I know Mr. Westcott," she said. "He used to be a real good friend of my daddy's before my daddy died. He may be willing to talk if I'm there."

"Or not," Raven said. "You are a reporter."

"Family comes first, Raven. And Antwone Westcott was like family. Hazel and I practically grew up together. Besides, he likes to look at my legs. Maybe he'll be so busy looking at my legs he'll slip up."

Raven scrutinized Tucker's legs. They were smooth and golden brown and very shapely.

"You give your legs a lot of credit," Raven said.

Tucker grinned. "I didn't say the man had taste," she said modestly. "I just said he likes looking at my legs. Maybe he likes 'em short, round and brown."

Raven turned on the engine and shifted the Mustang in reverse. "Just keep your mouth shut."

As Raven headed for the exclusive Big Bayou Lake neighborhood where Antwone Westcott lived, Tucker chattered as if it were just after Lent and she had just spent an entire month without speaking for her penance. She explained to Raven that her father was a pediatrician and her mother a high school teacher in 'da hood'. That's the way she said it – 'da hood' – while holding up her pink nails for air quotes.

Charlotte Tucker tried to get her daughter to follow in her footsteps but the straight-A student with a 4.5 average and a softball scholarship in her future had other ideas. She wanted to be a journalist — not a reporter but an investigative journalist who actually worked to find 'shit', as she put it, 'out'. She popped her gum the entire time, tried to get Raven to swing by her apartment so she could change out of what she called the monkey suit. When Raven protested that it was too much out of the way, Tucker said, "Well, fuck. Can we at least swing by my office? I have a change of clothes there." When Raven said yes, Tucker picked up the conversation at the point of her childhood as if she had never interrupted it.

When they got to her office, Tucker disappeared behind a screen and emerged a few minutes later wearing a white T-shirt and clean faded jeans with a pair of flat leather sandals.

"I thought Westcott liked your legs?" Raven said as they returned to the car.

"Honey," Tucker said, "today he's just going to have to use his imagination."

Once again on the road, Tucker paved the way by calling the house to make sure that Westcott would see them. As she pressed the button of her Android to hang up, she turned to Raven. "Here we go," was all she said.

Here we go, indeed, Raven thought. After that, they drove the rest of the way in silence. She could feel the unease coming from Tucker in waves. Raven couldn't help but wonder what she was so worried about.

CHAPTER THIRTY-EIGHT

A maid wearing a nametag that said 'Molly' answered the door. Raven remembered the conversation with Angel. She must have been the Molly who called the cops when Westcott was beating the holy crap out of his daughter, the same Molly whom the chief insisted they not talk to.

She left Tucker and Raven standing in the foyer while she went out to the patio. When she returned, she led them through the living room and out a set of paned French doors, her white orthopedic shoes whispering in the silence against the hardwood floor.

Westcott sat at a frosted-glass patio table with his hands curled around a glass of what must have once been whiskey and ice, but was now whiskey and cold water. He switched off the boom box that had been playing the blues when they stepped onto the patio. Raven could see he wore one of his Super Bowl rings. It was so huge she wondered how he had been able to lift the glass. At first he seemed to be staring out at the lake, contemplating the cypress rising from its slick surface.

But it wasn't the lake he was staring at, it was the boathouse. The back of his head was rigid and his back strained against the patio chair as if he would be willing to trade his soul for the ability to spring up and run far away.

"I'm thinking about burning the damn thing down," he said without turning around. "And if they won't let me burn it, I'm thinking about demolishing it. I want it gone all at once. One quick whack. Out of here." He waved the hand with the Super Bowl ring slowly in the air, and then he looked over his shoulder at them. "A thing like that shouldn't linger. Am I right?"

"Mr. Westcott," Raven said. "I'd like to talk to you for a few minutes."

"I've heard. And you've heard that I have a lawyer. Talk to him. Please."

"I'm afraid he wouldn't tell me what I need to know in order to find out who killed your daughter. You want that too. Right?"

He studied her before standing up and waving both her and Tucker over to two empty chairs. He sat down when they were seated and clasped his hands together on the table.

"Imogene," he said. "How are you?"

"Fine, Uncle Antwone," she answered. "But more importantly, how you holding up?"

He sighed again and rubbed his hand over his mouth. He was far from the same controlled man he'd been the night his daughter died. He was unshaven and his eyes looked as if sleep had been a stranger for days. There was no longer any righteous indignation in his face. He looked like a man who had been evaluating his life and was now thinking about what more reckoning there was to come.

"I'm hanging in there, little girl," he said. "Appreciate you and your mother coming to the memorial service. Tell her I said hello."

Tucker said that she would, her face composed into an expression of empathy. Raven was glad to see she had the good sense to keep her notepad in her purse.

"Please tell me you're not here for a story?" He stared at her for a long moment, suspicion along with betrayal moving over his face.

A look passed between Tucker and Westcott. It took her a second or two to recover. When she did, she shook her head and smiled wanly. "I'm just like you, Unc," she said. "Just want to find out who killed Hazel, so when Detective Burns said she needed my help, I told her that I'd pave the way for another conversation with you."

"Just like me, huh?" he said with a rough, relieved laugh. "I guess that should make me feel good, but it doesn't. I wouldn't want anyone in my shoes right about now."

"Mr. Westcott—" Raven started.

He held up his hand to stop her. "I already know what you're about to ask me," he said. "The chief has already been down here climbing my frame about me being in the hospital and Hazel being poisoned. You know what he wanted to know?" He looked from Tucker back to Raven.

"I can only imagine," Raven said, thinking it was yet another thing the chief hadn't shared with her. She wondered if she should be angry but knew it was nothing less than she would have done if someone suspected a friend of hers of murder. She would want to be sure. She would ask them personally, whatever her loyalties were to the job and protocols.

"He wanted to know if I killed her. If I got mad and shot her full of poison to shut her up once and for all. He told me that Angel told you a bunch of lies about me hitting her and messing up her face." He sighed so heavily that the top of his massive body heaved with the effort.

"What would Molly say?" Raven asked with skepticism. "And why would she call the cops if what Angel said wasn't true?"

"Molly would say that my daughter was troubled, Detective," Westcott answered. "If Hazel were still alive, I would have said 'daughters', plural. She would have said both of my daughters are troubled. Known them since they were babies, and she also knows how full of their own scent those girls are sometimes." He stopped. "I mean were – for one of them at least."

"So you're saying that Angel lied?" Raven asked.

He turned back toward the boathouse as if he were done with the conversation. "Of course I'm not saying that. I'm saying that she's troubled. Sometimes she just doesn't see things right."

Raven said, "Help me understand how she should have seen you striking your daughter."

He turned to look at her full in the face. "Just like that," he said. "Just like you said it. I struck her. Once. I'm not proud of it. I know Hazel is – I mean was – sick but sometimes in the heat of things...." He curled his hand into a fist and lifted it from the table. As it hung in the air, he said, "In the heat of it, you forget how sick they are and think maybe, just maybe they could help it if they wanted to. They would help it if they loved you, really, really loved you and thought something about you. You think that they are doing it on purpose to punish you for things you did or things you're about to do." His fist fell slowly back to the table. It lay there gently. "Like I said, I'm not proud of it." He looked back to the boathouse.

"Did you and the chief talk about Jabo Kersey as well?" Raven asked. "The fact that your daughter married a man behind your back?"

He twisted the glass around on the table, and said slowly, "You mean the man whose brains you blew out the other night?" He glanced up at her.

Raven sucked in her breath. She tried with all her might to keep her face still and her eyes focused on Westcott's bland face. "If I shot anybody," she said, "I wouldn't be sitting here talking to you. But, yes, the man who was killed the other night. Did you know your daughter was married to him before she died?"

He grunted. "Hell no," he said. "If I did, I would have had the damn thing annulled faster than you could say Jack Robinson." He turned his head back to the lake. "I certainly wouldn't have killed her." He looked over at her and barked a laugh. "Would have most likely killed him, though. Or had him killed. Maybe I should write you a thank-you note."

Raven pointedly ignored that last statement. She shrugged noncommittally before saying, "I can believe that you didn't kill Hazel."

He didn't turn back to her. He just said, "Then why aren't you leaving? I told you what you wanted to know."

"There is something else I had on my mind," Raven said.

"What's that?" he asked, without turning toward her.

"I need to know about the kiss."

He picked up the glass of whiskey and took a long swallow. It was empty when he placed it back down on the table. He gave her a long look. "Is this some sort of joke?" he asked.

"Absolutely no joke," Raven said. "During our first interview you told me that you and your daughter were fighting like cats and dogs before the party on the day she died."

He nodded. "I did."

"And then you said during the party she came over and kissed you on the cheek for some reason. Do you remember that?"

"Do I remember telling you or do I remember her doing that? If it's the latter, I'll carry that with me to the grave. That was the last time my daughter and I touched. What are you getting at, Detective?"

"Have you any idea why she decided to make up with you at that time?"

"I don't," he said. "But I have a feeling you do."

"Yes, I do," Raven said, leaning forward.

"Then why are you here?" he said. "If you know so much?"

"If I knew everything, I wouldn't be bothering you. But I do think that something happened at the party to make your daughter think about you, and think about you in a big way. Her deciding to put things right at that very moment where earlier you two couldn't be in the same room is telling. And then after she kissed you on the cheek, she got between you and someone trying to come over to talk to you."

"And who would that be?"

Raven shrugged. "We don't know. I was hoping you could tell us. For some reason, she didn't want you and that person talking. We're wondering if that was the person who killed her. We know that she knew the killer, but it wasn't someone she cared for given what she told her sister."

"What was that?" he asked. "What did she tell Angel?"

"She told her that someone threatened to spill their guts about something if she didn't meet with him in the boathouse," Raven said. "We thought it was because of something that Hazel had done and didn't want you to find out about. And we don't think it was about the fact that she had married Jabo Kersey."

All of a sudden his face closed. His eyes darkened as if someone had switched off a light behind them and pulled down the shade to keep a passerby from glimpsing the secrets within. He cupped the now-empty whiskey glass between his massive hands, rolling it back and forth. He looked from Raven to Tucker. He looked at Tucker for a long time.

"Uncle Antwone, may I trouble you for your restroom?" she asked him.

He waved a hand at her in a dismissing gesture. "Go on," he said. "You know where it's at."

Tucker told Raven she would meet her by the car and stood up. When she was gone, Westcott said, "Why wouldn't it be about Jabo Kersey? Maybe the person she didn't want talking to me was about to let me know what a mess she had gotten herself into again?"

Raven nodded. "Could be true," she said. "But her making up with you because someone was about to piss you off doesn't fit her MO. Like her sister said, she loved pissing you off, relished it, even."

"I wouldn't go that far."

"Come on, Mr. Westcott," Raven cajoled with a laugh. "You

even said that the only thing we two had in common was the fact that Hazel Westcott liked to drive us crazy."

"I don't know who or what my daughter thought she had to protect me from," he said with a frown. It wasn't a contemplative frown but one that said he was done with the conversation. He waved his hand at the French doors, beckoning Molly, who was standing just on the other side waiting. "I know you've been all over the business, the financials. Your flunkies questioned my employees, my accountants. They didn't find anything that would incriminate me, did they?"

Raven agreed with him on all of that. She said, "It could have been something else that may have been a worry to her but not to you. Did you see anyone there that night who could have made threats against you to get your daughter to meet with him in the boathouse?"

"No," he said.

She pressed on. "Anybody in a position to blackmail you?"

"You have the guest list," he said, as he started to stand.

"Was everyone at the party on the guest list?" Raven asked.

He was about to say yes, then he stopped and cocked his head at her. "You know," he said somewhat more agreeably, "now that I think about it, no. When we have parties like that, I call the usuals myself."

"The usuals?"

"Yeah, the usuals. People I always invite myself, because of politics, you know, and others because they're my friends and would be offended if I only sent them a formal invitation. It makes it more personal if I call."

"Who are the usuals, Mr. Westcott?" Raven asked coldly.

"Don't get like that," he said. "Nobody who could have done this. The chief, whom you know is a friend of mine, then the mayor, people in that circle. Scout's honor." He held his palm up. "No murderers."

Raven thought back to the security videos. "I remember seeing the mayor," *and his fat round belly*, she thought but didn't say. "But not the chief."

But she had remembered the chief telling her and Billy Ray that he had stopped by that night. She wondered how long.

"Oh, he didn't stay long," Westcott said, as if reading her mind. "He never stays long. About five or ten minutes. Just came in long enough to have a drink and shake my hand. Say hi to the wife. He didn't go outside."

"Any other usuals?" Raven asked, though she already knew.

"Yes, yes," he said impatiently. "That fella on the news sometimes, stocky black guy with greasy hair. Looks like a jerry curl or something. I can never remember his name, which is a shame because he's in some writing group my wife has at the house from time to time."

"Writing group?" Raven asked.

"Yes," he said. "She's been working on her memoir for what seems like forever, and he and a few other people who are working on writing meet in the library to jaw about it. If you ask me, it's just an excuse for her to get on my nerves and for him to drink up my wine. Why can't I remember that fella's name?"

"Lamont Lovelle."

"If you say so. I don't remember him staying long either. I had to call him personally because last time I had a party, my wife said she got a call from him and he was all sensitive that he didn't receive a personal invite like the chief. After that, my wife started writing down names of people that I had to personally invite so we wouldn't have another situation like that. I called his boss, too, I think. A mousy-looking fella that hung around with Hazel when she was going after you for that shooting. Horton or Holliday or something like that."

"Holloway," she said. She took out her cell phone and quickly punched up the Byrd's Landing Police Department's website. She showed him a picture of Holloway.

"Yes, that's him." He nodded. "He was there. He stayed for a long time but didn't spend time outside. Talks to my wife a lot, but I don't care for him much. I guess that's why I can't ever remember his damn name."

CHAPTER THIRTY-NINE

She left when it was clear that Westcott would not answer any more questions. After pointing out Holloway, he turned back to staring at his daughter's boathouse. Molly came and stood next to her, waiting for her to leave the man in peace.

But Raven stayed for a few minutes longer, long enough for him to push play on the boom box. John Lee Hooker's voice came through the speakers, a voice that was straightforward and unembroidered with sentiment. He sang 'Serves Me Right to Suffer' while Westcott tapped his heavy feet against the stone patio as if he couldn't agree more. Raven didn't leave until Molly touched her arm.

Tucker hadn't returned since the excuse of having to use the restroom. Raven met her outside, where she was leaning against the passenger side of the Mustang.

"You smoke too?" Raven asked her.

"Not all the time," Tucker answered. "I pop gum. When popping gum doesn't help, I smoke. Yeah, I know. Stupid, right? Want one?"

Raven shook her head. She made no move to open the driver's side door. She just stared as Tucker smoked. Tucker stared down at the paved driveway, studiously ignoring Raven's gaze.

"You sure were quiet," Raven said. "Quieter than I bet you've ever been since coming headfirst onto this earth."

Tucker didn't say anything.

"And he sure did a lot of looking at you," Raven said mildly.

Tucker nodded.

"But not your legs," Raven said. "And for someone so eager to come visit Westcott with me, you sure hightailed it out of there when the conversation got interesting."

Tucker finally looked in Raven's direction, but still managed to look past her. She took another deep drag from the cigarette before dropping the butt on the ground. She stamped on it with the heel of a leather sandal before wrapping the extinguished cigarette in a tissue and dropping the wad in her purse.

"I don't leave butts lying around," she said. "Pet peeve of mine. Nasty."

Raven said nothing.

"I'm a journalist," Tucker said, leaving out the proud-of-it phrase though her tone certainly implied it. "I find things out. But I'm also a human being, Raven."

Raven said nothing.

"You don't understand," she said. "It wasn't his fault. Looking at his face just now, I think that he thinks it was, that he's being punished for it. But it wasn't his fault."

Without speaking, Raven got into the car. She put the key into the ignition and waited for Tucker to get in. "You know," Raven said to the windshield, "Hazel Westcott couldn't stand me."

"That's not news," Tucker said.

"No it's not," she agreed. "To top it off she was the biggest witch of all the witches in the history of witchery."

"I don't understand."

"Yeah," Raven said as she backed the Mustang out. "There's a lot of that going around lately. A lot of misunderstandings. What I'm trying to say is that Hazel Westcott was a witch to me, but she loved her father and her father loved her. And she loved Quincy Trueblood. That shows that she was also human. No one, not anyone, deserved what was done to her. And even more, by taking Quincy Trueblood away from her, I owe her, Imogene. I'm going to find out who killed her even if it costs me everything that I have – no matter how much she hated me."

Tucker nodded. And then she said, "Like I told you, Raven, I grew up with Hazel. We didn't get along and we drifted apart after I graduated high school, but I still have a lot of memories. I'm going to tell you this because it sounds like you need to know it."

Raven waited. She could feel Tucker looking at her, but she willed herself to stay quiet.

"It doesn't have anything to do with the murder," Tucker said, before taking a deep breath and jumping right in.

Tucker's father and Westcott had been friends since they were children, Imogene started. Once when Tucker was sixteen she walked into the living room to see her father and Westcott sitting at the kitchen table with a bottle of whiskey between them. As she was walking in the room, she heard Westcott say something that haunted her until she was out of college and working as an intern for a newspaper in New Orleans. He hadn't said much, but it was the way he said it and the cold stop he came to when she walked into the kitchen. He was saying something about a body being three days lying before anyone found it. His voice was heavy as he said it, his face so guilty that Tucker wondered how long a person who had to suffer such guilt could live.

She would forget about it for a while and then Westcott's words would come back to her – *a body three days lying* – and she would wonder all over again. She thought about asking her daddy about it, but the way that they looked at her when she stumbled upon them in the kitchen told her that it was a subject that was off-limits for children, especially as Westcott so annoyingly insisted on calling her even now, a 'little girl'.

It was during her internship in New Orleans when she decided to do some research on Westcott. She wanted to find out what he meant by that *three days lying* bit. After all, she was in the place where Westcott grew up, a place where information would not be in short supply. She told herself that she was being silly, that he could have been talking about the traumatic experience of a relative not being found for three days after a gruesome murder, or maybe as she thought about the guilt on his face and her father's refusal to talk about it, a lover no one knew about, one who perhaps died alone. She realized that she was playing a silly little game, playing the part of the investigative journalist she had dreamed of being.

It didn't take her a long time to find clues regarding what Westcott was talking about, but without knowing what she had overheard earlier, she might not have been able to make the connection. There was an article in the local paper about the stabbing of a seventeen-year-old boy, the best friend of local football star Antwone Westcott. The boy's name was Blue Luther, and he wasn't a football star like his best friend, but a guitarist who lived in a small house with his four brothers, mother and grandmother. It was an unlikely friendship that started when Westcott heard Blue play in one of the juke joints that didn't care how old its patrons were as long as they could afford the drinks and the cover fee. The article said that the boy was found beneath a bridge abutment hidden from view. His body had been there a long time, potentially days. It was a crime that to this day remained unsolved.

But no matter how hard she tried, how many of Westcott's friends she spoke to, that was all she could learn. So she forgot about it and returned to Byrd's Landing, where Westcott had become a very wealthy man and, oddly enough, considering the line of business he was in, a philanthropist.

She stopped talking then, as if she had to come up for air. Then she said in a halting voice, "So I went to see him."

"Because you thought he had something to do with Blue Luther's death," Raven said.

"Yes," Tucker agreed. "It was because of what he said. *Three days lying.* Those words that I remembered. No one knew exactly how long Blue Luther's body had been there, I mean, the medical examiner could only pin down a vague time period. But from what Uncle Antwone was confessing to my father and the look of guilt on his face, it sounded as if he did."

"He killed Blue Luther," Raven said. "He killed him and left his body to decompose under that bridge."

Tucker shook her head. "Not quite," she said.

She continued telling Raven what had happened. Westcott and Blue Luther had gotten into a fight. It was Westcott's knife but he didn't pull it. He told her that the knife fell out of his pocket during the scuffle and Blue Luther picked it up and started taking swipes at him with it. Westcott, who outweighed his friend by at least fifty pounds, managed to wrestle the knife away from him.

But Blue Luther was wounded. It was the days before cell phones so Westcott left him there while he went to get help. But when he came back he couldn't find him. He had no idea that Blue had crawled behind the abutment and out of sight.

"Who did he come back with?" Raven asked.

"What?"

"You said he went to get help. From whom?"

"He couldn't find anyone and no one would answer the doors of the nearest houses, so he came back with some towels and bandages he had found at his own house. He didn't think that Blue Luther was hurt that bad."

Raven lifted an eyebrow.

"And that's exactly why I kept my mouth shut," Tucker said. "Because I knew that was the look I would get when I explained that it wasn't his fault. He didn't mean to kill him. You should have seen his face when he told me what had happened. It's something that he's been making up for all of his life."

By giving away his money, Raven thought, but didn't say out loud. That was why he had given so much of his money to Oral's charity, the one that helped kids like Blue Luther. She let the silence play and the town just rolled past their windows as if it were on display especially for them – the fits of live oak and cypress trees, the open fields burned yellow in the heat, the long, gray streets.

"Why did Westcott tell you this?" Raven asked after a while.

Tucker's shoulders slumped. "I pretended like I already knew. He made me promise to stay quiet. He's done so much good since then that I didn't have the heart to say anything. And...."

She stopped and looked out the passenger-side window.

"And what?" Raven prompted.

"My father had died a couple of months before. Stomach cancer. He died hard, he was in a lot of pain. I think that...." She stopped again as the surface of Big Bayou Lake flickered through her window.

Raven waited. Tucker started again. "I think that he couldn't, Uncle Antwone, I mean. He couldn't bear that secret alone."

"What about Blue Luther's family? His mom and dad? His brothers and sisters? You ever think about them?" Raven said. "What about him stabbed and dying under a bridge? Him missing while Westcott kept his mouth shut. What about all of that?"

Tucker looked at Raven's profile as she drove. "I didn't know Blue Luther," she said. "But I know Uncle Antwone. I know what a good man he is."

"Tell me one more thing," Raven said. "What were they fighting over?"

Tucker turned away from Raven to resume her gaze out of the passenger window. "Aunt Shelia," she said. "They were fighting over Shelia Westcott, Uncle Antwone's wife."

Raven let this sink in. She wondered if Shelia knew about it and decided that she probably did, and was using alcohol to hide from it. Perhaps that's why Westcott insisted that she wasn't to be questioned when Hazel died. She wondered if Shelia in one of her maudlin states ever told anyone, and if she had, she wondered who that person might be. When Hazel was making her life a living hell, she and Holloway became pretty chummy. She wondered if that led to Holloway meeting Hazel's mother, Shelia. She wondered if Holloway became friends with her too, and if they ever met alone when Shelia was drunk and vulnerable and talking about things she shouldn't.

"I don't think Shelia knows," Tucker said at last.

"Someone does," Raven said.

"It has to be someone like me," Tucker said. "Someone who's used to doing a lot of digging and research. I only found out because I put together what Uncle Antwone had said to my daddy and Blue Luther's murder, and then took a big leap. I tried getting my hands on the police reports while I was in New Orleans, but I didn't know how to get past all the red tape, not then. So it had to be someone experienced enough to find shit out. Like a journalist."

Or a cop, Raven thought. Someone like Holloway. It was likely that Shelia did mention something to him, and then he used his badge to talk to the investigator in Blue Luther's death, or maybe get a look at the evidence, including the interview Westcott had with the New Orleans cops after Blue Luther's body was found. Raven remembered Westcott telling her that he was questioned when his best friend was killed.

They rode in silence for a while. Raven imagined that she could feel the guilt about breaking a confidence emanating from Tucker in waves.

Raven left her alone. She began adding this new evidence to what they already knew about the murders. It made sense that the killer blackmailed Hazel into her boathouse bedroom by threatening to expose her father. And both Oral and Hazel had known their killers. She knew this because there were no signs of forced entry at either location. And at Oral's, there were the remains of dirty wineglasses amid the broken coffee table in Oral's living room. She remembered seeing CSI place them one by one in evidence bags. The DNA results hadn't come back yet, but she had an idea what they would reveal.

Another factor would be someone who was on the inside, someone who knew that she and Billy Ray were going to pick up Jabo Kersey at the Four Leaf Casino. And only five people were in that circle – herself, Billy Ray, the chief, Lovelle, and Holloway. One of them was the killer. Raven was betting on Holloway. Now all she had to do was prove it.

CHAPTER FORTY

It was already dark when Raven dropped Tucker off at her car in the BLPD parking lot. Raven was just about to leave the Mustang to go inside to see if Billy Ray was still working when her Android began its Zydeco 'Walkin' to New Orleans' ring tone. She answered it and pressed it to her ear only to hear Billy Ray say in a no-nonsense voice, "My place. Now," before hanging up.

She sat there for several seconds in the driver's seat, wondering if she should be offended by his tone. But in the end she wasn't. Something must have happened, she thought with a sinking feeling, something not good. She put the car in gear, whipped it out of the parking lot and drove to Billy Ray's double-barrel shotgun on Peabody.

When she got there, the place was lit up. The yellow light from the streetlamp splashed on the bottle tree Billy Ray kept in the front yard. The Christmas lights he used to frame his front door were on, blinking brightly in the increasing darkness of the humid night.

As she stepped onto the porch she heard the music of Buckwheat Zydeco blare through the open screen door. It sounded like the frenetic beat of the accordion and washboard on the song 'Ma 'Tit Fille', but she wasn't sure. She only knew the music through Billy Ray, who once told her that he agreed with Buckwheat – if you didn't feel the urge to move when listening to Zydeco, then there was something wrong with you. She wanted to move now. For some reason she wanted to run. The screen door rattled several times as she knocked but she knew Billy Ray couldn't hear her over the music.

The smell of olive oil and garlic greeted her as she walked in. She went straight through the living room and bedroom to find Billy Ray in the kitchen, standing at the stove with his back to her. He was shaking a pan against the burner, and there was a bowl of cleaned but raw shrimp on the counter next to the stove. She watched him work for several seconds, the muscles beneath his white undershirt rippling as he moved. He picked up the cell phone next to the shrimp and pressed a few buttons. Buckwheat's music became a feverish murmur over the oil bubbling in the skillet.

Then he said, "Are you just going to stand there all night? Or are you going to say hello?"

He turned to her. Raven drew in her breath at the intense look on his face, one he wasn't trying to hide. Something had happened, and though she wanted to ask him right away, her instincts told her to proceed with caution.

"I didn't want to startle you," she said. "Not with you shaking a pan of hot oil."

He grabbed the bowl of raw shrimp and threw them in the skillet. Smoke and steam sizzled upward.

"Can I help?" she said.

"No," he answered. "I'd rather do this myself. Grab some water or a beer out of the fridge if you want."

He pointed to a cupboard where she found a New Orleans Saints water glass. She went to the fridge to fill it. As water twirled into the glass, she asked, "What happened, Billy Ray?"

"You first," he said, his back still to her. She could see the orange flames leap beneath the skillet as Billy Ray scraped it against the burner.

He had finished the shrimp and was dividing them between two plates of baguette rolls already toasted and soaked with butter. Watching him, she told him about her visit with Westcott and what she had learned about Blue Luther.

"So, that's what the perp used to control Hazel," he said.

"Looks like it," she confirmed.

"I'm not surprised," he said. "Man looked like he was trying to make up for something with all that money he gave away."

"That's not all, Billy Ray."

He twisted around briefly to look at her and lifted an eyebrow. She started telling him about the fact that Holloway was at the party, but Billy Ray was shaking his head before she could get the words out.

"No," he said. "It's not him."

He sat the plates with the po'boy sandwiches on the Formica table. He went to the fridge, took out two beers and used an opener to flick off the tops before coming to sit down opposite her.

"How can you be so sure?" she asked.

He took a mouthful of beer. He held it for a few seconds before swallowing. "There is no way in everything that's bright in hell that man could've taken that shot from the trestle. He was a math teacher, remember? You even said yourself that the only reason the chief put him in IA was so he wouldn't shoot his own foot off."

"Who is it then?" she challenged.

"Now I'm not sure," he said. "But it's not Holloway. Not by himself anyway."

The music was still playing, softly, but playing. The piercing wails and uneven beat of Buckwheat's accordion were setting her nerves on edge. She was about to ask him to turn it off when he picked up a bag of plain Lay's potato chips and tore it open. As he was dumping the chips out over his plate, she realized that the entire time they had been talking, he had barely looked at her. He reached over to dump chips on her plate. She caught his wrist. He stopped.

"What's happened?" she asked him again. "Why am I here?"

She let go of his wrist and he turned the bag over. For the first time he leveled a steady gaze her way. She read fear and worry in his eyes, and something else. Secrecy. He was keeping something from her.

"You need to lay low for a while," he said.

"What do you mean, lay low?"

"Disappear. Get out of sight. Lay low," he said. "Not long. Just for a little bit."

She gaped back at him. "Billy Ray, are you outside of your mind right now?"

He sat the bag down, and picked up his beer again. "I've never been more inside of it."

"Why won't you just tell me what happened?"

"Not happened," he corrected. "Is. Is happening. You heard the chief this morning." He stopped and dragged a forearm across his sweating brow. "After you left, I got called to a meeting with the chief and Holloway and...."

"And?"

"Pam Jones."

"Pam Jones, the DA?" she asked, a finger of fear caressing her throat. "Without me?"

"Yeah," he sighed. "Without you."

"Why?" she asked.

"I think you know."

"And the chief was there?" she said, trying to keep the hurt from the chief's betrayal off her face and the agitation out of her voice.

From Billy Ray's look, she guessed that she hadn't done a good job of either. He shook his head. "I told you that no matter what you think about the chief or what he's done for you, that man's a politician. He's protecting his own house."

She sat back and stared at the sandwich on her plate. Her stomach lurched and for a minute she thought she was going to be sick. "He saved my life and now he thinks I had something to do with these murders?"

"I'm not sure what's going on in his head," he said. "But the evidence is all leading back to you, Raven. It may be circumstantial, but it's a problem. You've got motive and no alibis and — I hate to say it because I don't believe it has anything to do with you — a past that most people around here are starting to remember."

She nodded, fighting the urge to run again. "So it all comes right back down to Floyd," she said.

He nodded back, a troubled look on his face.

"Why were you there?" she asked.

"They wanted to know where I stood," he said.

"And where is that? Where do you stand, Billy Ray?"

"As if you have to ask. I stand with you, my partner," he said, "but I didn't tell them that."

They said nothing for a while. The Zydeco from the portable speakers on top of the fridge appeared to be whispering a frenzied warning.

"They're trying to build a case against me?" she finally asked.

"It's mostly Holloway. I don't think the chief would be so focused on you as the perp if that bastard didn't have his ear."

"I don't understand how the chief could think that I'm a monster like...." She stopped at the sound of Floyd's voice in her head – *You mean like your ole man, Birdy Girl? Maybe he thinks the apple don't fall far from the tree.* She put her hands to her temples and shook the voice away.

"You scared the chief at Oral's," Billy Ray said. "I think he saw something in you that he didn't like."

The thought of being locked up even for a short time made her frantic. She would suffocate in jail. No more long trail runs on Scorpion's Tail, no more gym sessions, and more importantly no more career, the one she had worked so hard on, and the one she had used to put men like Floyd away. If they arrested her, no matter what happened in the long run, her life in Byrd's Landing would be over. And so would her life as a cop.

Now her mind was whirring with the music. She felt like a trapped animal. "How much time do I have?" she asked, wondering if they were coming for her right now. She stood up so quickly that the table shook. Billy Ray reached out an arm to steady it. He caught the neck of the open bottle of beer in front of her before it fell to the floor.

"Wait, wait," he said. "You don't need to do anything right now. Just lay low. Leave town, even, while I try to work this thing out. But if you wait too long kicking around here..."

"...then I'm screwed."

"No," Billy Ray said. "You're fucked."

"And what are you going to be doing while I'm laying low?" she asked.

"Trying to find out who killed these people, Raven," he said. "What you think? Rita already calling in that favor to get the elimination samples of the DNA checked against the hairs found in Hazel's bed, including Holloway's. If it's somebody in the department, we'll get them. You just have to be patient and smart right now."

"No," Raven said. "This is my problem, Billy Ray, not yours."

She didn't wait for him to answer, but turned away and started for the front door. Billy Ray followed her. He tried to grab her arm, and even though he was her partner and ally in this, his hand felt like a manacle closing around her wrist. She shook him away, ran out of the door and into her Mustang. As she sped away she could see him in the rearview mirror staring at her with his hands on his slim hips.

A few blocks away from his house, she stopped the car next to a set of empty shotguns in the abandoned neighborhood. She flung open the car door and tumbled out. She sank to her knees on the broken asphalt, looked up at the clear sky bright with stars and asked the universe what she should do next. But it was Floyd who answered back.

CHAPTER FORTY-ONE

When she made it to her apartment from Billy Ray's that night she went back to where it all started – back to Floyd. She dumped the contents of the boxes she had retrieved from the storage shed onto her glass coffee table. A multitude of death row groupie letters, visitor logs, and notebooks of Floyd's sermons piled onto the coffee table and slid down to the floor.

She found herself holding the Michael Gorman book, *Straight Razors and Peacock Feathers*, and asked herself the hard question. Was she disturbed by the lies in the book, or because the author accused Raven of being a willing partner to Floyd's killing spree? After all, the author posited, some murders Raven had to have watched; some victims she must have lured. In the foreword, Gorman claimed that he had visited Floyd many times in prison, which was a lie. His name wasn't in the visitor logs. He might have written Floyd, but he never visited.

But maybe Gorman didn't lie about everything, Raven thought. Maybe Gorman had found her own true memories, the ones that she had been trying to bury all of these years by being a good cop, the ones that occupied her dreams. Floyd had used her to lure some of his victims. She was only a child, but she was complicit.

Heart beating, she threw the book as hard as she could against the wall. In an attempt to calm down, she listened to the breath scraping against her chest until it slowed. This is just what Holloway had wanted, she thought, to unhinge her before destroying her by putting her in a cage. That is why he had the book in his office. He was using it to find ways to torture her, to make possible her greatest fear that she was as evil as Floyd. What else did he have in store for her? *Now I rightly don't know about that*, a voice answered. *But if I was you, I'd be tryin' lickety split to find out.*

Raven waited until she thought the whole world had to be asleep before changing clothes and slipping into her Mustang. She didn't put the key into the ignition right away. She just sat there for a moment or two in the three o'clock in the morning darkness, thinking of Floyd. *So fuck it*, she thought, the unpracticed curse slicing through the confusion and fear in her mind. They would never let her escape her past. If they wanted her father, maybe that's who she should give them.

She looked over at the passenger seat. Floyd was sitting right there, as neat as a pin, so unlike the grinning, bloody disaster he had been at his death. He was wearing his favorite hat. The peacock feather, dark blue at its very center and fluorescent green around the edges, glowed from the hatband in the darkness of the Mustang's cabin. She watched him until the grin on his face and eventually the rest of him faded into the darkness.

She still didn't put the key into the ignition just yet. Instead she placed a peacock feather flattened between two sheets of wax paper on the dash. She smoothed the feather against the surface of the dashboard for several seconds. Then she unstrapped the hunting knife from her ankle holster and stared at its jagged tip. She wondered if it was anything like the knife Westcott used to kill Blue Luther. She held it by the handle and asked herself who it was really for. Holloway or the ghost who had just been in the passenger seat? She wasn't entirely sure.

She looked over at the passenger seat once again. Floyd, who was back, said solemnly, *I hope you 'bout to have a little fun, Birdy Girl. Lord knows you been boring the shit out of me lately.*

She drove the Mustang until she was several blocks from Holloway's tract home, parked and got out. Still on automatic pilot, she scaled the fading redwood side fence next to Holloway's house, wincing a little from the small pains caused by battered muscles still trying to heal from her adventures with Jabo Kersey.

Holloway's side yard was neatly kept with a narrow strip of grass rimmed by a funnel of white cement. She stood still for a while plastered against the stucco until she was sure that the neighbors hadn't heard. Even though it was late, there could be an insomniac or two sitting on their front porch or having a smoke on their backyard patio.

When Raven was sure it was just the moon, herself, and Holloway's perfect side yard, she peeled herself from the side of the house and considered the best way to enter. She had been waiting beside a window that had been slightly cracked to let in the night air. A blue light soft as a whisper floated from the window. Raven thought this was the best shot she'd have. She removed the screen using the knife from her ankle holster, lifted the window and wriggled inside.

She regretted her choice the moment she stood upright.

The room wasn't empty and Holloway's mother wasn't asleep. Trapped eyes moved over Raven's tight black jeans, the athletic black jacket, and the ski mask she had pulled over her head but not her face.

"It's okay," Raven said in a soothing voice though she knew it was ridiculous to try and ease the woman's fear. "I'm with the police." Even more ridiculous, Raven thought, feeling like the slime she arrested. "I'm not going to hurt you, I promise." Like her promises meant anything to the woman watching an intruder invade her house. "I'm just looking for something. I'll be on my way as soon as I find it."

Raven remembered the car accident. Jane Holloway's larynx had been crushed by the steering wheel of her new Cadillac. And that tragic mistake at the hospital left her paralyzed from the neck down with brain damage that appeared to allow her to understand but not respond. Unable to speak or write, she had become a mute prisoner inside the horror of her own body Now, a tear slipped down the side of the woman's face. Raven wiped it away with a gloved finger, thinking that if she was sent to hell for only one thing, it would be this.

Raven had never been in Holloway's house but she had obtained the plan for the tract home from the internet. Saving the master bedroom for last, she began a methodical search of the house. She started in the kitchen, looking in the pantries and the cabinets where he kept his dishes. His study was as unrelentingly tidy as the kitchen; the only item even slightly related to the murders was a file folder on the middle of his desk with her name on it, probably a copy of the one he had shown the chief in his office. She opened it and browsed through the pages as if reading about someone she didn't know. The folder held every negative article written about her along with newspaper accounts of the crimes Floyd committed.

She looked in closets, even returned to Holloway's mother's room to run her fingers under her body, surprised at how cool she was in the late summer heat, cool and dry. Yes, indeed Holloway took very good care of his mother. But she found nothing. No peacock feathers.

No silver cane with a wolf's head. And no signs of any manufactured evidence in the shooting of Quincy Trueblood.

She found Holloway's room at the end of a short hallway. His curtain was open. The frosted light from the moon allowed Raven to see him quite clearly. In spite of the heat, it looked like he slept in a full set of striped pajamas with the covers pulled up to his chest, his arms resting on top of the smooth blankets. One side of his face was pressed against the pillow. Raven could tell by the clear trickle of drool falling from the corner of his lips that he was deep in some dream. As she stood at the foot of the bed staring at his half-lit and half-dark face, she wondered what she would do if he woke up.

But she didn't let herself wonder about that too long. She walked around the bed until she was to the side of him. In one hand she had the hunting knife, in the other she held the peacock feather between wax paper. Floyd would have used both. She had planned to use only one.

She took the peacock feather from between the wax paper. She fanned it out with gloved fingers, noticing how the green tips glowed in the moonlight. Through the top of Holloway's pajama shirt, she saw the skin of his neck, as pink and smooth as a puppy's belly. How easy it would be to press the tip of the hunting knife to his throat in search of the first drop of blood, and then harder to get at the rest of it. A quick jerk up to the left and it would all be over.

And if the pain woke him Holloway wouldn't even have time to scream. She could watch him gurgle and clutch at his throat in an effort to hold in enough blood to keep life in for another second or two. They'd surely catch her, she knew, but the satisfaction of seeing him choke on his own blood would be worth it. She hadn't found any evidence that he was framing her, but at least she would have revenge. He had killed Hazel after befriending her, and then he had killed Oral after sitting down with him and sharing a glass of wine. And now he was finishing the job by plotting with the chief to send her away like Floyd was sent away.

She cocked her head to the side, wondering, barely realizing that the knife hovered over his throat at the very spot she was thinking about making that first incision. And then Holloway's face morphed into another one. He was Maylene Love. Jean Rinehart. She saw

Quincy Trueblood lying there sleeping peacefully with drool slipping from his lips, his hand curled innocently on his chest like a child's.

Her heart didn't thump as she realized what she had allowed to crawl inside her head. She didn't feel disgusted with herself like she had with Jabo Kersey. With the gesture of holstering the hunting knife, she simply moved the thought aside, gently, and reminded herself that there was still time to get Holloway the right way.

She picked up the peacock feather from the floor where she hadn't even realized it had fallen. She once again spread and smoothed the feather to make it a perfect specimen of what it was. She placed it on Holloway's chest right next to but not quite touching his curled white fingers.

It would be the first thing he would touch when he woke up in the morning. Maybe he would thank God for letting him wake up. Or maybe he wouldn't.

But Raven knew one thing for sure. His fingers would brush against the feather lying on his chest, and fear would close in on him. He would feel watched and marked, perhaps too afraid to kill again. She hadn't found Oral's cane or a stash of peacock feathers, but letting him know that the killer was marking him would give her time to catch him and put him away. And if he accused her of leaving the feather, he would have to prove it.

Before Raven left she opened the front door, the back door, the door leading to the garage. She opened the door to every room in the house to let in the moonlit morning air. She did so to let Holloway know that he may have been smart, but now he was vulnerable. He would never be able to bar any door against her.

She left him in peaceful slumber, sleeping like the dead.

CHAPTER FORTY-TWO

She was dreaming of Floyd. He was standing over the white porcelain sink at their house in Crampton singing the Barbasol 'closest shave of all' jingle. Maylene, Raven's mother, was in the kitchen making dinner. Raven sat on the closed toilet seat lid watching her father shave. The blade of the straight razor came perilously close to cutting the Adam's apple bobbing up and down in his throat as he crooned.

He stopped suddenly and turned to Raven. Light from the single bathroom bulb swirled in the Sheffield steel. His mouth filled with blood when he smiled. It stained his white teeth and dribbled down his pointed chin. He said, *I never thought of killing you, Birdy Girl. No matter what they said or what you thought, I never thought of killing you, not once. Killing you would be like looking in a mirror and slicing my own throat.*

She woke with a start on his last word, scrunching the damp, hot sheets to her neck, remembering the way Floyd died. She recognized the loud banging at her apartment door as the true reason she jolted awake. Heart pounding, she kicked the sheets away. She had been on the opposite side of that knock plenty of times, and knew exactly what it was.

She went to the bathroom and splashed cold water on her face before returning to the bedroom to slide into a pair of jeans and a clean, tight T-shirt. As she did so, the pounding went on and on. Not knowing why she bothered, after she had finished with her shoes she shrugged into her shoulder holster with the new Glock 22, and clipped the detective's badge to her belt.

When she opened the front door, she found what she expected. Two uniform officers stood there trying not to look pissed off at being kept waiting. She knew both of them, of course. The tall, younger one had even helped her on a couple of cases.

"Took you long enough," he said. "If we hadn't seen your car outside, we'd think you weren't home."

"What do you want?" she asked.

"The chief wants you down at the station."

"Why didn't he call me?"

He shrugged, and Raven saw his light brown eyes glance over her shoulder to Floyd's papers scattered all over her living room floor. "He didn't want to give you much of a choice about coming in today," he said.

"Am I under arrest?"

He shook his head. "I don't think so. He just said to pick you up and give you a ride back to the station."

"And if I refused?" she asked tiredly.

"He said to be convincing," he replied. "So, this is me, trying to be convincing, Detective." He tried to smile but failed.

"Give me a minute," she said.

They stepped away and she shut the door. She took her Android out to see if she had any missed calls from Billy Ray and found that she had been so out of it when she got home last night that she hadn't even bothered to charge it.

★   ★   ★

She rode in the back of a police car for the second time in her life. The first time had been when the chief had saved her from Floyd right after Floyd had killed her stepmother.

The two officers escorted her to the chief's office. The chief told her to have a seat after the officers had left. Raven did so slowly, noticing Pam Jones from the DA office and Billy Ray, who looked tired and haggard, in the room as well. Pam Jones had been friendly in the past but now she barely looked at Raven.

The chief picked up one of the Pappy Van Winkle bourbon bottles on his desk and rubbed at the label as if trying to clean it. "Where were you last night, Detective?" he asked after a while.

"What?" Raven responded. Her voice was much louder than it needed to be and she immediately regretted it. She knew exactly what she would think if a suspect responded to her in that manner. She would think they were about to lie.

"I believe I'm still speaking English," the chief said. "I asked where you were last night."

"Chief," Raven said, stalling for time – very obviously, she thought, stalling for time. "What's this about?"

"Raven."

"Why...." She could feel herself stumbling, groping for the right words. It was like looking for a doorway out of a black room. She knew the chief could read it all over her face. "At home," she said, and then more firmly, "I was at home."

"By yourself?" the chief asked.

In a fog, Raven nodded. "Yes," she said slowly. "Why wouldn't I be? What's going on?"

He nodded. "I see," he said. "So you're telling me that you were home last night. Alone. All night?"

She was about to answer yes when Billy Ray broke in. "No," he said. "Not all night. She came over to my place at about ten p.m."

She whipped her head toward him. He gave her a small shake of his head.

The chief leaned back in his chair. Pam Jones snorted and threw her briefcase on top of the chief's desk.

"All night?" the chief asked Billy Ray.

Billy Ray shrugged.

"Not an answer, Detective," the chief said.

"Yeah," Billy Ray said. "All night."

Jones clicked open the briefcase. She took off one Nike running shoe and then the other. "And you would be willing to make a statement to that fact?" she challenged him.

Billy Ray shrugged again. "I'd be willing to make a statement," he said. "Just let me know how you want me to do it. Pen and ink, smoke signals, bits and bytes. I'll tell it any way you want. She was with me all night."

The chief hadn't taken his eyes from Raven's face, but he spoke to Billy Ray. "You know you're talking about your career," he said. "Or should I say careers? Because either way you are fucked. If you're lying, you're going to jail for obstruction of justice. If you're telling the truth, you'll both have reprimands in your jackets for fraternization – right before I fire both your asses. So you want to answer my question again?"

"What's this about?" Raven asked, this time looking at the chief in challenge. She wanted him to say to her face that he suspected her of being the killer. She wanted to watch him turn on her, something he always promised never to do. She wondered if he would squirm as he did so. "You can haul me in here like a perp, but not tell me what's going on?" she asked. "You want to arrest me? Do I need a lawyer?"

Pam Jones was slipping a pair of black pumps with red soles onto her feet. "Okay, I'll play. Presley Holloway's dead. Someone killed him and his mother early this morning. You're looking like the prime suspect right now," she said in a dry voice.

"Close your mouth, Detective," the chief said.

"What? But...." She began, stunned. She was about to say that he was fine last night but stopped herself just in time. "How?"

"Looks like someone smothered them," the chief said. "There was a pillow over Holloway's face."

"And you think I did that?" Raven asked, flabbergasted at him being smothered. Her mind raced as she thought back to how this related to the rest of Floyd's kills. And again, smothering was violent for the victim, but clean for the assailant. Floyd, as her dream reminded her this morning, lived for the sight of blood.

"Nobody but you, precious," Jones said, admiring her newly clad feet. "You hated Holloway's guts. Your run-ins are legendary in this department. You almost bashed his head in at the Justice crime scene, and...." She gave Billy Ray an apologetic look. "Your alibi is weak as shit. Sorry, lover."

Raven's mind raced. Last night she was thinking that Holloway had killed all three of them – Hazel, Jabo Kersey, and lastly Oral Justice in order to set her up. But she couldn't find any proof even after breaking into his house. Now, Holloway was dead himself. And, of course, she was the best suspect. Even if Holloway was somehow still miraculously behind this, her head was right where he had left it after Oral Justice's death – on the chopping block. It was only a matter of time before the axe fell.

She looked up to see Billy Ray watching her closely. Did he think that she had killed Holloway? Billy Ray had said that Holloway couldn't have done this by himself. Could Holloway have had an accomplice who had gotten tired of him and taken him out?

"Did they find anything at the crime scene that would link

Holloway to the rest of the murders?" Raven asked, the feather she had left on Holloway's chest paramount on her mind.

"Like what?" the chief replied. "A feather? Yes, on the floor next to the man's body."

"And you think I did that?" she said, trying to make it sound ridiculous. "Why would I set myself up like that?"

The chief said softly, "I don't know, Raven. There's no accounting for what crazy people do."

Silence descended on the room and Raven looked at the chief for a long time. She tried to discern if he felt guilty about suspecting her, or if he had any doubt that she had something to do with the deaths of Holloway and the others. She found neither. No guilt. No doubt. She felt like screaming at the top of her lungs at the unfairness of it all. *Yep, Birdy Girl,* Floyd couldn't resist adding to her anguish, *no matter how deep you try to bury me, you got folks like the chief digging me up to remind you where you come from.*

Instead of screaming, she said softly, not taking her eyes from the chief's face, "Are you going to arrest me?"

The chief looked away from her and at the district attorney.

Jones said, "Don't have a warrant yet. My favorite judge is on vacation. Won't be back until next week. That gives you a couple of days."

"A couple of days for what?" Raven asked.

"To really take a look at this thing and see if there are other possibilities," she said. "It's because I like you, Burns. And I don't want to believe someone I like so much would have the heart to smother a man and his crippled mother while they slept in their beds. Bring the chief somebody he can hang his hat on so things don't get even more uncomfortable."

"Wait," the chief started in protest. "Pam, are you sure—"

She gave him a death-ray stare. "We are talking about one of our own here," she said. "You stood by Raven when they wanted to hang her out to dry during the Trueblood fiasco, and you were right then. Why are you so ready to turn your back on her now?"

The chief placed the Pappy's bottle he had been fiddling with back in line with the others. He said, "I hope you don't regret this, Pam."

"I don't plan on it." She stopped and looked at Raven. "Don't make a fool out of me."

Done, Jones retrieved her briefcase from the chief's desk and stood up. At the door she turned and gave the chief a stern look. "One more thing, find a different detective for the Holloway case. Even if it's someone from out of town." She waved her index finger at Billy Ray. "He," she said, shaking her head, "is to go nowhere near it. And Raven?"

Raven looked at her but didn't say anything.

"Don't leave town," Jones said.

CHAPTER FORTY-THREE

Raven sat for a few seconds after the district attorney left the chief's office. She wondered briefly if the next time she saw Pam Jones would be from the defendant's table in the courtroom. She turned back to the chief and studied his face. He returned her look, his mouth twisted with disgust and his eyes filled with what she took as angry betrayal. As if she were betraying him, Raven thought. Her throat closed with the tears she held back. She looked away from the chief, but try as she might, she could not look at Billy Ray, who had walked away from the window to stand by her chair.

The chief's gaze on her was as hot as a branding iron. His voice came from a long way off as she stood to leave.

"You can put your service revolver and badge right here for the time being," he said, pointing at an empty place on his desk.

Without surprise or protest, she unclipped her badge. "The Glock's mine," she said. "I bought it after Jabo. I lost the service revolver in the drink, remember?"

He nodded, but said, "I'd feel more comfortable if you left the Glock with me anyway."

She looked at him a long time. "Are you going to make me?"

He lifted both hands in the air briefly. "You know I can't do that."

"Then I think I'll keep it," she said.

She let the silence in the room play.

"You have anything to say?" the chief challenged. "Nothing?"

She tried to stop the macabre grin from spreading across her face but couldn't quite do it. It was what Floyd would have done. He would have grinned in the face of all this negative emotion and drama.

"What do you want me to say, Chief?" she asked. "Or do? Should I drop to my knees and beg for my job back? Ask you to believe in me while crying a bucketful of tears?"

"Now hold on," he said, lifting a placating hand. "I'm not firing you. It's just temporary, a suspension. What do you expect me to do with all this going on?"

"I don't know, Chief," she spat back. "Trust me?"

The office was quiet for a while, and then the chief held up three fingers. "This is strike three, Raven," he said. "I trusted you when Quincy Trueblood was shot, put my neck out there for you if you don't recall, and I trusted you again when Hazel—"

She let out a snort of protest.

"No," he said. "Hear me out. You lied about the phone call, didn't you? And now this department is on the line – not to mention that Holloway and his mother are dead after the entire force saw you threaten him at Oral's place. And you still running around here like a loose cannon asking me to trust you? Are you serious right now?"

"Wait," Billy Ray started. "There's no cause for all of this."

But the chief turned to him. "And you," he said. "You're lucky that your shit isn't right here on my desk besides hers."

Billy Ray went to respond but Raven placed a hand on his arm. It would do them no good if he ended up suspended as well. Without taking his eyes from the chief, Billy Ray said, "Come on, Raven. I'll give you a ride home."

★   ★   ★

Raven collided with the summer heat outside the glass double doors of the BLPD. A sweet but unpleasant smell hung in the air from the magnolia blooms sweltering in the heat. Sweat broke out on her face, and her T-shirt and jeans went immediately damp. Raven felt like she was burning, so hot that she wished she could jump out of her own skin.

All of a sudden Floyd like a mirage stood beside her. He puffed his chest out, put his hands in the front pockets of his dark brown pants and said in a speculative voice, *Don't worry, Birdy Girl. Badges are for sissies. Shoulda left your gun too. Best to stick with a blade. Always relied on a razor myself. Maybe you come 'round to my ways of doing things one of these hell-raisin' days.*

She wondered if she had finally lost her mind. He was really there. Right there besides her, his physical form wavering in the heat. As she stared at him, the figure of Floyd morphed back into Billy Ray. He took her by the arm and began to fast-walk her to his waiting car. The apparition had scared her. She felt as if she were no longer in control of her own mind. She tried jerking away from Billy Ray, but he held her fast.

"Don't be stupid," he said. "You need a ride home and I'm the only hope you have right now."

Billy Ray opened the passenger-side door of his Skylark. He stood there blocking her exit until she sank down into the passenger seat. As Billy Ray walked around to the driver's side, she rolled down the window in an attempt to get some air into the stifling car.

Billy Ray didn't speak until they were on Main speeding to her apartment.

"Raven," he said, his voice laced with anger. "What in the hell are you doing, girl?"

"Billy Ray," she started.

"No." He pointed a finger at her as he swung the car into the left lane and accelerated.

"Don't tell me you weren't over at Holloway's last night. It was all over your face back there. And I called you at least twenty times after you left my place last night."

She watched tall cypress trees fly by on either side as he continued to drive and rail at her at the same time. He did so for several long miles. The car came to a halt at a red light on Sugarloaf and he stopped talking. She didn't break the silence for a long time. Neither did Billy Ray.

Finally she said, "I had no choice but to go over to Holloway's after what you told me."

She gave him a pleading look and saw the muscle in his jaw jump. He said nothing. She continued, "But I didn't go there to kill him." *At least I don't think so*, she thought, but of course kept her mouth shut. "I went there to look for evidence – Oral's cane, the feathers, remember? And to see if I could find anything linking Holloway to setting me up. We have a killer out there and my ass was on the line...."

"And it isn't on the line now?" he said. "Even worse than before?"

The light turned green and he jerked the car forward. His face was set in stone, and she didn't remember ever seeing such an angry light in his eyes.

"I didn't kill Holloway," she said. "Please don't tell me that you actually think I killed that man and his mother."

"I don't think that," he said. "If I did, do you think I would be back there covering for your ass?"

She sighed in relief. At least he was still on her side. At least he didn't think that she was a monster. And then there was Floyd's doubting voice in her head. *Not yet, darlin'*, Floyd whispered. She grunted and put her sweat-dampened face into her hands to silence Floyd's ghost. She wondered if he would ever leave her alone.

"Who's doing this to me?" she said in a strangled voice.

Billy Ray didn't answer. He checked his mirror again and swung into the far right lane. He flicked on his blinker to make the turn into her apartment complex. She studied his face. The anger had dissipated. His face was flat and without emotion. She had seen that look many times as he interrogated suspects. It was a look that tried hard not to give anything away.

"You know something," she said.

"I don't know anything."

"What aren't you telling me, Billy Ray?"

He glided the Skylark into a parking space next to her red Mustang and cut the engine. He made no move to open the car door.

"I don't know anything for sure," he conceded. "But something just felt funny to me after I got the news about Holloway. I'm just checking on a few things, that's all. And waiting on something before I can say for sure."

"What few things?" she insisted, her heart speeding up as she searched his face.

"Now, I don't have any proof," he said. "But Holloway being gone makes me think we missed something right under our noses. Some things need working out before I can be sure."

"But you never suspected Holloway," she said.

"No, I didn't. Not by himself, anyway. But he could have been working with somebody."

Her heart dropped. "On the inside, you mean," she said. "Who? The chief?"

He let out a derisive laugh. "Don't be crazy, Raven," he said.

"Tell me!" she demanded. "Who?"

She had never heard Billy Ray raise his voice. He didn't now. Instead he twisted around in the car seat until he was facing her as fully as he could in the small space.

"Tell you, why?" he challenged. "So you can go after the perp like you did Holloway? So you can put the nail in the coffins for both of our asses? You're not in control, Raven. You have been lying to me since all this started. Telling you anything right now would make everything worse. You've left me no choice."

She sat back, stunned. He turned away then and got out of the car. She made no move to follow suit. He walked around and opened the door.

"Go on, now," he said, jerking his head. "Don't worry about nothing. I got this. Get some sleep and this whole nightmare will be over in a day or two."

She stumbled out of the car, still half believing that he would break down and tell her all. What would ever make him think that she would go meekly back to her apartment and wait once again for him to bail her out? She waited.

He said, "You want me to walk you to your door?"

She looked at him in stunned disbelief. "No," she said. "No, I don't need you to walk me to my bleeping door. I just need you to tell me what's going on."

But without saying a word he got back into the Skylark and backed out of the parking space. Before he left, he stuck his head out of the window and said, "I'm serious now, Raven. Leave it alone and let me do this. I got you."

She watched the Skylark whip toward the exit. She stared until it turned the corner to get back onto the main street outside of her apartment complex. As she watched the car disappear, she wondered if the life she had tried to build after Floyd would ever return to normal. And she realized the consequences of lying to Billy Ray these past several weeks. He had frozen her out.

CHAPTER FORTY-FOUR

Billy Ray had wanted to be her knight in shining armor but Raven couldn't let him do that. Finding her tormentor was something she was going to have to do herself. She sat on the living room floor of her apartment surrounded by Floyd's papers – the visitor logs, the fan letters, the book Michael Gorman had written on Floyd's life. Even though she was now engrossed in the dregs from the last years of Floyd's life, her mind was entirely focused on the investigation. There had to be some connection between what was happening to her now and Floyd's crimes. *You might be right about that,* Floyd's voice slid into her thoughts. *All those blasted peacock feathers ain't showing up for nothin'.*

She mentally reviewed the evidence at the Hazel Westcott crime scene. It had to be someone strong enough to carry Hazel's dead weight into her backyard, and someone who knew how to clean up after himself. He had to have access to the jumpsuits CSI wore at crime scenes, given the fibers found on Hazel's dress, and had to have done enough research on succinylcholine to know where to find it and how to use it. CSI could have worn one of the jumpsuits, yes, but Raven didn't see anybody wearing them when she was on scene. Nor could she remember anybody wearing one in the crime scene photos.

Her mind then moved to Jabo Kersey. Kersey knew his killer, even bragged about his connections to the BLPD as he stood knee-deep in the Red River. And the man who killed him would have had to have been a good shot to successfully take Kersey down from a railroad trestle.

And Oral Justice. He also knew the person who had killed him, perhaps shared a glass of wine with his killer before the bastard started chasing Oral around his own house with a scythe from Oral's prized collection of antique gardening tools.

Everything, she thought, everything had pointed to Holloway. He had been on the inside, he had access to succinylcholine from the hospital, and even the jumpsuits. Jabo had treated Holloway's mother in the emergency room. It was no question that they knew each other. Holloway had his computer erased after Hazel was killed, and Raven had believed he did that to cover up the research he had done on the succinylcholine.

But he was dead. And now she knew too late that she should have dismissed Holloway as a suspect after Jabo was killed. Billy Ray was right. No way could Holloway have taken that shot from the trestle. If her mind had not been so muddled by Floyd's harassing voice, she would have seen that sooner.

Who else knew enough about the investigation and hated Raven enough to torment her? The chief? Raven remembered Billy Ray's derisive laugh when she brought up the chief as a suspect earlier. He was right. The chief had never hated Raven, at least she didn't think that he did. He had saved her. She didn't know about how he felt now.

Could it be your good ole partner, then? Floyd whispered in her ear as if summoned. *Could it be Billy Pretty Boy Ray, Birdy Girl? After all, only thing standing 'tween him and his dream is his darn blasted loyalty to you. He'd be knee-deep in gumbo if you hadn't whined for him to come up here.*

"Shut up, Floyd," Raven said, and felt him leave her for a moment.

She was missing something big.

She returned her attention to Floyd's papers. They revealed no clues about the identity of the killer and her tormenter. The only thing new she realized was how often Michael Gorman, the author of *Straight Razors and Peacock Feathers*, had written to Floyd. Gorman's letters fawned over Floyd, they gushed as if Floyd were a talented movie star instead of a depraved serial killer.

Funny thing was Floyd never mentioned him. He loved talking about his fan letters — especially his regulars, as he would call them. There was one kid who sent Floyd pictures of himself all the time. He had so many piercings that Floyd wondered aloud *why the son of a sumpthin' just didn't go right ahead and put a bone clean through his skull and get it over with.*

The boy was obsessed with the murder of Jean Rinehart. *He keeps pestering me,* Floyd would tell Raven, *about how I came up with the idea to kill somebody with a high-heeled shoe. I'd tell him that Jean always complained about her feet killing her.* And then Floyd would cackle at his own bad joke.

There were the psychiatrists, of course. *A whole passel of 'em,* Floyd would complain, *who wanna get a peek inside ole Floyd's noggin'. But ain't nothing in here that they can handle.*

No, they surely wouldn't have been able to handle it, Raven thought, as her attention returned to Michael Gorman. Gorman must have bored Floyd to tears for Floyd to have never mentioned him. Floyd despised boredom. He used to say boring people could put you to sleep just by looking at them.

She flipped the book over and stared at the author photo on the back. Gorman posed in a blue-and-white pinstriped shirt with his Border Collie. The caption beneath identified the black-and-white grinning dog as Lizzie. Gorman must have bored the crap out of Floyd, Raven thought.

She didn't realize how stiff her body was until she stood up. As she stretched and bent to loosen up, she wondered what Billy Ray could be waiting on.

Her Android rang from the kitchen. When she got to the kitchen and looked at the caller ID, she saw that the call was from Imogene Tucker. She let it go to voicemail and left the phone charging on the counter. She was in no mood to talk to Imogene Tucker.

Her mind went back to the Justice crime scene. She flipped through the images in her head – the matted peacock feather under Oral's bloodied hand, the blood spatter on the bright yellow walls, and a CSI she didn't recognize placing two wineglasses in separate evidence bags.

She stopped in the middle of her walk back to the living room. All of a sudden her mind went blank as if it had short-circuited. The elimination samples. This case would all come down to the elimination samples.

If it was an inside job like both she and Billy Ray suspected, the elimination sample of the killer would match the hair samples found in Hazel's bed, and any DNA inadvertently left at the Justice crime scene. While a cop on scene could explain away any of their hair or fibers found in the boathouse or even on Hazel's body, it would take one tall tale to explain away hairs or DNA found in Hazel's twisted sheets. Or any matching DNA found on the wineglasses. That was what Billy

Ray was waiting on, the 'things he was working out'. He was going to push hard for the forensics results. Maybe pressure the chief and Pam Jones, the DA, to help hurry them up.

She went to the kitchen to retrieve the Android. When she lifted it from the counter, the Android began shaking and buzzing in her hand with another call from Tucker. She declined the call again, found the contact for Billy Ray and pressed the call button. She knew in her gut that she was right. But she wanted confirmation from him. He didn't answer. She pressed the end button and tapped the Android to her chin, considering.

She wondered again if a perp this clever would be stupid enough to leave forensics in Hazel's bed. But he would have had no choice. Hazel would not have let someone wearing a jumpsuit, a cap, and booties into her bed no matter what they were using to blackmail her. She would have known the perp had meant to kill her.

And even though he could have administered the drug at gunpoint, Raven couldn't see Hazel acquiescing to something like that. Not the woman who took on an entire department during the Trueblood shooting. Raven's hunch was that he had gotten Hazel in the position to administer the succinylcholine by pretending that all he wanted was sex. And while he may not have been stupid enough to leave seminal fluid, he would have been unable to help hairs.

Raven activated the Android and punched in Rita's number. She must have caller ID, Raven thought as the phone rang and rang on the other end without answer. News of her suspension must have gotten around. That was probably why Tucker had called earlier; she was looking for her comment.

Raven dropped the phone back on the counter and went back into the living room. She sat on the couch and put her feet on the coffee table, still clutching the Gorman book. She looked down at it as if she didn't know what she had. How did Holloway come to have a copy of this book in his collection?

She remembered back to when she found it. She was in the office he shared with Lovelle, asking Lovelle about the evidence Hazel claimed she had in the Trueblood case. The Gorman book was filed alphabetically with Holloway's other books. She remembered holding the book in front of Lovelle's face, calling it lies and telling him how she had squashed both the book and Netflix deal. She saw in her mind's eye Lovelle's strange grin as he made some remark about bodies and souls before turning away.

She stood up and started to pace, retracing every second of the visit to Lovelle's office in her mind. His desk was a mess, she remembered, and he had a stack of magazines on his chair. He thought he had cleared them all but he had left one on the seat. As she was handing the magazine back to him, she had glanced at the title – *Food and Wine*. She remembered it because she didn't think that Lovelle was the foodie sort. The image of the CSI placing the wineglasses in the evidence bags flashed in her mind once again.

She stopped pacing, and slowly sank back down onto the couch. *Could it be?* she thought. *No*, was the answer, and then a tentative *maybe*. Her mind began to scurry through the evidence. Oral and Lovelle had been friends. Lovelle and Shelia Westcott, Hazel's mother, had also been friends. What had Hazel's father said? Lovelle and Shelia were in some writing group, but he thought it was only an excuse for the both of them to drink up all of his good wine. Raven could see Shelia in a drunken, maudlin state telling Lovelle the story of how her husband had once killed his friend, Blue Luther. And she could see Lovelle using the story to blackmail Hazel into what Hazel thought was just going to be sex.

Raven jumped up from the couch. The book fell to the floor. She reached down to pick it up, her mind still racing. Lovelle was at both the Hazel and Oral Justice crime scenes. At Oral's, he looked harried and distressed, wearing long sleeves even in the scorching afternoon heat. To hide cuts, Raven thought. Had to be.

He had even appeared out of the blue at Hazel's crime scene. No one had called him, but he was there steering Imogene Tucker away from the body. He was nowhere to be found at the Kersey scene. *That's because*, a voice whispered to her, *he was too busy hightailin' it out of there after he blew Kersey's brains out.*

And Lovelle was a good shot. Raven had seen him many times beside her at the firing range.

But why? Why would he? She looked down at the book in her hands. Maybe Lovelle had known the author. Maybe he wanted revenge because she had squashed the book. Moreover, the man who had written this book was not only fascinated with Floyd, but suggested that Floyd's daughter was just as guilty as her father. According to Gorman, the only reason she was not in the gas chamber sitting next to Floyd was because she was a minor who earned her freedom by turning on her father. She fired up her laptop. Once her desktop appeared, she went to a browser and typed *Michael Gorman* in the search engine. And sure enough she found the author photo of Gorman and his Border Collie in images. She kept searching, her gut growing cold as more time passed. She could find no more pictures of Gorman. Other Gormans came up, sure, even a biblical scholar author, but no Gorman who wrote the life stories of serial killers.

After another forty-five minutes of searching, she felt her breath stop in her throat. The phone now lying beside her buzzed on the table. She glanced down at the caller ID. Imogene Tucker. She let it ring to voicemail.

She had found something so much more interesting than a conversation with Tucker could ever be. It was a photo of Gorman and his dog on a stock photo website. With the same Border Collie. With the same Carolina wood-frame house in the background. Wearing the same blue-and-white pinstriped shirt.

She sat back in her chair, aware of the chill coming from the whirring air conditioner of her apartment. *Couldn't be*, she thought. *Could it?* What did anyone know about Lamont Lovelle anyway? Only that he waltzed into the BLPD during the Trueblood fiasco offering his services as a media relations coordinator. How much of a background search had Holloway, the math teacher turned cop, done on him before Lovelle was hired? And the chief, with his hands full from dealing with the shooting and trying to build the department, how much involvement did he have in hiring him?

She picked up the phone and called Billy Ray's number again. It rang and rang. She pressed the end call button and tried again. Twice. More empty ringing. She checked the time on the Android. It was almost forty-five minutes after midnight. How stubborn could Billy Ray be?

She closed her eyes, and her eyelids felt grainy. She had been going at it all day and all evening. She hesitated for only a second or two and dialed Rita's number. It rang once, and the call went to voicemail. Rita had declined the call.

Raven sat with the phone in her lap, her mind racing, but for some reason, her heart felt calm, quiet. She was close, but she had to be sure.

Raven returned to her laptop hoping that she was wrong, her gut twisting in pain as if it were on fire. She searched until she found instructions on how to uncover the author behind a pen name. Following the instructions she navigated to the copyright database. And in a few minutes, she had her answer. She suspected, but it had surprised the piss and vinegar right out of her, as Floyd would say. Michael Gorman and Lamont Lovelle were one and the same person.

She didn't know if Billy Ray had known about the book, but wondered if he had suspected Lovelle by a process of elimination, and was now waiting on the forensic proof. He might have already realized that it couldn't be the chief because of his bum leg. He would never have been able to carry Hazel's dead weight. It couldn't be the chief's friend Westcott. Hazel's father wasn't on the inside. He wouldn't have been able to stay a step ahead of her and Billy Ray during the investigation. And it couldn't be Holloway because the perp had killed him. She wondered if Lovelle knew that time was running out. The possibility that he did made Raven's heart go cold.

CHAPTER FORTY-FIVE

Raven could have simply waited until the forensics were in. With it, Billy Ray and the chief would then be at least able to get a search warrant for Lovelle's place. She even considered it for a half of a second – but only a half. Billy Ray knew her better than she knew herself. Patience was never her strong suit, especially when the life she had tried so hard to build after her father's crimes tainted her was in danger of crumbling. And not when her very freedom was in the balance.

She drove to Lovelle's houseboat on an abandoned part of Big Bayou Lake. The houseboat was on pontoons with the front of it moored against the bank. Raven remembered him talking about the houseboat just before meetings while they waited for everyone to gather. He talked about the solitude, the fact that no one lived on that part of the lake because of the green muck teeming on the surface of the water, the pungent smell of the tall eucalyptus as they struggled to breathe amid the gunk, as well as nights so black he sometimes felt as if he alone owned it. He liked the peace, the quiet, and the slick surface of the water. He'd tell her about releasing the house from its mooring and using the outboard motor to take it downriver at night sometimes, and how beautiful the bayou was under the bright moon. Raven thought about how surreal that must have looked, a small frame house moving along the river with the rhythmic noise of the outboard motor cutting the silence of the night, the light of the moon transforming to silver the bark of the cypress trees hanging tall and ghostlike against the blackness.

He would tell her that it was there he felt himself. She wondered now if he was speaking of his Lamont Lovelle self or his Michael Gorman self. The porch swayed a little when she jumped onto it from the bank. The smell of stagnant water and earth was so strong that she found herself running her hand over her nose.

The house was black. Lovelle was either asleep or not at home. She knocked while concocting a story about an emergency down at the station and a problem with cell phone service. It didn't sound plausible, but it was all she had. She just needed to get inside, to walk casually around to see if he had been hiding anything while he dressed in his just-awakened and hopefully befuddled state.

But there was no answer. She waited several minutes and knocked again. When silence greeted her once again, she realized that no one was home. It was at least two a.m. by now. If he wasn't home yet, chances were that he was not coming home that night. Raven hoped with all her heart that she was right.

She tried the silver doorknob. And just as she thought, it was locked. Solitude or not, Lovelle did not strike her as the kind of man who wouldn't lock his doors. Using a tension wrench and a pick, she picked the lock, once again thanking her foster brothers and sisters for showing her how to get into places she wasn't supposed to go. She thanked them for the games troubled teens played.

Once inside, Raven turned on the light. A flashlight would be idiotic. If there were someone in this deserted part of the lake for one reason or another, they would be more suspicious of flashlight beams than just a houseboat with the living room lights on.

At first she could find nothing out of the ordinary. The place was nothing like his office. Lovelle was neat and kept everything in order. An old Indian blanket was folded perfectly on a chair covered in faded brown velvet. Every surface was wiped clean, the oak coffee table polished and the countertops sparkling. Floyd would have approved.

And everything seemed to be out in the open, which was hardly anything at all. There was no incriminating stash of peacock feathers. Oral's cane with the wolf's head and curving silver neck was nowhere in sight.

Then she went to the bedroom. Raven didn't know what to expect, but she didn't expect what she found. She was in the necessarily small space of the master bedroom. The queen bed stretched from wall to wall, with a narrow space that had barely enough room for walking. The bed was neatly made with a white and gray comforter pulled up to two fluffy pillows covered in white pillowcases. Oral's silver cane – black lacquered bottom and silver wolf's head with its mouth open on top – lay across the foot of the bed. It was as polished and neat as the rest of the houseboat.

And on the tiny side table was a photo album with a title of *My Memories* emblazoned across the cover in gold. Raven removed the leather gloves she had been wearing to break in and pulled out a pair of latex gloves from her pocket. She drew them on. She carefully picked up the album and flipped through it.

Photos from crime scenes. But these photos were not official crime scene photos. Hazel's eyes were still open as she stared at the camera from the bathtub, naked and perfect and dying. A bloody Oral Justice stared up while the camera looked upon him during his final breaths.

Holloway was the only one unaware. He slept in his photo, or more likely, it was one that Lovelle had snapped after he died. She wondered why Lovelle had gone through the trouble of killing Holloway.

But she knew.

Lovelle didn't want her in jail. But Holloway did. That was the other thing she had been missing. Holloway wanted her locked up because he thought she was a menace to society. But the person doing the killing wanted her free. If they were to arrest someone else for the killing or lock her up, the entire horror show would've been over. There would be no need for more killing. That's why Lovelle shot Jabo and killed Holloway. He needed to keep killing.

Outside the houseboat she awakened her Android. She pressed Billy Ray's number again. No answer. She took a deep breath and the rankness in the air almost made her vomit. She choked it back down, knowing what she had to do.

The chief answered on the first ring just as he always had. And he said what he always said.

"Sawyer."

"It's him," Raven said. "It's Lovelle."

"Raven," he asked. "Where are you?"

"At his houseboat."

"Come on," he said. "Now you're trying to pin this on Lovelle?"

"Chief," she said, "you know me. And with what you think of

me right now, I certainly wouldn't be dumb enough to call you without proof. We don't have a lot of time to waste here."

There was a slight pause, and then, "Okay, tell me."

So she did. She told him about Oral's cane in Lovelle's bedroom, and the photo album of the victims.

"Shit," he said.

"Where is he?" Raven asked.

"Raven, I don't know exactly," he said. She could hear creaking sounds as he lumbered out of bed. "When he said he had to go, I was too pissed off to ask or care. You stay put."

"I'm talking about Billy Ray, not Lovelle," she corrected him. "I can't reach Billy Ray. I've been trying all night."

The chief sighed. "Yeah, about that."

"Chief."

"Nothing bad, Raven," he said. "His sister went into labor. Finally. He had to head down to New Orleans after work today. You knew it was close."

"Exactly how long ago?"

"I don't know," the chief said. "About noon or so. Shortly after he dropped you off."

"Have you heard from him?"

"Heard from him?" he asked. "Why would I hear from him?"

There was silence for a few seconds. And then, "Raven."

"He would have checked in when he found out what was going on with his sister, wouldn't he?"

"He's all right."

"How long has Lovelle been gone?" she asked.

He said nothing. This time the silence stretched into what felt like screaming. "Raven, Chastain's fine."

"He would've called me," she said. "He would have told me if he had to go out of town."

"He wanted to give you some time to cool down," the chief said. "You would have grilled him here to Sunday about what was happening with the case if he called you. Now, you're letting your emotions get the best of you. He's fine. I'll have some units sent out. And I'm on my way myself. Stay there, Raven."

Raven didn't answer. She hung up the phone. There was a pit of fear that ran from her gut and lodged in her throat. Her hands shook as she put the key into the ignition. She knew where Billy Ray was. He wasn't making that trek to New Orleans either. And she'd bet anything that he was not alone.

CHAPTER FORTY-SIX

Most of the bottles clinging to the dead limbs of Billy Ray's bottle tree were broken. She could see that from the lights of her Mustang. The bottles that she had heard clink in humid breezes so many times now made fragmented and discordant sounds. The remaining bottles still clinging onto the branches by their long red and blue necks were bottomless and jagged. The rest lay in colored pieces of glass beneath the tree.

Raven cut the lights, and stepped out into the warm night.

She pointed the flashlight she had with her at the pile beneath the tree. The funnel of light revealed at first what she thought was a pile of rags. She un-holstered the new Glock 22 that the chief wanted her to leave with him. And she was glad that she hadn't. Weapon drawn and ready, she approached the crumpled heap beneath the bottle tree. She stopped when she realized what – no, who – it was.

She knelt down and looked at the old man for a long time, probably more time than she could afford. It was Billy Ray's next-door neighbor, the old vet who had shot a hole through the roof and had the uncanny ability to show up when dinner was ready. The smell of alcohol and feces and urine floated in a haze around his dead body, his face pressed against the shards of colored glass. Somebody crashed bottle after bottle over his old skull until he went down. When they tired of that, they reached down to slit his throat that was now open and gaping in a bloody grin.

Lamont Lovelle had eliminated Billy Ray's only neighbor for miles around, the other shotguns in the nearly abandoned neighborhood empty of anyone who might have called 911 or intervened. Raven speculated that Billy Ray had to have been taken first. Perhaps the landlord, hearing a noise or smelling a late lunch, had knocked on the door only to be chased down the sidewalk by Lovelle.

Her heart thumped a single beat in response to a loud mewling coming from the direction of the street. She whipped the Glock and the flashlight in the direction of the sound. It was a big black cat with a white tail held high and swaying gingerly in the black night, its eyes glowing gold as it tiptoed its way toward the body.

Raven lowered the flashlight and Glock.

"Go on, scat," she said in a harsh whisper. The cat considered for a moment before turning and trotting away.

She returned to the body and touched the landlord's wrist and hand. They were cold and very stiff. He was at the peak of rigidity, and had probably been dead for a while.

Raven turned toward Billy Ray's house. Someone had kicked out the porch spindles. The screen door had been almost pulled off the hinges. It now lay slanting across the open front door. Beyond the screen door Raven saw nothing but blackness.

★　★　★

On some level, Raven knew that Lovelle was probably in there waiting on her. He had probably seen all of those phone calls she had made to Billy Ray's cell, and knew that it was only a matter of time before she showed up to find out why he wasn't answering. If she was lucky, Billy Ray would just be a hostage that Lovelle was planning on using to torment her, not a murder victim. She should return to her Mustang, call for backup.

But she thought about Billy Ray being held hostage in his double-barrel shotgun house in the middle of a neighborhood destroyed by the act of abandonment. She thought about his expensive pork pie hats, his bowling shirts, ironed and flawless. His ceaseless ramblings when he was bored about his restaurant and his need to leave the job played in her head.

Through her mind went the fact that though he talked of leaving all the time, he never went. He even planted more roots with the renting and furnishing of what he liked to call his roach motel. They both knew why he stayed but never spoke of it aloud. He would stay as long as his partner needed him, would put whatever dream he had on hold until she let him go. He was that loyal. He had her back. She would not abandon him now.

Raven pulled the screen door from the last remaining hinge and threw it aside. She didn't care if he heard her. "If you're in there," she yelled into the darkness, "why don't you come out and get the real truth on who I am." She pointed her flashlight inside the maw of Billy Ray's open front door.

There was disaster on either side of her, broken furniture and plaster owls with the smooth inside of their bellies exposed. She kicked the debris aside. Billy Ray had fought like she knew he would, and he had at least a foot on Lovelle. Maybe he was successful in subduing the smaller man. But Raven remembered the landlord beneath the bottle tree. Billy Ray would have done everything in his power to save a civilian. Even sacrifice himself.

Everywhere she pointed her light, the Glock dutifully followed. But there was nothing trying to shoot her and there was nothing that she could shoot at. This made her feel even more afraid. So much for being strapped and ready for war, she thought.

She heard soft laughter in her head. It was Floyd. And he was laughing at her. *Just like in the movies*, he said. *What do they say, heart poundin' in their chests? Your heart's poundin', little Birdy Girl, poundin' so hard it makes my own heart hurt.*

"Not now," she said aloud, trying to keep the whimper out of her voice.

But he was right. Her heart was pounding in her chest as it had never pounded before. And she was sweating, the moisture slithering down her face and making her hands so slick that she had to concentrate on keeping a grip on the Glock.

She made her way past the living room and was instantly in the bedroom. She had been in Billy Ray's house dozens of times, but never had the transition from the living room to bedroom felt so bizarre. It was as if she were in a dream, being instantly transported from one place to the next. *Every time I walk into this place*, she heard herself say in some other life, *I always miss one thing.*

Yeah, Billy Ray laughed. *Hallways.* The bedroom was not as torn-up as the living room. But there was blood on the floor. The chifforobe lay on its side like a wounded elephant. The thick comforter was painted with blood.

And then she was in the kitchen. The Formica table, where she and

Billy Ray had eaten breakfast when she told him about the Trueblood killing, was knocked over. The back door that led to the porch was open. A cast-iron skillet lay facedown on the floor. Raven could see fire still burning on the stove, its blue flame the only living thing aside from herself in the entire house.

When she stepped outside onto the back porch, white light flooded the yard.

"Son of a bitch," Raven said softly.

Lovelle had rigged the backyard with motion sensitive floodlights. Her first instinct was to fall to her belly to get out of the way of the gunfire she was sure was coming. But before she could do that she heard a croak.

Over the porch railing the branches of a weeping willow spread and fell like rain. Billy Ray was tied to the tree with thick rope. In the floodlight, she could see that both eyes were blackened. Golf ball-sized lumps were at the corners of his mouth and eyes. His lips were swollen to thumb size, and streams of blood gushed from his mouth as he tried to talk.

"Raven," he croaked. "Gem off...."

She ran down the steps as if her feet were on fire. She could see him with effort try to raise his head again. "Rave...." he tried, "Gome...."

All she could think about was getting to him. But she stopped halfway. The backyard stank. Not of fear. Not of death. But with the nauseating smell of kerosene.

The fires.

It was not her father speaking but the child who grew up with Fire. The little girl who saw him burn down her mother's house while he watched the crackling flames and laughed. The girl who saw him kill Jean Rinehart. It was the victim speaking to her. *The Fire*, the voice warned again. And it was not only her as victim she heard inside her head, it was the other victims, Hazel, Jabo, Oral, and yes, even Presley Holloway and his mother warning her. *The Fire*, they repeated. She tried to make her feet move but they wouldn't. It was as if she had grown right there, sprung up from the ground and held by whatever roots that kept her alive.

"Gome...." Billy Ray muttered.

And she knew what Billy Ray was trying to do. He was trying

to warn her off. He wanted her to get out of there. She wanted to. She wanted to leave that place with every cell in her body. But she couldn't do that. She wouldn't. Even though she knew what was going to happen, what Lovelle had planned all along. With all the strength of the survivor who put men like Floyd Burns behind bars, she commanded her feet to move. Granted they were sluggish at first. But they moved.

"Birdy," someone said. This voice wasn't inside her head. It was all around as if it had become part of the white light. "Birdy Girl," it said again.

She turned slowly around to face the voice. Lamont Lovelle. It was Lamont Lovelle standing there with a gun to Imogene Tucker's head. In her hand she held what looked like a red-handled barbecue igniter.

A flicker of gladness went up in her. It only lasted for the briefest of seconds, but it was gladness and pride. Billy Ray had fought, she could see that. One of Lovelle's eyes was swollen shut. His face was beaten bloody, and his bottom lip was split almost in two.

"See," he said, the grin on his face exposing white teeth stained with blood. "I knew you could figure it out. You're smart, like your father."

Raven stared in amazement at Tucker, who was looking sideways in terror at the gun Lovelle held to her head. She was gripping the barbecue igniter with both hands. The faded jeans encircling her heavy thighs were torn in several places and crusted with blood. One sleeve of the bright pink blouse she was wearing was ripped from its seam, and she had a lump on her head the size of Texas.

Lovelle saw her looking at Tucker. He grinned. "Yep," he said. "She's the bonus prize tonight. She had heard you were suspended and came over here to interview your partner. And look what a mess you walked into," he finished with a loud stage whisper into Tucker's ear.

He returned a hard gaze to Raven. "Drop the weapon. Drop the weapon and I won't kill her," he said, his words wet with the blood in his mouth.

"Just like you didn't kill the landlord?" Raven stalled.

He laughed bitterly. "No," he said. "Didn't happen that way, my little Birdy. Your boyfriend wouldn't stand down. So I had to shoot the nosy bastard. That old man ran even with a bullet in him. Didn't even bother to open the screen door. And your boyfriend running after him to try and save him. That was a mistake. Don't you make another one. Drop the weapon."

Raven hesitated. He placed the muzzle of the gun hard into Tucker's temple. Tucker screamed.

"Okay, okay, Lamont," Raven said, as she stooped to lower the Glock to the ground. "Let her go. Let them both go. It's me you want."

He laughed. "That's where you're wrong," he said. "I never really wanted you, or anything to do with you."

"Then why are we here, Lamont?" she said. "Why all the hard work to get me here?"

"Be-*cause* I just wanted you to see who you are, to understand that *you* are your *father's* child. This," he boomed, waving the gun around the backyard, "is the only way I knew how to get you here."

The fact that he sounded so much like Floyd sent chills up her spine. And the fact that he was so full of crap stopped them.

"That's a damn lie, Lamont," Raven said, surprised her voice was level and mild. "You wanted revenge because I exposed that pack of lies you wrote about my father. That book you thought was going to put you on some map. I destroyed your chance to make a name for yourself."

He laughed. "See how blind you are?" he said. "I did hate you for that. At first. But the real reason you're here is because you betrayed your father. You sent that brilliant man to the gas chamber. I was just going to kill you, that's all. A simple shot to the back of the head. But then I started to watch you, the way you cut down that Trueblood boy."

"Shut up," Raven hissed.

"And I thought, why, she's just like her father and she doesn't even know." He smiled. "I had to show you, Raven. I had to show you your way back to your father."

"More lies," Raven said. "Just like the lies you told Hazel about evidence from the Quincy Trueblood shooting."

He laughed then. "Yes, that was brilliant," he said. "What a dumb bitch. She bought it hook, line and sinker. An anonymous letter with a promise that there was more to come. That's all it took and she was on the phone to you, setting you up for her own murder."

"And that wasn't Holloway's book in his office, was it, Lamont?" Raven asked to keep him talking while frantically searching for a way to resolve this without anybody else dying.

"No," he said. "I hid it there. I had it in my office but didn't want you to run across it when you were in and out during the Trueblood case. You know that little fucker never even noticed? As long as things were in neat little rows for him, he was happy."

"I called for backup, Lamont. You're over."

But he was shaking his head before her lips had closed over the last word. "No, no," he said. "Not over. You didn't call anybody. You were too busy trying to get in here to see what happened to your lover boy."

Raven said nothing.

He cocked his head. "And even if you did," he said. "I don't hear any sirens, not yet. We have plenty of time to do what we need to do."

She breathed slowly while thinking about her options. She was thinking faster than ever before in her life.

"How do you like my setup?" he said. "I did a nice job, didn't I?"

Raven looked over at Billy Ray. She could see his struggle to remain conscious.

"You did a magnificent job," Raven said, stalling for time.

"Why, thank you," Lovelle said. "A scene worthy of your father."

"I'm not so sure about that," Raven answered.

"Now who's lying?" he said. "Sure you are. He talks to you all the time. Isn't that what you told your shrink? I saw the psych reports Holloway pulled on you. Wouldn't Floyd be proud of me?"

She watched him but didn't respond.

"Answer me!" he demanded. He reached around and tried to take the lighter from Tucker's hand. Tucker closed her fist around it in a death grip. He pressed the gun once again harder to her temple. No scream this time, only a tiny whine.

"He would probably say you did all right," Raven said.

Lovelle grinned; his teeth looked wet in the bright lights. "You're lying."

Raven shrugged.

"Why can't you tell me the truth?"

"Okay," Raven said slowly. "You want the truth." She took a

deep breath, not knowing how he would react, but knowing that she had to keep him talking if she wanted time to find a way out of this. "He would find this entire thing foolhardy."

"Oh?"

"Oh," Raven said. "He didn't really like constructed drama. He'd say that you were working too damn hard." *For no damn good reason*, Floyd added in her head. *Tell 'im that.* "For no damned good reason," she repeated to Lovelle.

Lovelle's face contorted. He pressed the gun to Tucker's head. Tucker closed her eyes tight and whimpered.

"Light it," he growled.

"No!" Tucker sobbed.

"Do it!"

"No!"

Raven could see what was going to happen. Tucker was not going to light the barbecue igniter. And he would shoot Tucker. After he shot her, he would pry the lighter from her dying hands and set the yard on fire himself.

While he was doing so, Raven would have ten, maybe fifteen, seconds to disarm him. Her reflexes were good and the lighting, thanks to Lovelle, was spectacular. It was a good plan. But a plan that would mean Tucker would have to die. *I don't see nothin' too terribly wrong with that*, Floyd said in her head, in a wondering voice like a child's.

She answered that she did see something terribly wrong with that. And the thing that was wrong with it was that she was not him. She was not her father's child. If she only thought about her own life, another innocent like Quincy Trueblood would die, and maybe Billy Ray would die too. It was as if she was being given a chance to make the decision she made standing in front of Boones & Sons Grocery Market with her Glock trained on Quincy Trueblood's chest, all over again.

"Imogene," she said. "Give it to him." Tucker opened her eyes and stared wide-eyed at her. "Give him the lighter."

Tucker shook her head. Lovelle looked confused for a second. Then he smiled. He put his free hand across Tucker's neck and squeezed. "It would seem you have permission, my dear," he said. "A small reprieve."

Tucker, gasping for breath, gave him the lighter. He immediately tossed it to Raven. She reached out and caught it from reflex more than anything else.

He tossed the weapon he had been holding onto the ground. He pushed Tucker to her knees and put his knee between her shoulder blades. Before Raven could move he pulled a rope out of his pocket and wrapped it around Tucker's neck in a yoke. Tucker sputtered, waving her hand in the air.

"Light it or watch me yoke her to death," he said. "Isn't that what you cops say? Yoke? Much more fun than just plain shooting somebody in the head."

Raven didn't hesitate. She flipped the lighter and heard the hard click. A small blue flame flickered in the white light, a flame she would remember for the rest of her life. Her back to Billy Ray, she threw the lighter onto the tall, dry grass trying to get it as close to the back porch as she could and as far away from Billy Ray as possible.

Lovelle shrieked in protest, dropping the rope around Tucker's neck. Raven prayed in the few seconds she had to think. She hadn't smelled the kerosene earlier until she was in the middle of the yard. Maybe he hadn't drenched the porch so well.

But she was wrong. He had poured the stuff everywhere. And though the back of the yard nearest the porch caught first, the flames immediately streamed toward the weeping willow with Billy Ray tied to the base. She sprinted toward Billy Ray, hoping that Tucker could fend for herself now that Lovelle had dropped the rope.

She unstrapped the knife from her ankle holster and cut the rope in one clean swipe. Billy Ray fainted as she pulled the remaining rope from his body while the fire slithered closer and closer. No time to be careful or delicate. She needed to get him away from the flames. Heat seared through her T-shirt and jeans. She felt it on her arms. Somewhere, Tucker was screaming and screaming and screaming. Raven couldn't understand what she was saying, but if she was screaming that meant she was alive, and that was fine with her.

There were sirens too. Lots of them, the sound growing larger and larger as the cars came closer. Finally, Billy Ray was free. He slumped over at an angle. Raven placed both arms under his arms and around his chest and pulled at him with every ounce of training she had been through during the past year. Heat flooded her face and flames scorched her arms, but she ignored it. She had almost gotten him out of the path of the flames when she felt a force shove her backward. She rolled with it for what seemed like several feet. When she opened her eyes, Tucker was on top of her, sobbing.

And this time, it was Billy Ray. He was awake and he was the one screaming and screaming.

Both of his legs were on fire.

CHAPTER FORTY-SEVEN

She quit the day after she got out of the hospital. Her burns were not serious, but not so for Billy Ray. He had burns over twenty percent of his body, mostly on his legs. The gods spoke that night. The fire that had twisted over his legs suddenly shifted. And soon, the rest of Byrd's Landing Police Department was there with fire extinguishers from their squad cars.

But the burns weren't the worst of it.

Billy Ray had overpowered Lovelle after Lovelle shot the landlord, finally able to handcuff him to one of the porch spindles. It was a mistake Billy Ray probably wouldn't have made if he were not so worried about the landlord. As Billy Ray was tending to the landlord's injuries, Lovelle escaped by unseating the spindle and slipping the cuffs. The fight began anew. Billy Ray had almost subdued him once again when Imogene came walking on scene looking for an exclusive. Before he knew what was happening, Lovelle had the spindle pressed against Imogene's throat, telling Billy Ray to stand down or he would crush her windpipe. After seeing what happened to the landlord, Billy Ray complied.

Lovelle knocked Imogene out and tied Billy Ray out back where Raven found him. After he had him helpless beneath the branches of the willow, Lovelle beat him so badly that his brain had swollen inside of his skull. Then he went to finish off Billy Ray's landlord.

Though Billy Ray's brain didn't sustain permanent damage, it was clear that the road to recovery would be long. His twin sister, holding her new baby at his bedside, told Raven that she wished he had just done what he had been promising to do and walked back home to New Orleans.

As for Lamont Lovelle, his DNA matched both the hair found in Hazel's bed and the DNA found on Oral's wineglasses. A lot of good it did the BLPD. Lovelle ran while the fire was raging. He escaped. No one had seen him since that night. They were looking for him, but it was obvious that Lovelle had planned his escape well. The BLPD so far had nothing.

The day after she was released from the hospital, Raven walked into the chief's office and placed her resignation on his desk right next to the unopened bottles of Pappy Van Winkle bourbon he had vowed to share with her when he retired. That way the little girl he had saved, now a full-grown woman, and a cop like him, could toast with him. He wanted that full circle, he had told her, a fitting end to his long career. But the man now sitting behind the desk staring up at her was not the same idealistic man who had saved her from Floyd. With a busted knee and a jaded heart, he had made far too many compromises. She had no intention of sharing anything with him.

He must have expected her, because next to the bourbon was the badge he had demanded from her after Holloway and his mother were killed. Without speaking, he picked the badge up and turned it this way and that in the afternoon light flowing through the glass window behind his desk.

Finally, he said, "You sure this is what you want to do?"

Raven studied him. The voice came from a long way off because of a migraine roaring through her head. She had been having them since that night. The chief's serious face shifted and wavered in front of her as she tried with all of her might to fight with the freight train running along the tracks behind her skull. She heard him sigh.

"Obviously, you're still not well," he said. "You've been through hell. I know I put you through some of that and I'm sorry."

He threw the badge across the desk, intending for her to pick it back up.

"Think it over," he said.

But she shook her head. She was tired of trying to prove to the chief that she was worthy of saving, that she was not her father. Like it or not, some parts of her were from Floyd. This was her choice. She was at peace with that.

★   ★   ★

While Billy Ray's sister and family took care of him, Raven chased Lamont Lovelle across the bayous of Louisiana to the plains of Texas.

She was able to find out through her old contacts the new name on the papers he had forged. And her computer whiz foster brother, Cameron, helped her. Cameron called in results from credit card traces from computers he hacked.

Before she had an opportunity to catch up with Lovelle, he'd run again and soon ended up almost where it had all started – a California town called Modesto and close to Crampton, the place that had birthed Floyd 'Fire' Burns.

She asked herself several times why she didn't call it in. Every time she thought about making that phone call she saw her father in the gas chamber. She saw him draw that mirrored piece of glass across his throat. She wouldn't let there be another show with Lamont Lovelle, another celebrity serial killer for the groupies and copycats. And also, she had a promise to keep to Hazel and all the other victims she felt standing with her in Billy Ray's burning yard. For that, Lovelle's punishment would have to come just outside of justice. And it had to be clean. She would have to do it herself.

She watched him for an entire week in Modesto, impatient, wanting to get back to Byrd's Landing. But the perfect opportunity she needed, the clean shot she had been searching for, they appeared as elusive as ghosts.

But then he got a job working at a car wash, swirling a damp cloth across the glittering enamel paint of other people's BMWs and Cadillacs. It was somewhere he needed to be every day. And he remained a man of steady habits. That was the only thing she liked about him. That was the one thing she counted on.

*   *   *

Two days later she watched Lamont Lovelle from the roof of an auto shop as he exited his 1996 gray Corolla and jaywalked across the street to the Quizno's where he had bought his lunch for the past several days. The sky was a clean, clear blue. The day crackled with a dry heat. A trio of red, white, and blue balloons had broken free from some child's birthday party. They were now floating and floating higher and higher in the blameless blue sky.

She lay across the roof of the auto shop with the stock of a sniper's rifle against her shoulder and the gravel beneath her biting into her flesh. Not two blocks away was the Modesto Police Department, but the thought flickered in her mind just once. Police department or no, getting caught was not on her agenda. She wore gloves, had a go bag, and a rental car parked in an alley two streets over.

The heat, the rocks against the floor of the rooftop, the police department just around the corner didn't deter her. She barely felt herself breathe. Instead she focused on the scene made small and circular in the scope of the rifle. She remembered the sound of the barrel clicking into place, the snap of the stock being extended, how she put the rifle together in a way that was practical but loving.

Now a large drop of sweat rolled from her hair. She felt it trickle down along the nape of her neck and into her shirt collar, not stopping until it reached the back of her bra. She did not wipe it away. She did not move.

★ ★ ★

He was almost to the center of the street now. He had shaved his head, lost weight, the left half of his face deeply scarred from the beating he took from Billy Ray. He was thin and, though in that moment it had nothing to do with his weight loss, dying. Though revenge was on her mind, she was more interested in putting Lovelle underground so that his very existence wouldn't cause more hurt. It was what she should have done to Floyd 'Fire' Burns on his wedding day to her stepmother. It had nothing to do with revenge, and everything to do with keeping someone else from getting hurt. Then she didn't have the courage to finish her father forever. Today was a different story.

Maybe someone other than Raven would have paused. Maybe the chief, even Billy Ray, who was at this moment completing the arduous journey back to normal thanks to Lamont Lovelle. Maybe they would have had a moment's second thought.

But not Raven.

There was no pity in her at this moment. She watched him through the cross hairs. He was about four hundred meters away. She placed the target center mass – a better and bigger target than the top of his bald head. She waited until her entire body quieted. She wondered how many more Lovelles were out there – these Floyd groupies. Then she took a deep breath, sucked in all the air that her lungs would hold and slowly let it out. Between heartbeats, calmly and without doubt or hesitation, Raven Burns waited for the perfect moment in time to pull the trigger. And as she waited, the only voice left in her head was her own.

FLAME TREE PRESS
FICTION WITHOUT FRONTIERS
Award-Winning Authors & Original Voices

Flame Tree Press is the trade fiction imprint of Flame Tree Publishing, focusing on excellent writing in horror and the supernatural, crime and mystery, science fiction and fantasy. Our aim is to explore beyond the boundaries of the everyday, with tales from both award-winning authors and original voices.

•

You may also enjoy:
Second Lives by P.D. Cacek
Chop Shop by Andrew Post
The Bad Neighbor by David Tallerman
Night Shift by Robin Triggs

Horror titles available include:
Thirteen Days by Sunset Beach by Ramsey Campbell
Think Yourself Lucky by Ramsey Campbell
The Hungry Moon by Ramsey Campbell
The Haunting of Henderson Close by Catherine Cavendish
The House by the Cemetery by John Everson
The Devil's Equinox by John Everson
Hellrider by JG Faherty
The Toy Thief by D.W. Gillespie
Black Wings by Megan Hart
Stoker's Wilde by Steven Hopstaken & Melissa Prusi
The Playing Card Killer by Russell James
The Siren and the Specter by Jonathan Janz
The Sorrows by Jonathan Janz
Savage Species by Jonathan Janz
The Nightmare Girl by Jonathan Janz
The Dark Game by Jonathan Janz
House of Skin by Jonathan Janz
Dust Devils by Jonathan Janz
The Darkest Lullaby by Jonathan Janz
Will Haunt You by Brian Kirk
Creature by Hunter Shea
The Mouth of the Dark by Tim Waggoner

•

Join our mailing list for free short stories, new release details, news about our authors and special promotions:

flametreepress.com